ALVIN BAYLOR LIVES!

MAXIMILIAN GRAY

PECULIAR EPHEMERA

Alvin Baylor Lives! is a work of fiction. Any similarity to persons, living, dead, or not yet born is unintentional or satirical. If you're named Alvin Baylor, I wasn't thinking about you. I just made the name up. Cheers. Thanks for reading the fine print.

Edited by Carolyn Haley
Cover Illustration by Roger Betka
Gravedigger & Casanova fonts used by permission of Chequered Ink

Published in the United States of America
by Peculiar Ephemera
aka
maximiliangray.com

First and foremost this is for you, Mom.
Thanks for being my first fan and for putting up with my selfish bullshit.
This book couldn't exist without you. Neither could I.

And to those I will not meet again...

My father, who encouraged my love for the fantastic and instilled in me an
indomitable strength of character. I miss you everyday.

And Robert Copple, who saw me as an artist and helped me to finally see
myself. Thanks for helping me finish growing up.

I wrote you a fucking story.

The obstacle is the path.

ZEN PROVERB

ONE

One hundred ninety million miles from Earth, John Padre yawned. He rubbed his aching legs and looked up at the time. Seven hours, that's how long he'd been stuck in a tiny cockpit staring at the same two asteroids. His feet were jammed up against the controls of the stolen ship and his knees were swollen. At six-foot-five, he barely fit in the egg-shaped cabin. A year of microgravity had caused his joints to separate and muscles to atrophy. The damage would make readjusting to Earth gravity difficult. He felt it was worth it, though. Today's payday would cover his rehabilitation and anything else he would ever need.

He'd stolen the little rock hopper from an asteroid mining colony over a year ago. It was the first in a series of jobs for a well-informed client. Tasks that had the feel of audition. Today was the main event.

He wasn't sure of his handler's identity, but the promised billion in coin was evidence that this person was more than a disgruntled employee. Padre had spent his last few hours imagining the client's motivations. Perhaps it was a Chinese competitor trying to cut into the Alteris Asteroid mining trade. Or maybe it was Alteris itself. Maybe the tech didn't work, or an expensive employee needed to be wiped off the balance sheet. He'd seen contractors used for insurance jobs before.

Shit. All the time spent waiting was messing with his head. Why steal this thing all the way out here? Why not hack the network, dupe the plans, and print up a copy? As he pondered the bleak machinations that allowed him an income, the communications channel crackled to life.

"Yo, Pops! How long are we gonna wait? I'm running low on air and enthusiasm out here," Samantha Watkins whined.

That girl is a smartass.

"Till the fucking mark is here. Don't get your diapers in a bunch," Padre radioed back in his gravelly voice. "Cheng, you still breathing?"

"I do what I'm told and you told us to keep it radio silent," said Ajax Cheng over the comm.

Good-ol' Cheng. Great at taking orders.

"Good. Before this ship shows her sails, we need to be prepped. Are your lines anchored?"

"Yes, Mr. Padre, they've been fastened and ready to go for three hours," said Watkins.

"Well, check 'em again. We get one shot at this."

Rouja, baby where are you when I need you?

Padre pined for his usual girl. She was a better operative than either of these two, but she was on Earth and their relationship was strained. He'd have to make do without her today.

Minutes later he saw a blip on the scanners. Something was coming through the field.

"All right, kids, I'm going dark. Don't fall asleep out there." Padre chuckled. "Scopes show they should be in range within the hour."

He switched off nonessential systems to avoid detection and sat perched over his control console. Small lights danced across his face as he looked out the front window into the cosmos. He felt like a primitive hunter-gatherer stalking his prey. They waited in silence for the *Zzyzx*'s beacon.

An hour later, the ship appeared in Padre's view as it crossed between the asteroids. The bow was a massive solar collector that arched backward like a bronze umbrella. It was easily a mile in diameter. Padre furrowed his brow in anticipation and felt sweat roll down his forehead. He hated caring so deeply about something. It felt like weakness.

A steady ping of the ship's telemetry beacon sent Watkins and Cheng to their feet.

"Finally," Watkins whispered.

The massive dome of the *Zzyxz* glided between the asteroids and moved into view, exposing the body behind it.

Padre saw Watkins's laser signal illuminate first. He shifted in his seat and looked over to Cheng's asteroid perch. The soldier signaled, as well. Padre took a deep breath and turned on the rock hopper's systems. The craft spun in a somersault as its lights came up in the dark of space.

"We are go. Fire!" he yelled into the comm channel.

Two small rockets arched out from the asteroids and blew through either side of the *Zzyzx*'s umbrella sail. The bolts unfurled, releasing metal hooks that tore the solar collector in half as the ship passed between the asteroids.

Padre dabbed at the sweat running from beneath the black skullcap on his head. He felt a slight buzzing. His brain was linked to the hopper's controls and he willed it forward. It felt like an extension of his body as it shot toward his prey.

Luminescent appendages trailed from the rock hopper like the tentacles of a squid as it raced over the giant umbrella sail. The tendrils went rigid to form jointed legs and touched down at the rear of the ship. It ran six-legged toward the port side.

Padre was in the shit again, happy as a pig.

He wriggled his fingers and two of the tendrils split into clawlike pinchers. They reached over the stern and wedged into the top of the airlock door. Then a push with his fingertip cracked the seal.

The edges of the frame started to buckle as air poured out of the opening. Padre willed the rock hopper away from the door. Atmosphere flowed outward from the airlock, and in moments the metal door was whipped violently out into space. A belch of gas and debris followed.

"She's open for business, kids," he boomed.

He kept an eye on the airlock below while his team's camera feeds floated in space before him.

Watkins and Cheng fired up thrusters and lifted off the asteroids. They covered the distance to the ship using the jets built into their suits.

Cheng touched down first and affixed his magnetic boots to the hull. He looked ahead with his pulse gun at the ready. Sam Watkins came next. Her camera lingered on her feet as they snapped to the ship.

The duo made the sticky-footed walk to the airlock. Each took a side of the round opening, and Cheng leaned over to peer inside. The inner door was still sealed tight. He motioned to Watkins.

"Beginning system intrusion," Watkins said.

She stepped into the airlock then pulled a thumb-sized card from her belt and connected it at the inner door. Watkins took control of the ship's systems and began scanning for life.

"Okay, I see the crew," she said. "Five readings, they're in the central cabin." She used eye movement and blinks to lock down the cabin doors using a menu that floated in her view. "I'm ready to crack the inner seal."

Watkins stepped out of the airlock to join Cheng outside. They scuttled away and she opened the inner airlock. A furious vortex of air and glittering debris twirled out of the cargo hold and into space. They waited for the discharge to stop and moved back toward the opening.

"Proceeding with boarding," radioed Cheng.

He stepped through the airlock and into the cargo hold. Cheng scanned every crate and rippling tie-down strap through the sight of his pulse gun.

Watkins followed him into the hold.

"No gravity on the cargo deck," said Cheng.

"Of course not, only in the crew quarters on this model," said Watkins.

They continued to clomp forward with magnetic steps. They scanned the rows of pallets strapped to the deck, and Cheng fired a few laser blasts to disable the nested security cameras. They popped apart in a spray of plastic and glass confetti that drifted through the air.

"You know I can just turn those off," said Watkins.

Cheng huffed and kept walking.

"Comin' up on bio forms," radioed Watkins.

Padre watched through the camera feeds. He examined the cargo bay and spied a bulkhead door ahead. "There," he said. "Get to that door."

The pair moved forward and Watkins sealed the inner airlock again. The cargo hold began to repressurize. She kept an eye on the loading dock's environmental status in her heads-up display. When the pressure equalized with the crew cabin, she nodded to Cheng. He tightened his grip on his weapon and hunkered down at the crew door. Watkins pulled her sidearm and began breathing heavily in her helmet.

"Okay, opening it."

"Remember, we need the guy alive," said Padre.

A moment passed as Watkins examined her heads-up display, her breath quickening.

"It's not opening," she said.

"I thought you had control," said Padre.

"I do. It's unlocked. It should have opened."

"Try to push it, then," snapped Padre.

Cheng rammed his shoulder into the door. It didn't budge.

"They must've barred it," said Watkins. "They have gravity on the other side."

"I got an idea," said Padre.

He turned his rock hopper around and ran it along the top of the ship. Ahead, an oblong capsule, thirty feet long, revolved around the ship on a metal line.

Cutting that should dislodge whatever they used to bar the door.

"Get ready," said Padre.

He moved in close to the spinning tether, then manipulated one of the hopper's legs out before him. He watched the capsule swing swiftly round and round. The cable anchoring it swung past his tendril. He paused his open eye over the icon for the plasma cutter. He felt the sweat on his brow again.

Ah, fuck, it. Rouja, baby, I'll be home soon.

He blinked and a white-blue plasma stream shot out of the tip of the rock hopper's limb. The cable swung through the heated plasma and melted through in an instant.

"*Now!*" Padre yelled.

Cheng ran forward and smacked against the door. It swung inward. Beyond the doorframe, everything was embroiled in a dizzying physics experiment as the centrifugal gravity drive failed. The five men inside lifted into the air and slammed violently into the far wall. A coffin-size med pod followed after them and splattered one of the men's heads on the ceiling as the gravitational focus moved around in the small space. The crew was sent pinwheeling in changing directions.

Topside, Padre had only melted partway through the thick spinning cable. Suddenly the capsule arced toward him. He fired the hopper's thrusters and darted off. The giant pod careened into the spot where he had been, then snapped loose and flipped end over end into the black starry expanse.

Everyone was quiet for a moment.

"Uh, how'd that go?" asked Padre.

He looked down to make sure he hadn't shit himself.

The camera feeds of Cheng and Watkins peered into the open room. Splotches of red smeared the white walls. Battered bodies floated about the cabin surrounded by red bubbles and debris.

"Door's open," said Cheng.

Five of the bio readings in Watkin's display went dark. A sixth was still pinging.

"Fuuuck!" said Padre. "Move, now!"

"Stepping in," said Cheng.

He crossed the threshold and went straight for the nearest floating body.

"You know, I could have disabled the gravity using my access," said Watkins as she followed.

Padre scowled and shot back, "There was no time."

Little redheaded know-it-all. Did I just blow it?

Cheng knocked debris out of the air with his elbows as he trod around with his weapon at the ready. Watkins ducked and bobbed to avoid floating blood bubbles.

"All right, give me the roll call," ordered Padre. "We're looking for an engineer named M. Rinsler."

"Mohammed Rinsler? The brainiac who invented quantum intelligence? Didn't he croak in '07 before the secession?" asked Watkins.

"Enough with the smart talk," said Padre. "This guy's bio-locked to a mining prototype."

Cheng pulled the closest body toward him by the lapel. He scanned the face with his Opti-Comp. "Singh," he read off the identity lookup that appeared in his view.

"No," growled Padre.

Cheng pushed the body back through the air, where it drifted into a corner. One by one, they scanned the corpses—Crown, Kim, Montenegro, Frist.

"I'm still reading another one," said Watkins as she paced the small room.

"It's our mark, find him," said Padre.

There was little more than six hundred square feet in the cabin and the man was nowhere to be seen.

"Got him," said Watkins.

She pushed aside the floating medical pod to reveal an obscure alcove. A flashing light appeared in the center of her view. It read, "Occupied."

"Ha, the fucker's taking a crap!" said an elated Padre. The lights from his console lit up his pearly whites like a Cheshire cat's grin. "Get out the can opener."

Cheng took up a ready position beside the door while Watkins navigated the ship's control system with eye movements.

"I can't peep it," she said. "This lock's manual."

Cheng stepped forward and pulled a small handgrip the size of a box cutter from his belt. It produced a six-inch heated blade that wavered in space as he moved it around. He stuck it between the door and the frame and quickly swiped down, cutting the bolt. Black fumes obscured Padre's view.

"I can't see shit," said Padre.

Cheng whipped his hand through the smoke, clearing it away. Then he reached forward and pulled the door open.

Inside the cramped zero-g toilet sat a shaggy-haired, unshaven man. His black hair floated about his head and face in the microgravity. His eyes were still open and in his hands he grasped a black sphere, three inches in diameter. He gave a final exhale and the bio-light on Watkins's display went out.

The man was dead.

"Pops, that's him," said Watkins. "That's Rinsler. The famous one."

Padre wanted to cuss, but all that came out of his mouth was air.

"I'll be damned," said Cheng.

What the fuck?

"I'll check his med log," said Watkins.

"Looks like a heart attack," said Cheng.

Watkins fidgeted with the man's wrist to initiate a download of biometrics.

Padre hoped it was just a heart attack. They could try to shock him back.

"Confirmed. Heart stopped. Also, his implant says his name is Mohammed," she said.

Cheng spoke up, "You want us to take this black ball?"

"No," Padre replied. "I want you to fucking resuscitate him!"

"I'll try," said Watkins.

She reached out to pull the sphere from his grasp and it rippled red at her touch.

"Don't touch that thing! The client said there's a self-destruct mechanism if it leaves him," said Padre.

"I can't shock him without shocking it, too," said Watkins.

Jesus, what have I gotten myself into?

Mohammed Rinsler, the most brilliant mind of the last century, was still alive . . . and they had just killed him again. Padre knew two things now. The device was no simple mining tool, and his handler was lying to him. The stakes had just changed.

"Fine, leave him be. I have to make contact. Watkins, bridge me through the *Zzyzx*'s antenna," said Padre.

"Affirmative. Stand by."

Padre saw the link connection status come through on his display. He navigated to a historical automobile auction site and logged in as *deadguy3337* to bid up an auction for an old Chevy big-block engine. Had the job gone well, he would have bid as *twointhehand13*, but Rinsler was dead and so he was *deadguy3337*. He'd have to wait for his bid to relay down to Earth and then back. It would take about thirty minutes.

"I'm going to look around," said Watkins. "Maybe there's some other valuables."

"What's your little ball do?" said Cheng as he stared into the dead man's eyes.

After thirty minutes of fruitless pondering, Padre's inbox received a message. An ad directed him to download a bit-currency gambling game. After another wait, the install completed and he found it was actually an encrypted chat app. A call came through immediately. He had received only text communications until now. He pinched his earlobe.

"Hello," he answered.

A silhouette appeared on screen. "Status," said the specter in a digitally modulated voice.

Where is this guy? There are no ships or bases in range.

"We have the prototype, but your guy had a heart attack," he said.

There was a moment of silence. Padre began to feel a strange buzzing in his head.

"And the rest of the crew?" asked the silhouette.

"Retired," said Padre.

"This is a serious situation. Success was of the utmost importance."

"What could I have done? The man had a heart attack. There was no way to do this without giving him a scare. It's not like we went in there guns blazing."

The silhouette went silent again for a moment. The buzzing in Padre's head became a subtle headache.

What kind of connection is this?

"You'll be required to clean up this mess, Mr. Padre."

"That's not a problem. I can bring you the sphere. Just tell me how to unlock it."

"No," came the stern reply. "I'll send someone else for that."

"Listen—" began Padre.

The silhouette interrupted, "Disable the ship's communication systems and do not touch the prototype. You are to guard the wreckage until I say further. Manage that and there's still a paycheck in it for you."

"How long are we talkin' about?" said Padre.

"Six months, maybe more. I have to send someone with another bio-key. I will contact you as necessary."

Padre rubbed his kneecaps. "Are you shitting me? I should sit here and guard this wreck for another six months?"

"If you want to stay in my good graces," said the silhouette.

And who the fuck are you?

Padre suppressed the urge to scowl. It was rumored that Rinsler's QI had cracked faster-than-light communication for Washington. If the dead man really was Rinsler, then—

This chat is coming from Earth and this spook is a G-man.

The silhouette continued, "I have no religion as to how many operatives it takes to retrieve the prototype, but I will eliminate outstanding risks."

Motherfucker. Do you expect me to share my payday with another merc?

Padre snarled his lip. He couldn't help it anymore. "I can watch the ship. Who are you sending?"

"Someone expendable," said the silhouette.

The call ended. Padre felt the throbbing in his head cease.

"Uncle Sam ain't screwing me over a second time," he grumbled.

He flipped on the comm and radioed his team. "Watkins, hack that prototype."

TWO

Alvin Baylor hovered in front of the office coffeemaker. It was 7:00 a.m. and he was exhausted and itching for the vacation that awaited him at the end of his shift. He stared bleary-eyed at an animated hologram floating before him. A cartoon asteroid-man gave him a thumbs-up over the blare of trumpets. "Honesty! Integrity! Teamwork! Excellence! That's the Alteris Way!" shouted the animated logo. It looped over and over, commingling with the sound of Alvin's percolating coffee. He waited for the fluid to finish dripping into the cup, then turned away quickly so his Opti-Comp would break line of sight with the projection frame mounted above the coffeemaker. The asteroid-man and his trumpets ceased.

Alvin's stomach rumbled. He'd been drinking the night before. He'd been doing it a lot lately. He grabbed a doughnut from the counter and headed to the red vinyl booth in the corner of the kitchenette. He plopped down on the seat with a little bounce and felt his gut touch the table.

I gotta cut back.

A glass wall divided the kitchen from the test floor, and he could see Thompson giving a tour to a woman in a blue hat shaped like a giant flower bulb. They were holding up work. Work that needed to be completed before he could leave. They walked along the guardrail that overlooked the rock hopper staging area. The enormous industrial hangar was located in Old North Hollywood, an industrial district in the Southern Californian Corporate Collective. Synaptic controls for asteroid mining vehicles were installed here. That was Alvin's job.

Two of the egg-shaped crafts were suspended above the floor by a thick harness. Each rock hopper had eight tendrils and over seven thousand flexion points awaiting calibration. The complex business of aligning mental control with leg motors was waiting for the tour to finish. Following configuration, the vehicles would be sent to the stars while Alvin would go home to relax for the holidays. His first vacation in over two years.

He sipped his coffee then blinked twice and a virtual newspaper appeared in his Opti-Comp on the table in front of him. He picked it up and flopped it open as though it were a real old-fashioned newspaper. His eyes zipped past holiday sales and examined the headlines.

"Homeless Riot Over Sidewalk Taxes!"

"Lawyers Strike to End Contract Automation!"

"Alteris Asteroid to Ride with China!"

The last one caught his attention.

China?

When he peeped it, an advertisement leaped out into the air.

"Alvin Baylor, roll the years away with nano-rejuvenation!" a voice said.

A hologram of his face appeared in front of him. He scowled, and the floating doppelgänger mimicked it. He ignored the voice as he studied the thinning hair and pudgy cheeks, the almond eyes that focused like lasers, and a chin that jutted out like a rock. As the sales pitch continued, he watched his face grow younger and younger until it reminded him of a time when the spotlight was still on him and his future was golden. Those dreams were dead.

.

The doppelgänger popped out of existence and his mind snapped back to the present. The news article was revealed, and Alvin skimmed it.

Alteris was sending payloads to Earth on Chinese ships. The atrophied U.S. Government had filed suit. Washington survived on defense contracts while North America fractured into Corporate Territories. It had been ten years since the secession, when a group of CEOs had joined forces and used fear of artificial intelligence to split the nation. AI was outlawed to protect human employment, but little else remained that wasn't governed by a balance sheet. *Greedy bastards don't care if we get nuked.*

Alvin picked up his doughnut and took a bite. He watched Thompson out on the test floor laughing with the woman in the stupid hat.

"Hurry the fuck up so I can get to work," he grumbled under his breath.

He cocked his head as the duo stopped next to the synaptic control station. Thompson was enticing her to drive one of the unfinished hoppers. He reached out to pick up a rubbery skullcap as the woman removed her flower hat.

"Hell no," said Alvin.

He dropped his doughnut on the table and blinked at a floating button labeled "PA" in his Opti-Comp.

"Hold up," he said. "Are you rated?" His voice echoed over the test floor.

The woman looked at Thompson with surprise. Thompson pressed a button on the wall and glared at the kitchen. "It's fine, Baylor." His voice came from a speaker by the coffeemaker. He smiled at the woman then swatted in Alvin's direction. She placed the synaptic cap on her head.

"I asked you a question. Are you rated for hardware control?" said Alvin.

The woman walked to the public address at the wall, turned to face the kitchen, and answered, "I'm rated for VR Level 3 and Hardware Level 1."

Alvin ran a facial recognition scan on her and saw that she was Asha Lakshmi, the head of the dev team that wrote microcontroller code for the legs.

Great... now I got two corpos holding up the line.

Management rarely touched hardware. Like most of the big salaries, they were telepresence-commuters, using virtual reality or other technology to avoid the blight and overpopulation of the city centers. Most of their time was spent calling meetings so they could bitch at people about deadlines like the one they were holding up now.

"It's not calibrated," he said. "At Level 1, the feedback would be too—"

"She's fine," interrupted Thompson. "Her team writes code for these legs. Go ahead." He motioned to Lakshmi, and she gave a thankful smile as she walked back and connected her cap to the console in front of her. She tapped the screen and began moving her index finger. The hopper hanging beyond the guardrail moved a single leg. Her eyes opened wide in excitement and she turned to smile at Thompson.

Alvin shook his head and went back to the news.

Dumb-asses.

The next headline he saw was, "Zuck Dominates Final Match!"

He read it immediately and learned that Rick Zuck, star cyber-athlete and heir to a data-mining empire, had led the Los Angeles Voidwalkers to a win in his final game. He was retiring with a half-billion payout and an all-expenses-paid trip on *The Hope,* a Chinese luxury starship.

Lucky no-talent bastard. Like he needs another dime.

Suddenly a scream blasted from the coffeemaker.

Alvin looked through the glass wall to see Lakshmi's arms

flailing ahead of her Frankenstein's monster. Her face contorted as she wailed.

The hopper rocked from side to side as a tentacle swung through the air. The arm was dangerously close to hitting Lakshmi.

He dashed out the door and felt his temples warm as the synaptic implants in his head activated. He overpowered her control and the hopper ceased its fight. The leg dropped back down to hang limply beneath the ship.

Lakshmi passed out, hitting the ground with a thud.

"Get it off her!" Thompson screamed as he backed away.

Alvin ran up and pulled the connection. As he knelt to take the cap off the woman, she opened her eyes and gasped.

"Thank god!" exclaimed Thompson. "That cap is defective!"

Lakshmi brought her hand to her forehead. Thompson came forward to help her sit up. "She could have been killed," he said.

"Let me check it," said Alvin.

He placed the cap on his head and disabled his implants with a peep. He wiggled his fingers. Nothing happened.

"Oh," he said, remembering the cable.

He plugged the cap in and looked at them calmly.

From behind him, the hopper reached out with all six tentacles and grabbed on to the guardrail like an oversized squid. It pulled itself forward, stretching the suspension harness to its limit. Thompson screamed and ran to the far wall, abandoning Lakshmi while she backpedaled on her hands in terror.

"Nope, cap's fine," Alvin said with a shrug.

He released the hopper's hold on the rail. The two-seater pod swung backward like a pendulum suspended from the ceiling.

"I told you. It's not calibrated yet. The feedback's out of range for neurotypicals. I hope you feel better, Ms. Lakshmi, but I really do need to get to work. These ship out tonight."

Thompson composed himself and helped Lakshmi to her feet. They scuttled back along the guardrail toward the kitchen. She grimaced, holding her hand to her forehead while throwing fearful glances back at Alvin.

"I don't like him," he heard her say.

"Nobody does. He's an idiot savant. Former cyber-athlete, we got him cheap after he cheated and lost his license," said Thompson as they reached the kitchen door.

The words stung Alvin.

The woman stared at him through the glass wall as she scanned his face with her Opti-Comp. He read her lips saying, "Alvin Baylor . . ." and knew that soon his sordid history would float before her. He turned around and gritted his teeth. He would always be a pariah.

"Vacation in ten hours," he said to himself.

He wanted a drink.

THREE

Rouja Natastae strode through the bustling Hong Kong dining hall past servers hunched over dim sum carts and patrons stuffing their faces. Her statuesque figure and beauty attracted attention as always, but few suitors had the confidence to do more than gawk. That was just as well—she had work to do. She ignored swooning looks from diners as she passed them by. She was tired of this city, and she would be leaving today.

In the corner booth was the man she had spent a year tracking, a notorious pimp and illegal goods dealer named Jianju Leung. An overly made-up girl in trashy, schoolgirl attire blathered in his ear. Leung possessed accounting data for a ring of sex slavers, information that would help Rouja retrace her past and correct a mistake. His fat head looked down the aisle at her, lasciviously scanning her figure. He didn't recognize her, not yet, anyway. She stopped in front of his table and his gaze rose to meet hers.

"Hey Ju," she said.

He looked puzzled. Perhaps he recognized her voice or something about her demeanor, but not her face or blond locks. He'd never seen the green-eyed visage that smirked down at him now.

Leung cocked his head and smiled back while the schoolgirl

went wide-eyed at the sight of Rouja and began nagging at him in Cantonese. Rouja found the girl's voice shrill and irritating but kept her gaze on Leung.

"Time to pay up," she said.

Leung sat up straight with a concerned look. His mole-flecked upper lip twitched, but before he could speak, his temple was perforated by the metal stiletto of Rouja's boot. His head bounced sideways and then he fell forward into his soup bowl, splashing sweet and sour liquid all over the girl beside him.

Rouja leaned over the table and sliced his wrist with a blade. The smart-band fell off and his flesh parted. She dug inside and removed a bloody strip of holographic foil.

The tablecloth took on a darker, richer hue as blood spurted from Leung's wrist and spread across its surface. The girl froze, her caked-on makeup looking like a painting. She began panting hysterically.

"You're free," said Rouja.

She swirled her bloody fingertips in a glass of water, then turned and strutted away with the confidence of a model on the catwalk. She'd killed plenty of people in plain sight before. The trick was to be nonchalant.

The clamoring of all-you-can-eat gluttony was soon overpowered by the girl's screaming. People craned their necks for a look at the commotion, but Rouja was already through the dining hall.

She felt her smart-band buzz. The name "Daddy" in digital letters floated in her view. She hadn't spoken with Padre since he'd left for his "big" job and she considered ignoring it, but the timing was too rich. She tapped the implant in her earlobe and answered. She felt an odd buzzing in her head.

"I got it," she said pocketing Leung's data store.

"Hey doll, wasn't sure you'd answer," said John Padre.

"I found her without you," she said.

"You did?"

"Leung had the sales manifest just like I told you. I need to buy a decrypt of his DNA hash."

"Still a little work to do, then," Padre replied.

His indifference irked her. "And your once-in-a-lifetime opportunity? How's that working out?" she said.

"It's still that and I'd like to offer you a cut," he said.

"Oh, would you?" *He must have fucked it up.*

"Check your inbox in a few, for travel arrangements. You're going on a little recon tour."

"Shit," she said as two of Leung's men walked through the front door. She turned away from them and toward the kitchen. "John, I'm gonna have to call you back."

"Listen, I'm serious," he said.

"So am I," said Rouja.

"I'll hold, doll."

"Of course you will."

"Can I watch?" he asked.

She rolled her eyes.

Rouja pressed at the outer edge of her eye socket, turning on the camera in her Opti-Comp lens. Padre would see what she saw now. She looked back over her shoulder as Leung's hooker ran to the two heavies and pointed at her.

Rouja stepped through the kitchen's double doors and assessed her surroundings. The cooks immediately took notice of her. They moved to and fro across a walkway banked by stainless steel tables and appliances. She stepped to her left and backed up toward the wall while they watched.

The doors swung inward and her pursuers entered. They stopped in place to scan the room. Each was the size of a refrigerator.

I'll need to separate them.

The heavies traced the gaze of the kitchen staff to find Rouja with one arm raised up behind her and one jutted out in front in a flashy wushu stance. She gave a little wink to entice the bigger guy.

"You first," she said.

He nodded at his partner then smiled and stepped forward to take the bait. He raised his arms like a boxer. Before he got half a step, she dropped her arms and her smile and kneed him in the nuts. He groaned as his head fell forward and she swung her right leg over the back of his neck and cracked it with a twist of her hip. She stepped back to let his gargantuan body slump to the floor.

His partner's eyes went wide. Then he charged her. She side-stepped, causing him to slam into one of the metal preparation tables. He came to a halt as the wind was knocked from his lungs. Flour clouded the air.

She stepped to him as he was bent over, coughing. He snarled and went to attack and she stuffed two knuckles right into his throat, crushing his trachea. He gasped as he fell to the floor in a clatter of metal bowls and airborne particulate.

Rouja adjusted her black skirt, brushing the white powder from her stockinged legs as the man rolled about on the floor suffocating.

"Very nice," growled Padre.

"All in a day's work," she said.

She walked down the aisle, giving cute little smiles and winks to the team of cooks. They were silent and gaping, returning like the tide to the cramped area for a look at her as she strutted out the rear exit.

Padre saw what she saw. He chuckled in her ear.

As she passed through the doorway, she lifted the black silk hoodie from her back and covered her head. Then she tapped at the choker around her throat and felt the muscles of her face stretch and twitch as nanotechnology reconfigured soft tissue and pigment. Her scalp follicles tickled. She coughed as her throat tightened while the collar injected miniature robotic plastic surgeons. By the time she had traversed the trash-strewn alleyway out to the bustling street, the process was done. She removed her hood to reveal raven hair and brown eyes with epicanthic folds. The morning light hit her and began to sooth the remaining itchiness in her face. She pulled a red scarf from her purse, wrapped it around her neck, then continued into the crowd.

"Okay, what's the deal?" she said.

Padre answered, "Alteris Asteroid has a ship that went missing out past Armstrong Station. I need you to figure out what they plan to do about it."

"Who's the mark?" she asked.

"I don't know. That's what I need you to find out. They're sending someone to replace me."

"So you fucked up?"

"Rouja, don't give me any of your crap. This is the last job and I'm coming home for good."

"Wait a minute. Where are you?"

"I'm out here with the package," said Padre.

She slowed her walk down the crowded sidewalk. "So take it. What the fuck?"

"It's locked with some new synaptic scheme. I put my new girl Watkins on it and she passed out. She's moaning about a migraine and won't touch the thing. There's some sort of self-destruct. I need you, doll."

"Why should I help you?"

"Because Washington is paying the bounty," he said.

"You're working for those assholes again?"

"I didn't know. I thought it was a Corporate job. This is our chance to fuck 'em."

"For how much?" she asked.

"The contract was one billion. We can get more from the Chinese."

"One billion in coin? What is this thing?" She had never encountered a payday that large. Purchasing an old quantum cryptographic machine to hack Leung's data would cost her in the hundreds of millions. It was as if the universe had created a path for her.

"Some sort of experimental mining tool," said Padre.

"Did Alteris cheat on their Continental Defense Taxes? Why's Washington after it?"

"I don't know. I just know it's my chance at revenge." His voice softened. "Our chance."

I don't want revenge. I just want to make it right.

"Fifty-fifty. You split your half with the team," she said.

"Deal. Now listen, I want you to stick with this guy all the way to Armstrong."

"I'll get on it."

"Attagirl," said Padre.

"One more thing," she said. "If you're out there in the belt, then how are you talking to me in real time?"

"Faster than light, baby. I'm on Uncle Sam's network."

"And you don't think they're listening?"

She stopped walking and lowered her head.

"Watkins says our encrypt keys will hold. Don't worry."

Damn it, he's sloppy.

"Don't contact me this way again. I'll be in touch." She tapped her earlobe and ended the call. An odd tension left her head as the connection dropped.

Padre's job sounded like a long shot, but it had come at the right time. She felt the knot in her gut tighten. Nothing would stop her from finding her daughter again. She stood up straight and disappeared into the crowd.

FOUR

Fifteen hours later, Alvin was finally out the door. The incident with Thompson had soured the day. As usual, he had been forced into overtime because of shipping delays. He'd had both hoppers ready in eight hours and secretly wished that AI had not been banned from freight jobs. Bots were so much more reliable than humans, but if one said that aloud the union would label you anti-humanist and send you packing. He was exhausted and eager for two weeks of homebound bliss, during which he wouldn't have to deal with a single demand from work. But first, he needed a drink.

He headed to his neighborhood bar, the Budapest, for the salve. It was a shithole dive for working-class loners and failed human beings. Waste-oids roamed the perimeter and slept in the alley out back. He could have gone home to drink, but it wasn't the booze he really craved. He hated to admit it, but he needed to be around people to forget himself, and he needed to be drunk to slough off his hardness. It was the only socializing he welcomed anymore.

Alvin sat down to order a bourbon from the dour-eyed woman behind the bar. He sighed under the soft glow of the Christmas lights strung above the mirror. The place was windowless with two doors opposite each other. One led in and the other led out into an alley. It reeked of sweat and marijuana. A couple of synth addicts at the end of the bar chattered to each other through rotten black teeth while a single augmented-reality panel flitted through different ads. Alvin turned off his Opti-Comp so he could instead look at the wall of ancient tin and neon signage show-casing obscure beer brands that weren't sold anymore. It felt like a defeated place, passed by in the twenty-second-century rush. It felt like home.

The heavy-chested barmaid placed down a shot and gave him a soft smile. He'd been with her once. A drunken escapade. He knocked back the shot and asked for a bourbon and cola.

The rear door swung open as a couple of toughs from the local Mexican-Armenian gang wandered in. The sounds of an over-crowded city blared over the din of drunken conversations. Alvin's sleep-deprived mind wrestled with the noise, then the door swung closed again and the chatter returned. The thugs sized up everyone and their eyes landed on Alvin. He'd seen them before and they'd never given him any trouble. He gave them the hard look that had become his public face, and they nodded in respect.

He considered the consequences of another hangover. He was done with work and he could go to bed drunk at 4:00 a.m. and no one would care, but he knew he was killing himself. Then the warmth hit his gut. He felt a rush of contentment swallow his conscience.

The older woman leaned over the bar and handed over his next drink. She smiled at him silently, allowing her breasts to brush his forearm. She spoke very little English, so he simply smiled back. She was warm and she smelled good, but he was not drunk enough to take her in the back again. He didn't want it tonight. He was happy to be off for two weeks; plenty of time for carousing if he got sick of VR hookups.

She walked away to serve the end of the bar. He saw his face appear in the spot of mirror left bare in a sea of paper flyers admonishing patrons to "pay up" ahead of time. He looked angry. It surprised him. He thought the shot had softened him up. He lifted the glass and stared at the ice cubes as he chugged it down.

After several more rounds he got up to piss. Standing in the rat-shit-dotted bathroom, he tried not to breathe in the aroma of the toilets. He could hear Wayne through the window talking to himself out back.

I could use a toke.

He finished up and stepped out into the dark alley to say hello to the homeless man.

"Alvin! You wanna hit this?" asked the white-haired man. Wayne looked clean enough today, no visible sores around the mouth. Alvin always checked, always told himself the alcohol would kill the spittle on the end of the joint.

"Sure, man." He took a puff and passed it back. "How ya been?"

"I'm good. Trying to wind down. Been partying since dawn. Where were you last night? It was packed. Girlies even," said Wayne.

"Had to work early today, so I drank at home."

"Shoot. Well, I guess you gotta pay the bills. They had the game on. Did ya see it? Zuck was tearing it up!"

"Naw, didn't see it. Zuck ain't that great. I played with him in school."

"Well, he was fucking 'em up bad last night. Got five head shots in a row."

"Yeah, he always liked to hang back. Was Rita here?"

"Yeah, she was working. Got her a new man," said Wayne.

Alvin made a disappointed face.

Wayne took a long hit off the joint and offered the nub back. "Shit, man, you look tired. They must be working you hard."

Alvin nodded. "Yep," he said as he declined the toke. "Gotta get back to my drink."

"Sure thing, boss. Merry Christmas and keep away from the old cow. I hear she gots the drips."

"Will do," said Alvin. As he walked to the door, Wayne got on his knees and crawled back into the plastic toolshed he called home.

Just one more.

He walked in to find the barmaid pointing a baseball bat at the gang toughs. He passed them with a beady-eyed stare on the way to his seat. They cursed and she cursed back and they walked out the back door.

"What was that about?" he said as he sat on the torn red bar stool. A fresh drink was waiting for him.

"No money," she muttered in her broken English. She turned back to the register and began bopping her hips. She'd started on the sauce.

No way. Not again.

His sharp edges were rounded down to nubs. He stared around the room bleary-eyed. He didn't feel his smart-band buzz. He hoisted his drink in cheers to the bar. The synth addicts down at the end toasted him back. When he finally chugged the brown poison back, he looked down the empty glass and saw the message on his wrist.

"Alvin, where you at? Barton." The words circled around like a mini rotating marquee on the black strap.

"Fuck!" he shouted.

The bartender gave him a look.

His first damn night of vacation and he was going back into the office. He knew it. *What blew up?* He hoped it was something small, something he could turn on and off. *I have to sober up before responding. Please don't let it be a coding issue or I'll be there all weekend waiting on a fix.*

His wrist buzzed again and new words appeared.

"Have you been drinking?"

They're monitoring me.

"Sonofabitch!" he shouted.

The bar patrons turned to look at him.

He knew when he'd agreed to the health tracking that he might sometime be monitored, but Alteris had never said anything before. Why should they care what he did to himself on vacation? How dare they! Was it Thompson's doing?

I'm hacking this thing.

Then the band buzzed with a different rhythm.

"Incoming call—Barton Aimes," read the floating marquee.

Alvin scowled, then suppressed it and took a deep breath. He tapped his temple to wake his Opti-Comp lens. A quick blink answered the video call.

His boss appeared, perfectly coifed and clean shaven in a suit. Barton Aimes's elbows splayed wide across the image, as if to obstruct the view behind him. "Alvin, we need you to come in. We have an emergency."

"What emergency merits this kind of privacy invasion? You know I'm on vacation."

Aimes looked shaken. "Listen, Alvin, this isn't the time for—"

"I want to see his face," said a female voice.

Barton looked back over his shoulder.

"Who is that? I want to see *her* face," demanded Alvin.

Aimes moved aside and an older woman walked up to the camera. She was fashionably dressed, and her delicate features were framed by a blond bob. She crossed her arms.

Oh my god—it's Meyer.

He quickly brought his face into something resembling a smile.

"This is the man who was selected?" she asked with disdain.

"Uh . . . hello, ma'am," Alvin stammered. He was not important enough for Sabrina Meyer, CEO of Alteris, to know he existed. Something unusual was going on.

"Young man, you'd best get your act together. We have an emergency on hand," said Meyer. Then to Barton, "Get him briefed and out the door. If there are any problems, terminate him immediately." And with that she walked out of view.

Alvin was stunned. Alteris was the only company that would employ him without a degree. They overlooked his past indiscretions in exchange for his synaptic competence. They sponsored his apartment and his citizenship. His anger vanished. He needed the job. He hated it, but he needed it. Barton again filled the screen.

"This is serious, Alvin. It's never been more serious. I know you're burning it at both ends, but you're the only one we trust to get this done."

Trust?

Alvin had never heard anything so close to a compliment from his boss. He hardly spoke to the guy. Once a month at best. Heck, he only saw him in person once a year during the man's visit to the hopper facility.

"I hear you, Barton, but I can't get a day off. What is this about?"

"Did you hear Meyer? You do this and you'll be a hero to the company. This is the kind of opportunity a person gets once in their career. Get yourself here to the spaceport ASAP. Your launch window is at 5:00 a.m."

"What? The port? Launch to where?"

"Just be here. You heard her. Don't be late or you're fired."

"Yeah. I got it," he said as he ended the call.

He would have to leave now to make it to the spaceport in time. He'd only been to New Mexico once, let alone outer space. His high was dashed.

I hate traveling.

"Goddamn it!" he shouted as he slammed his fists on the bar.

"Three hundred," said the bartender. "Then go."

He looked at her as if to say *sorry*, but she wasn't having it. He bumped his wrist to the tab then walked out the door.

FIVE

Alvin dragged himself out onto the cracked pavement of the parking lot and signaled an autocar with his Opti-Comp. It had begun to rain.

The Budapest's neon sign sizzled as water drops hit it. Purple letters reflected in a puddle at his feet. The pedestrians scattered like rats from the street. They abandoned foot for cars and seized up traffic. Alvin had a feeling he'd best start walking. He'd find his ride somewhere in the line.

He walked down the sidewalk enjoying the solitude. No one looked at him in the rain. The streets sparkled and the storefront colors popped; even the graffiti looked nice. He longed to retire elsewhere to escape overpopulation, but prices were unfathomable. He would never earn enough to stop working and, besides, his skills were needed on-site.

Outer space. Shit.

That's where Aimes had said he was going. The thought of going into orbit scared him. So much to go wrong. *Cautious optimism*, he reminded himself. Perhaps his fortunes were changing at work. *Hope for the best, but for now, enjoy the rain.*

A small driverless car pulled over and he felt his wrist buzz.

He tapped his band to the door to identify himself, got in, and slurred the word "home." The car pulled out into traffic. Row after row of tiny, single-doored cars sat bumper to bumper. The travel time floating in his view reported one hour.

Not bad.

He purchased a train ticket to New Mexico using his Opti-Comp, then set an alarm and closed his eyes for a nap. Sixty minutes later a tone blared in his ear as the car pulled up to his building. He stumbled out and bumped his band against the lobby doors. His nap, while mildly refreshing, reminded him all the more that he needed to rest. He'd have to catch those zzzz's later to get to New Mexico on time.

Once inside he took the elevator up to his apartment. He tapped his band again at his door and the company lodging bill came up. They'd raised the interest on his daily mortgage. *Cheap-skates.* He paid the two thousand from his bit-wallet and entered. Then he logged his implants out of the Alteris network and snorted a bump that he'd been saving for New Year's Eve. The company didn't need to know what he was ingesting. They knew he was coming and that ought to be enough. The boost got him packing. He hurriedly stuffed a few days' worth of clothes, his multitool, and a set of VR goggles into a shoulder bag.

He did another line, finishing off his emergency stash, emptied his bladder and bowels, picked up his bag, and walked to the door. He stopped to look at his two-hundred-square-foot home. The bed looked so comfortable.

"Security mode on," he said.

The AR projection frames throughout the room turned off. The TV, the artwork on the walls, his ferns—all the augmented reality disappeared, leaving only that comfy bed. He felt butter-flies stir in his gut. He turned and hightailed it down to ground level.

Another ride took him to the North Hollywood station, where he hopped on the metro. He half wished he hadn't done the coke so he could rest, but he knew he'd sleep through another alarm. He rode the train thinking intensely about how he could prevent the company from monitoring his smart-band and just what kind of job he was being pulled into.

He arrived at Union Station just before midnight and worked his way past the oblivious holiday travelers staring at every flashing, screaming advertisement that hit their Opti-Comps. The coke was beginning to wear off and he felt jittery and exhausted. He dodged around them and hurried to the maglev so he could start working on a smart-band hack before he left LA.

He followed the floating arrow in his view that led to the high-speed-train station outside. He pushed his way out the front doors, where the stench of sidewalk dwellers hit him hard in the nose. They hoisted signs demanding living wages and an end to squatter's taxes. They were such a disgusting rabble that he wondered who would want to hire them and why they would scream about it at this hour. He wanted out of the pack and shoved aside a man carrying a sign that read, "No Jobs, No Future" then ran for fresh air.

Up ahead he saw the checkpoint for the maglev. He began walking again. Running toward security would get him shot.

There were three doorways through the freestanding wall that led to the platform, one for California's Corporate-sponsored citizens, one for non-citizens, and one for the other North American Territories. Each entry was fronted by a tall block of glass that encased a virtual security agent. Beyond that, a body scanner and two armed guards waited.

He was never so glad to have his Corporate sponsorship. The line was the shortest and Corporate passengers got to skip the automated personality interrogation and move straight to the body scanner. Money did all the talking.

Only one woman remained ahead of him when a commotion broke out at the North American entrance to his right.

"Am I armed? Of course I'm armed, you virtual bitch!" yelled a white man wearing a cowboy hat. "They don't stand for this horse shit in the Republic!"

He was obviously from Texas, where automation was even less popular, and ironically he was screaming at the virtual screener that was meant to detect unstable personalities.

Seems like a positive diagnosis. Alvin crouched to the ground in preparation.

Two guards hefted their assault weapons at the Texan as he dropped his bag to reach into his waistband. He was riddled with bullets before his hand came out of his pants.

Alvin stood up again as travelers all around him dove to the ground in a panic.

It's over, slowpokes.

A computerized voice came over the loudspeakers. "Security has been restored. Please return to your business."

That seemed to end the matter. Everyone stood up and went on as if nothing had happened. Alvin felt a twinge of concern when he realized that his multitool might be considered a weapon.

The woman in line ahead of him passed through the check-point while he stood watching the guards throw a tarp over the dead Texan. Blood pooled around the body.

This is why I don't travel.

"Corporation?"

The words startled him. He looked ahead at the clear rectangle jutting from the ground. A holographic blond woman embedded in the glass block was asking the question. He looked past her at the body scanner and the armed guards and answered, "Alteris Asteroid Excavation Company."

"You may pass, Corporate citizen," said the virtual woman.

Alvin walked forward to the guards. "I have some tools that might—"

"You're Alteris, right?" interrupted one of them with a smile. He looked mixed race.

Alvin's look was similar. Although he was mostly Ashkenazi, he had enough Mongolian blood to benefit from the favoritism.

"My boy's gonna work there one day," said the guard. "You gotta have the tools for the job." He took Alvin's bag from him. "Go ahead, friend."

The other guard just yawned.

"Thank you," said Alvin.

He stepped into the scanner and was green-lit. The man handed back his bag on the way out and said, "Merry Christmas, Mr. Baylor."

Alvin nodded and hurried ahead. He figured he'd get a ping someday asking him to help the man's kid into a job. If that was the only cost, then so be it. Security checkpoints were death zones and he was happy to be through the gate.

One long workday had given way to the starless LA night. He felt loopy and nervous. *Was Aimes's call a dream?* He wished.

He felt his stomach rumble and turned his thoughts to sustenance. He needed something in his system besides drugs and alcohol. A line of printing kiosks stood in front of the train platform. Wedged between a Toy Box and a Smart-Band Express was a Vend-A-Meal. He got in line behind a mother and her young child. The boy was watching the Toy Box with his goggles. Various action figures battled it out in AR while waiting to be chosen for on-demand printing.

"Ms. Righteous . . . The Man . . . Agent America. Mom, they have Agent America!" the boy pleaded as his mother scoured the food options.

She hushed him tiredly. "We can't afford it."

"But Mom, I want something real to play with."

"That's a pro-government toy. Play in your goggles."

She pulled a package from the Vend-A-Meal slot and hurried off, dragging him by the arm.

Alvin stepped forward and looked at the menu.

He preferred real food when he could afford it, but he might as well get used to 3-D-printed amino-acid crap. Nutri-Paste was all there was to eat off-planet. Bland slop hardened and colored like a pizza would have to do. He tapped his band to pay and retrieved the small disc from the slot.

He boarded the train, threw his bag under the seat, and slumped down with relief. One disgusting bite of the rubbery pizza was enough. He wrapped it back into the package and shoved it into his bag. He'd eat it later; right now his mind was an addled mess.

His thoughts bounced around from the shooting to the unknown job ahead to the smart-band hack he'd been considering. He checked the train's entertainment stream and peeped Play on an old film. *Horse Feathers* started up in his Opti-Comp. He tried to watch, but he was restless. The drugs were fading. He resolved to get working on the smart-band hack before he crashed. At this point it seemed less risky than allowing Alteris to know what he did to himself nightly. Honesty had not paid off in the past.

He went into his bag for his multitool. Then he popped open the hand and got to work adding a new memory module. When it rebooted he started an operating system download and a script to virtualize the Alteris code. When the process finished, he would have control over what they knew about his habits.

I need to stop thinking now.

He closed his eyes to the sounds of the Marx Brothers and drifted away. Sometime later, he felt a jolt as the maglev train began its journey. At nearly four hundred miles per hour, he would be in New Mexico in a couple hours.

SIX

Alvin was awoken by a smack in the head. He opened his eyes and found himself hanging halfway into the train aisle. A rotund woman towing an overstuffed red shoulder bag banged into each passenger as she exited. He sat up straight as his thoughts coalesced. When he took a breath, he coughed up phlegm. His eyes were still tired.

I gotta stop killing myself.

He pressed a finger to his temple. His Opti-Comp woke up. It showed 3:00 a.m. in New Mexico. No Alteris logo appeared.

It worked.

He peeped through the menus and allowed location-reporting to his employer to commence, but he blocked the biometric data. He could show up dead now. As long as he showed up.

He hunched over in the alcove above his seat as he put on his jacket. A sparse stream of travelers finished exiting then he made his move. He stepped out onto the black lacquered floor of the spaceport. Chrome beams supported the glass ceiling. The clear night sky was visible above.

Wow, so many stars!

A man walked into him with a thud. "Excuse me," said the man without making eye contact.

Throngs of people passed through the station. Nothing halted the space trade, not the holiday nor the time of day. Launches were scheduled according to the position of orbits, not the circadian rhythm of humanity.

Alvin spied a water fountain to his right and made a beeline to it. He sidestepped a janitor mopping the floor and kept his head held high with a stern expression. His glare deterred the few travelers who were not lost in their Opti-Comps; the rest he dodged.

"Alvin! Good, you're here," said a voice from behind him.

Already spotted. I can't believe he's awake.

Barton Aimes trotted up next to the water fountain and stuck out a sweaty hand. Alvin shook it.

Alvin smiled broadly with bloodshot eyes and Aimes recoiled. Alvin took his drink and felt his boss eyeing him as he slurped up water.

"So what's this all about?" asked Alvin when he finished his drink and straightened.

They started walking through the terminal.

"We're sending you out with a delivery. We have an RnD test that has gone off schedule."

"Barton, I'm not trained for space."

"We need your synaptic skills. You're our best. No doubt about it," said Aimes.

Yes, I am. He hadn't heard words like those since his gaming days.

"I know you should be on leave and I promise you will be taken care of," Aimes continued.

"How so?"

He put his hand on Alvin's arm and gestured forward. "This is big league. Come on, Meyer is waiting."

"For me?" said Alvin.

"Yes." Aimes guided them toward the hover tram and they

boarded. "Excuse me, I need to send out a message." Aimes took on the aura of a robot in standby as he worked in his Opti-Comp.

Alvin felt his mood lighten as his mind raced over the possibilities. They wouldn't send him to outer space without a bonus. Asteroiders were granted retirement for risking their lives in deep space. He would be doing the same and not because they needed any human to fill a quota, but because they needed him.

The belt was very far away, but the chance to reclaim his dignity and change his fortune made the mission more than mandatory—it made it attractive. For the first time in years, he was getting some recognition.

Ten minutes later the hover tram pulled up in front of the Corporate concourse. It housed the twenty-second century's greatest space-bound companies. They stood in a towering block-long semicircle of glass, metal, and extruded synthetic materials. They sparkled in the moonlight.

Alvin admired the design of the company headquarters as he and his boss started up the long path to its entrance. It had been constructed only a few years ago, as part of CEO Sabrina Meyer's public relations outreach. She was a master of style. The building was over two hundred stories of intricately woven materials. The skeletal, cobalt-blue scaffolding seemed to rise to space itself. Large 3-D fabricators allowed the construction to feature numerous surface openings and outer decks. At this early hour, the building disappeared into the sky, leaving only the speckling of illuminated windows.

As the path curved around manicured faux-lawns and plastic trees, the company logo came into view. A series of onyx rectangles rose like staggered steps from the artificial turf. The iron sculpture of a comet rose steadily over each block. Its tail formed an asymptotic line reaching for the sky. No cartoon asteroid-man on this marquee. This was the power logo, overdesigned and created by committee. Alvin wondered when and if Meyer would touch that redesign job.

"I need you to clean up before we see her," said Aimes.

Alvin wrinkled his brow. "Sorry, I had no time."

"I have no religion about it, but Meyer is gonna have a fit if you walk in there looking like you just came off a bender."

Where does he come up with these sayings?

"I can shave and change into my dress hoodie," said Alvin.

He eyed Aimes's fitted business suit nervously. The boss was from Washington, D.C., a city that had refused casualness.

Aimes's mouth smiled, but his eyes didn't move. "That'll have to do," he said.

Fuck, I didn't think I'd be meeting with Meyer.

As they approached the double doors security became visible. Aerial drones swirled about the building like fireflies. Beyond the glass was the human contingent. A small coterie of black jumpsuits stood behind a giant console. They looked like field marshals surveying the battlefield. The lobby around them held a smattering of Opti-Comp multitaskers who roamed around bumping into things.

Alvin and Barton passed through the outer doors and entered a holding area. Another glass door stood before them.

Aimes stepped forward and a computerized voice said, "Hello, Barton Aimes. Please provide retinal identification."

He leaned forward into a concave impression beside the door and rested his chin on a small perch. A light turned on and examined the pattern of blood vessels in the back of his eye.

"Entrance granted, Barton Aimes. Please step forward," said the voice.

The translucent door opened.

Aimes stepped through into another small room, waited for the door behind him to shut again, then the one ahead of him opened and he was finally into the lobby. He turned to wait for Alvin.

Like rats in cages, thought Alvin.

"Hello, Alvin Baylor. Please provide retinal identification."

He placed his head in the chin cup and stared ahead through his right eye. He waited for what seemed too long.

"Unidentified pattern," said the computer voice.

Alvin pulled his head back and looked at his boss through the glass. He shrugged and flipped his palms upward to indicate his confusion.

"Alvin Baylor, please provide retinal identification," the voice demanded in the same monotone.

Alvin stuck his head forward again, hoping to avoid a scene.

"Unidentified pattern," it said.

The outline of the doorframe began to glow a pulsing red and an alarm went off. Alvin looked through the glass wall and saw the guards remove their sidearms. He stared bug-eyed at his boss.

Aimes gesticulated wildly while talking to them. A single guard passed through the doorway, gun in hand.

"What's the problem?" he said.

"Bad scan," said Alvin.

"Try the other eye," said the guard.

"Yes, sir," said Alvin.

I don't wanna die because of a computer glitch!

"Please provide retinal identification," commanded the voice.

Alvin again stared into the light, this time with his left eye.

"Unidentified pattern."

The black jumpsuit tightened hold on his handgun.

"Wait—it's my Opti-Comp," said Alvin.

He tapped his temple to turn it off.

"Entrance granted. Please step forward."

Alvin exhaled hard.

The guard motioned to him with a tilt of his head and they walked through the doorway together.

"What was that about?" said Aimes.

"I had to use my left eye," said a breathy Alvin.

The guard shined a flashlight into his eyes.

"Ack . . ." He grimaced as he looked away from the light.

"Bloodshot. You party last night?" asked the guard.

"Yes," he answered.

"You do it a lot?"

"On occasion," said Alvin.

"Uh-huh. Long-term abuse will change the blood vessels. Best to get rescanned," said the guard.

Aimes shot a glare at Alvin.

"I'm sure it's a stressful job," said the guard. He walked away.

Aimes shook his head. "Time to cut back."

Alvin nodded.

You control my work time, not my free time.

They continued on toward the bank of elevators and boarded the express car to the top floor. A guard waved them on, and when they entered, Aimes had to pass another retinal scan before he could speak the floor name.

"Penthouse," he said.

Fuck, this is real, thought Alvin.

The elevator doors parted to reveal a white plastic room. The shocking brightness of the decor kept Alvin in place. He wasn't ready to be seen. Ahead, a desk rose out of the floor in one continuous piece. A perfect-looking secretary sat behind it. A well-dressed guard stood beside her.

Aimes stepped off the elevator. "Clean up," he said, pointing forcefully.

Alvin hurried off the elevator. His shoes squeaked as he crossed the floor to the restroom. He pulled his fleece dress hoodie from his bag then dug around for an electric shaver. He began buzzing off his beard growth while staring at the mirror, which doubled as an AR promotions feed. It detailed the accomplishments of Alteris and Meyer. He knew the story, but read it anyway to quash his anxiety before meeting the CEO.

Meyer had built a reputation as the head of QuickFoods, the company that cornered the market on amino solutions for 3-D food printers. The floating media display christened her as the nutritional savior of the poor. It moved on to explain how she would now lead Alteris to market dominance in the energy sector.

He knew what it left out.

The death of her predecessor—murdered while visiting a mining colony near the asteroid belt. A disgruntled employee had sneaked aboard the executive shuttle and planted an ax in the man's brain over a contract dispute. Everyone had seen the video snippet of the blood-covered asteroider. The leak caused consternation among cause-oriented consumers. So Alteris brought on Meyer to polish the company brand. The public came to believe the 'roiders were simply unstable people, and a PR blitz wiped any talk of workers' rights from the news. Asteroiders were necessary but expendable brutes. Automation would eventually eliminate them.

He put down the clippers and brushed his fingertips over his now smooth cheeks.

His eyes were still bloodshot so he practiced a broad smile, squeezing his almond eyes down to slits. Meyer would be intimidating, no doubt, but she had rushed him here for his synaptic skill and he had no lack of confidence about that. He could have been the best neural jock ever, had his gaming career not been cut short.

He stepped back into the white room. Aimes stood up near the reception desk. The well-dressed man was now patting him down.

I'm sick of this shit.

Alvin walked over slowly.

"Arms up," said the man in an accented voice. He looked at Alvin with disdain.

Alvin stared blankly at the man's sunken cheeks as he was poked and prodded.

"Your bag stays with me," said the guard.

"Can I trust you with it?" said Alvin.

"What's that?" said the security man. He said it like he didn't care to hear the answer. Then he pulled the bag from Alvin's shoulder.

Fuck this guy.

"Nice work if you can get it," said Alvin.

Aimes's eyes went wide.

The guard glared at Alvin. He finished his pat-down and motioned toward the door.

"She doesn't like to be kept waiting."

"Then I won't tell her you kept me," said Alvin.

Aimes grabbed Alvin's arm and ushered him forward.

They stepped inside a small alcove, leaving the security man behind.

"Jesus, did you not take your meds today?" whispered Barton.

"I don't take meds. I'm fine."

"That's right, Mr. Baylor. You were a cyber-athlete," said a stately female voice. It echoed from the next room. Alvin froze.

Shit.

Aimes tugged him forward over the floor and through the next doorway. His shoes stopped squeaking when they hit the carpet.

"Minor issue with security, Ms. Meyer," said Aimes.

She smiled broadly from behind a golden desk. Her blue eye shadow didn't move. She radiated cold.

"The male ego is so fragile," she said.

Alvin stared awkwardly.

She was in her eighties, but easily passed for sixty. A bright-yellow collar rose up around her neck and stopped just below her blond bob, framing her head and giving her a regal look.

Alvin flinched against the power of her presence but continued with Aimes toward the golden desk and extended his hand to her. She looked at it and said, "Have a seat."

Alvin broke off eye contact as he sat down. The wall behind her was all glass. Off to the side, a wooden case housed a menagerie of awards in mismatched styles and sizes. He looked back and his gaze fixated on another award sitting on the corner of her desk. It was a silver slice of pizza perched on a stump, which recalled his train station snack. The plaque read, "People's Choice for Best Synthetic Pizza—Sabrina Meyer/QuickFoods."

Yuck.

"Mr. Baylor, Barton tells me you're the standout in synaptics. No doubt due to that cyber-athletics career."

He turned to grab a look at his boss, who nodded in agreement. Alvin did not want to discuss his past.

"Thank you. I always put the team first. That's what any job's really about," he said.

Her eyebrow raised.

"To what do I owe this meeting, or should I say . . . opportunity?" Alvin smiled.

Barton looked on, expressionless, while Meyer spoke.

"Indeed, Mr. Baylor, this is a very important opportunity."

"It must be to get me here at this hour," Alvin joked.

No one laughed.

She looked over at Aimes and he began speaking as her gaze returned to Alvin. "We have a research-and-development project at 243 Ida and we need someone self-directed. Someone with excellent synaptic skills," said Aimes.

Ida? That's where the hoppers end up. "That's a long haul," Alvin said. "I thought this was just an orbit job."

Barton said, "It's a six-month trip and a week of work. As I said, we need someone who can execute without assistance.

You've got the necessary tool set and you've been supporting LA solo."

Meyer stared on silently. Her head fidgeted occasionally. Alvin wondered if she was conducting other business in her Opti-Comp.

"Who will support the hopper calibrations?" he asked.

"Mr. Baylor"—Meyer tapped a finger on her desktop—"we have someone to cover your duties here. You are needed up there." She pointed toward the ceiling.

Alvin's mind raced over thoughts of a miserable haul to deep space. He admired the resilience of asteroiders, but he wasn't one of them, nor did he wish to bump elbows with a bunch of maniacs.

"It's not something I'm trained for. Six months in zero-g on a mining frigate—"

"You're going on *The Hope*," said Aimes.

"What?"

"That's why we need you here this morning. *The Hope* is the only ship that meets our time frame," said Aimes.

"The Chinese luxury cruise?" asked Alvin.

Aimes smiled. "Yes, you can relax and study up in the VR trainer before you reach 243 Ida. We're prepared to give you an asteroider's retirement for completing the job."

"What?" Alvin was stunned.

"This is a generous offer for a man of your skills," said Meyer.

This can't be about rock hoppers.

"You're going to send me to the edge of civilization on a pleasure cruise and then retire me out there?"

"Alvin, you'll retire at Luna Colony or Musk City. No one stays in the belt. It's only a week's work," said Aimes.

I'd never go outside again.

"A week plus everything I ever planned to do," he said.

Meyer leaned in. "This is an important project. What is it you require?"

Don't push her too far.

"I like Earth. I like . . . air. I don't want to live with retired 'roiders on Mars. I have an apartment. I waited six years in the housing queue to get it."

"That's what this is about? Your apartment?" said Meyer.

She didn't move in her seat. She sat there staring at him with her head cocked.

"I'm not sure a person of your stature can relate, but it is damn hard to get an apartment in LA as a single male. I literally waited six—"

"Yes, six years, Mr. Baylor. And who sponsored you? Who holds the deed? Hmm?"

Fuck. "Alteris, ma'am," he said.

She began again, "Complete this task and I'll give you the apartment deed."

Holy shit, they need me bad. "And the retirement pension?"

"Good housing is reserved for workers, Mr. Baylor. If you don't wish to contribute anymore, you can do so off Earth. Or we can simply take you off the payroll altogether."

"I'll take the apartment. I have a lot left to contribute," said Alvin.

"I'm glad you were able to come to that realization. Gentlemen, you are excused."

She waved her hand toward the door. Then her eyes went blank. Nothing but breathing and the batting of eyelashes remained. She was in her Opti-Comp.

Meyer's security man entered and ushered them out.

Alvin felt uneasy. *Did I really just close a twenty-five-million mortgage? What kind of equipment test is this?*

They stopped in front of the elevator.

"This must be serious," said Alvin.

"It is, and you're the guy for it," said Aimes. "Welcome to the middle class, Alvin."

Alvin Baylor smiled.

Holy shit. I wonder if I can sell the apartment when I get back?

Aimes went rigid. "Hello," he said. He was in his Opti-Comp on a call. "Yes, okay."

"Oh wait, my bag," said Alvin.

He turned around and the guard tossed it at him. He caught it with a smirk.

Aimes abruptly returned to the conversation. "We're headed to your briefing now."

"Good, I'm curious."

The elevator arrived, and Meyer's security man eyed him dourly as they boarded.

"The pizza lady's not so tough," said Alvin as the doors closed.

Inside the elevator, Aimes spoke up. "You really like to ride that line, don't you?"

"The guard was asking for it," said Alvin.

"He's unpleasant, but he's licensed to play alpha male. You're not."

"Yeah, I know the rules."

"Good, then keep it between the lines. There are other synaptic engineers," said Aimes with an annoyed shake of his head.

The elevator chimed and they exited and walked into a conference room. A red-haired man was waiting for them. Alvin's Opti-Comp identified him as Stephen Grimes, an executive travel planner. He had beady eyes that broke away when Alvin looked at him.

"Mr. Aimes, Mr. Baylor, please have a seat. We have a tight schedule," said Grimes.

Alvin took a chair and stared at the soft white glow that hovered over the conference table. A moment later, a 3-D model of the solar system floated above it.

Grimes began speaking. "Your launch is today at 5:00 a.m. CST. The shuttle to Luna Base will take eleven hours. There you'll board *The Hope* en route to Armstrong Station for one hundred and thirty-five days. At Armstrong you will take another company shuttle bound for 243 Ida."

"Excuse me," Alvin cut off Grimes. "If I'm going on *The Hope*, am I getting a stipend? Because there's no way I can expense—"

"You're going first class and you're fully comped," said Aimes.

"First class . . ." Alvin's voice trailed off as Grimes nodded excitedly.

"Mr. Baylor, everything you've heard is true. The accommodations are outstanding. You're clearly a valued member of the family," said Grimes. He looked jealous.

"That's amazing, but may I ask, if this mission is critical, why wasn't a private ship sent?"

Grimes paused with an inquisitive face and looked toward Aimes.

"Alvin, there are elements of this project that cannot be revealed until you reach Ida," said Aimes.

"So what will I be doing for the next six months?"

"Enjoying the ride," he said. Then he motioned to Grimes to continue.

Fucking weird.

Alvin sat back as the man resumed his dull description of navigation routes through the solar system.

Alvin would spend half a year on a luxury cruise for trillionaires with nothing to do but enjoy himself. Sounded too good to be true, but he wasn't going to beg to be put in medical stasis. He caught Aimes eyeing him and he focused back on Grimes.

"At a distance of 1.769 AU, you will reach 243 Ida. It's a binary asteroid in the Koronis belt between Mars and Jupiter. It has a small moon named Dactyl," Grimes continued.

The AR solar system model zoomed in on an odd peanut-shaped asteroid. A small object orbited around the peanut, stately and spherical by comparison. The projection zoomed in further. A round metal plate resembling a screw head was buried into the rock.

Must be the entrance.

"Record," said Alvin quietly. He saw the text "Recording Disabled" flash in his Opti-Comp.

Aimes leaned in and said, "We don't want this going anywhere."

Alvin nodded. "Got it."

He reached down and pinched his smart-band. He kept his fingers depressed until he saw an options menu floating in front of him then he blinked quickly three times in his newly hacked operating system. The text "Now Recording" was visible only to him.

"243 Ida has low density, allowing for underground deployment of the mining camp." Grimes pointed toward the giant metal plate. "The entry and egress point is found here near the southern pole. The regolith provides solar shielding as well as a supply of basic life support materials. Due to the odd geologic formation of Ida, there are some characteristics you should be aware of. Any trips topside will require accompaniment by an appointed safety officer."

"A what?" said Alvin.

"A safety officer. The gravity is minimal except at the poles, and safety precautions must be adhered to."

"Minimal how? Like, I float away?"

"Yes, sir. A jump could take you into orbit. EVA suit thrusters must be used at all times. As I said, a safety officer will be assigned to you for any EVAs."

"And will there be any extravehicular activity?" Alvin probed.

"I can't say. I do not know the nature of your business. However, we have provided you VR training materials to familiarize yourself with operational practices. You should have plenty of time to review them on the trip."

"Right," said Alvin.

They're not gonna tell me anything.

"That will be all, Mr. Grimes. Please enjoy the holiday," said Aimes.

"Thank you, sir. Enjoy your trip, Mr. Baylor." Grimes grinned and bounced on his toes before exiting the room. The table went dark.

Aimes turned to Alvin. "Go ahead, ask."

"What exactly will I be doing?"

"You're delivering company assets."

Alvin made a face.

"So where's this asset?"

"You'll pick it up on the way to Ida. The shipment is locked to you with a new synaptic encryption. I'll send you a tracking app. When you reach the pickup point, run the tracker."

"Where's the pickup point?"

"It's on the way. That's all I can say for now. Just consider that this may be the last job you'll ever need to take."

"Oh, I have," said Alvin.

Aimes gave him a look, then stood and offered a handshake. "You're a good engineer, Alvin. I trust you can handle this job, but don't be late for the shuttle. *The Hope* won't wait for you."

SEVEN

"We're here Mr. Baylor," said a voice.

Alvin felt a tap on the shoulder. He opened his eyes. The flight attendant was over him.

"Feeling rested?" she said.

His Opti-Comp showed eleven hours had passed. There was no location status.

"Yes, good nap," he said. He yawned.

"We'll be docking shortly. I've called a transport for you. *The Hope* departs in thirty minutes."

"All right, thanks again."

She glided away.

Am I already here?

He opened the shaded porthole window beside him. The monotonous repetition of stars that had helped put him to sleep was gone. The Moon occupied his view. He marveled at it.

Floating above it in space was the giant white ring of Luna Base. It was divided into marina-like inlets for docking ships. The outer edge was dotted with industrial ships transferring cargo. Yachts and shuttles circled the inner spokes of the ring. Some were attached to the structure at airlock ports, others were simply tethered to keep from drifting away. Alvin thought there must have been nearly a hundred different vessels.

At the centerpiece of the ring was a cluster of enormous towers that stretched downward to touch the lunar surface. Alvin recognized them as elevator shafts built to heft payloads into orbit. The bold design had been a theoretical possibility for years, but it found its realization on the Moon when the Chinese went crazy for helium-3 production.

Then he saw the unmistakable form of *The Hope*.

On the far side of Luna Base, a long yellow cylindrical body shimmered and writhed in space. It was divided into rotating slices with uneven surface features, giving the ship a corkscrew appearance. At either end sat the torch-shaped laser propulsion engines. Alvin thought *The Hope* looked like a yellow sapphire.

"Now approaching Luna Station," a recording announced.

Alvin's heartbeat quickened.

While he admired the romanticism of the frontier, the limitations of man-made ecosystems were disconcerting. Death in such fragile environments was only an accident away. To add insult to potential injury, communication with Earth had slowed gradually as he traveled out into the stars. He checked his smart-band. The content downloads he'd queued before leaving were still running. *Damn.* By the time he reached 243 Ida, his Opti-Comp would showcase old data. He would be out of touch and surrounded by 'roiders.

"Now docking at Luna Station," said the recording.

The porthole window shutters closed and he felt reverberations as the shuttle made contact with the dock.

"Time to disembark, Mr. Baylor," said the flight attendant. She was floating in the aisle above him.

She reached across to unfasten his seat belt and his butt floated up off the seat. He felt his stomach drop.

He was now the farthest distance he had ever traveled, and eleven hours was all it had taken. The next leg was unfathomable.

I need a drink.

She handed him his bag then took his arm and pushed him toward the exit. His head began to spin.

"Mind the handholds, Mr. Baylor."

He grabbed onto a ladder affixed to the door and a platform ascended.

"Have a pleasant trip," said the woman. "And enjoy the holiday."

He nodded as he was lifted through the ceiling. "You, too."

What fucking holiday?

He rose into a brightly lit airlock with walls lined in dark rubber. He felt the weight of his body return gradually. The floor sealed below him. *Thank god.* He walked to the end of the rubber tube and the door slid into the wall. An Alteris employee was waiting in a gray jumpsuit. She was beautiful with dark-brown skin and long black hair.

"Only the one bag, sir?" she asked in a prim English accent.

"Yeah," he said with a smile.

She did not return his smile.

They walked toward the center of the concourse. A small four-wheeled transport was parked there. They climbed aboard and drove down the wide walkway. The station's walls were punctuated by expensive artwork and gaudy Christmas shopping displays. The ground curved up ever so slightly. It was quiet. He'd expected more people.

"I guess they want me there in a hurry?" said Alvin.

"Yes, sir. That was the request."

He didn't like being called *sir*, at least not by her. It made him feel old.

"Call me Al. So where is everyone?"

"Having Christmas supper I imagine," she said.

"Thanks for doing this, then. I'm sure you have better places to be."

"No, I work every Friday."

He nodded. She seemed intent on driving and not much else.

"Not religious, then? Neither am I. I'm an atheist."

She nodded. "I'm a lesbian," she said.

"Oh. Well—I hope your girlfriend has the night off, then."

She laughed. "No girlfriend."

They pulled to a stop in front of the gate. He slung his bag over his shoulder and looked over at a couple of attendants. The man and woman were perfect-looking, tall with alabaster skin and delicate features. They looked like Chinese high-fashion models.

"Welcome, Mr. Baylor!" they said in unison.

Good, they're not security.

"Keep all four wheels down, miss?" Alvin said to his driver.

"Layla." She smiled. "Have a good trip, Mr. Baylor."

He nodded and stepped off the vehicle toward the gate.

"Is this where I report for vacation?" he said. The attendants both laughed like they were flirting with him. "I guess so," he continued.

"Right through here, Mr. Baylor. You will be escorted to your room," said the man.

Alvin walked past their outstretched arms through the circular doorway. It led down a sloping hallway lined with more dark rubber. At the end he saw another woman waiting for him. She looked as perfect as the two outside. Then he saw her shimmer and suddenly she was a blond Nordic type like in his last VR hookup.

Almost had me.

"Mr. Baylor, you are an esteemed guest. Allow me to show you to your room," said the virtual girl.

What a crock.

He walked through her image and stepped onto a hotel carpet busy with patterns. Ahead of him he heard the ringing of slot machines. He looked out over the cavernous room and saw that it sloped upward at the far end. His eyes followed the wall as it rolled up and over. There were people on the ceiling.

He felt dizzy.

Suddenly the virtual girl was back in his Opti-Comp blocking the view. "We recommend you don't look up at first. Acclimation to artificial gravity makes some people nauseous. Please follow me." She walked ahead of him into a covered hallway. He chased after her, relieved to be under a ceiling rather than an upside-down casino.

That's better.

He continued after her. The walls shouted in Cantonese and English as his Opti-Comp passed over AR projection frames. He didn't think it was possible for an empty hallway to feel more crowded. His eyes bounced from the carpet pattern to the virtual girl's ass to ads for restaurants and shows. Suddenly "Location: Hope: Room 237" appeared in his Opti-Comp.

"Here you are, Mr. Baylor," said the virtual girl.

Alvin swiped his wrist past the door sensor and it slid open. He stepped into the dark room.

"Enjoy your stay," said the girl.

He shut the door on her smiling face and plopped down on the bed.

The walls came alive with virtual fireworks. "Welcome Esteemed Customer, Mr. Alvin Baylor!" leaped at his face in 3-D starbursts. He groaned and turned off his Opti-Comp. Silence reigned for a moment, and then the walls began playing back standard video. There were dozens of ads running over every square inch.

He looked around the now illuminated room. There was no escape from the noise.

At least the furniture is real. Time for that drink.

EIGHT

Alvin brought the cold glass to his lips and took a sip. "Very nice," he said to the bartender as he placed the concoction down with a gentle clink. It was one of those overly priced mixed drinks that people order on vacation. Ordinarily he wouldn't bother his wallet with more than a bourbon and cola, but everything was on the company tab now. The Nova Smash tasted great and he knew he'd have to pace himself. He could imagine the certain spiral into nausea if he looked up after one too many.

He pressed his fingertips into the bar top and leaned back on his stool. Half of the casino rolled overhead. Centrifugal force pulled everything toward the rotating walls in an effort to fake gravity. The surface was covered with game machines and video floor tiles. At times enormous garish advertisements lit up the tiles. Visual noise had replaced the grandeur and beauty of the ship's exterior. He found it loud and bereft of charm. It was like a cosmic Vegas. He watched the smattering of tourists drift from one empty card table to another. The greatest density was in front of the AR slots. The players yanked invisible lever arms and stared at spinning dials only they could see.

His Opti-Comp showed 6:00 p.m. Los Angeles time. It seemed to be a pointless metric out here.

"Always this busy?" he asked the bartender sarcastically. The bar was empty of customers save for him.

The bartender's tiny mouth drew into a smile. He flopped his jet-black hair back and stepped closer, eyeing Alvin.

"It's Christmas Eve, folks are shopping. They gotta get those moon rocks, you know? It'll get busier when we get out of port."

Alvin nodded.

"This your first time out for the company?"

"Yeah. That obvious?"

The bartender nodded. "So who do you rep?"

"Rep?"

"Yeah, man. Whose products are you selling?"

"Oh, nothing. I'm not a salesman."

"I thought you said it was your first company trip."

Better not discuss this.

"I won a vacation is all—on the company dime." He flashed a toothy smile.

"Ah, all right, man. I thought you were chasing the big money," he drawled as he pointed to a couple of retirees walking on the ceiling.

Alvin chuckled. "Nope, just chasing this." He lifted his glass.

"Another Nova Smash?"

Alvin nodded.

"You got it. So, is it all expenses paid or what?"

"Yep, pour 'em heavy." Alvin's voice drifted into melody as he sang, "'Cause I'm on vacation."

"All right, then," said the bartender.

Alvin leaned back and exhaled loud and slow. His buzz was on. "So what kind of trouble can I get up to on a ship like this?" he said.

"Any kind. We got gambling, shows, a spa, boys, VR pods. We even have girls."

"You mean VR pods for gaming?" he asked.

"Yeah, if that's your pleasure." The bartender paused and eyed him. "I'm guessing you're a fan. Maybe combat games?"

"Haven't played in a while, but I used to enjoy them." Alvin knew he'd been face-scanned.

The younger man stopped for a moment before saying with a wink, "Well, let me know if you play so I can put some money down."

"I'm a little rusty," Alvin said. He missed playing—wished it had been his career. Losing that still stung. The bartender laid another Nova Smash in front of him.

Alvin sipped it, and the booze numbed him. "So tell me about the girls," he said.

"There are women on this corkscrew who aren't billionaires and they work for a living," he said with a lopsided smile.

"They sanctioned or just . . . under the radar?"

"Hell, man, this is a Chinese party in deep space—anything goes. No one is gonna ask questions as long as you have the coin."

Alvin finished a sip. "Don't tell anybody, but the company gave me a bit-wallet and I'm gonna live it up."

"You got the right attitude. You won't have any trouble spending it here. Hey—I'm Ryan," he said as he stuck out his hand.

"Alvin."

"Don't you mean Zeus?"

Alvin let go of the bartender's hand and gulped down the last of his drink. He hadn't been called by his gaming handle in years.

"I used to be Zeus, not anymore." He hated being recognized, but this guy was different—respectful. "Ancient history," he said through a forced smile.

"I'm a true fan of the Olympians, Mr. Baylor. LA born and raised." The man flashed a small tattoo on the underside of his wrist—the initials "LA" in a stylized font that resembled lightning bolts. It looked faded and hastily drawn. "I did it myself. I was in junior high."

"Dedication," said Alvin.

Ryan paused and cocked his head. "Wow, man! Fuckin' Alvin 'Zeus' Baylor! So where you been? After '05 you just disappeared."

"There weren't a lot of options for me."

"Because you overclocked your feed? Shit, everyone does it now."

"Yeah, well, they didn't then."

"Oh, no judgments. You were the fucking *man*. No one could tolerate that many frames per second. Faster than real time! You changed the game."

"Didn't exactly pay off," said Alvin.

Ryan made a face, like he expected more enthusiasm. "You know Rick Zuck is here on his retirement tour. Bet the two of you could bring some real heat to the tournament."

That asshole. Alvin remembered reading about Zuck in yesterday's news.

"What tournament?" he asked.

"The VR Gaming Tournament, man—first year. Zuck's here to christen it. There are ads everywhere. I'm surprised you didn't know."

"Lucky guy, that Zuck." Alvin wasn't hasty to return to public view or to get reacquainted with his old rival. Besides, Alteris expected him to keep his head down. "Lemme get another," he said.

"Sure," said Ryan.

Alvin looked around the casino in a daze. It was getting busier. An alcoholic fog dulled his thoughts, and his focus shifted overhead as he heard a crowd shriek in delight. Pivoting on the chair, he looked up to see a large swath of the ceiling illuminate. An advertisement for Privacy Guard lit a path on the vid-screen-paneled surface. A backscatter scanner in the illuminated area undressed the patrons in Alvin's Opti-Comp. The more demure customers dashed away and created a ruckus. Ryan looked up and guffawed.

Alvin found his eyes drawn to a moving figure. A tall woman dressed in white took graceful strides down the ad's path. Most of the customers were elderly and out of shape and wore undergarments that preserved their dignity. This woman shared no such concern and proudly bared all as the ad worked its magic. She was stunning even upside down.

"Wow," Alvin muttered.

"I see that," said Ryan as she walked overhead.

She looked up at them and her blond locks fell back toward her shoulders, revealing the bounce of her breasts as she walked. Alvin felt the giddy excitement of an ogling schoolboy. As she passed directly overhead, she made eye contact and smiled seductively.

"Here's that cocktail," said the bartender.

"Here's to Privacy Guard," said Alvin.

He raised his glass then took a gulp.

"You might wanna slow it down if you wanna get your money's worth," said Ryan.

"You think she's . . . ?"

"Man, I told you. The Chinese don't care about female prostitution, but you'll pay through the nose."

"Got it," said Alvin.

Excess was not an indulgence on *The Hope*, it was an expectation. He just needed to warm up to it.

NINE

Rouja stepped along the lighted path, following its slope downward toward the bar. The tracker had brought her to a nearly empty bar in the middle of the casino floor. She'd followed the smart-band's serial number through Alteris launch records, finding it very suspicious that a shuttle would send a single employee out to the Moon on Christmas Eve. Now she was face-scanning the man who owned that band.

"Alvin Baylor," she read off her Opti-Comp. *Disgraced cyber-athlete. Interesting.*

If the guy hadn't boarded so late, she might have been able to get the job done while still in dock. Instead she was stuck onboard for six months. He looked drunk and alone. An easy target. She gave him her best *I want to fuck you* look and let the hair fall back from her face as she walked beneath him. His almond eyes popped open.

Sold.

By the time the bar was at her feet, he looked even more inebriated. She walked past him toward empty stools.

"This seat taken?" she said.

Ryan's eyes perked up before Alvin turned to look at her.

"Uh, no," Alvin said.

He looks like a frightened boy.

She sat down. "Vodka with lime. Make sure it's the good stuff, none of that Chinese shit."

Ryan nodded and got to it.

Rouja waited for Alvin to hit on her, but he didn't.

"So, you staff too?" she said.

"No. On a business trip."

The bartender returned with the drink. "Two hundred fifty, please."

"I'll get it," said Alvin.

She nodded and saw the bartender give a wink to the man.

"Thank you," she said. "What kind of business are you in?"

"Shipping. Long haul, deep-space stuff—obviously," said Alvin.

She caught him eyeing her figure while she took a sip of her drink.

"Well, aren't you gonna ask me what I do?" she said.

"I think I know." He chuckled and went back to his drink.

God, he's a weirdo.

"Oh really?" she said.

"Well, I saw you coming from all the way up there," said Alvin.

"That's because I wanted you to. A person should never be shy about what they want."

"People don't generally get what they want," he said.

"No, they settle before it comes, but I'm here now. So why not settle for me, baby?" She batted her eyelashes.

He looked her in the eye and she saw his nostrils flare before he looked away.

Too strong.

"Money, money, money," he sang, then finished his drink and waved off the bartender before he could bring a replacement. "Nice talkin' to ya," he said. He wobbled for a moment as he got off the stool, then walked away without looking back.

He still thinks he's hot shit.

An approach developed in Rouja's mind. She would coax him out of his solitude and learn what he knew about Padre's mysterious device, but she would take her time. Ending it quickly would leave her too poor to enjoy the cruise. He obviously had some cash flow, why not empty his bit-wallet before disposing of him?

"Hey, barkeep, where can I find the gaming pods?" she said.

TEN

What was the word she used? Settle? thought Alvin.

It ticked him off. He staggered away from the bar in a fog. He was over his limit—a talking zombie in the blackout zone. He wouldn't be able to get it up now, anyway. Best to leave before he committed himself to embarrassment.

He needed food.

He stumbled down the hallway with his eyes on the floor below. If he looked up at the rolled ceiling, he'd retch. An AR ad for women's shoes enveloped his feet with virtual pairs as he walked the floor tiles. A pair of red heels popped onto his feet.

"Woo-hoo! Nice stems!" said a voice.

Alvin looked up. A couple of young men dressed in translucent blouses catcalled him.

"You look fierce, Papi," said one of them.

The other one stuck his tongue out and wiggled it.

I guess those are the boys.

Alvin laughed and kept walking. A short while later, he came to a row of finely dressed waiters. They stood at attention like Buckingham Palace guards in front of a red restaurant with laurel wreaths in the windows.

What the hell are they doing?

It looked like an establishment he could not afford on Earth. He could smell the wafting scent of food. Real food.

He stumbled up to the hostess outside. "Hi, you serve steak here?"

She looked taken aback by the question. "Sir, all of our dining establishments offer a full range of cuisine. Perhaps the Soweto Grill, would suit you better."

Sir?

"No. I'm interested in eating here. Never had a steak at a swanky restaurant before. And I want that guy." He pointed to the tallest waiter. The man looked back at him curiously, and Alvin's eyes narrowed to slits.

"Are you sure you wouldn't—" the hostess began.

She froze when he turned his dagger eyes on her. "Do I look like the kinda guy who isn't sure?"

"No. Follow me."

She led him from the walkway and up to the restaurant doors.

"Do you work?" he said to the tall waiter as he walked by.

The man's name tag said, "Frederick." He didn't answer and instead gave a snooty, irritated look.

The hostess hurried ahead and Alvin stared at the back of her shoes as their click-clack picked up tempo.

"Can I get a window seat?" he asked as he followed her inside.

"We have no window seats," she said.

"I was told there were window seats in this joint," he said loudly.

They passed by a table with an elderly couple, who stared at him as he went by bleary-eyed and disheveled. Alvin managed a crooked smile at them.

"I'm sorry, sir, I'm not sure who would have told you such a thing."

"The company, lady. The company told me this was a nice trip. Nice trips have windows."

After passing a series of dining rooms, they arrived at a tiny table in the back room. She pulled out his chair and stepped aside quickly.

"The display panels in your stateroom can switch to exterior views," she said.

"Really?"

"Yes. The front desk can assist you with them."

"Of course, just pushin' buttons, I imagine."

She crinkled her brow, then walked off. The tall waiter had followed behind them and Alvin overheard her say to him, "Another Alteris comp."

Another?

Alvin looked away and swiped his finger through the air, spinning the AR menu display for a few revolutions—long enough to realize he didn't recognize any of the names. His waiter arrived.

"Good afternoon, sir. May I answer any questions about our courses?"

"Well, Fred, I'm not much into goose or pate or whatever these things are. I'd like a steak."

The waiter's eyebrow arched. "Sir, our holiday menu is served without substitution. I think you may find the Soweto—"

"Yeah, yeah, I'm sure I'll get to this Soweto Grill. Tonight I want a steak and I want it here."

Alvin looked the man in the eyes.

The waiter stared back at him with disdain.

"I think there must be a misunderstanding. We have a fixed menu. There are numerous offerings throughout the dining quarter if you wish to choose your courses."

"Right. I get that you want to serve me a series of small appetizers with funny names. I want a steak. A nice filet mignon. I hear that's the best kind. Is that so?"

"A serving of filet mignon may exceed your daily stipend, sir," he said.

"My stipend?"

"Yes, you are one of the Alteris's comps, are you not?"

"One of?" said Alvin.

"Yes, sir. Are you not a guest of Alteris Asteroid?"

I thought this trip was secret.

"I'm with Alteris, yes, but I have no stipend."

"Well, sir, past guests had similar expectations. I would advise you to manage your money wisely or you may find yourself unable to afford the return trip."

"Uh-huh. Fred, let's just run up my bill and see if I have enough for the tip. I like it medium rare."

"Shall I bill the room?"

"No, I'll pay the table."

"Very good, sir." Frederick's eye darted around in his Opti-Comp, then he stood there waiting.

"Ah, I get it," said Alvin. He tapped on the table and brought up the bill. It was over four thousand in U.S. coin.

"You tell no lies, Fred. Let's say I give you a fifty percent tip and you tell me who else Alteris sends on these trips. Deal?"

The man arched his eyebrow again. "Oh, what a happy holiday," he said.

"Let's make it a hundred percent," said Alvin. He bumped his band to the table and swiped his finger up on the percentage.

"Ah, a Merry Christmas to you. How can I be of assistance?" asked Frederick.

"Who else has Alteris comped?" asked Alvin.

"One other," said Frederick.

"Right. And?"

"I don't recall a name. He was tall, gap-toothed. I believe we sat him at this same table. He was . . . difficult, like you."

Asshole. I'm not difficult. I just don't like people.

"Thanks for being honest, Fred."

"Indeed, sir."

"Now, I'll take that steak," said Alvin.

Frederick walked off with more energy.

What the hell is Alteris up to? I need to talk to Aimes.

He peeped through his Opti-Comp, but the cursor bounced around erratically. He was too drunk for eye control.

"Fucking thing," he grumbled.

He brought up his left wrist and activated the touch-field display in his smart-band. It projected out along his open palm. He typed in a message—"Need to talk" and hit Send.

How long, at this distance, until he would receive Aimes's response? The ship was barely out of Luna dock. Surely it couldn't be more than ten minutes before Aimes would get the message, plus another ten for the return trip.

Twenty minutes—at least.

The last time he'd been without a live uplink was when the power grid had gone out, sending Alteris's NoHo office into lock-down. Security doors had sealed, leaving him sitting in a hallway for hours. Now not only could he not contact anyone, but also his entertainment apps were deauthorized. He pondered the disconnected nature of technology at cosmic distances.

Damn it. I guess I'll spend their money on real food and mind-altering substances.

"Your filet, sir." Frederick placed an ornamentally arranged plate on the table in front of him. "Is there anything else I can get you?"

"Yes, Fred, I'll have another Nova Smash."

"Oh, but of course."

Alvin hunkered down and cut off a piece of filet mignon. The steak was smaller than he had imagined, but the flavor was sublime. Normally, eating animal protein on his salary was out of reach—if he could even find a place that dared to serve it.

Minutes later, Frederick returned with the drink and set it down. He watched as Alvin chomped down with glee.

"Will that be all, sir?"

"Yes, that'll do it. This is amazing. Really tasty, nothing like the lab-grown stuff."

"So glad you approve."

Alvin gave him the finger as he walked away, then finished his meal in delight.

When it came time to leave, he stumbled out and back to the guest rooms. He was careful not to look up the entire way. His ground-level stare found him a new treasure, though—drug and alcohol vending machines. They were tucked into alcoves everywhere. He purchased some cappers for the night and stuffed them in his pockets.

He found his hallway, bounced a shoulder off the doorway, stumbled into his room, and kicked off his shoes.

He wasn't ready to knock out yet, though. The mystery had him jazzed. Who was the other employee who had flown *The Hope?*

Tall, gap-toothed, difficult.

Best to connect to the company servers now, before the ship got any farther away. He tried peeping in his Opti-Comp.

Eyes too tired.

He walked to a desk in the corner of the room and slurred the word "keyboard." A holographic key raster splayed out across the desk. Then he fished the fifth of whiskey from the vending machine out of his pocket and took a swig. He told the room to play The Doors.

Alvin sat down and connected to the Alteris servers via command line. Each flashing cursor prompt hung around longer than the last before returning a response. In between each press of the Enter key, he danced around like a maniac. Forty-five minutes later, he was logged into the system and he was fading from consciousness. The whole process would have taken him maybe ten seconds on Earth.

He queried the system for project reports pertaining to 243 Ida then walked over to the bed and lay down.

"Can I get a window?" he said.

The ceiling transformed into a view of the stars. He reached into his pocket and pulled out a cannabis bar, unwrapped it, and ate it.

Nice hotel.

ELEVEN

Alvin opened his eyes. The colorful gases of a nebula swirled around overhead. Red, blue, and yellow forms expanded, contracted, and merged with one another to give way to blackness speckled with pinpoints of starlight. The dots radiated intensely amid the changing patterns. He felt a heavy throbbing in his head. When he sat up, he found himself in bed.

Ah yes, he remembered now—at least partly. After dinner, he had self-medicated from a vending machine. He remembered turning on the nebula playback loop in his room. The view was something like a window, only he'd set the nebula to maximum speed to get a different perspective on the passage of time. That was what had sent him into the spins. He might have thrown up. He couldn't really remember. Things had gone black after that.

He crawled slowly to the edge of the bed and fumbled with the controls on the end table. When he switched off the space view, it was replaced by ads of differing shapes and sizes drifting about the walls. Each image glided around, occasionally bouncing off a corner or flipping over to be replaced with another ad. All of them were targeted at Alvin's consumer record and reflected his boyish interests. As he gazed about, he was thankful that no AR imagery jumped out or began looping in his ear. His Opti-Comp was still asleep—the wall sensors still in video mode. It was quiet.

Then his device powered up and the AR ads began to leap into his brain. VR gaming pods spun around his head like little animated birds as a breathy voice announced the entertainment deck. He felt his nausea crescendo and ran for the toilet, leaving the animated halo behind. After several minutes of his loud retching, the room spoke up.

"Do you require medical aid, Mr. Baylor?"

He crawled away from the porcelain throne and back onto the carpet. "Connect me to the front desk."

There was a click followed by a cheery voice. "How may I be of assistance?"

"How do I turn off the ads in my bedroom?" he mumbled.

"Oh, sir, those are mandatory for our comped rooms. Are you not enjoying the value addition that they provide?"

"No. Listen, I'm hungover and it isn't helping. Turn 'em off or I'll figure out how to turn them off."

"I'll send someone up right away, sir."

"Thanks."

The call disconnected.

Alvin sat up against the wall and took slow breaths to calm his stomach. He kept his Opti-Comp eye closed. After a minute or so, he began crawling back toward the disaster he'd left in the bathroom. Every movement sent a shudder of nausea through him, and he felt he would throw up his guts if he moved another inch. He crumped down in the fetal position and decided to wait for whoever was coming.

The door buzzed minutes later, and he leaned against the wall and tapped the controls to open it. A classically dressed bellhop presented himself and handed Alvin a small metallic can.

"Desk says you had a rough night. Here's a pick-me-up. Enjoy the morning after with Refuel!"

The bellhop grinned as Alvin took the can.

"What about the panels? How do I turn them off?"

"Oh, I'm sorry, sir, I have no idea how to do that." The man walked away and called, "Merry Christmas!" over his shoulder.

Nonplussed, Alvin shut the door. It was down to him and his ingenuity if he wanted those ads to disappear. Right now he had to recover. He chugged down the milky substance from the tin and gagged at the metallic taste. But it seemed to settle his insides on the way down. He took slow steps toward the bathroom, feeling steadier on his feet, and thought there must be truth to the "fast-acting hydrating agent" claims. He got into the shower and let the warm water soothe him.

After returning from the bathroom, clean and renewed, he felt his stomach grumbling but his headache was gone. He pulled on his pants and noticed a computer terminal floating in the corner of the room. He had forgotten his search for answers from the night before.

The screen showed a list of project reports pertaining to 243 Ida. As near as he could tell from the titles, the asteroid was a home base for mineral extraction. Nothing unusual—except something was not the usual here there was too much urgency and money being thrown around. If there was specialized equipment already out there, then someone had gotten it there.

Maybe there's a shipping log?

He strung together a database query and hit Enter. The answer would come slowly.

Time to eat something greasy.

He felt a spring in his step and nearly bounded out the door.

Damn, that Refuel does work!

TWELVE

After scarfing down a burger at the Soweto Grill, Alvin felt satiated and whole again. He now understood the promptings to visit the restaurant. The clientele were mostly off-duty crew members soaking up booze and puffing water pipes. It was comfortable, but he'd made a lifetime of lowbrow tastes. He'd be back when he got tired of exploring how the elite lived.

He exited the faux-shantytown shack that housed the Grill and stepped onto the main path. Vid screens and AR advertisements burst out everywhere. The section was carved into a long street that curved up and down the cylindrical ship. Smaller alleyways cut through this sweeping path to create a dense shopping district. Everywhere he looked was another restaurant, clothing shop, or spa. It seemed the ultra rich had the same religion—consumerism, only they worshipped without limit in floating spaceships. The Christmas Day sales were in full bloom.

Alvin ignored high-priced shoe and purse stores, nano-rejuvenation centers, and hair salons.

What a bunch of crap.

His gaze wandered to the ceiling above him. Centered in the

mass of wavy pathways was a circular clearing. Six black pods, each the size of an autocar, clung like warts to the surface.

Gaming pods?

His heartbeat jumped. It had been a while since he'd sat in one. He ducked down an alleyway lined with vending machines and began moving toward the pods.

After several minutes navigating the labyrinthine paths, he was greeted with a broadside view of one of the black pods. The stencil of a red dragon on its side announced it was a FlameWar Pro model. He paced around the pod anxiously, then brushed his hand gently across its glossy black curves.

"You break it, you buy it," said a voice.

"Huh?" mumbled a startled Alvin.

He looked over to see a beautiful young woman with warm-brown hair and bright eyes. She smiled as she walked toward him, her hips swaying from side to side. He was mesmerized and quickly removed his hand from the pod.

"I'm kidding. You were being so delicate," she said.

"I, ah, used to play," he shot out of his mouth nervously.

"You still look young enough to give it a go," she said as she stopped next to him. She was a couple inches taller and she leaned in and whispered, "Not like most of the old farts around here."

Her breath smells like bubblegum.

Her name tag read "Katy" and below it the words "Game Host." He caught himself staring at her bust and quickly looked up into her blue eyes.

"So what does a game host do, Katy?"

"I strap you in, make sure it's tight." She smirked. "And I keep an eye on you so your brain doesn't boil. You game to break the rust off?"

"I've had my time in the chair. I'm good."

"Oh, I know you're good, Mr. Baylor. Or should I say, Zeus?" She tipped her hips in a little pose and leaned against the pod.

She'd scanned him and she wasn't telling him to get lost. That was novel. A gorgeous gal, the kind he'd expect to see on the arm of a pro gamer, was chatting him up.

He looked at her pensively.

She responded, "We're not on Earth. The laws don't apply here."

It can't hurt. Where else am I going to play, South America?

"Let's do it," he said.

"Good call, Al." She chuckled and Alvin laughed along with her, having no idea what was funny. He just wanted to keep the vibe up. She motioned for him to follow.

"Say, did I see you on the casino floor the other night? You seem familiar," he asked.

"Oh, I don't know. Did you?"

She pressed a red outline on the surface of the pod and the side wall slid outward a few inches and then moved back to reveal the chair.

"I guess not, but you do stand out," he said.

"That's what they pay me for. It's all advertising. Hop in."

Alvin ducked to enter the dark interior of the pod. He sat down into the reclined chair and Katy entered behind him. The space was limited, just large enough for her to maneuver in front of him. He felt his pulse quicken as he looked at the dark walls of the pod. It was a setting he thought he'd never see again.

She slipped restraints over his wrists and ankles, then tied down a set of straps that pressed him into the chair, locking his chest and hips in place. Next she began to place a synaptic skullcap on Alvin's head.

"Don't need it," he said. He felt his cheeks flush from being so close to her.

Katy paused and examined his face. She pinched his chin and turned his head side to side to look at his temples. "Nice install."

"Oh, it's just for company work now."

What the hell am I saying?

She lowered the chair back so Alvin's body lay almost straight.

"Good luck, company man," she whispered in his ear.

Bubblegum.

He tried to catch a view of her rear end as she bent over to exit the pod, but he couldn't angle his head. The door closed, leaving him in total darkness.

"I'm on vaacationnnn," he warbled quietly to himself.

A faint blue light glowed at the periphery of his vision and his temples warmed. He closed his eyes and felt the world drop away.

When he opened them again, he was lying on a hospital bed being prodded by mechanical arms while humans with clipboards stood around and took notes. He was now in virtual reality. A bunch of shoulder-high red letters crashed to the floor spelling out the word "Hostage."

The game was about to begin.

One of the doctors held out a clipboard in front of him and handed him a pen. It said, "Tutorial" with check boxes for "yes" or "no." He checked "no." A long list of legalese medical disclaimers appeared on the page informing him that he was playing at his own risk by skipping the tutorial and synaptic calibrations. He signed off on his rights and stood up dressed in black tactical gear. A pistol materialized at his hip and an automatic rifle appeared slung over his shoulder.

He jogged around in search of game options and ignored the narrator as the objective was explained. He was already familiar with the genre. Somewhere in the building there was someone who needed saving. The floors could be filled with terrorists, zombies, or mutant monsters. Once he had even played a mod against porn stars and unicorns. This instance was modeled on the economic warfare of the twenty-first century. Nothing supernatural.

A bank of elevators ahead of him beckoned. The buttons on the wall said "Solo" and "Group." If any of the other pods had been occupied, he'd have seen those players.

Playing with bots.

It was just as well. He hadn't played with another person in years.

This will be easy.

He pressed "Solo" and waited for the elevator. He looked over to see the stairwell—a sign on the door said, "Nightmare Difficulty."

Let's do it.

He ran and kicked in the door.

"Save the CEO's Daughter," said the narrator in a melodramatic tone.

One step in and Alvin tripped down the stairs. He wasn't ready for the smoothness of the newer pods. He heard laughter over the spectator channel.

He jumped to his feet in the middle of a dilapidated warehouse and was shot dead by a homeless terrorist. Game over.

Shit.

"Come on now, Al. Don't tell me that's all ya got," said Katy's voice over the spectator channel.

It jarred him back to reality. Years of rust and advances in sensitivity had made him clumsy. He was embarrassed.

"I'm ready for another run-through. That was a warm-up."

"Sure thing, Al, but we have a five-minute cooldown between sessions. Don't wanna bake your noggin."

"I'm good. It's been a while, but I'm warmed up now."

He lay in a virtual medical bed as his body was repaired: the five-minute cooldown.

"Okay," said Katy. "You know what you can handle. You've got another play credit." Alvin saw the timer drop to zero, and his free credit appeared. This time when the doctor with the clipboard approached, he checked "yes" for the tutorial.

He was sent to a firing range in the next room where he engaged in a series of targeting and calisthenics tests. The pod's controls were more sensitive than the last pro models he'd played in. He'd been thinking too hard, giving his virtual self the shakes.

He just needed to play with a little more looseness. When he eased up, he found the interface was smoother than ever. His shots landed easily now. He finished up the tutorial and went back to the Nightmare staircase.

He heard spectators giggling expectantly. He did not trip down the stairs this time, and the bum at the bottom did not survive the encounter. He worked his way through the grungy warehouse, clearing room after room of pipe-swinging activists and gun-toting sidewalk warriors seeking revenge on a captain of industry. Alvin gave little thought to the real events that had inspired the scenario. He just wanted to impress the girl. Five minutes later, after he killed the last kidnapper in record time, he heard only cheers and clapping.

"You just qualified for the tournament," said Katy.

Tournament?

Alvin rushed to the corner of the virtual room to save the CEO's daughter before she was fed arms first into an industrial shredder. He rolled her off the conveyor belt onto the floor and untied her bound hands and feet.

"Ah shit, Al, you just hit the top spot. First place on the scoreboard. The last guy lost her pinkie."

Katy's voice was buffeted by more applause in the background.

The game ended and he sat there sweating in the darkness. It felt amazing to be in the action again. She entered the pod to unfasten him.

"That was the best run I've seen all week. You've got the stuff . . ." She paused. "You're here for the tourney, aren't cha?"

"No. Don't care about it."

"Don't be silly, you could be a contender."

No way.

"I'll take it under advisement."

"You should. Big win, big money."

He followed her fantastic behind out of the pod. Three kids

and a couple of old ladies were clapping for him. He nodded and returned some enthusiasm.

"Some friends and I will be at the Kowloon Cowboy later if you wanna come have a drink," she said.

"Yeah. I can have a drink."

"See ya later, Al." She winked and strutted away.

Who needs a tournament? I just won the grand prize!

THIRTEEN

Alvin slammed the empty pint glass down on the bar top. He hollered in victory as he threw his arms up.

"Such a gracious champion," chided Katy as she gulped down the last of her pint. "You win the beer challenge."

They sat in the back corner of Kowloon Cowboy, a Western-themed dive bar crowded with off-duty crew members emptying ice-cooled booze towers and sucking on vapor pipes. Everyone was loud and drunk. No one paid them any mind as they rubbed up against each other in the corner booth. Her "friends" had failed to materialize, and Alvin took it as another sign of his rising fortune. He was having a terrifically good time with her despite the possibility that she was another hooker. He didn't have the nerve to face-scan her yet.

"So when you said you used to play, you were being modest," said Katy.

"So you read my history?"

"Just a peek. I'd rather hear it from you."

He smiled. "It's been a long time. It was fun to play again. I guess it was good to have a win again, too."

She leaned in close. "Oh, you stopped on a losing streak? Shame, shame, Al."

Alvin stared back into her gaze. He felt oddly comfortable. "No, I didn't lose. That was the problem."

"If you're that confident, why'd you stop?"

Her blue eyes focused on him. He couldn't remember feeling so much the center of a person's attention.

She really hasn't read my whole social . . . or she's being polite.

"I was banned for cheating."

Alvin waited for a change in demeanor.

Instead she asked, "Did you?"

No one ever had asked if he did it. They'd just read the archived news and assumed the worst. Katy seemed genuinely interested in his side.

"Technically, no."

"Technically?"

"The game pods were modified, but not by me. One of my teammates hacked the pod server for overclocking. I was the only one who could handle the synaptic feed. I won the match by myself. The other team groused and an investigation . . . pinned it on me."

"You won by yourself?"

She looked impressed.

"For the most part. My teammates picked off one guy before passing out from overload. I beat the other seven."

"Amazing, but I don't get it. What's the scandal? Everybody overclocks . . . the pros, anyway."

"Not back then. The speeds weren't regulated and gamers weren't trained for it. This was the first time it had been done— forcing the brain to play faster than real time. Besides, this was University. They were freaked out about neural injuries. A few of the guys on my team had temporary brain damage, and one of them died."

"It killed someone?"

Alvin watched her full lips as they formed the question. She was so damn sexy.

"Not instantly. It was the guy who did the hack. It fried him. He went batty and killed himself a few weeks afterward."

"Wait . . . so why'd you get the blame?"

"Chad Henry, the one who died . . . his dad was our team manager. The school hired a private investigator."

Katy laughed out loud and then caught herself. "I'm sorry, are you serious?"

"Yes. I pointed them in the direction of Chad. I knew he was into home-brew synaptic mods and . . . I felt so guilty, I let him know what I had said. A day later, his father fired me for interfering with the investigation. To everyone on the outside, I was the guy who did it."

"So this guy, the manager . . ." started Katy.

"Carroll Henry was his name," Alvin interjected.

"This guy framed you to save his son?"

"Yep. They couldn't prove anything one way or the other and they wanted someone to hang for it."

"And his kid killed himself?"

"Yep. After the investigation the government went into my head and locked down the bandwidth on my synaptic implants and expelled me. I'll never overclock again."

"That's so fucked . . . so you coulda been . . ."

"Fucking rich. How about another round? It's on Alteris," he said with a wink.

She nodded and Alvin motioned to the bartender.

"So what's the deal with Alteris?" Katy asked. "What kind of business are you up to on a cruise ship?"

"There's some sort of snafu. They're being tight-lipped about it, and this was the only ride."

"Ride to where?"

"Some rock in space. My gig's boring, really. I'm in synaptics."

"Ah, no wonder with your implants. What do you operate?"

"Oh, I don't—I'm maintenance and support. You know, friend to the machines. I help test the tech and keep it running. It's the kind of integral job that no one appreciates because they only talk to you when they have a problem."

"Well, it must pay better than game host," she said.

"I suppose it could be worse, but then I don't get to spend my time in a flying resort."

"Hate to break it to you, Al, but you do now."

He grinned. She grinned back.

The bartender returned, plopped down the drinks, and gave Alvin an encouraging wink behind Katy's back.

"Thanks," said Alvin with a nod. "So enough about me. How'd you get the game host gig?"

Katy turned to grab her drink and caught the bartender's eye leering at the name tag on her ample chest. She turned back to Alvin, removed the name tag, and stuffed it in her pocket.

"I knew a guy who knew a gal. Nothing special, really. It's all about the look."

Alvin caught the bartender still staring at them and he looked at him hard. The man turned and walked away.

"Well, you certainly got that. Seems like you have to beat 'em off with a stick."

"Yeah, I'd rather not advertise when I'm off duty. What do ya say we get up to some serious fucking off?"

"Lady, I think you and I speak the same language," he said through a wide smile.

Katy nodded in the direction of a mechanical bull in the corner.

"That thing?" questioned Alvin.

"Yep. You ever rode one?"

"No, can't say I have. You?"

"Not the mechanical kind," she said demurely.

"Yeah, right."

"Oh, I only did it a few times. My uncle had a ranch."

"Really, wow. I thought they'd been outlawed."

"Only in the U.S. Anyway, I got thrown on my ass."

"That's probably what'll happen to me," said Alvin.

"C'mon, it's fun," she said as she stood up.

"I don't like being the center of attention. I get face-scanned and then I get shit from sports fans."

"Get over it." She dragged him out of his seat.

"Wait—we're not gonna be able to hold these," he said. They chugged back the pints and he finished first again. "See, I don't lose."

She laughed. "You're gonna lose to me at that."

She pointed to the ruckus in the corner as a man went flying off the mechanical bull onto the mat. The crowd went wild at the sight of defeat.

"C'mon," she said.

A few minutes later, it was Alvin's turn. The room roared with jeers and cheers as he was thrown over backward. He landed with his ass up in the air and his face buried in the soft mat. He'd lasted a good second or two. He was too drunk to be embarrassed and he jumped to his feet with a smile. Katy laughed as he stumbled toward her on the soft footing. She gave him a hug.

"You're better in VR," she teased.

"All right, tough gal, you're up," he said.

The game operator called her name and she hopped up on the saddle and gave a little wink to Alvin.

The bull started to gyrate, and the crowd grew. Every drunk in the place was looking at her. She certainly made a more attractive rider than he had.

As the bull picked up pace, it became clear that she was great at riding it. She held on with ease, and the cheers grew louder. The machine began pitching wildly and still the operator could not knock her off. Alvin's salacious thoughts turned to astonishment. The crowd roared and Alvin hollered along with them as the man at the controls egged them on.

After nearly a minute, the operator exclaimed, "All right, beautiful, let's give someone else a chance. I don't think you're comin' down, unless I ask!"

The bull came to a slow halt and she kicked her leg high overhead and hopped off. Alvin clapped slowly while shaking his head in disbelief. The crowd whistled and cheered.

"Amazing!" he said.

She strode across the mat and grabbed him in an embrace.

"How did you do that?" he said under the cheering of the crowd.

She leaned in close to be heard. "Oh, it's easy . . . if you have strong legs. I have very strong legs." She brushed her thigh against his and pushed into him then grabbed his hand. "Let's go somewhere else, it's getting loud in here."

As they moved around and between the patrons and past the long bar, a man stepped out of the crowd and into their way. He was tall and lean with sleeve tattoos and he was dressed too fashionably for the Kowloon Cowboy. He was about Alvin's age, but he clearly took better care of himself. Alvin recognized Rick Zuck, the retired cyber-athletics star on his retirement voyage.

"You look like shit, Baylor," he said.

"What the fuck do you want?" growled Alvin.

"I heard you qualified," Zuck said as he folded his arms.

"Yeah, so what?"

"I was number one on the scoreboard until you pulled your number," said Zuck.

"So I've beaten you twice, then?"

"Yeah, how's that worked out for you?" said Zuck.

Alvin scowled. Katy looked at him with concern.

"I know your deal, Baylor, and now I know you have someone on the inside to help you cheat again." He looked at Katy.

She looked pissed. "Fuck off, Dick."

"Okay—enough, Richard, I'm not playing in any tournament," said Alvin. "Get out of the way."

"You're gonna get caught again if you do, Baylor. That's your lot in life."

"Fucking jerkwad," spat Katy as she shoved Zuck. He fell over backward, crashing into a table of people. When he jumped to his feet, he began screaming, "Do you know who I am?" at them.

Jackass. Alvin laughed.

"C'mon," said Katy as she towed him away by the hand.

"That trophy is mine!" yelled Zuck.

The bar went quiet.

"Richard, you're lucky I'm havin' a good night or I'd lay your ass out," Alvin shouted from the exit door.

The crowd "Ooooooohed," and Alvin and Katy walked out.

As they walked down the exit ramp, she said, "How do you know Rick Zuck?"

"He was on the other team—the one I beat in my last game."

"Oh, I see. He's being paid to play in the tournament."

Alvin shook his head in irritation. "I'm not entering that thing."

"Don't worry about it now." She gave him a peck on the cheek. "Tonight I want your undivided attention."

"Yes, ma'am. You lead. And I'll follow."

"Ooh, I like that kinda talk," she said. "Keep it up."

FOURTEEN

A week had passed since Alvin arrived on *The Hope*. In the inter-vening time, the search for answers about his job had turned up nothing useful. His boss had simply responded to his inquiries with, "We'll talk later. Enjoy the trip." He'd continued on with Katy and was enjoying himself, but there was a nagging sense that something unpleasant awaited. Each day he'd send out a long-distance query to the Alteris database, go for a luxury excursion at the spa, visit the dining quarter, and return to parse the query results. Oftentimes he'd get nothing but another prompt to hit Enter. It was as tedious as it was unrewarding.

His last idea to check for shipping logs showed nothing going outbound. Only minerals returning via *The Hope*'s vast cargo hold. None of the signatures on the manifests were Alteris employees. All of them were non-union Chinese stationed at Luna Base, and there was no record of how the minerals reached Earth. It was some funny business to be sure, but it had nothing to do with his mission or *The Hope*'s previous passenger.

The only thing he hadn't accessed were the files kept by the Human Capital Department. Those were beyond his clearance. They were also the best place to look. He squirmed in his seat.

Enough fucking around.

He logged into the domain system and looked up his human capital representative. He could clone the credentials, but he'd need to cover his tracks. It would require him to sit for hours to complete the process, but it was his best bet if he wanted to find the mysterious Alteris employee who had preceded him on *The Hope*. Alvin highlighted the ID code and copied it. He spent three hours feeding strings of text into the terminal and waiting for each confirmation until he had his new permissions.

During the downtime the constant procession of ads began driving him batty. He scoured the room until he found a small gang box near the front door. Using his multitool, he unscrewed the bottom half of the plate, swiveled it aside on its top screw, and reached inside to tug the cables loose. The AR ads disappeared from the room.

Thank god.

He sat back down in the corner in peace and silence. When his permissions were ready, he queried for employees stationed at 243 Ida. It took forty-five more minutes to get fifty-one names back. Half of them were already retired. The rigors of space were not kind to the human body.

As he scanned the list, he recognized only one name—Carroll Henry.

"Wha . . ." he muttered as he stared at the screen.

It can't be.

He scratched at the scruff growing on his chin, then selected the entry and sat for an interminable wait as the portrait displayed. His stomach grumbled. He needed a break, but this was too intriguing. He looked down after a while to find a man with wavy salt-and-pepper hair and a buck-toothed grin. It was him. He was older, but it was the same Henry. His university gaming coach.

"Damn it!" he yelled.

"Is something wrong, sir?" said the room.

"No." He stood up and paced.

That sonofabitch.

He exhaled and sat back down. Henry's file listed him as Lead Drill Op.

Just a worker bee. Maybe a few men to push around. Good.

He sucked it up and moved on. Next, he cross-referenced job titles. No one on Ida was in research and development—not a single name.

He groaned and sent out another request, but this time he popped an asterisk in for the location. It would look for RnD workers stationed anywhere. He paced until forty-three names came up on screen. He stared at the locations—all were on Earth.

He sighed heavily. His stomach grumbled.

"I'm drawing a blank here," he said.

The cursor popped back and erased his asterisk.

A final idea occurred to him. If the guy wasn't anywhere, maybe he was nowhere. He could query for employees with blank location data. It was likely a fruitless play, but he had nothing else. He was famished and needed to get out of the system before someone caught him. Before hitting Enter he modified the command so it would log out and dump the logs after returning the search result.

He dressed himself and went to shave his scruff off. The bathroom mirror began feeding out ads.

Gotta find the cord for this one.

Fireworks exploded out of the mirror and a voice announced his choices for "Ringing in the New Year." The voice jabbered about various ballroom parties throughout the ship.

I should ask Katy.

That was the proper thing to do. Make plans, go out, do things. He was, after all, going to be here for months. He couldn't just loaf around the spa and visit her at the gaming pods.

As he went through his grooming, the New Year's ad shuffled off to be replaced with one for cosmetic surgery, then specialty mood-altering cocktails, then a Mixed Martial Arts event, and finally the VR Gaming Tournament. He ignored the tournament ad as always and left the bathroom and then his room.

As he strolled down the hallway and off to the dining quarter, a couple of old men nodded and said hello to him. Then a younger couple also waved. He found it odd.

Am I putting out a warmer vibe?

He walked the synth-stone hallways until his nose caught the wafting scent of pizza. He followed it to a service window and ordered a slice.

"Here you go, Mr. Baylor," said the clerk.

He took a bite while leaning up against the small counter.

"Mmmm, nothing like the printed stuff," he said.

"Oh, no. That's stuff's the worst," she said in agreement.

She's friendly.

It was the best pizza slice he'd ever eaten.

A couple walked by with a child in tow. They were discussing what to eat, and the boy looked at Alvin. He was wearing an old pair of oversized Opti-Comp goggles and grabbed at his parents for attention. Together they all looked at Alvin and waved.

He smiled and waved back.

What is going on?

He looked at his reflection in the mirrored window of the pizza shop. A quick peep of his face highlighted it with a yellow selection box. A pop-up showed his name and declared him the current favorite in the VR tournament. *The Hope* had updated his records. People thought he was going to play. They were rooting for him.

Oh hell.

He peeped the tournament details in his Opti-Comp for the first time. There was a portrait of Rick Zuck and a bunch of blank spots.

Shithead, asshole.

The pot was two hundred million in U.S. coin—eight times

the cost of his apartment. It was chump change to *The Hope*'s travelers. To Alvin it would mean never working a day again. He could return to Earth, sell his home, and move to South America.

He stared at the glowing golden button that said, "Enter the Fray."

Alteris might not like the attention, but it was harmless. Besides, he'd been told to enjoy himself. Worst-case scenario, if they reneged on the agreement for the apartment, he could tell them to fuck off—so long as he won.

If I lose, I'll still be the same schmuck.

It was a risk, but the payoff would be life changing.

This is a second chance.

He selected the golden button and prerecorded cheers erupted. All at once, the walls of the ship displayed a new ad for the tournament. It showed his portrait and Zuck's. The other players were still blank.

Nothing like jumping in with both feet.

The Hope had multiple bustling parties on New Year's Eve. The ballrooms were so packed with revelers that long lines ran out each doorway. Alvin squirmed in his rented tuxedo jacket as he and Katy walked across the synth-stone floor.

Fucking crowds.

He had been invited to the most exclusive party after enrolling in the tournament. The invite listed *The Hope*'s owner, Chan Xi-Michaels, as the host. There were billionaires who couldn't get into the room, and though Alvin was not keen on bumping elbows with *The Hope*'s luminaries, he figured it would impress Katy.

As they approached the ballroom at the end of the hall, he didn't see a line streaming out the door; instead there were armed guards. They wore tuxedo jackets with their gold-plated rifles.

He grimaced and stretched his arms out in front of him. The fabric wanted to give.

"It's not supposed to be comfortable," said Katy. "It's for looking good."

"What's wrong with both? I can hardly put my arms out," he said.

They approached the door and the guards nodded politely.

"Welcome, Mr. Baylor," said one of them.

Alvin nodded hello with relief as they entered the room. Then he stopped in place, stunned by the sea of partygoers ahead of them.

"C'mon," said Katy as she cut through the crowd.

He kept his eyes on her in her stunning blue dress. Plenty of other eyes were on her, too, and he found himself sending dagger stares. She looked back and frowned at his antics.

"You need a drink," she said.

As they made their way across the room, Alvin heard a shrill laugh.

At the center of the room, Chan Xi-Michaels was holding court. His cherubic face towered over the surrounding guests. A floppy black bowl cut topped the smile. Alvin could hear a whirring sound mixed with the high-pitched laugh as they got closer. He saw wheels down on the floor where Xi-Michaels's feet should have been. The cluster of sycophants around him obscured the rest of his body.

"That's *him*. Is he on a scooter or something?" whispered Alvin.

"No. I heard he had an accident a few years back. Those are his feet," said Katy.

A waiter walked by carrying a tray of champagne. Alvin snatched two flutes and nodded in thanks. He handed one to Katy.

"Shit," he said. "There's Zuck."

He motioned to a table in the corner. Zuck hadn't seen them

yet. He was talking to a heavyset black woman in a cardinal's frock.

"Is that Oona?" Alvin asked.

"Oona Amaru, first female cardinal of the Catholic church? Yep, that's her. She bet big money on Zuck before you made the cut."

"Great. Let's not go over there."

"That's fine. I'm not here to dote on the rich and spoiled. I'm here to be with you," said Katy.

"Say no more." He smiled.

Zuck finally looked over and saw them. He smirked.

Alvin glared back and Katy tugged his arm to take him in another direction through the crowd.

"That looks cozy," she said, pointing to a roped-off corner of the room covered by a satin overhang. Underneath were several unoccupied booths. They made their way to the ropes, where an usher eyeballed them before letting them into the covered area. They took a seat at a black-velvet banquette in the corner.

"So when are you gonna start practicing? You can't just chat me up at the pods if you wanna win," she said.

"I just decided today. I'll start soon."

"C'mon, Al. You're ready to rumble. I can see it in your eyes."

"I'll start training day after next."

"You gotta go after things or they don't happen," she said.

"I know. Look, sometimes I just want to hide away from everyone."

"We're doing that now. When you get over your hangover tomorrow, go hit the pods."

"Okay, Mom." He chortled.

"They're going to be gunning for you. Zuck especially," she said.

"He takes it too seriously."

"Yes, he does."

"Point taken. I'll come by and start practicing."

"Don't worry, Al. Tonight, we'll just drink the free champagne."

"Cheers," he said.

They clinked glasses and guzzled down the first drink.

"Two hundred million's a heck of a lot of coin for folks like us," she said.

She's using the word "us" now.

"Chump change to this crowd," he said. "They'll make more betting on the match than I can make winning it. And if I do, more than half will go to taxes and fees. The rest—well, I guess I could retire in Chile."

"I hear Antarctica is melting and flooding the coast," she said.

"That's why it's affordable."

She laughed then said, "Oh my god—look at the fashion show over there."

She pointed to an elephantine man holding his wife's purse. He was wearing a white tux with advertising patches all over it. His wife was dressed in orange that matched her husband's hair. She gesticulated drunkenly while speaking to a group of Chinese in transparent plastic suits with multicolored fabrics beneath. They complimented one another on their attire.

"That guy looks like a parade balloon," said Alvin.

"Maybe his wife's purse is weighted to keep him from floating away," she said.

As if he heard them talking, the man looked over. He smiled and waved, then fashioned his fingers into gun barrels and pantomimed shooting at Alvin.

"Uh-oh, you got a fan," she said.

"Yeah, I seem to be picking 'em up lately."

A waiter came by and offered more champagne flutes.

"To new fans," said Katy.

They clinked glasses.

"Enough about me," he said. "Where were you before you came to *The Hope*?"

"I was in China . . . for a while."

"Oh, really? Must've helped you get this job."

"The truth is I'm ready for a change," she said.

He wondered if she was just on *The Hope* to land a whale and retire.

"So what's next for you?" he asked.

"I've gotta get back to Earth. I need to pay off a debt. That's why I took this. Pay's good, so long as I live lean up here."

"I can wine and dine you and call it company business for a little while."

"I won't stop you," she said.

"So what will you do when you get back?"

"I don't know. I never finished school. Without a degree I don't have many options."

"I didn't finish, either."

"I think it's different for men. People feel sorry for you. Too ADHD and aggro to help yourself and all. Women have to make it on their own."

"Hey, I didn't get my gig on charity."

"No, of course not. That came out wrong. I think you're different."

"How so?"

"You're the one holding yourself back."

Her words felt like a gut punch.

"I'm know. I'm lost."

"Everybody is, Al, but they don't have the luxury of complaining. You have a gift you should be using."

"I tried. I was kicked to the curb. I guess I've been lying in the gutter all this time."

"You've got a second chance now. Take it."

"Yes," he said.

"Good."

They spent the next hour getting drunk and cozy until the man in the patches stomped up to the table.

"Mr. Alvin Baylor, put 'er there!" he shouted with a thrust of his hand.

Alvin was boozed up and met the man's handshake with gusto.

"I hear you're a regular ringer. Social says you used to play in college." His voice slowed as he got to the end of each sentence. He kept pumping Alvin's hand up and down.

"I did play in college," said Alvin.

He looked over at Katy, who smiled politely, then back at the man, who was still holding on and saying, "Yeah, that's what I hear. They say the smart money's on you."

"I can't say if the money is smart. I just play," said Alvin.

"Hah! Hahahaha!"

His laugh was sickening, but he let go of Alvin's hand.

"If you'll excuse us, we were just going to dance," said Alvin.

He got up from the table and cut in front of the man on his way to Katy. She stood and the man looked her up and down with a lascivious expression.

"Ooooh! My money's on you, Zeus!" he shouted at Alvin's back as they disappeared into the crowd.

"Horrifying," whispered Katy.

"Hold me," said Alvin with hound-dog eyes.

She laughed and they slow-footed it among the other dancers. It was near midnight, Beijing time, and the vid screens began their countdown. The room went still and the crowd began counting backward as the number ten lit up a thousand times across every surface in the room. As the numbers reached zero, the shout went out.

"Happy New Year!"

Every inch of vid-screen-paneled wall, floor, and ceiling pulled back to reveal the stars outside. This ballroom had real windows. Chan Xi-Michaels's laughter could be heard above the gasps.

Alvin and Katy kissed as "Auld Lang Syne" began playing. They danced in silence among the crowd. The light of a thousand stars sparkled in her blue eyes.

After a few songs, the room began to thin and Alvin could see the cardinal from Chicago, Oona Amaru, over Katy's shoulder. Zuck was gone. Oona beckoned Alvin with a wave.

"Oona calls," he whispered to Katy.

"It might be easier to indulge her. She likes her way."

"Okay, I'm drunk, anyway," he said.

They walked over to the table. Oona was upbeat. She looked cartoonish with a tiny cardinal's hat perched upon a giant afro. She was seated with a petite woman dressed in a revealing set of black straps. The woman could barely keep her head up.

"Why hello, Mr. Baylor! It's a pleasure to meet you. Please," she said motioning for them to sit. "And a hello to you, Ms. . . . ?"

"Katy's fine. Your friend looks a little tired."

"She'll be fine. We've had a long day."

Oona laughed and rubbed the girl's thigh with a fat hand. The woman's head wobbled and her mascara ran down her cheeks.

Katy's eyes narrowed at the scene and Alvin second-guessed the decision to chat.

"Your Eminence, it's getting late, perhaps . . ." he began.

"Oh, nonsense, it's New Year's Eve." She pushed the words off her tongue with regal countenance. "Call me Oona. They say you're a favorite in the tournament."

"That's what I hear," said Alvin.

"Yes, people do talk. Earlier, I was discussing the very topic with my friends Rick Zuck and Chan Xi-Michaels. Chan was disappointed that he didn't get to meet you tonight."

"He seemed occupied. I didn't feel it was my place to interrupt."

"Yes, we all have our place, but tonight you belong here. That could change, of course." Oona kept her smile.

"I imagine it will if I don't perform, but you shouldn't worry about that. It's up to me," said Alvin.

Oona laughed and puffed her chest out.

"You are an interesting man, Mr. Baylor. Are you so sure of yourself?"

"I am when it counts."

He felt his blood pressure rising. Katy stood still, wearing a barely neutral expression.

"Oh, how very masculine," said Oona. She turned to her girl-toy and said, "Don't you think?"

The woman nodded, but she didn't know to what.

"Well, Oona. It was illuminating, but it is getting late."

Alvin pressed his hands on the table, preparing to leave.

"Oh, don't go, Mr. Baylor. Stay, entertain me with your thoughts. What makes Alvin Baylor tick?"

"Hmm, maybe it's aggression?" He cocked his head slightly.

"Aggression? I thought we'd taken care of that with grade school medications," she said.

His eyes narrowed and he splayed his hands out on the table. "I don't need medicating, lady."

"How charming. I respect all people, even men who've skipped their doses."

He sneered at her and she leaned back and smiled.

"Al . . . let's go." Katy grabbed his arm.

"But she wants to know what makes me tick . . . tock, isn't that right?"

His gaze was square on Oona.

"Please, indulge me with your experience," said the cardinal.

"The struggle is won by the most aggressive participants. It's nature's way, not man's."

"A reasonable misunderstanding, Mr. Baylor, but cunning has always been the determining factor. You're not going to win. Richard has already topped your score. Isn't that right?" said Oona.

Alvin looked at Katy questioningly. She nodded.

"Good for him," said Alvin. "Now excuse us, please, we have to go fuck and I think you have some business of your own."

He motioned toward the passed-out woman at the table.

Oona Amaru maintained her smile. "Of course. Don't let that booze go to your head. We want you to make the tournament."

His head set lower; eyes glaring.

"He'll be there," said Katy. She pulled Alvin away.

"So Zuck passed me?"

"Yeah, I didn't want to upset you, so I didn't say anything." She hugged him tight as they walked toward the exit. He was rigid with anger. Katy said, "Don't let her get to you. She's worried about the money she bet. I don't think they expected someone like you to come along and spoil the fun."

"She can have fun losing," he said.

"You're one hell of player, Al, but don't be naïve. They won't just let you win."

He stopped at the door and gave one last glance to the star-speckled ballroom.

"You're right. I'll see you at the pods tomorrow. I'm gonna go get some rest."

───────

Alvin awoke on New Year's Day with a hangover. It irritated him. His thoughts were focused on the tournament.

Posting the high score had lasted all of a week. If he didn't cut back, lose the gut, and get himself tuned up, he wasn't going to take down a twenty-year pro like Rick Zuck. He needed to practice.

He ordered up a can of Refuel from room service and got himself dressed. It was time to take the tournament seriously. Time to kick the boozing. He had nearly six months of Katy and the good life ahead of him. There was no reason to stay drunk.

He walked back from the bathroom and answered the door.

"Here's your Refuel, sir," said a chipper bellhop. "Say, is there something wrong with your panels? I can ask maintenance to—"

"No." Alvin grabbed the can and bounced his wrist off the wall. The pocket door slid closed.

"Have a nice day, sir!" yelled the kid.

Alvin chugged back the can and tossed it at the recycle bin in the corner. He missed and it banked off the edge and hit the desk. The vibration woke the floating terminal screen.

He walked over to pick up the can while mourning his fruitless search for answers from days past. Then he remembered.

Carroll Henry. Bah.

He scowled as he bent over to fetch the can and toss it in the bin.

A new search result was waiting for him onscreen. His blank database query had returned a result. There were two employees in possession of an empty location field.

The first was him. The second was Mohammed Rinsler.

His heart jumped in tempo.

There were few details. Only names and dates of hire.

Rinsler? The Mohammed Rinsler?

He knew the name, anyone literate in science did. The man had cracked faster-than-light communication and built an artificial intelligence that led to protests that accelerated the breakup of the United States.

He peeped a quick lookup of the scientist in his Opti-Comp. It came back with *The Hope*'s cached bio and a photo. The man had shaggy black hair, an awkward smile, and a gap between his front teeth.

Looks like that waiter's description.

The article detailed Rinsler's various Nobel Prizes in quantum mechanics and his strange beliefs about the nature of consciousness. He claimed a contentious theory called Orch-OR had led to his development of the first conscious computer, the QI. He worked for the U.S. government until his death during the secession riots on 4/13/2107. There was nothing about mining.

Then Alvin noticed a detail. Rinsler's date of death matched the hire date on the Alteris terminal session.

"Whoa," he said.

"Is something troubling you, esteemed guest?" said the room.

"Get me the published works of Mohammed Rinsler," said Alvin.

"*A Quantum Theory of Everything* and *Objective Reduction & Quantum Consciousness* are now available on your bookshelf," said the room.

Damn it.

Alvin walked to the doorway, swung open the electrical plate, and plugged in the AR panels. A virtual bookshelf appeared along the back wall. The two books by Rinsler appeared on it. He had new homework and a tournament to win.

FIFTEEN

Alvin heard the shower running as he lay in bed. His eyes fluttered open and he flopped over on his back. He felt his head throb and he coughed. Five months ago when he boarded *The Hope,* his liver had been pickled. Now three drinks had given him a hangover. He regretted his act of sabotage, but today was the player's luncheon and his social anxieties had gotten the better of him.

He'd had no contact from Alteris in weeks and he'd kept his socializing to Katy. While that relationship bloomed, his research on Rinsler had come to nothing more than a layman's study of esoteric science. Had the brilliant scientist faked his death to work for Alteris? Maybe. Right now he was just a name in a company record. Rather than stay troubled by the uncertainty, Alvin enjoyed the vacation and rehabbed his gaming skills daily— until today. There would be no more practice. Tomorrow was the tournament.

The shower stopped and Katy exited the bathroom wrapped in hotel towels.

"These are really nice," she said while thumbing at the thick towels.

"You're not used to them by now? Ooooh, my head," said Alvin.

"We don't get these in the crew quarters. You want a Refuel? You look terrible."

"Anything. Make it stop," he groaned.

She grabbed a can from the mini fridge and tossed it toward him.

"Look alive," she teased as it landed on the edge of the bed.

He moaned as he reached for the can.

"I thought you were gonna take it easy last night," she said.

"Yeah, I planned to, but—the best laid plans and all."

"Huh?"

"Nothing, it's from an old book. I'll be fine."

Alvin chugged down the drink and rolled off the bed sideways onto his feet. He braced himself on the wall. The throbbing in his head grew more pronounced.

"Well, the game's not till tomorrow. Don't do it again," she said.

"Food'll help. I got twenty minutes to make the player's luncheon."

"I don't know why you wanna eat with those rich assholes. Just take their money at the tourney."

"I told you. I need to size them up. Besides, it's free." He winked at her.

"Nothing's free, Al. Be careful they don't drive you to drink again."

"I can control myself."

"Can you?" she asked.

"What's up your ass?" he said.

"I don't like seeing you sabotage yourself." She arranged her clothes on the bed.

"Babe, I'm gonna win."

"You're such a cocky shit."

"After I win we'll go out and celebrate. How 'bout the Twenti-eth-Century Rock Review?" he said.

"You're dying to go to that thing . . . you win and I'll go watch your holographic relic show."

"You'll love it. I promise."

He could feel the Refuel beginning to clear his head. He got up and wrapped his arms around her.

"I'm sure I will. Just do it, Al. Whatever it takes." She kissed his cheek, then continued, "You hate being called a cheat, but I don't think you can handle being a loser."

His chest tightened. Isn't that what he'd spent most of his adult life being—a malcontent? A loser?

"Thanks for giving it to me straight," he said.

She kissed him full on the lips, then turned around, bent over the bed, and dropped the towels from her wet, naked body.

"I suppose you're trying to make me miss that lunch," he said.

———

Alvin flashed a smile as he walked up to the doormen. He was late and feeling okay with it. Katy had a way of changing his priorities.

"Welcome, Mr. Baylor. The banquet hall is to your left," said the taller man. He leaned over conspiratorially and whispered, "We got money on you, Zeus." The other fellow just winked.

Alvin was pleased to see his status as blue-collar disruptor had charmed security. "Drinks on me if I disappoint, gentlemen," he said with a nod.

He entered a white synth-stone room and instantly felt every-one's eyes upon him. The Grecian-styled hall was occupied by a long dining table heaped with food. It struck Alvin as ostenta-tious—something out of a bacchanal. Several contestants were picking their way through mounds of fruit, seafood, and pastries at tables scattered around the room. Some stared intently at him, others tried to be more discreet. Looking around, he did not see a single vid-screen-paneled surface.

No freakin' ads anywhere. It's good to be rich.

His eyes stopped on Oona dressed in a white gown and sitting at the center table. *Why is she here? I thought this was for players.* She nodded to him and he nodded back. A tiny woman sat beside her and whispered in her ear.

New girl-toy?

This one looked more alert, less slutty. She wore black eye shadow that was exaggerated with long sharp swoops. A streak of orange ran through her black hair.

The man seated across from Oona had tattooed arms. Alvin recognized Zuck, who turned around and scowled.

"Well, you showed up!" he shouted.

Beside him a skinny old man in a cowboy hat looked over and twirled the end of his white handlebar mustache.

Alvin paused and cocked his head.

"Is that you, Richard?" he said.

"You're not winning this thing," answered Zuck. He sneered and turned back to Oona.

Alvin ignored them again and began digging into a pile of seafood at one of the small tables. The guests returned to various small conversations.

As he dug through the pile, a fast-talking voice spoke up from behind. "Try the lobster."

Alvin looked over to see a brutish-looking man with cornrows and dark eyes wearing a sparkling-orange jogging suit. He balanced a plate of seafood in one hand.

"I think it's real, yo."

He smiled goofily and wiped at his mouth before reaching the same hand out to Alvin.

"Chico," he said.

Alvin's eyes lingered on the man's titanium teeth for a beat. He looked down to see rough, bruised knuckles. Chico Perez, as foretold by Alvin's room advertising, would defend his MMA title aboard the ship. His ears were cauliflower and his head was shaved and misshapen. "I'm Alvin."

"Yeah, I know."

"I've seen your mug plastered all over the place, too," said Alvin.

Chico smiled. "Tha's right. I'm gonna be champ twice, yo!"

"Nah. Just once," said Alvin. He stuffed what he assumed was the lobster into his mouth then continued talking. "Oh, you're right. This is good."

"Players, can I have your attention please," said a soft-voiced man.

He was immaculately dressed in a white linen suit with a gardenia springing from the chest pocket. His oiled black hair shone under the lights as he gesticulated.

"Mr. Xi-Michaels will be joining us shortly. If you would all gather at the table, we have a schedule to keep."

He gave a disapproving look at Alvin, who figured his tardiness was not appreciated.

As Alvin walked toward the table, he noticed another man taking his time at the fondue station. He wore a rumpled navy suit, and his tousled silver hair sat over a bushy mustache. He looked like a poorly tailored Mark Twain impersonator and seemed more concerned with strawberries dipped in chocolate than listening to the natty messenger.

"Mr. Vance, can you join us, please?" said the man in the white suit.

Vance turned and winked and then stuffed another bite into his mouth. He mumbled something that sounded like "sure" and walked over.

"I am Hong Chow, Mr. Xi-Michaels's personal attendant. I welcome you to *The Hope*'s first annual VR Players Luncheon. If everyone will please stand for Mr. Xi-Michaels."

Those seated at the table stood to join the others at attention.

Alvin heard whirring gears and looked over to see the old cowboy rise up. His withered legs were wrapped in a skeletal exo-suit that whined as it did the lifting. The man held his hat across his chest. He was very old, perhaps in his nineties.

Too old, thought Alvin.

He watched the far door through which Chow had entered, but no one came. Instead, an electric warble sounded from the center of the table and a spherical hologram resembling a crystal ball bounded into the air. Chan Xi-Michaels's rosy-cheeked face sprang up in the middle and exclaimed, "Hello everyone! So happy to have you!" His holographic head whirled around and nodded at all present. The strands of his hair flopped about as he giggled.

"Mr. Chow, please introduce me to our illustrious guests," he said.

"Of course, sir. To my left, we are very proud to have Ms. Oona's . . . protégé, Rita Takata."

The young woman flashed a hand gesture at Xi-Michael's floating head as if she were posing for a photo. Then she blinked to show a set of green cat eyes painted on her lids.

"Meow," said Xi-Michaels. "So wonderful to have you in competition today, Rita, and a warm welcome to you, Ms. Oona. I hope you are enjoying the caviar!"

Oona laughed and nodded. She motioned for Rita to sit. They both took their seats. Alvin recognized the name. Rita was number three on the leaderboard. A distant number three.

"And here we have Mr. Tex Holloway of Holloway Modular Designs," said Chow.

Alvin knew that Holloway's storage clusters supplied data and temperature control for the Alteris NoHo office.

Good products.

"Ah, yes, yes," said Xi-Michaels in a vague way, suggesting to Alvin he had never heard of the man's company.

The old cowboy nodded and took his seat with the aid of the noisy exo-suit.

Chow moved on. "Rick Zuck needs no introduction. After retiring from pro competition, he's been kind enough to entertain us with his skills and provide a quantum analysis of the match."

"Hello, Mr. Zuck!" said Xi-Michaels. "How goes the transition to the family business? Finding more social metadata in deep space, no doubt."

"I'm still focused on playing for the time being, sir. There's plenty of time to expand the product and the clientele."

It was the most humility Alvin had ever heard out of Zuck. He took his seat and Chow moved on to Chico.

"The fighter, Mr. Chico Perez."

"Hold on now, dog. That's the undefeated, pound-for-pound best—Chico—from Puerto Rico—Perez."

He threw two thumbs up and flashed his titanium grin at the table, then turned around to make sure he didn't miss anyone.

"Yes, Mr. Perez, I know you—very impressive ground-and-pound," said Xi-Michaels without losing his plastered-on smile.

Chico nodded and looked around with bravado as he sat back down.

Chow turned his attention to a mysterious woman dressed in all black and covered by a niqab. "Visiting from the Islamic State is Noura Al-Tahtawi."

She sat with a Middle Eastern man wearing a collarless fitted suit with no tie. He looked to be made of muscle. She bowed her head gracefully and the man spoke. "The house of Al-Tahtawi is honored to be among such accomplished company."

Alvin tried to read Noura, but got nothing. Only her elegant brown eyes were visible.

He heard Oona scoff under her breath and saw her throwing sideways glances while she rumpled her nose. Whether it was Christian or feminist ire, he couldn't tell. Perhaps it was both.

"Next we come to Alvin Baylor," said Chow.

Alvin straightened up and nodded at the cherubic head in the holo-sphere.

"Ah, Mr. Baylor, we finally meet. I am very excited to see what you can do! But no overclocking tomorrow!"

He said it with a glee that irritated Alvin.

"Thank you. I'm happy to participate." He smiled and sat down.

"Finally, we come to Mr. Anton Vance. Mr. Vance is a journalist for the *Yellow Letter* and quite the fan of cyber-athletics. He'll be covering the game."

Nearly everyone at the table guffawed and sneered at the man in the navy-blue suit across from Alvin. Zuck and Oona were visibly upset.

"My personal affairs had best remain personal," said Oona with a touch of contempt.

"Your Eminence, I don't give a rat's ass who you're fucking," said Vance with an accusatory finger covered in some sort of sauce. He sucked it off his digit with a flick of his wrist and Oona fashioned a look of disgust. Alvin liked him immediately.

"Oh, Ms. Oona, nothing to worry about," said Xi-Michaels, never losing his boyish smile. "Mr. Vance is a benefit to our promotions. Advertising, if you will. You have my protection from any unwarranted news gathering. But you, Mr. Perez, you'd better behave! All of this is fair game for prefight reporting."

He said it with a chuckle and everyone but Chico grimaced. Instead his mouth parted wide to flash those metal teeth.

"Not a problem, sir, I'm a man of the people," said Chico. "I live my life for them. For my fans."

Alvin couldn't tell if he was really that much of a fool or if he'd just studied self-promotion.

"Oh, that is wonderful, Mr. Perez. There will be many fans watching this event, as well. We want to give them a good show. That is why we will have special team competition!"

Alvin's eyebrow arched up.

What is this about?

"I thought this was a winner-take-all death match," crowed Tex Holloway as he smacked his withered hand on the tabletop.

For the first time, the smile left Xi-Michaels's face.

Mr. Chow answered, "Mr. Holloway, the solo competition is intact. We are simply adding a team phase."

"Team phase? What team phase?" asked Holloway.

"We want to entertain our guests. This will ensure a longer match . . . for spectating purposes," said Chow.

"Ha!" barked Tex. "They think they got this one figured already, folks."

"Figured how?" asked a tense Oona.

Zuck dropped his eyes down. Oona glared at him and the table slowly followed suit. The Zuck family were the operators of a data-mining consortium. Rick was heir apparent and soon to be running the family business.

Oona's gaze left Zuck and she addressed Xi-Michaels directly. "What has the data predicted?"

Xi-Michaels took up his smile again. "Ms. Oona, it is best to leave the odds to the odds-makers," he said.

"Enough. What was the prediction?" She looked over at Zuck and back at Xi-Michaels.

Zuck flashed an angry glance at Alvin.

I must be the winner.

"What's the prize for second?" said Alvin jokingly.

"Good of you to ask, Mr. Baylor," said Chow. "The top three players will receive monetary prizes."

"See, folks, nothing to worry about," said Alvin.

"You're a cheater," said Oona.

Xi-Michaels spoke. "Mr. Baylor did not cheat to place in the tournament. I have no reason to block him. In fact, his participation has attracted interest."

"A rival for the champ here, eh?" interjected Anton Vance.

"Don't go muckraking, Vance," scolded Zuck. "This isn't newsworthy."

"Anything is newsworthy if the right people are involved." Vance looked first at Alvin, then at Zuck, and finally he smiled at Oona and Rita.

"Hey, man, I'm not looking to—" started Alvin before being cut off by Oona and Zuck's overlapping retorts.

"One call to your parent company," said Zuck.

"One word, you dirty little man," said Oona.

Alvin sighed and dropped his attempts to communicate. He didn't want to be in the news, either; the attention could upset Alteris. Best to shut up now.

"Relax. I'm here to promote *The Hope*, lady," said Vance. "I don't need to print anyone's dirty laundry."

"You can print mine," said Chico.

Vance nodded with a smile and resumed talking. "So answer the esteemed cardinal's question. What's the prediction that required a team phase be added for entertainment?"

A worried Chow looked toward Xi-Michaels and received a nod.

"Thirteen seconds," said Chow. "Data analysis predicts that Alvin Baylor wins in thirteen seconds."

The stunned group turned to stare at Alvin.

He gave an awkward half smile and pointed at Zuck. "He's the one who predicted it."

The table turned to look at the ex-pro and now data magnate.

"I've seen bad analysis and that's what this reeks of," whined Holloway.

"I don't care what the computer says, I am a champion," said Chico.

"Richard, why didn't you tell me this?" asked Oona.

"Sometimes the algorithm gets it wrong . . ." said Zuck.

"Mr. Zuck, would you care to explain the vagaries of fuzzy data analysis?" asked Chow.

Zuck shook his head.

"Hot damn," said Vance. "So what are you charging people for?"

Zuck snapped at the comment. "My data is always accurate. This is an extreme case . . . the calculation—"

Xi-Michaels cut him off. "This is an indicator we must respect. We will ensure an excellent show for our spectators!" His face drew into the widest smile yet. For the first time his white-gloved hands rose up into the hologram, and he clapped quickly in a gesture of completion. "Thank you, everyone. Mr. Chow, please make sure our guests have very pleasant meal. But don't eat too much before competition!" He laughed shrilly and his holo disappeared.

Chow bit his lower lip as he looked at the players. The group exchanged pensive, angry stares. Then Chow took a deep breath and raised his arms. The doors behind him opened up as the wait-staff entered bearing the first course.

"Oh yes!" said Vance.

Alvin looked around the table as the food was served. Oona and Zuck regained their composure in front of the help. The others ignored him, except Noura Al-Tahtawi, who returned his stare. Her eyes were smiling from the black niqab. She seemed to be enjoying the chaos.

SIXTEEN

The next morning Alvin reported to the entertainment deck for the tournament. A row of male and female dancers performed a kick line around the pods while virtual fireworks exploded from the walls. There were a smattering of old ladies and young kids, but the crowd appeared to be mostly crew. He hung back while Katy and the other game attendants began putting the players in their pods. Anton Vance ran from pod to pod trying to get quotes from everyone. When the rest were all in, Katy walked over to him and led him to his pod. Vance jogged along with her.

"Baylor, any final words before the match?" said Vance.

"No."

"You're the only working man in the contest, does that give you extra motivation?"

"No. I enjoy competition, that's all."

"Is it really competition when the odds have you so far ahead?"

Alvin stopped at the door to his pod, one leg in. "What's the difference? I still need to beat them."

"That you do. Good luck, kid," said Vance.

Alvin nodded and stepped in. Katy followed after.

"Not interested in stardom?" she said.

"I don't need that bloodsucker writing me into public dramas."

She laughed. "So how was the lunch?"

"Well, we all had one thing in common," said Alvin.

Katy began tying down the restraints. "What's that?"

He gave her a wry grin. "We dislike each other."

"Yeah, that I saw coming."

She leaned over him to secure his torso. "What about Oona? She give you the business again?"

"No. She was cordial. She has that Rita girl playing for her."

Katy leaned close and snapped in the chest strap. "Rita's hot stuff, but you're better. Be careful, Oona's free with her money when she wants something."

"You speak from experience?" he teased.

"I only have eyes for you, Al. Any other brilliant observations?"

"I got a read on most of them, but I left after the salad."

"All that 'I must go study them' crap—and you walked out?"

"It got uncomfortable. We were told the bookie algorithm had me on top in thirteen seconds."

She stopped and cocked her head.

"Thirteen seconds . . . the muthafucking champ!" She socked him in the shoulder.

"Ouch . . . I'm gonna need that arm."

"Not really," she said as she secured his head. "Shit, that's fast, Al. They didn't say it was that fast. You think you can pull it off?"

"I don't know. It mighta scared them a bit. The only one I couldn't figure was that Arabian princess."

"So, she'll take you an extra couple seconds."

Alvin gave a smile. "Let's do this."

She lowered the chair and gave him a peck on the cheek, then stepped out of the pod.

Alvin heard it seal shut with a clunk. He tried to relax, but his adrenaline was pumping.

"Contestants, the competition is about to begin. Please prepare for synaptic redirection."

He closed his eyes and felt his head start to buzz. When he opened them again, he was lying on his back in total darkness. The sound of his breath filled his ears. He pushed up into the black against a hard surface and it cracked, filling the darkness with light.

Alvin sat upright and looked around the room.

His pod was long and low, like a coffin. As his eyes adjusted to the virtual world, he saw the blurry silhouettes of players rising from their own black sarcophagi. They were outfitted in black suits that rose up to cover their skulls, leaving only their faces and the tops of their heads exposed.

Their avatars were idealized renditions of themselves. Alvin used an actual scan. He was fit enough now that he'd dropped the boozing and some extra weight.

Who the fuck is who?

Zuck jumped out of the far pod. His athleticism was distinguishable from the others and he too used a real scan. The pros always did for licensing and endorsement purposes. Alvin's vision cleared enough to see the aggression on his face. Then his heads-up display kicked in, followed by the cacophony of the crowd and a droning announcer. They were surrounded by a stadium of virtual spectators. Every object and person in the room momentarily received a digital outline as it was scanned. There looked to be hundreds watching.

Alvin muted his audio feed and stared at the cheering faces and the fumbling of the players in silence, then closed his eyes and took a deep breath. There was cross-play between his physical body and his virtual one. Concentrated breathing helped him to unify the two. As he breathed deeply his physical body did so as well, and his mind relaxed into the virtual environment.

When he reopened his eyes, he saw colored piping illuminating the players' uniforms. Red versus blue; those were the teams for the first phase.

On each side of the circular platform, a doorway filled with colored light. Alvin turned up the volume as his heads-up display finished self-diagnostics.

"Choose your weapons and enter the arena," said an announcer.

He walked to the blue side and removed a rifle from the wall rack, then took a step toward the exit and through the shimmering blue field into a small room.

A young, sturdy man wearing a cowboy hat entered after him. It was Tex Holloway, seventy years younger.

"Yeehaw!" he yowled as he gave Alvin a little elbow to the ribs. He twisted the ends of his mustache just like he did in real life. Alvin smiled and kept his eyes on the door.

A stocky, dark-complected man entered. The pair stared at him curiously.

"It's nice to finally say hello," he said in a deep baritone.

He leaned up against the wall and crossed his legs in distinctly feminine fashion.

"Noura Al-Tahtawi I presume?" said Alvin.

"Yes, Alvin Baylor." Her avatar smiled.

"So ya do talk?" asked Tex.

"When custom allows, Mr. Holloway."

"You folks got funny customs," said Tex.

"A rude American—how unusual. Or are you just a Texan now?" said Al-Tahtawi.

She laughed and Tex grimaced and pulled at his mustache. Alvin ignored the animosity. He felt assured by his decision to leave lunch after the salad.

These people are a bad mix.

"Attention, players. We have a last-minute ruling for tonight's tournament. We are allowing overclocking for capable players."

Alvin heard the words and felt his spirits drop. The countdown in his display started ticking down from sixty.

"You clocking it?" asked Tex.

"No," said Alvin.

"But they did that for you," said Tex.

"No, not me. My implants have a limiter installed."

"Richard Zuck," said Al-Tahtawi. "He and Oona were whining about you."

"Shit," said Tex.

"Let's stay out of tight corners and play a distance game," said Alvin. "The reflex advantage works best in a surprise encounter."

The duo nodded then stood silently while the timer counted down.

We're fucked.

The countdown finished, then a flash of light blinded him.

He was no longer in the small room. He stood on a rocky perch overlooking a valley. Pinpoints of starlight dotted the black sky. In the valley below sat a crashed starship surrounded by large crystals that jutted through the wreckage. Starlight glinted off them, casting light patterns on the dusty gray surface. The game field was an alien moon.

Man-sized letters suddenly dropped from the sky and crashed to the ground in front of him. They spelled "Relic."

"All right, we got a capture-and-return match," said Alvin.

The letters disappeared and a green ring of light, nine feet in diameter, took their place. Then a slow ping sounded in his ear while an arrow appeared in his view indicating the direction of the relic.

A blaring horn declared the beginning of the match.

"Move to that ship and keep to cover," said Alvin.

"Yeehaw!" exclaimed Tex as he charged down the hill.

"Seems I have the longest gun. I'll hang back and snipe," said Al-Tahtawi.

She smiled as she swung the rifle forward over her shoulder and took a knee.

A red muzzle flashed and the cowboy dropped face forward to the dirt.

Alvin ducked behind a boulder.

This is a free-for-all.

"You see that to the left?" said Alvin.

Before he got the words out, Al-Tahtawi let loose a shot from her rifle and he saw Tex's killer fall. It was Chico.

Alvin ran out from the boulder and dashed down the hill. He crossed the field going from rock to rock. He heard another, "Yee-haw!" as Tex used his boot thrusters to leapfrog overhead. He had respawned.

The cycle of death and rebirth would continue until the relic entered the green circle. Two captures would end the match.

Okay, old man, you're the bait.

Alvin dashed for the crashed starship.

A shot crossed the field from beside the wreckage. Tex leaped over it. Then from the same spot came another shot headed for Alvin. He ducked it with a front roll, and when he came up Tex was face down in the dirt and Zuck was standing next to him.

Damn, that's fast.

Zuck fired.

Overclocking bastard.

Right through Alvin's forehead.

Back on *The Hope* proper, Hong Chow and Chan Xi-Michaels watched from a regal bedroom with decor purchased from the Palace of Versailles. Chow wore linen dress slacks with suspenders and an undershirt. He was comfortable on the edge of the enormous canopy bed. His dress shirt and jacket hung over the one of the baroque chairs. Xi-Michaels, dressed in a black overcoat with tails, spun around in circles on a set of prosthetic wheels and clapped his white-gloved hands excitedly.

Both men were transfixed by the six player feeds of the game floating before them in their Opti-Comps.

"Ooh. I'm so excited! I need to be emptied," said Xi-Michaels.

Chow got up from the bed and removed the man's overcoat, revealing an ovoid translucent bag that hung from metal collarbones. Save for a head and the organs contained in the bag, Xi-Michaels was all metal skeleton and tubes.

Chow neatly folded the overcoat and placed it on the antique bureau before retrieving a round container and a tube. He inserted the line into a port at the bottom of the man's metal pelvis, then turned the gasket knob. Dark waste began flowing into the receptacle.

"Mr. Baylor is dispatched so easily," said Chow.

"Yes, he's very cautious. I did not expect that," said Xi-Michaels.

"Do you think he really has a chance?" asked Chow.

"Mr. Zuck certainly thought so after running the analysis," said Xi-Michaels.

A tone sounded. Rita Takata had captured the relic.

"He's just lost the first round of a team match. Mr. Zuck is overclocking. How can Baylor win?" said Chow.

"Quantum computers calculate the possible as well as the probable, Hong. Why do you think the Americans destroyed theirs? Nobody likes being outsmarted. It doesn't matter either way. If Baylor loses, I cover the house with the money Alteris is paying me to ferry him. And if he wins . . ."

"Then Ms. Oona and Mr. Zuck will want their bribe money back," said Chow.

"Yes. She will make noise and Vance will have a story about a commoner being cheated. Then I will find out why Alteris sent Baylor," said Xi-Michaels.

"You really think Meyer is trying to double-cross us?"

"She's up to something. First that scientist and now this man. The payloads have been light for the last year. She's slowing the deliveries. I think she's trying to cut us out with some sort of automation."

"How can she? Alteris doesn't have a big enough fleet. She needs us," said Chow.

"Yes, and we need her business. It's too expensive entertaining these guests. Without our percentage of the rare metals, I can't keep this going," said Xi-Michaels.

"Perhaps we can add a new convenience fee for the guests? A twenty-five-percent oxygen tax?" said Chow.

"Hahahaha! That is why I love you, Hong, you are terrible person just like me! I will consider it."

Hong Chow watched the next round begin. This time the players rushed into the ship before firing. He focused on Zuck's and Alvin's feeds.

Rick Zuck ran solo through the cramped corridors. He leaped a crevasse and came upon the other team. He fired, sending Noura back to the spawn point.

Then Chow gasped as Alvin kicked Tex into Zuck and unloaded over the man's shoulder. Zuck's head was reduced to digital pulp.

"That's unsportsmanlike," said Chow.

"Ooh. I like him," said Xi-Michaels. "I'm finished."

Chow disconnected the tubing and sat down on the bed to continue watching the game from his Opti-Comp. He placed the container near his feet should his master need to be relieved again.

Back in the game, Tex gave Alvin a dirty look.

"Don't do that again," said Tex.

"Start using your fucking brain and I won't."

A clanking noise from down the hall ended the discussion as the two took up ready positions at the doorway.

Alvin peered down the ship's wrecked corridor. A reflective crystal shard punctured the craft. It had torn through the vessel's decking and hull, giving a clear view to the outside. Alvin's display showed a flashing icon and he heard a pinging sound. The relic was near—beneath the punctured mess.

"Noura, see the hole in the ship?" said Alvin.

"Yes, but no one is there," she said from the hilltop spawn point.

"They will be," he replied.

Alvin pointed to the crystal shard jutting through at the bend in the corridor. It reflected the dark hall to the right. Tex looked puzzled as he crouched on the other side of the doorway. Then Alvin pointed to his own teeth and then back at the crystal. The cowboy nodded. He saw it too now, reflecting out of the dark: a titanium grin.

Alvin motioned for him to stay back, then ran and leaped down the hallway.

He arced high through the air and caught a glimpse of his own reflection in the crystalline stalagmite as he bounced a grenade off it and around the corner. Chico and Rita rushed forward straight into the blast. Their avatars were sent to respawn.

Alvin landed where the floor had torn open. He stooped in the crevasse made by the crystal breach and waited for the smoke to clear. The pinging in his ear was a constant tone now. Something green and spherical shimmered in the darkness to his right.

There it is.

A noise came from the edge of the crevasse and he fired.

Zuck stepped forward into the shot. A millisecond later Alvin took one to the head. He lasted just long enough to see a red dot appear on Zuck through the open wall. Then blackness.

Little blocks of light popped into existence. They came hurriedly, and in a matter of moments his vision of the battlefield

had returned. He stood back at the green circle of light, next to
Noura Al-Tahtawi on the rocky perch.

"I got him," she said.

"Good."

In the distance, he saw Chico walk into view through the
damaged hull. Noura tensed up as she aimed, then a shot from
across the field went right through her scope. She dropped and
her body rolled down the rocks and dematerialized.

Alvin leaped out of the way as another blast hit the rock face
beside him. He scrambled to cover and heard a tone howl.
Someone had the relic.

"Yeehaw!"

He peeked from behind his rock. An explosion blew through
the opening in the hull, taking out Chico. Tex came leaping out
after it with a green orb in his hands. He hit the ground, rolled,
and managed to keep his hat on.

"Stick to cover!" yelled Alvin.

Zuck fired again, catching the top of his head.

Damn it.

When Alvin rematerialized he saw Tex run behind a gray
boulder.

Noura was on the field laying down covering fire.

Rita jumped down through the hull breach.

Chico ran around the right side of the ship at the far end of
the field.

Alvin dashed down the hill to join them.

Tex ran from his hiding place in the rock field and entered the
open just past Zuck.

"Sheee-it!" he yelled as Zuck put him down with a shot to the
back. He flopped to the ground and the glowing orb rolled from
his grasp.

Zuck charged for it in a zigzag pattern to evade the incoming
shots.

Damn, he's fast.

Alvin rushed toward the orb and popped the pin on a grenade. Zuck came straight at him and fired before diving to the ground to scoop up the relic. Alvin's body fell and the blast from his grenade sent Zuck back to respawn.

Alvin rematerialized on the hill across the battlefield. The relic had dematerialized. It would reappear inside the ship in moments.

Bet that pissed him off.

He saw an explosion at the entrance to the ship. Noura bounded into the smoky doorway.

Tex ran down the field behind her. Rita and Chico were down momentarily.

A tone sounded.

"In hand," said Noura on team chat.

She rushed back out of the same doorway. Tex leaped over her on his jet boots, scattering shots inside the ship.

Alvin charged across the field. He saw Chico coming out of the torn hull and sent a shot right into his head.

Noura ran back with the orb. She was halfway home.

Alvin looked back at the doorway. Tex held it for a moment longer before being mowed down by a barrage of shots. Zuck and Rita came through.

Alvin aimed up on Zuck and missed. The shot landed on Rita, knocking her back. He fired again and sent her to respawn. He fired again at Zuck, but he couldn't hit him.

Then he heard Noura say, "What is it you say in Texas, old man? Touchdown?"

She wasn't at the green circle yet.

Don't get cocky.

Alvin was littered with shots as Zuck ran up on him. He felt pinpricks all over his body as his vision went black. When he rematerialized, Zuck was rushing away with the orb. He'd taken Noura down.

Alvin was too far to give chase. He fired from the hilltop.

Zuck passed the orb to Rita before turning and shooting back at him. Noura and then Tex respawned in the chaos. They dodged around Zuck's shots until a booming tone echoed across the field signaling the relic's return.

Rita had just won the match.

Alvin dropped his rifle to his side. Zuck shot him in the head as the game ended.

How the hell am I gonna beat him?

SEVENTEEN

Alvin heard the whine of motors as the pod door opened beside him. His nostrils caught Katy's sweet scent as she entered the pod.

"Fuck, Al," she said.

He felt the chair rise. Then her hands were working at the straps across his torso. Sweat flowed down his forehead and temples.

"You okay?" she said.

He opened his eyelids. Her blue eyes were looking right back at him. Her smile looked pained. He felt a throbbing in his head and grimaced.

"Was I at least entertaining?" he said.

"They loved it, Al."

He relaxed back into the chair and she undid the straps on his wrists and ankles.

"Why did the rules change?" Alvin asked.

"Oona paid off Xi-Michaels. She bet big on Zuck before the predictive analysis was revealed. She has a real dislike for you."

"So you turned on overclocking?"

She looked uncomfortable. "I had to."

"I'm not sure I can beat him," he said.

"You can't, Al. There's more . . . they're going to gang up on you. Oona bought them all off, even that Arab lady," said Katy.

"Not a surprise. The level of duplicitous . . ." He trailed off to silence.

"Al, I'm sorry."

"Don't be. I got to play again. For months I've had something to look forward to."

"But you'd win for sure if they'd only play fair," she said.

"Call it karma. Besides, I already won. I have you."

She smiled softly. "You have thirty minutes before you need to be back in the seat."

"I think I'll rest here. Maybe something will come to me."

He reached down and picked up a can of Refuel he'd brought in to the pod. He swigged it and closed his eyes.

"Okay, then, I've got to disembark the others," she said sadly.

She stepped out and closed the door.

Think, Baylor, think.

He replayed the match in his mind, pondering the players and the map. He walked through the downed starship in his thoughts, examining the corners, looking for an advantage. When he heard the pod door again, Katy had returned and he had found the answer.

He opened his eyes and checked the time.

Three minutes to go.

"I've got an idea. I need you to load me a copy of Zuck's avatar," said Alvin.

"What are you going to do with that?"

"Become Zuck," he said.

She cocked her head and smiled. She seemed almost proud.

"Here." She fiddled at the controls in her Opti-Comp.

He received Zuck's avatar and loaded it up.

She began reaffixing his restraints. He looked past the floating character model in his eye to see her looking worried.

"This will even the score. If they want to gang up on me, they have to find me," he said with a wink.

"I always fall for the cocky ones," she said shaking her head.

She affixed the final torso strap, kissed him, then lowered the chair back.

"Either way we'll have a great dinner tonight," he said.

She stepped backward out of the pod and blew him a kiss. "Kick some ass."

The door slid shut.

He finalized his new avatar and waited for the pod to connect to his mind.

He felt calm. That's what pressure brought him—peace of mind. Two Zucks would sow confusion. If he could gather everyone together, he could break their alliance.

"Contestants, prepare for synaptic redirection."

Alvin closed his eyes and felt his head start to buzz. When he opened them, he was lying on his back in the coffin. He stepped out onto an empty dais. Each player entered the final match alone. The crowd roared and then a hush started to fall.

He scanned their faces and saw looks of shock. Oona stood up and shouted angrily, fist in the air.

Alvin looked down at his skinny arms—Zuck's arms. He smiled at her.

Seated near Oona was Anton Vance. The writer slapped his knee in laughter.

Alvin walked to the wall and grabbed a pulse rifle, the model Zuck preferred. He exited through the lit doorway and waited in the small room while the countdown began in his display. His vision went black.

A haze of particles appeared. They grew structured and formed the same gray plateau. He looked around. The crashed ship sat in the distance. He'd spawned exactly where he had during the team game. Large letters suddenly dropped from the sky and crashed to the ground in front of him. They spelled out "Last Man Standing." A tone sounded and the match began.

Alvin jumped down off the perch and ran around back of the rock face to hide. His display showed warning messages indicating the time benchmarks for payouts on the match. Should he finish in under thirteen seconds, he would make somebody rich. After thirteen seconds, he would make someone else rich. He didn't give a shit what the data analytics had forecasted. He needed to be patient if he wanted to win.

In the distance, he saw Chico run toward the ship and then from the other side came Tex. The two saw each other, but they didn't fire.

They're definitely working together.

Alvin scurried low around the rock face to take a look from its left side. He saw Rita move slowly from one boulder to another and thought of picking her off.

Not yet. I need everyone to shoot Zuck at once.

It looked clear now. He took off running toward the ship. A tone blared across the field. Thirteen seconds had elapsed.

He saw spectator chatter in his display. Some razzed him, others complained about lost wagers. He ignored the distraction and continued on to the vessel's side where it was torn open. He lay down flat, just below the gouge in the hull, and peered over the edge. The players were checking the rooms together and they were using open chat.

"All clear," said Chico. "We should hold position and wait for him to move out there."

"I'm not sitting in here. It's too dangerous in one spot," said Zuck.

Might have to surprise him.

Alvin slid away from the opening and ran down to the aft exit of the craft. Seconds passed and no one came.

He must've gone through the other side.

Alvin entered the ship and walked calmly across the deck. Tex saw him first.

"I thought it was too dangerous in one spot," he said. He looked at Alvin, but what he saw was Zuck.

Alvin shrugged his shoulders and kept on walking.

"Coward," grumbled Tex.

Alvin moved toward the corridor where the mirrored crystal spire jutted through. He exchanged glances with Noura's male avatar while continuing to keep his cool.

Thanks for the idea, lady.

He hopped over the crumpled deck, past the torn hull, and stopped in the corner. He turned around, his back against the mirrored crystal. He could see easily down both hallways now. It was a minute and a half into the match.

A flurry of censored chatter continued to appear at the bottom of his display. Given the amount of garbled characters being censored by the system, it was clear the crowd had something to say about his avatar. He ignored the chatroom and stood, silent and still, as he watched the players pace the ship like ants mapping their territory. None of the others ventured outside. They looked edgy.

C'mon, Zuck. Get back here.

Finally someone cracked.

"Zuck, maybe you should go back out there," said Rita.

Shit.

Alvin felt his heart jump. He turned calmly to look at her and said nothing.

She glared at him.

It had been an easy enough effort loading Zuck's skin, but mimicking his voice required more time than he had to work with.

Plan's about to change.

"I said, maybe you should go back out there. He's obviously

not in here," said Rita.

Alvin waved her off with his hand and she furrowed her brow.

The others looked at him. His heart beat faster. He waited for them to gather.

Two hundred million, Baylor.

Rita walked closer. Chico followed behind her. They stopped opposite him just before the caved-in floor.

"Zuck!" she yelled. "Go outside."

"I am outside!" shouted Zuck over open chat.

One minute and forty-seven seconds had elapsed.

Rita froze and Chico's smile fell away as Alvin fired his rifle. She absorbed the blast and knocked Chico into the crevasse. They fell in a tangled mess. Alvin sent another shot into Chico's metal-toothed grimace. His face disintegrated.

Tex came running. He fired and Alvin rolled away while lobbing a grenade. The cowboy ran into the explosive and was obliterated by the blast.

Alvin scrambled to his feet as Noura wounded him in the hip. He crumpled, but returned fire. She went down.

Where's Zuck?

Alvin placed his back against the mirrored crystal.

Which side is he coming from?

A clank rang out ahead.

Before Alvin could act, Zuck bounded over Tex's body and up to the edge of the crumpled floor. He stood in the wafts of smoke opposite Alvin, his eyes roving side to side, but he didn't fire.

He doesn't see me. He thinks I'm his reflection.

Suddenly, Zuck turned to aim out the hull breach and off into the distance. It broke the illusion. He did a double take, his eyes pinging back and forth from Alvin to the outside.

Now.

Alvin squeezed the trigger and dropped to one knee. At two minutes into the match, Zuck yelled, "Bay—" as he was hit square in the chest. He fired back on his way down, shattering the crystal. Alvin stood up amid the raining shards and shot him in the forehead. Zuck's body went still.

A tone sounded. "Alvin Baylor lives!" said the announcer.

Fuck yeah, I do.

EIGHTEEN

"Took you long enough," said Alvin. He was bound up in the pod chair with a pleased grin.

"There's drama out there," said Katy.

She leaned in to him with a finger across her lips and motioned toward the open pod door with a tilt of her head. A group was speaking just outside.

"Who made you a fool? Quantum analysis was available to everyone before the match. Are you telling me you don't trust Mr. Zuck's data?" said Xi-Michaels.

"You predicted thirteen seconds. Something was wrong with the analysis," bellowed Oona.

"Actually, Ms. Oona, it was 12.8 seconds, measured from Mr. Baylor's first shot. So no need to question the accuracy, merely the interpretation," said Chow.

"Oh, hot damn," said Vance.

Alvin winked at Katy.

She planted a kiss on his cheek and hugged him hard.

"I can't believe you just pulled that off," she whispered.

"Where's our winner?" sounded Xi-Michaels's voice from outside.

Katy finished unfastening him and they exited. He followed her out with his arm at the small of her back.

Xi-Michaels was at the center of the pods, surrounded by Oona and the other players. The defeated eyed him solemnly.

"Ah, Mr. Baylor, you do not disappoint!" exclaimed Xi-Michaels.

He raced forward on his wheels with Chow, Oona and Vance walking swiftly behind him. The players stayed put.

Vance examined Alvin and Katy's embrace curiously. She shook Alvin's arm off.

"So you got a prize for me?" asked Alvin.

"Yes, Mr. Baylor. A new chain will be added to your wallet," said Xi-Michaels. "You were very impressive. Alteris must be proud to employ a man of such talent."

"I wouldn't say proud. I'm a necessary evil. So how much did you two make?" asked Alvin.

Chow looked perturbed. Vance laughed.

Xi-Michaels answered, "It would be unethical to bet on my own tournament. What kind of a man do you take me for?"

"The smart kind," said Alvin.

Xi-Michaels's smile froze.

"That sonofabitch cheated! He's a fucking cheat!" shouted a muffled voice. Alvin recognized Zuck, still inside his pod.

They all turned to look across the dais.

"Is that a sore loser I hear?" said Alvin.

Oona glared at him.

"I'll get him," said Katy. "He's still cooling down."

She walked away quickly to Zuck's pod.

Oona stepped forward and pointed a finger in Alvin's chest. "You are a dirty player."

"I took your advice about cunning," he said.

Vance waved his finger through the air like a stylus. He was taking notes in his Opti-Comp.

"Settle down, everyone," said Xi-Michaels.

Chow looked uncomfortable.

"So where'd you get the scan?" asked Vance.

"No comment," said Alvin.

Zuck came tumbling out of his pod and crashed to the floor with his ass in the air. Katy stepped through after him.

"Take it easy. Overclocking has you out of whack," she said.

He got back up on shaky legs, sneered at her, and walked straight into the next pod.

"Your funeral," said Katy.

Vance turned on his heel and went for the drama. Everyone followed. Alvin joined them at Katy's side.

Zuck sat on the ground, leaning back against the pod wall. His shoulders were hunched and hanging, and his head turned rapidly on his neck.

"How you feeling, Rick? That was a long time to overclock," said Alvin.

"You cheated!" shouted Zuck. He tried to stand, then buckled and threw up in his lap.

"Ooh boy," said Vance. He looked excited as he stepped away from the bile.

"Mr. Zuck, please rest for your safety. We have medical personnel on the way," said Chow.

Zuck lifted his head as the expulsion ceased. He looked angry and exhausted. "He's a cheater, always was."

Xi-Michaels clapped his gloved hands. "Now now, Mr. Zuck, Baylor did nothing illegal during the match."

Alvin's smile grew broader.

I'm free.

He looked around the pod floor and spied Noura with her black niqab in place. She was standing at the edge of the stage watching the drama. She nodded at him before her manservant escorted her away. The crinkle around her eyes told Alvin she was smiling.

I'm fucking free.

"There are no rules about borrowed avatars," said Chow.

"Yeah and it's not as if he conspired with everyone to beat you," said Katy.

The group looked at her curiously. Vance's eyebrow raised.

"Thankfully for all of us, nothing like that happened," said Xi-Michaels.

"Really?" said Vance.

"Yo, I woulda wrecked house if we played a fighter match," interjected Chico.

"No doubt, Mr. Perez," said Vance. "Anything to say about these allegations?"

"No," said Chico.

"Ms. Takata?"

Rita gave a sheepish look that made her elongated eye shadow contract. "I gave it my best," she said.

Oona glowered at her.

Vance's eyes drifted to Tex.

"I've had enough of this horseshit." The cowboy clomped off the stage in his metal leg supports.

"Mr. Baylor, you were quite a challenge for this group. Surely you have something to add," said Vance.

"Not really. I played my part. Now excuse us, we have celebrating to do."

Alvin grabbed Katy by the hand and pulled her away. The players stared after him with looks of jealousy and shock. Zuck was pallid. Oona's face was almost red with anger. Vance scribbled notes in the air.

"Enjoy your celebration, Mr. Baylor," said Xi-Michaels. He was jubilant.

Alvin and Katy walked away.

"Not interested in fame?" she whispered.

"Fortune will do," he said.

"I'm with you. So we're going to that rock show, right?" she asked.

"Yep. The Twentieth-Century Rock Review. You're gonna dig it," said Alvin.

"Dig it?"

"Twentieth-century word. You're gonna love it."

"Oh, don't worry, Al, I can dig it."

NINETEEN

Alvin and Katy ate dinner in a high-backed red booth at the Twentieth-Century Rock Review and Supper Club. The ads promised holo-legends would reignite the spirit of rock-and-roll. The club was half empty.

"These booths are nice and private," said Alvin.

"Is that why we're here? For the private booths?" said Katy.

"I like the classics," he said. "I can't help it if holo-rock is out of favor."

He looked around the theater while they waited for the show to begin. His eyes moved over the stage, the proscenium, and the lights.

"I don't see any projectors. I wonder if this is just an AR show? I thought it was holographic."

"Does it matter?" she said.

"I like old tech. I think it's cooler when it's real."

"A hologram is realer than augmented reality, Al?"

"You know what I mean. When it's out there, not just an image floating in my Opti-Comp."

"I'm sure we'll dig it either way." Katy winked.

He laughed. "I'm sure we will."

An ad touting the gamers tournament flashed across the stage. "Watch the legend, Alvin 'Zeus' Baylor, return to action," it said. "Replays are now half off!" Alvin's face was thirty feet across, staring back at him.

He sighed.

"Get used to it," said Katy.

"I can get used to the money," he said. "And to you. You look beautiful."

She blushed.

Things were changing. He was as happy as he'd ever been.

"How's your steak?" she asked.

"Real," said Alvin. "How's yours?"

"Real good."

They giggled.

He studied her as she worked at her plate. The two hundred million in winnings could buy them a lifetime if they stayed to the unincorporated areas of Earth.

Is that all she's after?

She was beautiful and fun and she understood him.

Does it matter?

"When my job is done, we can quit together and head back," he said.

"I found my champion." She smiled sweetly at him. "That's still a little ways away. Besides, what if you meet another gal out there?"

Her reticence confused him. "I don't think the miners are gonna have legs like yours. Maybe some of the attitude, though."

He cut off another piece of steak.

"Miners, huh?" she said. "That's where you're going. An asteroid?"

"Some rock called 243 Ida. It's a delivery job. I'll be there a week and then I turn around on *The Hope*."

She looked at him silently. He couldn't read her.

"I meant what I said. When I'm done with this job, I'd like to see you."

"I'd like that," she said gently.

"I can pay for us, but it won't be luxury. Can you give this up?"

"This? Of course, but I need a job. I've always taken care of myself."

"If you wanna work, that's cool, but I'm just gonna enjoy life."

"You should. You need it. What do you think you'll do?"

"I always wanted to learn to tap dance."

"Shut the fuck up," said Katy.

The server returned to the table and waited for their laughter to stop. "Another round?" she asked.

Katy nodded.

"I'll just have a soda," said Alvin.

Katy arched her eyebrow.

"One's enough," said Alvin.

She laughed. "Are you for real? You're set for life. Live it up."

Alvin nodded to the server. "Okay, one more."

"Yes, Mr. Baylor."

She nodded and walked away, revealing a young boy standing behind her.

"Zeus?" said the boy.

"Yes?" said Alvin.

"Can I get a pic with you?"

"Sure, kid."

Alvin placed his arm around the boy's shoulder while he snapped a pic with his band.

"Thanks, Zeus!"

He ran off.

"How sweet. You're a role model," said Katy.

"Then that kid's gonna have a rough life."

"Don't we all," she said.

"Katy! Where you been?" a female voice called out.

A young blond woman ran up to the table. She was casually

dressed with a server's uniform under her arm. She squinted as she looked at Katy.

"I'm sorry. I thought you were someone else," she said slowly.

She walked away, but glanced back. Katy's eyes followed the woman then turned back to Alvin.

"That was weird," she said.

"Least she didn't recognize me," he said.

"Al, I'm so proud of you, but I'm getting drunk tonight." She swigged the last of her drink. "I'm gonna run to the ladies' room. Don't want to miss the beginning."

He nodded and watched her lithe figure strut away. He wondered if they were falling in love. He'd had a few relationships in person before, but this felt different. There was no denying it.

TWENTY

Rouja left Alvin at the table and strode down the aisle catching attention from fat old men and rich old dykes, lascivious at the thought of renting her for a night. Normally she fed off the attention. It was flattering for a woman of her age, but she was on a damage-control mission and didn't need the extra attention. Whoever the little blond busybody had been, she had obviously tracked Katy Macintyre's smart-band. And now the busybody knew, albeit with much confusion, that someone else was in possession of Katy's smart-band. She had to be stopped before she could squeal to anyone.

Rouja wasn't surprised that someone had finally questioned her; she was just pissed that it happened in front of Alvin.

So sloppy

She could have blown the job. Padrie's urgent call had forced her to rush her planning. After failing to entice Alvin with the prostitute routine in *The Hope*'s bar, she'd found the perfect cover to seduce the disgraced gamer in Katy Macintyre, Game Host. Unfortunately, facial bone structure not a match and a nanite-filled plastic-surgery collar could do only so much. Rouja had chosen instead to wear her own face, albeit the way it had looked nearly twenty years previous. It complicated the job for her.

She caught her reflection in a mirror. A woman who had abandoned her own daughter stared back at her.

I'm off my game.

She saw the blonde enter a narrow hallway near the restrooms and followed, slowing her walk to peer around the corner. The woman was stopped at the end of the hall, near a backstage entrance talking to a hulking security guard with a tribal tattoo on his neck.

Shit.

Rouja turned back into the restroom and surveyed the stalls to make sure no one was inside. Then she tapped the side of her choker and her face twitched and stretched as nanites re-formed the soft tissue. She held the edge of the sink and coughed. When she looked up into the mirror, she had black hair, brown eyes, and the face of the Chinese hooker she'd killed on her way to track down Leung, the pimp who sold her daughter into slavery.

A borrowed avatar. Just like Alvin.

She was afraid to admit it, but Alvin was growing on her. Fake a relationship long enough and it became real. Add in similar values and it became dangerous. She was glad she hadn't gotten all the details out of him yet. That kept the tension away.

She removed the red shawl she had been wearing and tossed it over a stall door, then walked out.

Rouja went around the corner where the little blond busybody was still conversing with the guard. She moved closer, lingering in the hallway while playing with the settings on her smart-band.

"Can you please check her location logs? I think she might've had her ID swiped," said the blonde.

"I'm not authorized to do that," said the guard sternly.

"But you can, can't you? You can look up any *Hope* employee."

"I can for the boss, not for you. Go report this at the main security desk."

"But this imposter is here now! Don't you understand I haven't seen my ex in months?" The woman looked pained. She tucked a folded uniform under her arm then pulled a pill bottle from her purse. She began fighting with the lid. The guard eyeballed her until she got one of the pills into her mouth.

"Maybe there's a reason for that," he said.

The exasperated woman dropped her pill bottle to the ground in a clatter. She knelt and began collecting the little capsules as the guard stared down at her in disdain.

Lucky break.

Rouja rushed over to help collect the capsules from the floor. "You poor thing, let me help."

The woman was sobbing. The guard stayed out of the conversation, but Rouja could feel his eyes on her.

"Come with me and we'll get you cleaned up," she said.

She gently grasped the woman's wrist, then led her down the hall like a lost child. She glared at the leering guard. He pressed the side of his temple and went back to staring into space.

"In here," said Rouja.

She pointed to the restroom.

"I've got to get to work," mumbled the blonde. She looked dazed.

"Let's clean you up, first." Rouja pulled her into the room and let the door close. Then she locked it.

The woman stopped sniveling and stared with wide eyes. "What are you doing?"

Rouja pressed her wrist against the woman's. Their bands vibrated on contact. Confusion rolled over the little woman's face. Her blue eyes bulged as she shrieked and pulled away. Her band had gone off because she had touched Katy's, but this woman was not her Katy.

"Who are you? Where did you get that?" the woman asked.

"I took it from her," said Rouja.

The blonde opened her mouth to scream and Rouja grabbed

her hard by the throat, squelching her voice. She shoved her head back against the wall, turning on the blaring noise of embedded hand driers.

"Let's not make this messy. What's your biometric override password?"

TWENTY-ONE

"Yes, I think she's done," said Alvin. The busboy nodded and added Katy's plate to his tray. Alvin watched him speed away down the aisle, past Katy on her way back. She looked stunning.

I can't believe that's my girl.

She took her seat next to him, leaned in, and gave him a peck on the cheek.

"They came by for the plates. You weren't still eating?" he asked.

"No, it's okay, I'm finished."

"You look amazing. Back in the twentieth century, they would have said you ought to be in pictures."

"Pictures?" she asked.

"You know, movies. Vid streams."

"Ah, I get it. 'Pictures,' because they were 2-D, like paintings and photos. Where'd you get this fixation with the past?"

"When I was kid, my dad used to show me the old 'this day in history' news streams. I really enjoyed them. Just little square videos with only one thing playing! That was how they got information. I got hooked from there and started watching more about the period. I've even read a real newspaper or two." Alvin was proud of that, so he smiled. "You know it makes your finger-tips dirty?"

"The news is depressing," she said.

"I know, ignorance is bliss. But I like to understand how events progress."

A loud guitar chord rang out then pulsed rhythmically.

They looked to the stage as fireworks exploded. The dining table lowered into the floor and they got to their feet.

The hologram of a long-faced man wearing a Union Jack suit rose from the stage. He swung his arm in a wide arc and the guitar sound became a rhythm. He was joined by three other holo-performers and the music grew in loudness and complexity.

Alvin could feel the bass in his teeth. He'd heard this group before—a rock band from the 1960s.

"Who is that?" asked Katy.

The music was so loud Alvin couldn't even hear her voice, but he got the question.

"Yeah, it is. I think," he yelled.

She wrinkled her brow. "Who?"

"Yes!" he yelled.

She shook her head and he turned back to the stage. He went to peep Record in his Opti-Comp and saw that it was disabled.

"Can't record," he said.

Alvin pantomimed that she should watch. He tapped out the override gesture on his smart-band and rebooted into his custom code, then gave her a thumbs-up.

She nodded.

He peeped Record and gave her another thumbs-up.

They bopped to the music for several loud songs before the next act came out. A holo-man walked from the back of the stage as the band disappeared. He wore a red bandana and a white fringed jacket. He strummed the guitar with his left hand and it became clear who it was.

"I know that one," said Katy.

Alvin started bouncing up and down. "This is fucking great!"

The whine of electric guitar continued for several songs before the man performed a riff on the old United States national anthem. When he finished, he sat down on his knees and lit his guitar on fire.

Alvin spun Katy around and held his wrist out for a pic with the Jimi Hendrix hologram in the background.

The show continued for almost an hour. At the close, Alvin and Katy applauded for the holo-performers.

"Yell 'encore!'" he said.

She looked at him, puzzled, then joined in as he shouted, "Encore! Encore!"

The hologram of a pale-skinned man with a painted face and a red mullet floated from the floor in the fetal position. He somersaulted slowly upward and uncurled as a slow ballad began.

The floating holo-man sang of the prettiest star in a lilting English accent.

Alvin had never heard the song.

How beautiful.

He pulled Katy into an embrace and looked into her blue eyes lovingly while the pulsing lights cast shadows across her face.

TWENTY-TWO

The next morning, Rouja sat in her room, or, rather, Katy's room. It was a four-foot-by-eight-foot box with vid-screen-paneled surfaces and a loft bed that hung overhead. She sat at a tiny desk brushing her hair using a video mirror. The other surfaces blazed with advertisements.

John Padre would be contacting her soon for an update. Her wrist buzzed and she slumped before reaching up to pinch her earlobe. The connection caused a buzzing in her head before he even spoke.

Goddamn it. He's calling with that government link again.

"Rouja, baby. How goes it?" said Padre's gravelly voice.

I can't believe I ever found that voice sexy.

"Can't see ya, babe," he said.

She really didn't want to look at him, but she came out of her slouch and tapped her band to the vanity mirror. His face appeared in the lower corner of the frame.

"Getting comfortable, I see," said Padre with a smirk.

He had not laid eyes on her since she left Earth.

"Yeah, I'm into the classics now," she said.

"Almost as young as when I met you," he said.

"Not quite," she said with irritation.

"So? Tell Daddy what he needs to know."

Creep.

She picked up the brush again and returned to her hair.

"He's not a professional. He doesn't even know what he's been sent to deliver," she said.

"Did he say where he's taking it?"

"An asteroid—243 Ida. I tagged the stream where he said it."

"So he doesn't know what it does, either?" asked Padre.

"If he does, he's not letting on. I tapped his band last night. He finally showed me his override. There's some maps and training manuals, but nothing about that device."

"Nothing?"

"Nothing. He's just an Alteris employee being kept in the dark."

"Are you sure? It took you longer than usual. You slacking or being played?"

She rolled her eyes. "Please . . . he's exactly where I want him. Besides, you're not the one stuck on this ship for six months."

"Eh, from what I hear, it's a pretty good place to get stuck," said Padre.

"Yes, well, it is if you're with a nice guy who can pay the exorbitant prices for you."

"Exorbi . . . what? He's nice, huh?"

She smiled.

"I hope you aren't enjoying yourself too much," said Padre.

"Business, baby, you know that."

"Good, I don't want you pouting when I tell you to whack him." His face was stern.

"I can't risk any more trouble on this trip. Some dyke tracked my band with a social app, ex-girlfriend of my cover. I took care of her, but I'm two bodies deep now."

"Baby, you gotta finesse 'em."

She stopped brushing her hair and arched an eyebrow. "The

game host was last minute. He didn't go for the usual routine. I was lucky. Katy Macintyre had the perfect job for a psych-op on Baylor and my measurements. I got her right before she started work."

"And what happened to her face?" he asked.

"She was ugly."

"Oh." He seemed surprised by the answer.

"I stashed her body in one of the protein recyclers and scrubbed her pic from the database. Her ex was a surprise. I had to leave her in a bathroom."

"A bathroom?" he said.

"She was depressed. So depressed she took too many pills and died vomiting into the toilet."

"Jesus. All right, girl, keep your head down," said Padre from his floating portrait. "I'll send Cheng and Watkins to collect him at Armstrong Station. You know his shuttle number?"

"Not yet. But you'll need him to unlock that device."

"Watkins can fabricate the bio-key with some of his DNA. He dies at the station. Send over the number as soon as you get it."

"Sure, but how are we gonna sell it if we don't know what it does?" she said.

"There's a thousand buyers who will gladly pillage Uncle Sam's corpse."

"I suppose so. How close are you?" she asked.

"I'm still babysitting the wreck. It's a couple days away," said Padre. "I'll send Cheng and Watkins out tomorrow. They'll meet you at Armstrong."

"That's what I thought. I told you not to call me on this stolen relay," she said.

"Babe, don't worry. It's encrypted. Send over Baylor's data the old-fashioned way if you want. I can wait the twenty."

He disconnected.

Rouja felt the tension from the communications link leave her head. She breathed out heavily.

Padre had grown so freaking cocksure and lazy over the years, and it was going to get them caught. And over what? A need for revenge. She had no interest in Washington. Their meddling in the Greco-Islamic War had cost her a daughter. The chance to correct that would not be sidelined by his feud.

There was nothing to do now but wait out the four days while playing girlfriend. She pouted then reached for the hair curler. She needed to make the ends of her hair wavy. Alvin liked it that way.

Hours later Rouja and Alvin lay in bed. He stared up at the ceiling, unmoving. He took long slow breaths.

Something is wrong.

"What's buggin' you?" she said. "You were quiet all through dinner. And you drank."

"I got a message from work. They found out about the tournament," said Alvin. "I waited to see if they were serious."

"Serious about what?"

"They pulled my winnings. My boss was apologetic. He said he had no religion about it, that it was the CEO's choice."

She was shocked by his words. "What a fucking creep. Can they even do that?"

"The funds are gone from my bit-wallet. They own me. They sponsor my citizenship. They hold the deed to my apartment. I can't get even get home without them."

"Alvin . . . I'm . . . I don't know what to say. I'm so sorry."

"I can't pay for us. I can't quit," he said. "No South America."

"I never expected that from you. That's not why I'm with you."

She rested her head on his shoulder.

"Thank you for getting me into that game pod," he said.

She felt his body tense as he stared at the ceiling in silence.

"I needed to know what I could have been. Even if it was . . ." His eyes welled up. He hugged her.

Six months ago, Rouja remembered, playing him was easy, like always. Now she felt a gnawing inside. The more she came to see him as an innocent, the more the feeling grew.

How cruel am I? How cruel has Padre made me?

Her frustration turned to anger. "We can't let them do that."

"How? How can I stop them? You think *The Hope* cares? They got their money back."

"Alvin . . ."

"They're going to stop me from coming home."

"Why would they do that? It's nothing. So you played a game."

"They wanted to put me off Earth before I left. I fought for a return. Everything is a secret with this damn job and I think I know why."

She looked at him curiously.

He does know more.

"It has something to do with Mohammed Rinsler."

Rouja shook her head. "But he's dead, Alvin. He was killed during the U.S. riots. I remember hearing it on the news."

"No. He's alive and he works for Alteris. I broke into their personnel database and found a record. They poached him and covered it up."

Is this the scientist Padre killed?

"How long have you known this?" she said.

"I discovered it a few months back. I hit a dead end, so I buried myself in gaming sessions."

"Why would they risk that?" she said.

"They told me it was a mining tool. Maybe it is. He cracked faster-than-light communication and artificial consciousness. So I imagine it does the job well."

"Al, this is so bizarre," she said.

"I know. Everything about this project is bizarre."

She felt the itch again. "So what are you going to do?"

"I don't know. I'm at their mercy. I hope I'm just paranoid. I don't want to be stuck on Musk City or the Moon," he said.

"Would it be so bad? If you didn't have to work anymore?"

"To never feel the breeze or the sun? To live inside plastic bubbles and space suits? I think it would be," he said. "They need me to get this package to Ida. I'm safe until I do."

She felt her insides burn with tension. "Al—never let anything get in the way of what you want."

"Easier said than done. I don't even know what I want."

"You want me, don't you?"

He nodded.

"Then enjoy our last few nights on *The Hope*." She kissed him.

His mouth moved down her neck, stopping on the cool metal of her nano-collar. He tugged at it gently with his finger.

"What is this choker you're always wearing?" he said.

She pulled his hand away and placed it on her breast. "It's special. My daddy gave it to me," she whispered.

They made love and Alvin didn't ask about it again.

TWENTY-THREE

Alvin hated waiting. For the last several days, his mind had drifted over the pretense of caring about his job. The last two hours aboard had been the longest. Time enough for anxious thoughts to creep back. Now the day had come. Six months of living it up ended here, at the casino bar. His bag was as light as the day he'd left Earth. No knick-knacks, no new clothing. Just memories . . . and Katy. She was up at the pods. She'd be down soon to see him off.

"Another Mexican Coffee, Zeus?" asked the bartender.

"No thanks, Ryan," said Alvin. "I'm taking off soon."

"So this is it, huh?"

"Yep, time to get back to work."

"It was amazing to see you back in action," said Ryan.

Alvin smiled. "It was good to get that feeling back."

"Amen, Zeus. Sometimes it's the journey, not the destination, that gets us where we need to be. Let me know if you need anything else."

"Thanks, man."

Alvin bumped his wrist to the table, paid for the coffee, and left forty thousand for the tip.

Fuck you, Alteris.

He thumbed through the newspaper projection displayed on the bar top. It was current as of thirty minutes prior. He felt like a dignified man of the past reading old news with his coffee. An alert flashed on the screen. Something from the ship's local news service. Usually, a lost earring on the pool deck or a big win at the sports book. This was different—Chico Perez had died. He'd won his middleweight match a few weeks before. It had been a clean fight. He'd put on a clinic, really, but there it was—he'd died from a cerebral hemorrhage.

Wow, he was young.

Chico had given him and Katy a pair of ringside seats, and he liked the guy despite the foul play at the tournament. Perhaps they might not have become buddies, but in this fancy world they were brutes in solidarity. He wondered if he'd have it as easy with the asteroid miners. Was he salty enough after six months of the good life? He could get on well with the worst types, but felt a rising apprehension.

I coulda been a short-timer with those winnings. Fuck. Just finish this and get back to Katy.

She was worth more than any pile of money.

"Hey sexy!"

Alvin turned around to see her walk down the short steps into the bar. His face lit up.

They kissed and he lifted his bag up onto his shoulder.

"You got time to walk me out?"

"I'll take you into the station. It's kinda confusing in there. I'm on a break, though. Someone booked a match at two and, of course, he demanded me."

"I would have," said Alvin.

They began the trek across the cylindrical floor. He looked back at the bar as it came over his head and the bartender waved.

"Aw, you made a friend," she said.

"I'm not that disagreeable. Besides, he was a fan from way back."

"Oh, okay, then." She giggled.

They continued on in silence for a bit.

"Did you hear that Chico died?" said Alvin.

"Chico? Oh, the MMA guy. Died from what?"

"Cerebral hemorrhage. I guess he must've been hurt during that fight."

"Live by the sword, die by the sword," she said. "He wasn't that great, anyway, just a rock-paper-scissors fighter," she said.

"Damn."

"Sorry, I'm not at my best saying good-bye."

"I get it. I don't want to go, either."

They approached the exit tunnel and stomped up the narrow corridor. At the door to Armstrong Station stood the same two greeters he'd met when boarding.

"We hope you enjoyed your stay Mr. Baylor," the man and woman said in unison.

The woman looked at Katy. "Ms. Macintyre, your ID lookup appears to be corrupted. The picture isn't there."

"I know. I reported it when we left, but no one has gotten to my ticket yet," said Katy.

"We'll make sure to take care of that," said the male greeter.

"Thanks. I'll be back soon, just wanna make sure he finds his way."

They stepped out into the hallway of the space station. The wall showcased a video mural depicting the history of space exploration. It began with a funny ball with four antennae and ended with an image of stacked discs rotating in space—the station itself.

They made their way to the end where the hall opened into a lounge area with red and orange seats. Guests of *The Hope* bustled about the room looking at curios celebrating Neil Armstrong. A couple of waiters walked around handing out drinks. Alvin found it ironic that he had made it farther into space than Armstrong himself.

"Over to the right," said Katy.

Alvin looked to see a glass doorway, beyond a downward sloping hallway that lacked aesthetic design. The party ended at the door. He snatched up a champagne flute from a passing waiter, then downed the bubbly and put the glass back on the tray.

Anxiety showed on his face.

"It'll be over before you know it," Katy said. "C'mon."

They walked through the door and down the sloping hallway. It was silent. At the terminus Armstrong opened up into a multi-level spoked hub; once again centrifugal force substituted for gravity. The soft rumble of people movers could be heard all around. They wrapped the curved white walls of the station. One escalator sloped down, another up, with long stretches of flat conveyor belt looping overhead in all directions. There was no one around.

"Whoa," he said.

He looked up his boarding pass with an eye blink. The shuttle bay was listed out on the mercantile hub, and a floating arrow appeared in his Opti-Comp directing him forward.

"I told you. This place is a maze," Katy said. "First we head down, then back up."

They took the escalator down. Below, he spotted a maintenance bot cleaning the floor.

"I guess the union never made it out here," he said.

His palms were sweating. Fewer than a thousand humans had ever ventured to Armstrong Station. The number who continued to 243 Ida was lower still. He would be number fifty-two.

They reached the bottom. The arrow directed him across the concave floor and back up an escalator on the far side.

"Hey, wrong way, buddy. That's a private terminal," said a redheaded woman.

Next to her stood a muscular Asian man. He was armed and didn't seem friendly. Neither did the gal handing out directions. There were no other people around.

Alvin paused. He looked at the freckled redhead, who pointed to another escalator beside her.

"It's okay. He's a company man," said Katy.

The redhead narrowed her eyes. The muscle-man's lip twitched and he gave a permissive nod.

"I'll take you up, then I have to say good-bye," said Katy.

"Are you sure we're going the right way?"

Katy nodded and they stepped onto the escalator. "Don't worry. The folks out here are just soft on social skills."

He looked back down at the soldiers and smiled. No smiles came back his way.

Guess so.

At the top they were alone again. Alvin stopped walking and hugged her.

"I love you," he whispered in her ear.

He didn't want to let go. He felt a silly sense of paranoia, like she might disappear the moment he turned around.

"You'll be so busy with work. This will all seem like a dream," she said.

"I will think of you every day, Katy."

He felt her tense in his embrace.

She pulled away, her hands gently cupping his face.

"I love you too, Alvin," she said. "Go now and don't look back."

She took the downward side of the escalator, riding it backward. He watched for as long as he could see her. Before she left his sight, she waved then turned around and cracked her neck from side to side.

She's as upset as I am. She just hides it better.

He turned around and stepped onto the people mover. The long conveyor belt took him to the end of the open area. The arrow in his Opti-Comp pointed ahead through a glass door and into another beige hallway. He passed through. This one grew narrower as he continued toward the door at the far end. There were no murals depicting the history of exploration. No cushy seats, no drinks, no babes, and certainly no casinos.

The frontier is on the other side of that door.

He peeped the station map and tried zooming out past the door ahead of him, but the map ended there. When he reached the door an announcement sounded. "Warning. Alteris personnel only beyond this point. Entry requires authorization."

The door had Alteris's swooping asteroid logo emblazoned upon it. Below that a red circle with a slash through it and inside a stick figure hitting its head on the ceiling. "Zero-g Zone" was written above the image.

Alvin tapped his wrist to the door panel, which informed him, "An escort has been summoned."

He was no pro at zero gravity. He'd slept off his hangover on the shuttle ride to the Moon. Other than a long nap, he'd had no experience at all. He just hoped he didn't puke.

TWENTY-FOUR

Rouja stepped off the escalator. Jax Cheng and the redheaded woman, presumably Padre's newbie, were waiting near a maintenance door below the hub of people movers.

"Inside," said the redhead. She tapped her band to the wall and a short panel slid aside. It was half the height of a person, used by the maintenance bots.

They ducked down and went inside. The room was large and wide with low ceilings. There were dozens of bots sitting idle. A service tech's body was dead on the ground.

"What's the deal? We were supposed to take Baylor here," said the woman.

"You must be Watkins," said Rouja.

"Yeah, and you better explain yourself," Watkins said.

"Change of plans. Washington had an undercover agent on *The Hope*. He was masquerading as a pro fighter. I killed him last night. We're going to have to let Baylor retrieve the device first. They're watching us."

"How?" said Watkins.

"They were able to track the FTL link you encrypted."

"Impossible," said Watkins.

"You're not as good as you think," said Rouja.

"Padre said you might try something," said the redhead.

Cheng eyed Rouja with suspicion.

"Please. I've worked with John for longer than you've been alive. I get a billion. How much is he paying you?" said Rouja.

Surprise showed on Samantha Watkins's face.

"You're lying," she said.

"No. He's been lying to you all along and you didn't notice. Where'd he get you, some cheap hacking school?"

"Listen bitch . . ." said Watkins.

Rouja threw a left hook and knocked the redhead over a parked bot and onto her ass.

"How bad do you want to fight me, little girl?" said Rouja.

Watkins sat upright and wiped blood from her mouth. Rouja looked at Cheng. The muscles in his forearm started to twitch. He was no dummy.

It's time.

Cheng's crossed arms opened up and he lunged at Rouja, knife in hand. She sidestepped and struck him in the nose with her palm.

It knocked his head back long enough for her to kick him in the ribs. He winced.

She went to swing her rear leg at his head, but felt the weight of Watkins's grip on her ankle. The girl was fighting from the floor. Rouja's leg came halfway up, enough to keep Cheng out of range as he whipped his knife at her throat. She bent backward as he extended his reach and fell over on top of Watkins.

Rouja lifted an elbow and brought it back down on Watkins's temple. The redhead went still, and Rouja rolled off as Cheng stomped right on the woman's unconscious body.

Rouja rolled in a backward somersault and stood up as Cheng stomped again, hitting the deck with a thump. She kicked the knife out of his hand and it skittered across the floor.

He lunged at her with open arms and gripped her in a bear

hug. Then he head-butted her in the forehead and she nearly went out.

Her legs went soft for a moment as his muscled arms squeezed the air from her lungs. She pressed her heel down, and a blade popped from the toe of her boot. She lifted her bent knee high and in close then raked the blade down the inside of his leg, cutting the femoral artery. Blood rushed to the floor, but his grip didn't loosen.

He head-butted her again, breaking her nose.

She raked the knife blade down the other leg and felt his grip loosen. Then she brought her hands together, interlacing her fingers and pushed them up through his hold. At the top she parted her arms and broke the bear hug, then shoved him back as hard as she could.

He staggered back a few feet then reached down to his holster. She kicked him in the nuts with the boot blade. His expression changed and he doubled over. She kicked again and buried the blade in his face. His torso went upright again and he reeled back. He was missing an eye. It was stuck on the end of her boot.

Blood pooled all around his feet.

Cheng gave an odd expression and wobbled backward. His testicles rolled down his pant leg and unraveled in a stringy mess at his feet. Then he reached for his pulse gun again and got it halfway out of the holster, before slipping in his own blood.

He lay on his back and raised the gun at her. She kicked his hand, then stomped his trachea. He wheezed, air escaping from his lungs. His arms dropped limply back to the ground.

"You're both liars," he whispered in a crunchy breath.

Then he died.

"Fuck," said Rouja.

She reached up at her throbbing nose, then took a step back and steadied herself while sliding in Cheng's blood.

The girl.

She turned around and Watkins was gone from the floor. She was running to the exit.

Rouja hopped the blood puddle and went after her.

Watkins reached the door and it opened. She placed a hand above the frame and ducked low to pass through.

Rouja spotted Cheng's discarded knife, went down in a forward roll, snatched it up, then threw it. It went through Watkins's hand, pinning it to the top of the doorframe.

She screamed in pain, then whimpered, "Please don't kill me."

"Shut that fucking door," said Rouja.

"Please," begged Watkins.

The door slid shut again.

Rouja grabbed her by the collar. "You're going to tell me everything."

Watkins reached over toward her pinned hand and tapped a button on her wrist.

An electric shock jolted through Rouja. She felt her teeth snap shut and her hand clamped down like a vise as electricity poured out of Watkins's suit.

Then it stopped. Rouja's muscles went soft and she dropped to the ground.

Her breath was fast and shallow and she felt her heart beat uncontrollably. She stared blearily as Watkins pulled the knife from her pinned hand.

The girl turned around and leaped on her with the blade.

Rouja rolled her head and the point hit the ground next to her ear with a loud ping. She turned back and bit down on Watkins's nose, tearing it off.

The redhead screamed. She dropped the knife and grabbed at her bloody face.

Rouja rolled her over into a choke hold. The girl's neck was hard to grip in the gushing blood, so she reached up and jammed a thumb in her eye socket. Then she wrenched Watkins's head to the side until her gurgling terminated with a loud pop.

"Never mind. I'll figure out the plan myself."

They lay in a heap on the ground. The electrocution had left Rouja's insides burning. She rolled over and tried to stand, but her legs trembled and she fell back to the floor.

Fucking eel suit.

Padre was still waiting at the disabled ship—where Alvin was headed.

Have to call him away. Have to get out of here.

She peeped Padre in her Opti-Comp. The floating display was filled with static. She pinched her earlobe and nothing happened. Watkins's eel suit had damaged her implants. She went back to the floating display and typed out the text message, "need you here now. they know. C & W dead," in ghosted letters.

He won't kill me.

She peeped Send. Then she crawled to one of the janitorial bots and powered it up. It was time to clean up.

TWENTY-FIVE

Alvin waited a few minutes at the Armstrong Station terminal door before it opened. He was greeted by a floating man in a bright-red jumpsuit. His face featured a neatly trimmed Vandyke over a serious expression. A caduceus was imprinted on his front breast pocket.

"Baylor?" the man said quickly.

Alvin nodded.

"Ito," said the man in red. "Put this on, then come inside."

Alvin dropped his bag and stepped into the loose green jump-suit. He rolled up the overlong ankles and sleeves then zipped it up. He picked up his bag and stepped over the threshold. His right foot came down inside and then he lifted his left leg. While pressing down on his heel, his weight shifted oddly; and as he came through the doorway, he lifted off toward the ceiling. The burden of his bag disappeared first and then he felt it in all his limbs. No gravity. His stomach dropped.

"Whoa," he said.

Ito pulled the door closed and spun a wheel locking it. Then he tapped the wall and two metal plates closed off access to the outer door. They were in an airlock.

"Give me your hand," said Ito.

Alvin gripped the man's outstretched hand.

Ito pivoted in the air, crouched sideways against the doorframe, and kicked off. They glided down the long hallway and up to another circular door at the end.

Alvin's stomach made loops. "I think I'm gonna be sick."

Ito spun himself so they were both upright. "Look me in the eyes."

Alvin stared at him. He could see Ito's hands doing something at the periphery of his vision. The door ahead opened. It was dark beyond.

"Close your eyes. I'll be right back," said Ito.

He did as he was told.

Sweat began to bubble at his forehead, but it did not run. It felt like growths on his face. He coughed and his heart pounded.

"That corpo better not puke in here!" echoed a gruff voice from inside.

After ten seconds of heavy breathing, Alvin felt his sleeve being pulled up.

"I think I'm gonna lose it," he said.

"They come in different colors," said Ito. "I like red."

Alvin opened his eyes. Ito's neatly trimmed facial hair was staring him in the face. The bright red of his jumpsuit sat below it.

"You don't say," said Alvin.

"What's that?" asked the man.

"What's what?" asked Alvin.

"Sorry, I didn't understand that. English isn't my first language."

Alvin nodded. "I was just saying that it was obvious."

"Oh. Yes. I suppose it is," he said. "I was just trying to distract you."

Alvin felt a pinch in his arm as Ito withdrew a needle.

He felt a rush of calm come over him. The nausea was gone. He dabbed at his forehead.

"What was in that?"

"Dimenhydrinate and ketamine. It will prevent motion sickness, panic, and intracranial pressure. We don't have time to acclimate you before our spacewalk."

"Spacewalk? What do you mean, spacewalk?"

"You will need to retrieve the hardware. It is keyed to you," said Ito. "Didn't the company tell you?"

"Yes . . . I mean, no. They didn't tell me it was floating in space," said Alvin.

"I think it is actually in a ship, but the ship has been damaged. Probably no atmosphere."

A damaged ship with no atmosphere? That means the crew must be dead.

"Is the crew dead?"

"I think so," said Ito. He laughed and pulled Alvin through the next door and into the ship. He tapped the wall and the entry sealed.

Alvin gazed around. It was dark and cramped. He would have been terrified if he wasn't so relaxed from the drugs.

Ito looked at him. "Don't worry, we have a security man to protect us." He pointed to someone floating in the corner up near the ceiling.

Alvin spotted him. A dark-skinned man in blue spun slowly in a lotus position. He had a grim look on his face. He didn't look interested in an introduction.

Must be the voice I heard.

"Is he friendly?" Alvin whispered.

"Doubt it. He's stationed here at Armstrong, only seen him a couple times. What's your name, security man?"

The man placed a palm against the wall and stopped his spin abruptly. His folded body opened up like a carnivorous plant. His limbs were massive.

"Don't fuck with me, 'roider. I got license to shoot who I please—even corpos on secret missions."

"I just asked your name, gunman," said Ito.

"My name is Bossman, muthafucka." His eyes bulged when he said it.

"All right, Bossman, stay frosty," said Ito. "Let's go get your EVA suit, Alvin."

Ito grabbed Alvin's sleeve and pulled him aside. He glided through the cabin, towing Alvin along.

Alvin looked back at Bossman's glower. They rounded a corner away from his evil eye.

"What's his deal?" whispered Alvin.

"Security don't get aggro meds. Most people out here get that way . . . if they don't take their meds."

The thought was disconcerting. Alvin had avoided personality reframing because of his cyber-athletics career. He'd managed to escape it his whole life.

I guess that shot did help. "You're on medication?"

"Naw. I don't put that poison in me. I use cannabis," said Ito.

Alvin laughed.

"That doesn't cause you problems?"

"You are funny, Baylor. If one forgets something out here, they're dead. So pay attention."

"Got it. Call me Alvin."

"Toshiro. I go by Tosh."

Alvin felt helpless in zero-g, but being pulled along with the nausea gone made it almost enjoyable.

They stopped inside a larger room. Spacesuits of various colors were affixed to the far wall. Each featured different colors, patterns, and exterior molding. They were a mix of metals and soft fabrics.

"Now listen up," said Tosh. "The jumpsuits we're wearing are the inner layer. You'll need one of those to survive the vacuum of space." He pointed at the wall of suits.

"Which one is mine?"

"None of them. You ever use a Tailormatic on Earth?"

Alvin nodded.

"Same method. Suits and liners are customized. You can replace that old green thing. That's your fitting station." Tosh pointed to an upright glass cylinder in the corner. "Print job takes about an hour."

"Good. This thing doesn't even fit. How long till we get where we're going?"

"About a day to the crash site. Just make sure you play through the manuals. Especially the chapters on propulsion and air supply."

This is coming fast now. No red tape. No bureaucrats.

"You're talking to tech support here. RTFM is not a problem," said Alvin.

"Good. We've lost people who didn't take this seriously. Synaptics are used to control the propulsion packs. I will be with you for support, but nothing will prep you like the VR trainer. I had a guy pass out from the strain once during a spacewalk. Don't do that to me."

He hasn't pulled a search on me.

"I don't think you'll have that problem with me." Alvin pointed to his temple implants.

Tosh nodded. "I see why they sent you. When you're done with the tailor and the manuals, get some rest. Watch some streams or whatever you do to chill. When we get to Ida, you'll meet the rest of us. There's only a few corpos, so it's chill."

Tosh turned away then stopped himself, "Sorry, I didn't mean to . . ."

"Don't worry, I'm not C-class, I'm maintenance," said Alvin

The man nodded. "Right. Peace!" He pushed off out of the room.

"Hey, where can I get something to eat?" said Alvin.

Tosh replied over his shoulder, "Food printer's in the main

hold. The recipes are limited, though. The one at the base is better. Peace!"

Nutri-Paste, yuck.

Tosh floated away.

Must be in a rush to go get high. He's all right, certainly conscientious for a stoner.

Alvin looked back at the row of suits. His thoughts were racing.

A fucking spacewalk. Jesus.

He gripped his way along some pipes to the translucent Tailor-matic tube and touched its surface to wake it. He entered the cylinder and cycled through the color options. It offered countless customizations. His mind drifted to thoughts of Katy as he dialed through the settings.

What is she doing now?

He missed her. She always kept him calm.

Does she miss me?

Then from the back of his mind came the urge for a drink. He pushed it away. A designer space suit would have to be his solace for now.

Alvin approached the airlock wearing what he believed to be the snazziest custom EVA suit ever designed. He'd colored it in metallic blue with golden lightning bolts that ran the length of his limbs.

Toshiro Ito was waiting for him, helmet in hand, decked out in red and white. His mouth hung open when he looked at Alvin.

I think I look good in my old team colors.

"Too much?" said Alvin.

"Man, they gave me hell when I said safety ops should be all red," said Tosh.

Bossman laughed. He was outfitted in black with "Security"

emblazoned in white on the front and back of his suit. He was armed with a pulse rifle.

"I thought I could design it however I wanted," said Alvin.

"Punk fool," said Bossman.

Tosh grinned. "Dude, you look like a superhero. It's badass."

"Thanks."

Alvin made a face at Bossman, who just shook his head and put his helmet on.

"You go through the sims?" asked Tosh.

"Yep," said Alvin.

"Good. The wreck is orbit locked in an asteroid field. Autopilot can't move the ship any closer so I'm gonna take us out there."

Tosh attached a tether line to Alvin's waist then hooked it to his own.

"Helmet on," he said.

Alvin did as he was told. The room ambiance fell away, leaving only the sound of his own breathing. Then Tosh pressed his face guard right up against him, looking into his eyes.

"Do not use your thrusters until I tell you to do so. I will power us there." His voice echoed slightly. It was coming over the comm channel now.

"Understood," said Alvin. After a night's rest and some zero-g acclimation, he had just gotten comfortable. Now he was faced with being spun every which way in the black void of space.

Just don't puke.

The men stepped forward to the door.

"Stay the fuck out of my way," said Bossman. "I go point and if there's trouble, I take care of it."

"Sure thing," said Tosh.

The hulking man tapped the wall. Two overlapping crescent-shaped panels parted and slid back into the circular doorframe. He went through first, then Tosh, and finally Alvin. All three floated in a line down the cylinder.

Tosh and Bossman kicked their legs down and locked magnetic boots to the deck. They stood up normally. Tosh nodded at Alvin.

He peeped the proper command in his heads-up display and felt a small reverberation as his feet clamped down on the floor.

That's better.

"All in," said Tosh.

Bossman tapped the wall and the metal panels arced back down into place behind them.

Perspiration clung to Alvin's temples. He stared at the ground as they marched forward. Suddenly he felt a tugging and was surprised when he looked up to find no one touching him. The door ahead was open now. The sensation had been air pressure rushing out into space.

He took a deep breath, then clomped his boots on the deck and stopped behind Tosh. Beyond the two men was an open circle of stars. Alvin was conscious of the sound of his own breathing— the stillness—and the infinite expanse that lay ahead.

Bossman jumped first. He floated outward for maybe ten feet, then small plumes of dust shot from the thruster jets along his limbs as he dove down out of view.

Fuck.

Toshiro tugged at the waist tether and Alvin stepped along-side him at the edge. The small tunnel opened to the vastness of space.

His guts swirled around in nervous tension. He felt the affixed drops of perspiration wiggle on his face.

Tosh looked at him. His visor had turned copper to protect against the stellar lights. "Release your boots," he said.

Alvin obeyed and he came up off the ground, knees bent. Then Toshiro Ito jumped. Alvin was transfixed by the caduceus on the man's back as he flowed out the exit. He hardly noticed the tether at his waist as it drew away. It pulled him right out the door, surprisingly gentle.

His view broadened as the expanse of twinkling space enveloped him. He looked down at a vista of spinning rocks that overlapped stars and a mangled bronze solar collector. The ship spun slowly below amid the debris.

This is not so bad.

Alvin thought of childhood snorkeling in the Caribbean. How beautifully clear the water had been and how crisp the reef and sea life had looked below him. He also remembered his fear of the dangers that lurked beneath the surface.

Then Tosh crossed down into his view with thrusters firing and Alvin gritted his teeth. He prepared himself to be yanked downward, but again found the motion to be surprisingly mild. His nerves softened.

I'll have this damn thing soon and be on to Ida and then back to Katy.

Tosh fired the thrusters lining his limbs harder, and the two men rushed past enormous rocks that had spun off from the nearby asteroids. This small spot in space was crowded with a dance of debris, both natural and man-made.

The ship spun lifelessly below, its nose aimed up at them. Bossman touched down at the bow. Beyond him the shaft was visible sporadically through the tears in the solar sail as it rotated.

"Major damage here," Bossman radioed.

"Copy that," said Tosh. "From up here it looks like the gravity-axle is missing."

"Torn the fuck off," said Bossman.

Tosh slowed twenty feet from the ship as Alvin continued to coast toward him.

"Fire your jets and try to stop here next to me," he said.

Alvin turned on his thrusters and recalled the VR training. He stopped immediately.

"Whoa, brakes are better than I thought," he said.

It had literally taken a thought, though the control effect didn't feel like the body extension of a rock hopper tendril or the full immersion of VR. This was something else. He felt like a superman with feet in two different worlds.

He fired the gas jets again and slowly drifted over to Tosh. As he moved up next to the man, he thought of stopping—and the thrusters on his arms adjusted direction and stopped him.

I got this.

"You're pretty good with that thing. I expected you to hit the ship," said Tosh with a laugh. "Let's go."

They jetted over the bow and through the torn solar collector toward Bossman, who was crouched down at the midpoint. He was examining the missing gravity-axle. On the way they passed over curious scratchings on the hull.

They stopped and affixed themselves to the surface with their mag-lock boots. Alvin took a clunky step. It felt pedestrian after flying.

"This looks like a clean cut, and those markings look more like metal on metal than dents from rocks," said Bossman. "Stay here, I'm going to the airlock."

Alvin considered the situation. If this wasn't an accident, then what had happened? The hardware he was retrieving was certainly valuable to be bio-locked. Who would or could hijack a ship like this? Other than a couple of terrorism incidents in low Earth orbit, no one had ever forced their way onto a spaceship. Out here the criminals were white-collar robber barons, like Chan Xi-Michaels, not space pirates.

"The airlock's been blown. I can see clear through to the crew cabin. Going inside," radioed Bossman.

"No air, they're dead for sure," said Tosh.

Alvin's mind processed the possibilities. If the device hadn't been taken, then it had either been hidden from the attackers or it had been left deliberately. If the famous scientist, Rinsler, was really involved, it could be something of unimaginable value.

They're waiting for me to unlock it.

He looked at the rocks floating around him.

Are they watching?

He felt a chill run down his spine.

"Shit," said Alvin quietly to himself.

"What's that?" asked Tosh.

"Nothing, just—what is this thing I'm picking up?"

"You don't know? I don't know what it is. They told me test equipment."

"That's what they told me. Experimental. Listen, though, what if they're just waiting for me? You know, to unlock it?" asked Alvin.

"Who?" asked Tosh.

"Whoever did this." He stared at Tosh's coppery face guard. He couldn't tell what the man was thinking.

"Calm the fuck down," said Bossman over the radio. "Ain't nobody else here. It's secured, move in."

He'd forgotten that the security man could hear him, too. "You scanned outside?" said Alvin.

"What is this, amateur hour, muthafucka? Course I did."

Thank god.

Tosh chuckled over the radio and they flew off toward the port-side airlock. They reached the back of the ship and clamped their boots down again.

The damage was extensive. It looked like something had wedged its way into the doorframe. The interior cylinder jutted out from the ship at its top edge, and a rubber accordion-like inner layer stretched outward in a freeze frame of the moment of atmosphere expulsion. Alvin's breath quickened.

He followed Tosh down the hull of the ship toward the broken seal. The damage had created sharp edges around the top half of the airlock. Tosh positioned himself at the lower edge of the opening, where the damage was minimal. He bent down to grasp the rim, released his boots, and pulled himself inside with his hands.

As Tosh floated across the threshold, Alvin thought he saw

something move out in space. He looked out into the blackness and saw a star blink twice, then stop. He thought it odd, then realized his nerves were probably getting the better of him.

When he looked back to his feet, the tether had drawn away from him into the ship.

"Hold up," he said.

Tosh spun around and planted his feet on the interior wall. He walked sideways back along the tube and stuck his hand out.

Alvin grasped it, released his mag-locks, and flipped head over heels into the ship in a somersault. He became disoriented, and upon thinking that his spin must be stopped, his hip thrusters pivoted back and forth to bring the motion to an end. He floated at ease in the middle of the airlock.

"I like this suit," he said.

Tosh pushed off the wall over to him. He unclipped the tether from Alvin's hip and said, "I don't think you need this anymore. Just be careful using the thrusters inside." Then he jetted through the tunnel and clamped his boots down in the next room.

Alvin followed him into what looked like a storage area. He did not come down to the floor, but instead flew up high and surveyed. The ship was lifeless. Emergency lights outlined walkways and doorways; nothing stirred. He could see Bossman waiting deeper inside, just outside a doorway. The security man stood with a pulse rifle at the ready. Tosh walked over to him.

Alvin peeped his Opti-Comp controls and started the device tracker Alteris had given him. A slow ping began.

Time for a game of hot or cold.

He floated around the rectangular storage dock. The read was negligible. He moved nearer to the doorway and the ping accelerated. Tosh and Bossman stepped inside and the emergency lights kicked on within the room.

"Found the crew," said Bossman.

Alvin saw a pale hand pass by the doorframe. He gasped. He did not want to enter, but the ping grew faster.

If there were someone to shoot, Bossman would have done it already.

He floated down, moved on through, and was startled by the sight of a frozen man drifting toward him. Bossman stepped between them, but then kept walking and the corpse continued toward Alvin. It got within a few feet of him when he panicked.

At his thought about getting away, his thrusters fired, sending him backward. He hit the wall hard and something gave behind him. Something crunchy. Whatever it was had dampened his impact.

"What the heck, Baylor!" yelled Tosh.

Bossman just chuckled.

Alvin tried to spin himself around, but his arm was caught on something. He pulled it free and found it wrapped in long black hair. Clinging to the hair was a frozen human head. He instinctively snapped his arm away and the hair untangled. He watched the head float away and rebound off the cabin wall. Red particulate drifted after it.

Nausea overtook him. He began panting and looked away. Then he saw the rest of the body—frozen hands and neck stump.

Alvin breathed faster. He was sweating.

"Don't you fucking puke," said Bossman.

"Seriously man, don't do it," said Tosh.

Alvin closed his eyes.

It's just like a VR game.

He took long slow breaths.

It's only a game.

He opened his eyes and became aware that there were more bodies floating in the cabin. He closed his eyes again and listened to the steady ping of the tracker. After a moment he looked around. The nausea was abating. He was in control again. He turned on his mag-locks and clamped to the floor.

"You all right?" asked Tosh.

"I'm okay. Just never seen a human popsicle."

"I understand," said Tosh. "I remember my first time."

"Let's move it. We have a schedule to keep," said Bossman.

"How'd they die?" asked Alvin.

"They got their heads smacked in when the gravity went out," said Bossman.

"How can you be sure?" said Alvin.

Bossman pointed up.

Alvin looked at the ceiling. It was covered in red blotches. He could see where a man's head had hit. Black hair and a cloth turban were affixed to the ceiling via frozen pieces of scalp. He exhaled heavily and went back to minding the tracker.

The ping took him to the back of the room and into a small hallway. A few steps further and it sounded a solid tone. He was standing in front of the bathroom door.

"I think it's here," he said.

"Is it locked?" asked Tosh.

Alvin looked at the melted doorframe. The deadbolt had been cut.

Someone was here.

"No," he said and opened the door.

More black hair sprouted from another popsicle.

His heart skipped a beat.

It's him. It's Mohammed Rinsler.

The most famous scientist of the twenty-second century was dead, again.

His frozen torso was folded over grasping a black ball.

"Can you give me a hand? I think he's holding it," he said.

Bossman walked over and put one hand on the corpse's leg and the other on the chest and pushed. The man cracked in two and the ball came away, floating. A ripple of rainbow colors like an oil slick washed quickly over the surface of the sphere. Then it turned so black it appeared two-dimensional like a fist-sized hole in space.

"Let's go," said Bossman.

"They didn't tell me how to unlock it," said Alvin.

"Figure it out on the ship," said Bossman as he grabbed at the device in midair. The sphere pulsed red as soon he touched it.

"Wait!" yelled Alvin.

He knocked Bossman's thick arm away and the pulsing stopped. Bossman stepped back, his silence acknowledging the need for care. Alvin examined the ball closely and noticed a thin cable, the thickness of fishing line, hanging from its rear. It ran back to the corpse's head.

"Looks like a synaptic interface," said Alvin.

He tugged at the cable and the man's head pulled toward him. It was connected to a skullcap. His hair was intertwined with it. Alvin disconnected the line from the mesh cap and some strands of hair pulled free, sending bits of frozen scalp about. He grimaced and momentarily felt a pang of nausea again.

He plugged the cable into his suit, creating a connection, and his visor turned off. Everything beyond his nose was black. His heartbeat jumped. Before he had time to panic, the view came back.

Thank god.

The sphere was still floating in midair, unchanged. He had no idea what to do.

He knew how to control a rock hopper tendril, a gaming avatar, and now a thruster suit. They were all as easy as a thought; perhaps the device worked the same way.

Unlock, please.

A green pulse rippled through the sphere and it went black again.

"I think you did it," said Tosh.

Alvin touched the ball with his finger and it remained black as pitch. He felt a buzzing sensation in his head.

How in the hell?

He carefully placed his gloved palm on the floating orb and waited. In his ears, he heard what sounded like the ocean, as if he were listening into a seashell, then came something like voices whispering. The synaptic implants in his temples got hot and he felt the buzzing increase.

My head. This thing hurts.

"Okay, let's go," said Bossman.

"Hey, you guys hear that?" asked Alvin.

"Hear what?" asked Tosh.

"Sounds like an echo or something, like someone's comm channel is stuck open."

"No, probably just solar interference," said Tosh.

Alvin felt a tingling in his palm. Somehow an energy passed through his glove.

"Enough, let's get off this tomb," said Bossman.

Alvin disconnected the synaptic cable and his visor shot to black again for a quick flash. The noise was gone. He felt the headache subside and his synaptic implants cooled. He'd never felt them get so warm.

He grasped the device carefully, pulling it from the air, and felt his fingers pass through the sphere's sides. He thought he might have damaged it, but when he examined it, everything looked normal. The odd feeling persisted as they trekked back to the airlock with Bossman at point. The more Alvin worried about his grip on the black ball, the deeper his fingers seemed to penetrate.

As they climbed out of the airlock, he paused on the hull for Tosh to hook the tether to him. He stared out at the sea of stars and tucked the device in a pouch on his belt. They leaped off into the black ocean for the swim back. Alvin felt like "it" in a deadly game of tag.

TWENTY-SIX

Barton Aimes sat at his desk in his freshly pressed suit and watched as a security drone relayed footage of Alvin Baylor. The man held Rinsler's Alkahest in his hands while crouched on the hull of the wrecked sail-ship *Zzyzx*. He stared straight at the drone's camera, his copper face shield revealing nothing of his intentions.

Aimes was a half-hour ahead in the knowledge that his subordinate had successfully acquired the device. The computer systems at the Alteris office had no access to the faster-than-light communication network that Washington utilized. Aimes's home office made a superior and safer command center for his true work.

He grimaced as Baylor dove from the hull and glided off with two other men. The mercenary, John Padre, was nowhere to be seen. Aimes directed the drone to perform a radio sweep of the area. It picked up an Alteris shuttle, but no sign of any other ships. He pounded the top of his desk, and the video display that floated above its surface shimmied from the impact.

Where is that fucking man?

Baylor was on his way to Ida to complete the job he had been assigned. If he were to reach his destination, matters would complicate.

Aimes could not take the Alkahest after Baylor reached the mining colony without an open attack on Alteris. That would risk tipping his hand to his employer and engendering all-out rebellion from the Corporate Territories. It would cost the American government its Continental Defense Taxes and that could finally kill them off, leaving North America to Corporate rule. The world would not survive if left to the vagaries of consumer trends. So said the machine. Rinsler's machine. The machine that had cost them the union.

Fucking Rinsler.

The scientist had abandoned Earth for reasons not fully understood. Aimes did not like mystery. He felt himself to be the commander of secrets. Yet he searched for the scientist's latest invention all because the QI told them to do so. The damn machine that knew everything but never gave a straight answer.

He disconnected from the drone feed and searched for the mercenary's ID via the FTL relay network. It would show his last location. Padre had used it to make private calls to someone aboard *The Hope*.

Is he working with Baylor?

Within moments the merc was located somewhere in the vicinity of Armstrong Station. A precise location would require a new ping. Aimes called him through an encrypted chat app and silently cursed his reliance on another one of Rinsler's inventions.

"You motherfucker!" Padre screamed.

Aimes stared at Padre's raging face on the screen in front of him.

"Excuse me?" he said.

"What kind of spook bullshit are you pulling?" said Padre.

"Why aren't you at the site, Mr. Padre?" asked Aimes. "I told you to wait there. I need the package. Your job is not finished."

"Is that where you planned to kill me?"

No. I would have done it closer to home.

"Kill you? The package is getting away. I have no religion as to who reclaims it. Is it going to be you or not, Mr. Padre?" said Aimes.

"You killed two of my men at Armstrong. You're a sono-fabitch," said Padre.

Well . . . the latter is true.

"I killed no one, Mr. Padre. We sent a man via *The Hope* to unlock the device. A patsy. You were instructed to remain at the crash site and await further instructions. Instead, you used our relay to communicate with someone aboard *The Hope*."

"I know all about your boy, Alvin Baylor," said Padre. "And your second man, Chico Perez. You ain't double-crossing me, you government trash."

So that's what happened to Mr. Perez.

"Our agent was only there to protect Baylor during transit. You were to be the recipient of the bounty," said Aimes.

"He's a fucking liar," said a female voice on Padre's end.

"Who is that?" asked Aimes.

"It doesn't matter who I am. You're Alvin's supervisor and your name is Barton Aimes," said the woman.

How the fuck . . .

Aimes's head began to spin.

"I am going to murder you," said Padre.

"Mr. Padre, I have dealt with quite a few disgruntled and misinformed contractors in my day. Threatening me is not going to get you anywhere."

"You're a dead man," said Padre.

Aimes hung up the call. He had a solid trace.

He switched the FTL relay back to drone control and fed it Padre's transmitter ID with an order to kill. It might take a few days, but drones would find Padre's ship and get the job done with no questions asked.

Who have you told about me?

Aimes ran through the FTL logs. All of Padre's messages had gone to *The Hope*.

Presumably all to this woman. The whore seen in Baylor's Opti-Comp streams?

Nothing else showed up.

I still have time.

The job was now disaster control. Aimes had kept his cover at Alteris for seven years. It had to end sooner or later. It was time to inform Mother.

First I lose Rinsler and now the Alkahest. She may kill me herself.

TWENTY-SEVEN

Rouja reclined on a bunk aboard Padre's ship, the *Cronus*. A moist towel lay across her forehead. Her body ached from electric shock.

"How did you know?" said Padre.

"Because the asshole uses the same phrases. Alvin made fun of him for it. 'I have no religion'—who the fuck talks like that?"

Padre nodded and a wry grin spread across his face. "We're gonna make Washington pay."

He gripped the chair back hard with hands. She watched the muscles in his thin forearms flex. He looked so old and skinny. Not at all like the man she had once loved. Spite and zero-g had taken their toll.

She sat upright and sipped at a bottle of Refuel.

Back at Armstrong Station, she'd stuffed Watkins's and Cheng's bodies in a supply closet with the maintenance tech they'd killed. Then she let the janitorial bots mop up the blood while she waited for her former lover. She told Padre the maintenance man was Chico Perez, despite having killed him onboard *The Hope*. It was best to have an element of the truth in any lie.

You taught me that.

She said, "You're taking this lightly. I told you not to use that government comm channel. That Perez guy took out two of us and nearly killed me. You think that spook Aimes is just gonna sit back while we screw up his plans?"

"We're gonna put an end to him right now. I'll send the chat dump from our conversation over to Alteris," said Padre.

"Baylor told me the assignment came straight from the CEO. Send it to Sabrina Meyer and copy Aimes," she said.

"Copy him? Why?"

"Because that asshole doesn't like to sweat," said Rouja. *And he deserves it for taking Alvin's winnings.*

"Ha, it's payback time," said Padre.

"I don't give a shit about Washington," she said. "Let's forget this goose chase and head back to Earth before it's too late."

"You don't want revenge? For what they did in Greece?"

Don't you dare.

"You pulled us out of there," she said.

"Because the place was overrun and Washington disavowed me. It's their fault we lost your daughter."

You bastard.

"Our daughter, John. Our daughter."

He looked away.

"Babe, we know they need this device. If Uncle Sam needs it, then everybody will pay to keep it from them. This is the last job," he said. "We're getting too old to keep this up."

Too old . . .

Their daughter would be almost twenty now. Would Lia even forgive her? It didn't matter. Lia needed her. She couldn't let that continue to fester. Leung's sex-trade ledger was the only chance she had to find her. An off-network decrypt of his DNA would cost a fortune and this job was uniquely valuable.

He's right. I don't have time to earn the money any other way.

"We still don't know what it does." She groaned and pulled the towel from her face. Her broken nose throbbed.

"It doesn't matter," said Padre.

She tapped the wall and examined her face in a video mirror. There were bags under her eyes and her cheeks were beginning to sag.

"I look terrible," she said.

She set the nano-collar to work at returning youth to her face and repairing her nose.

"I say we hightail it to that asteroid and take it by force," said Padre.

"That's your plan?"

"We have to act fast."

The nanites hurt like hell as they ran under Rouja's skin, pushing bone back into place and repairing tissue. Normally it itched, but this was something else; the pain of weeks of healing in only minutes.

"We're a team of two now. We don't know what kind of fire-power they have at that base," she said.

"By all accounts it's just a mining camp. Like the one I stole this ship from. We'll kill anyone who gets in our way," said Padre.

Alvin's innocent; he doesn't deserve this.

"They'll see us coming in a stolen ship. I need to scout it alone," she said.

Padre nodded. "All right. I knew you'd be up for it." A wry grin spread across his face. "As long as I have you, babe, I can pull this off."

"Yeah, you have me. Babe," she said.

The nano-collar made a clicking noise. Then it shorted and died. She looked at the mirror again. Her face was youthful again, but her nose was still bruised and swollen.

Watkins's eel suit must have fried the collar.

"Shit. It didn't finish," said Rouja. "I need to get to Baylor before my face comes undone and I look as old as you."

TWENTY-EIGHT

Barton Aimes sat down on the edge of his bed. Light from a window illuminated his expansive loft apartment. He stared at the far wall. Christy's *Scene at the Signing of the Constitution of the United States* filled his view. It was so large that he felt like one of the assembled signatories gathered around George Washington. The painting had always given him courage. Its enormity conferred the impact of that meeting almost three hundred years ago. The greatest nation in history was not finished. Not yet.

He tapped his right temple, activating his government-issued Opti-Comp, and opened a direct line to Washington. An older woman with medium-length brown hair and a hard expression appeared before him in space.

"Hello, Mother," he said.

"Hello, Bart," said Margaret Aimes. "Is it in hand?"

"No. Our contractor has gone rogue."

She cocked her head to the side and glared sternly.

"Kill him," she said.

"I sent a drone."

She nodded. "Has Baylor retrieved the Alkahest?"

"Yes. We'll have to acquire it at the Alteris facility and get rid of Baylor there."

"You can't kill him. You need to send him home quietly before you take it or this will become a media feeding frenzy."

"I don't understand."

Her eyes narrowed. "Alvin Baylor is something of a showboater."

"You mean the gaming tournament? We quashed that. Meyer pulled his winnings and had her pal Xi-Michaels take him off the records."

"He upset some very big names. Rick Zuck is the best player in the world, is he not?"

"Mother, I told you he's been wiped off the record. The info never made it to Earth. Baylor's a washed-up nobody."

Her mouth drew even tighter than usual.

What does she know?

"Not for long. There was a reporter on *The Hope*, a hack named Anton Vance. We just got word of an article. He's calling the tournament a scandal—a poor working man robbed by the upper classes. It will be all over the Earth-net in minutes. Baylor will be the most famous has-been in the world."

Barton Aimes felt his stomach drop.

"Have your inside man kill Vance," she said.

She's going to kill me.

"I . . . can't."

"Why not?" she asked.

"Because he's dead. Killed by some woman working with our rogue contractor."

Her lips parted just a hair and he could see her teeth.

"Go to Meyer. Have her tell her buddy Xi-Michaels. He'll kill Vance for us. He won't allow that kind of negative publicity to go unpunished."

You mean you won't allow it.

"Get details about the test of the device," said Margaret

Aimes. "I need to plan something that won't make noise. Time is short."

Yes it is. How long till Meyer knows about me?

"Okay, Mother. I will do this. She'll want Baylor off the project when she gets wind of this. Maybe that will help us."

"I hope so, Bart. You've really fucked this up."

"I know, Mother. I'm sorry."

The connection dropped.

Barton Aimes stood up from the bed and walked over to his desk. He pressed a hidden button in the leg and the electronics inside shorted out with a pop. A small waft of smoke rose from the desktop. Then he opened the top drawer and pulled out a translucent ultrasonic pistol. He placed it in his inside chest pocket, adjusted his tie, and buttoned his jacket.

If Meyer knows about me, she dies. Mother will understand.

"Room off," he said.

She won't forgive, but she'll understand.

Various objects around the giant room disappeared. All that remained were his bed, the smoldering desk, and a twenty-by-thirty-foot painting created for posterity. He looked at George Washington's face for a moment and then out the window at the blue sculptural headquarters of the Alteris Asteroid Excavation Company. Then he turned, chin held high, and walked out the door. He didn't bother to shut it.

Barton Aimes entered Sabrina Meyer's office with a sense of urgency in his gut. His window of innocence would close soon. She was seated in her high-backed chair, a pleasant smile on her face as she poked around her Opti-Comp. It would have been concerning to find her undistracted. She couldn't hold a meeting without running a chat or checking company correspondence or the news. She was barely focused on him.

She doesn't know yet.

As he walked down the short steps leading to her desk, her security guard, Rashad, stepped behind him and shut the door. Barton paused a small distance from her desk and looked back. Rashad was dapper as always in his fitted suit, but his eyes told a different story.

He'll be the one when the time comes.

Aimes nodded at the security man and sat down. Meyer cocked her head and looked through him. She was quiet.

Drones glided by outside the wall of glass while bright cumulus clouds drifted slowly in the distance. The top floor had been designed as a sky lounge to entertain guests, but when Meyer was brought on she scrapped the plans and took the whole floor for herself. She knew how to make an impression. PR was her strength. Aimes knew that he didn't command her kind of charisma, and he found her casualness repugnant. Alteris was involved in the theft of United States property, and like any common criminal, Meyer's day would come. Perhaps her office would be an entertainment lounge again.

"Have you heard the Baylor news?" he asked. "Who knew that reporter Vance was going to make a scene like that."

"Chan Xi-Michaels informed me of the possibility. It adds a new wrinkle," she said.

"It's an undesirable bit of publicity. Do you think we can manage it before anyone gets too curious about Baylor? Perhaps Xi-Michaels can assist," said Aimes.

Meyer's eyes roved around in her Opti-Comp. "Hmmm, hold," she said.

Aimes reached up to adjust his coiffed hair and masked a quick blink that enabled his direct line. It began streaming directly to Mother. He noticed a new message had come in. He ignored it.

"Is there a problem with Baylor? He should be nearly to Ida by now," he said.

Meyer went on looking in her Opti-Comp. Then her eyes focused forward. She was looking at him squarely now.

"I'm concerned," she said. "There are breaks in Baylor's Opti-Comp feed. He's been hiding something. He's started a relationship with some dubious woman and there's this business with the gaming tournament. It's as if he wants someone to find out about him. Such attention seeking. Why did we pick him again?"

Certainly not for attention.

"We had few options. Rinsler's device sent back a short list of names from my department. Baylor was the one with the best synaptic skills and he had no family."

"Mr. Rinsler is a complex man with paranoid delusions. He must have chosen those names for a reason. He correctly suspected someone would attempt to kill him, yet he didn't suspect Baylor of duplicity. Curious."

"I don't understand," said Aimes. "Do you really think Alvin Baylor is up to something?"

"Mr. Aimes, this is a difficult job. Very tough. Tougher still if I can't rely on discretion."

Aimes shifted in his chair, conscious of the weight of the plastic pistol in his pocket.

"Dr. Rinsler warned me not to disclose his involvement . . . to anybody," she said.

Aimes's heart rate jumped.

Why is she still focused on me?

His eyes wandered to the message indicator floating in his view. "Losing him was lamentable, but we've recovered his device. Everything is finally moving again," said Aimes as he peeped open the message. He skimmed it.

She knows.

A drop of perspiration formed at his temple.

"Oh, we didn't lose him. We lost his double. Rinsler is safe at Ida waiting for his delivery," said Meyer.

Aimes felt his heart pound in his chest.

What? Mother, are you watching this?

"Rinsler's alive?"

"I agreed to some extreme measures to calm his paranoia," she said.

"What kind of measures?" said Aimes.

"Really now, Mr. Aimes . . . I thought you were my problem solver, but it seems you're somebody else's."

The bio-implant in Aimes's arm began sending alert signals. He saw the words "Elevated Heart Rate" flash in an ugly red font across his Opti-Comp projection. A drop of perspiration began to roll down his temple.

"Sabrina, please explain. I'm afraid I don't know what you mean," he said.

Aimes shifted in his seat and leaned forward slightly, allowing the gun to pull away from his chest.

"You killed his brother," said Meyer. "And you've received this same message, yes?"

Meyer activated the touch-field display on her desk with an upward swipe of her finger. The output from Aimes's Opti-Comp appeared above her desk. It multiplied his vision like a hall of mirrors.

The message from John Padre floated there, and then "Warning: High Heart Rate" flashed over it and echoed a thousand times.

Rashad stepped to Aimes's side. A black-gripped handle dropped into his hand from under his jacket sleeve.

"You have created a difficult situation for me. I am not well practiced in violence or interrogation. Thankfully, Rashad enjoys this kind of work. He tells me his weapon won't stain the carpets, either."

Mine will.

"*Sic semper tyrannis!*" yelled Aimes.

He drew the ultrasonic pistol from his pocket and kicked off the desk. As his chair fell backward to the floor, he fired. There was no sound.

The ultrasonic blast vibrated the golden desk until the wood supports splintered. Meyer's bronzed Pizza award went flying and bounced off the window behind her, cracking the glass. She made an animalistic noise as she shielded herself from the flying debris.

Rashad whipped his arm and an electric blue arc flew from the black handle. The blue line snapped through Aimes's outstretched arm and the gun went airborne with his finger still on the trigger.

The severed limb fell to the floor still firing. It blasted Meyer in the shoulder. She screamed in pain as Rashad leaped atop the weapon. His nose and ears began dripping blood as he ripped the gun free from the tensed hand.

Rashad stood, then fell backward against the cracked window. He panted and the whites of his eyes turned pink. "Are you okay?" he said to Meyer.

He sat on the floor while she sat in her chair, wincing from the pain.

"Yes," she said while rubbing her left shoulder.

She wasn't afraid, she was angry.

Aimes grimaced as he saw his arm ended at the elbow. The stump was cauterized, no blood to be seen. Rashad aimed his pistol back at him.

Mother will retrieve Rinsler and finish you.

"You can't steal this nation," said Aimes.

"I'll tell your mother you died for the company," said Meyer.

"She knows I died for my country. She's watching."

Meyer roared with anger. She picked up an award from the floor and ran at him through the debris of her desk. With an over-hand swing, she buried the metal pizza slice in his eye socket. His Opti-Comp sparked.

"Rashad, we're going to have to clean the carpet," she said.

TWENTY-NINE

Alvin awoke from a nap, floating above the surface of his cramped bunk onboard the Alteris shuttle. His Opti-Comp showed he'd been out for several hours. A few feet away, the black orb floated in the air. Its deep black surface caused it to disappear into the shadows. Since the unlocking there had been no further light shows from the device. He reached out and tapped it with a finger and felt a tingling. Then he wrapped both palms around it. It felt like static electricity. He considered using the synaptic cable again, but was not anxious for another headache.

He was clueless as to the sphere's use. It might be amazingly important to Alteris, but what could one do with it? He'd expected a revelation by this point in his journey, something to clarify the significance of this task. Knowing its creator to be Mohammed Rinsler generated nothing but more questions and a new fear. Who killed the scientist and when might they come for him? He thought it best not to handle the device until he understood it. He released his grip and it went back to hovering in the air. The tingling in his hands ceased.

Hopefully they'll send the damn manual and some answers soon.

Alvin's apprehensive mood was exacerbated by the shuttle's drab interior. He missed *The Hope*.

This place is toxic.

He missed Katy.

I need to get in touch with her.

He hit Record and aimed his wrist to capture a video stream of himself and his environs. He spoke of how he was thinking of her and how this place held no distractions. "I'll call again when I'm there," he said.

Talking to her again felt good, even if he'd have to wait for a reply.

He pressed Send on the message and slumped back into his bunk. For two minutes he looked through his Opti-Comp at the empty inbox floating in space and straight through it at the blank wall of his cabin. Then his Opti-Comp flashed and alerted him to a new message.

Yes.

He peeped it. The message was from Alteris. Disappointment hit him.

The text showed an odd return address. It looked like an automailer from the system.

Finally some details?

He opened it.

Dear Valued Employee [Alvin Baylor],

This notice serves to inform you that your supervisor has been changed. Effective immediately you will report to []. Your new supervisor will contact you about any changes to your work schedule.

Thank you,

The Service Desk

He was dumbfounded.

What the hell happened to Aimes?

"Fuck! I need leadership and I get a stupid automailer that isn't even filled out?" he said aloud. "I'm contacting Meyer."

He opened his recorder for a hurried voice message.

"Meyer, it's Alvin Baylor. What's this about a new supervisor? You got me out here. Are you gonna get me home? It doesn't say who to contact. Get back to me. I'm not interested in being another dead employee."

It would take at least an hour to get a response. He wanted a drink bad. He wanted Katy. He wanted anything but to be where he was.

Trapped at work.

He heard a knock at his door.

"Come in."

The door slid back into the frame and Tosh floated inside.

"You good in here?" he said.

"No. They still haven't sent me the manual and I don't think they're going to," said Alvin.

"I'm sure they'll send it. I have more ketamine if you need it."

"I'm not going squirrelly. Check this out." Alvin swiped upward on his smart-band. The message from Alteris displayed on the ceiling.

Tosh gripped a handhold and spun himself to read the text.

"Damn. That's weird," he said.

"Especially for a mission they deemed so important. Something stinks," said Alvin.

"Hey! You guys holding out on me?" yelled Bossman.

The security man bounded off the hallway walls toward the doorway.

"We're just talking," said Tosh.

"Don't be holding out. You're getting ready to vape again," said Bossman.

Tosh shrugged his shoulders in ignorance.

"I know you're growing it down in that greenhouse. Don't make me bust you. Sharing is caring," said Bossman through a mouthful of teeth.

"What're you, on a work release program?" said Alvin.

"What chu say to me?"

"I asked if you were an ex-con, Bossman." Alvin's voice hardened at the appellation and he glared at the man.

"Hehe. You got nuts, little man. I'm on contract from the penitentiary, but we're all friends here," said Bossman.

"Now you wanna be friends?" asked Tosh.

"We did our thing. Now let's chill," said Bossman.

"I have to do something with this restless energy," said Alvin. He set his Opti-Comp for bathroom privacy with a peep.

Tosh pulled an electric pipe from his zippered pocket and took a puff. With a mellow grin, he exhaled water vapor into the cabin. Then he handed it over to Bossman.

Alvin snatched the vaporizer away from the big man's hand.

"Gimme that, you're next," he said.

Bossman chuckled. "Where you from?"

Alvin pulled a drag and exhaled.

"Earth, muthafucka."

He passed it back to Bossman.

"A company man." Bossman inhaled.

"Man, fuck the company. They think they own me," said Alvin.

Bossman exhaled. "Haha. I like this one. He different."

"As different as they come," said Alvin.

Tosh's grin grew wider. "The company doesn't care, so long as we make the deliveries on time. Check it out." He tapped the wall and a video display appeared. "That's where we're going."

A gray oblong rock with red mottled streaks appeared. It turned on its long axis. A circle of lights surrounded a metal plate at its lower center. A few small lights floated near the asteroid.

"Ida?" said Alvin.

"243 Ida," said Tosh.

Alvin felt comforted by the lights that meant human life. He'd seen a ghost ship. And he'd half expected to find a ghost town at his destination.

"That metal disc is the dock. The design comes from the Alteris 3-D print library. Everything is fabricated from locally sourced materials," said Tosh.

The miners were akin to primitive hunter-gatherer societies of the not-so-distant past. They lived in harmony with the most inhospitable environment ever braved by mankind and they were considered lowlifes by the people of Earth.

"Does the 'roiders' reputation bother you?"

"You mean mindless brutes mutated by the rigors of a thousand unfathomable hells careening through space?" said Tosh.

Alvin laughed. "Yeah. That."

"It's VR play bullshit. We're machine techs, dude. We spend our time surveying in rock hoppers for suitable conditions. Then we send in drones to drill. Most of us are just here for the thrill of the frontier."

"Or work release," said Bossman with a smile. "You all a bunch of robot tenders. Least I get to use my own hands."

"Yeah, for what?" said Alvin.

"For beatin' fools down. Sometimes I even strangle a mutha-fucka before I shoot him."

"Take another hit," said Tosh.

Alvin had only met only one 'roider so far. Toshiro Ito appeared to be anything but a brute. Corporate Security was another story.

Bossman puffed and passed the vaporizer. "Can't wait to put my feet down again. Tired of this floating shit. Makes you weak."

"I thought there's no gravity there," said Alvin.

"Inside it's Earth equivalent," said Tosh. "Ida's rotational period is fast enough to power a gyroscopic gravity drive."

"I'm good with that," said Alvin. "The suit's fun, but I'd like to feel my weight once in a while."

"You're going to Dactyl," said Tosh. He pointed to one of the tiny lights and zoomed the display to show a small gray ball. "Not much gravity there. Sorry."

Alvin nodded and took his turn on the vaporizer. It didn't matter much. One week was all he was scheduled to spend there. No need to be preoccupied with atrophy. "What's on Dactyl?" he asked.

"A comm tower and a habitat dome," said Tosh.

Alvin stretched out in midair toward the image. He squinted at a sliver of red light emanating from a crater on the small moon.

"And who's there?"

"Beats me. We aren't allowed to set foot on it and there's radio interference from that tower blanketing the place," said Tosh.

"Maybe it's a hot lady," said Bossman. He elbowed Alvin in the ribs.

"I'll let you know," Alvin said with a smirk.

"The rumor is the company's testing automation," said Tosh. "Something to cut the staff. So be ready for some hard looks. Some of the crew are worried about losing their jobs."

"Great," said Alvin. "You know, I can relate. Maybe that thing doesn't need an operator. Maybe I was just an errand boy. Aren't you worried about what we saw back there? The lock was cut on that bathroom door."

"Don't get paranoid. We have security," said Tosh.

He hammered his fist against Bossman's chest.

"There could be real danger coming," said Alvin.

"We live with real danger every day, dude. Besides, you and the device will be on Dactyl."

"Oh, thanks. How long till we get there?"

"Eight hours. Time enough to get some rest before we meet the crew." Tosh motioned to Bossman and the two floated to the doorway. "Peace out, Alvin."

Alvin gave Tosh the two-fingered peace sign, then turned it backward at Bossman.

"Hehe," said Bossman. "Don't let your nightmares ruin the trip, little man."

The door slid closed.

Alvin brought up the inbox in his Opti-Comp. Nothing new. He stared through it at the video display of Dactyl and watched it in a haze until he drifted off to sleep.

THIRTY

Still no gravity.

Alvin's magnetic boots clung to the exit ramp as he followed Tosh and Bossman out of the shuttle and onto the floor of Ida's cargo hold. The conical bay was a hundred feet in diameter and it narrowed as it drilled deeper into the asteroid's core. He felt like he was descending into a hole.

"So where's the gravity?" he said.

"Through there, it's no help in here," said Tosh.

He pointed ahead to a door at the bottom of the cone. A long balustrade ran straight away from it and wrapped around the room in a circle. Parked all along the railings were rock hoppers. The shuttle was the largest vehicle. Nothing else could carry more than two people.

My babies.

"I calibrated those hoppers," said Alvin.

"Ain't you special," said Bossman.

"They're nice machines. Couldn't do the job without them," said Tosh. "Let's jet."

The men stepped off the ramp to the deck and then lifted off with their suit thrusters. They flew toward the door at the bottom, passing between straps of black fabric that crisscrossed the midsection of the hangar like a spider web. Restrained in the web were metal shipping containers being prodded by drones. The drones resembled alien insects as they loaded chunks of rock and minerals into the bins with tentacled limbs.

A few miners floated about, directing the action with hand waves. They watched him.

The men reached the door and it opened automatically.

"Set down," said Tosh.

They affixed their boots to the deck before stepping through the doorway. As they passed through, Alvin felt the weight hit his knees first. The sudden sense of up and down disoriented him. He unlatched his helmet and tucked it under one arm. The sphere was safely hidden in the travel bag slung over his other shoulder.

"This suit's heavier than I thought," he said.

Tosh nodded and removed his helmet. "Release your boots," he said.

Alvin disengaged the mag-locks and felt his knee shoot up with ease. They were under artificial gravity now and the magnetic boots were unneeded torture.

"It's leg day," said Bossman. He puffed with each step as he pulled his magnetic boots away from the deck.

They began trekking down a sloped hallway that swirled into the asteroid like a corkscrew. The angle was steep and disorienting.

At the bottom of the slope the ground flattened out. A line of people in gray jumpsuits were waiting for them in a room with ceilings thirty feet high.

Three levels of catwalks wrapped the asteroid walls in metal. Bunk beds were embedded in the rock face. Smatterings of people leaned over the railings and watched him. He felt every eye on him.

Under the white lights, his lightning bolt paint job made him look like an action figure. He removed his helmet and a musty scent hit his nostrils.

"Folks, I give you Alvin Baylor," said Tosh.

He saw eyes narrow into slits.

A short, balding black man stepped forward from the group.

"Nice suit," he said in a pinched tone as he reached out for a handshake.

Alvin awkwardly tucked his helmet under his arm and shook the man's hand.

"Welcome, Mr. Baylor. I'm Jamie Beckman. We've been anticipating your arrival for some time."

He was dressed in brown slacks and a button-down shirt, unlike the other jumpsuits.

Must be the Man around here.

"Thank you. I'm glad to finally be here. It's been quite a trip."

"I understand *The Hope* is spectacular," said Beckman. "I expect to ride it home one day."

"I got a contract!" yelled a voice from up above.

Beckman turned on his heel with military precision.

"Stow it, Chickowski," he shouted up at the catwalk behind him.

Alvin followed the voice up to see a shirtless man with rippling muscles grip the railing. He was bald with a tattoo of a cog on his forehead. Beside him stood a tall, mean-looking brute with long black hair and a goatee over olive skin. He took a hit on a vaporizer and passed it into shadows to another man beside him. That guy took a drag and a blue light lit up curly gray-white hair that framed a buck-toothed grin. It sent a chill through Alvin.

I know that grin.

After all that had happened, he had forgotten about the discovery of his old gaming coach in the crew logs for Ida. The man whose son had died from overclocking. The man who had made him a pariah.

Carroll Henry.

The buck-toothed man continued to smile as Beckman yammered. "These individuals form my administrative staff. I am the executive in charge."

Alvin brought his attention back to ground level as Beckman motioned toward the gray jumpsuits. He exchanged nods with each in turn. A woman in a lab coat, made no expression while she waved her fingertip through the air. She was taking notes of some kind. Another man with intense green eyes stared at him. None of those assembled seemed welcoming so he greeted them with a simple nod and turned back to Beckman.

"Come with me. I'll show you to your room," said the executive.

"Peace," said Tosh.

Bossman gave him the two-finger *up yours* gesture.

"Later, fellas," said Alvin.

He walked with Beckman. The man spoke in a casual tone as he asked about the weather on Earth. He seemed starved for someone to talk to. All the while, Alvin stole glances back at the catwalk above as they crossed the room.

Beckman continued on to work details when Alvin didn't grab at the small talk. Something about material drop-offs to be made at Armstrong for *The Hope* to ferry back to Earth. Alvin couldn't focus on Beckman's words. He was distracted by the man who had ruined his life.

Beckman returned to comments about *The Hope* itself, eager to discuss its grandeur.

"Yes, it's quite nice," said Alvin.

They arrived at a group of doors located across from the toughs on the catwalk. They appeared to be private quarters. Everyone else had a bunk on the wall.

"Take the room on the left," said Beckman.

Alvin turned around, his back to the door. He looked up again. Carroll Henry and his two pals were staring.

"Don't worry about those shitheads," said Beckman. "Henry, get your men back to work!"

The buck-toothed man hunkered down over the rail, illuminating his entire face for the first time.

"We're on a smoke break, don't cha know!" he said.

His face and Philly accent were unmistakable.

Carroll Fucking Henry.

"Your associate is waiting on Dactyl, Mr. Baylor. You can rest for a few hours until breakfast. Then we'll prep you for transport," he said.

Associate? You don't know who it is, either.

"Thank you," said Alvin.

"I am here to assist the company in any way I can," said Beckman.

The officious little executive departed and Alvin stepped inside the room. Henry and his goons were still watching when he shut the door.

Alvin lay on his bunk pondering his anxieties for nearly two hours. No new communications came from Alteris.

Did Meyer see my message? What the heck do they expect me to do? I should just head to Dactyl. But what if someone is after this sphere? They might kill me there. But who might they be? And who's up there waiting for it?

Five minutes before, he had ignored the blaring breakfast announcement. He wasn't interested in eating.

Henry's gonna cause trouble.

He rolled over and grabbed his head.

When is Katy going to get back to me?

He felt a buzz at his wrist. The sight of a new message banner made his heart jump. He peeped it open. It was from Meyer.

"Hope everything is going well. We had to let Aimes go. I'm

sorry I can't say more now. I'll have someone assigned to you as soon as possible. What I will say is that I am pleased with your progress. Please send an update when you reach Dactyl. And try to keep a low profile. We don't want any grumblings from the union about your work. I'll be in touch."

That's it? Who the fuck am I meeting and what am I doing?

A banging at the door startled him. He sprang up off the bunk and answered it. Beckman's face was shoved right up close to the frame. A Star of David swung from his neck and glistened in the light. Alvin stared at the necklace rather than make eye contact. His mother had worn one just like it.

"Mr. Baylor, you didn't answer the breakfast call."

"Yes, that's because I was asleep."

"Space lag, no doubt. After breakfast we'll need to discuss transit to Dactyl."

"Yeah. Let me get myself together and I'll be out."

"Good."

Alvin shut the door on Beckman and fell back on the bed. Despite his apprehension he needed to get on with it. Whatever it was. He sucked up his pride about the lack of response from Katy and went to put on his shoes. Then he peeped out a message.

"Yo, Tosh! Where do I find something to eat?"

The reply came quick. "Come meet up."

A map of the base was attached. Alvin stepped out the door and a floating arrow appeared in his Opti-Comp. He stopped to push his arms into the sleeves of his hoodie. The crew deck was sparsely occupied. There were about five to ten people spread across the walled bunks. Most of them looked at him discreetly. By the time he went down the exit ramp, all of them were staring. He wanted away from them. He'd go to Dactyl and get his head straight. A little work would focus him.

He walked down the sloping metal halls, and a short jaunt later a flashing "X" appeared in his view. The door said, "Surveyoɪ." He knocked. As he waited his eyes drifted up to a hand-scribbled sign above. "Abandon all hope." There was no mention of "ye who enter here."

An alert young man with a plume of blond hair and an avian look answered the door.

"Password?"

Alvin shrugged his shoulders.

"I'll give you three guesses."

"Swordfish."

The man's eyes opened wide and he giggled. "Come in, Alvin Baylor. Marx Brothers fans are always welcome."

Alvin walked in to find Tosh and two others. They were playing a card game with miniature projections of army men running across a small table.

"Hey Alvin!" greeted Tosh.

Alvin walked over to them while studying the room. In the back was a work console and what looked like a small food printer.

"I thought the dining area would be bigger."

"It is," said the hawkish man. "I like to prepare my own Nutri-Paste. The mess hall never gets the consistency right."

"I'm a stickler for texture, too," said Alvin.

"Alvin, this is Yumi and Ravi and you've met Buzz," said Tosh.

Alvin exchanged nods with Yumi, an energetic young woman who was more interested in the game board, and Ravi, a petite man with a dusky complexion topped by a bowl haircut. Ravi eyed him uncomfortably.

The hawkish young man walked over smiling and Alvin stuck out a hand.

"You've washed that thing I hope," said Buzz.

"Many times."

"Excellent," Buzz said before returning the handshake.

They sat down at the table.

"Are you named after the astronaut?" asked Alvin.

"No. I like to hum frequencies," said Buzz.

Alvin arched his eyebrow and nodded.

"We're just finishing up a game," said Tosh.

"So you're part of the big secret on Dactyl?" said Ravi.

Tosh looked over at Ravi with a grimace.

"I'm not in on it, if that's what you mean," said Alvin. "I'm just a messenger. Why? What do you know about it?"

Ravi sat back. Tosh continued to stare at him disapprovingly. Buzz had a smile. His eyes darted from Alvin to Ravi.

"I know that you work for the company and they don't want us to know jack shit about what they got up there."

"Then we know the same things," said Alvin.

Ravi looked irritated as Buzz and Tosh chuckled.

Yumi looked up at Alvin suspiciously. "You mean, you don't know why you're here?"

"No. I'm delivering something. I might help set it up, but I'm not sure."

"See, it is a test," said Ravi. He looked around at the table in search of approval.

"Rav thinks you're deploying automation to replace us. Is that what's up?" asked Yumi.

She chewed gum and seemed more intense in her aloofness than Ravi had been by being direct.

Toshiro leaned forward. "I'm sorry, Al. We don't get many visitors. People have concerns."

"It's fine. I understand. I'm on this job because the company was in a bind. I don't know the grand plan."

"That sounds plausible," started Buzz, "but your arrival is troubling to many of the crew."

Toshiro rolled his eyes.

Buzz lifted an eyebrow at him and continued, "I took the liberty of researching you, Alvin. Do the rest of you know that he used to play on the league circuit with that creep Henry?"

"That true?" asked Yumi.

"Yes. And it's also true that he's a fucking creep. Listen, I'm just here doing what I'm told. I have no secret agenda or opinions about any of you."

"Except Mr. Henry," said Buzz.

"Yeah. Except that fucking guy," said Alvin.

"I think this dude needs a toke," said Yumi.

Alvin shook his head. "I'm on the job today. So . . . what's the game?"

Buzz said, "A delightful little game called—"

"Domination!" said Yumi. "I win."

A plane flew over the game board and dropped a bomb. A mushroom cloud sprang up and wiped all the other pieces away.

"You always win," said Buzz. "Now get out of my bay and go eat your breakfast. I have work to do."

She stuck out her tongue at him and stood up. "Let's go. I'm starving."

"That's because you smoked," said Tosh. He gave her a peck on the cheek.

"Stay out of trouble, Alvin Baylor. We have no other fans of the Marx Brothers," said Buzz.

Alvin nodded. "Why certainly," he said in a Brooklyn accent.

"That's the Stooges," said Buzz as he closed the door.

Alvin chuckled and followed the three of them up the hall. It grew brighter and wider as they climbed the slope away from the operations area. The base was mostly graded circular ramps and dull metal hallways. Occasionally a bit of rock face was exposed. They passed only a few doors along the way.

The smell of metal and moisture dissipated as they arrived at an arched doorway. Beyond it the decking transitioned to a rubberized green surface that had recently been hosed down. Circular tables with attached molded seats sprang up like daisies around the room. Everything was a nauseating green. In the center of the room stood a Vend-A-Meal machine with one dispensing station. It was crowded with personnel who dragged ass through the place. Beckman approached looking alert in his dress grays.

"Mr. Baylor, I see you found your way here."

"I had a little help."

Beckman gave a severe look at Tosh, Yumi, and Ravi. They quickly walked away. So did everyone else. The 'roiders eyed Beckman but kept their distance as if he were a rock in the middle of a stream.

"So what's on the menu?" Alvin pointed over to the dispensing station.

"We have it all. That machine will print a perfectly balanced meal with any recipe you choose," said Beckman. "The company takes nutrition very seriously."

"So do I, Jamie. I don't mind telling you I take it very seriously," said Alvin.

Beckman smiled awkwardly. "Come see me when you're done eating. I don't want you kept from your work."

"Sure thing. Question: Have you received any messages for me from HQ?"

"Wouldn't they contact you directly?"

"Yes, normally, of course. I was out of range for a period and I thought they might have made an effort."

"Nothing, Mr. Baylor. Enjoy your breakfast."

Alvin continued forward through the clusters of tray-bearing workers. Most eyed him. A few stood their ground and made him sidestep. He got in line and shambled forward with the group. The printers gave off a hot moist aroma like freshly baked bread. That was a pleasant surprise. The stuff he'd had on Earth was odorless. He felt a shove from behind that knocked him into the queue of 'roiders.

"We're onto you, corpo," said the man with a cog tattoo on his forehead. His beady red eyes made him look like a rat.

Alvin returned the glare, but didn't make an expression. "Chickowski, right?"

"Don't look at me, you corpo fuck. This job here is what I got and you ain't taking it away."

Alvin shook his head. "I'm not after your job. I'm after breakfast."

Chickowski tapped his finger on Alvin's chest and his red eyes opened wide.

The chow line curved into a circle with Alvin and the bald lunatic at the center.

This guy only understands crazy.

"Don't fuck with me or I'll eat you for breakfast," said Alvin.

The line of 'roiders chattered with excitement.

"Chickowski! Knock it off!" a voice shouted over the crowd.

Beckman passed through the circle of men and broke up the confrontation. The observers went silent and scattered.

The rat-faced man skulked off grumbling under his breath. He pounded a fist into his other hand.

Beckman looked at Alvin's angry face. "You good, Baylor?"

Alvin nodded.

Beckman stepped in close and whispered in his ear. "Then hurry up and eat. I don't want a riot on my watch."

He walked away through the parting crowd.

Alvin stared after the path he'd cleared. In the distance, at one of the molded dinette stations, sat Carroll Henry with his arms crossed. Chickowski muttered something and sat down beside him. Beckman followed over to scold him. He got a few words out before Henry waved him off. Beckman straightened and left the room.

Alvin turned back around in line. A minute later he was up at the Vend-A-Meal. He ordered eggs Benedict and heard razzing from the guys behind him as they waited for his request to finish.

Fuck these assholes.

When the Nutri-Paste was done baking on the plate, a chime went off and Alvin snatched up the tray. He walked off in the direction opposite of Carroll Henry and looked for a seat. At the back of the room he saw Tosh and company. He went over and sat down with them.

"I'll catch up with you guys later," said Ravi as he abruptly left the table.

Alvin stared after him. Halfway across the room he looked back nervously.

"What's his deal?" asked Alvin.

"Duh," said Yumi.

"He's afraid of being associated with you," said Tosh.

"Henry pulls weight around here. He says you're trouble," said Yumi.

"I'm just passing through. Carroll Henry doesn't know shit about what I'm doing here."

"Hey, don't kill the messenger or whatever. You wanted to know."

Alvin pushed his food around on the plate. As it cooled it changed consistency and the seams where it had been molded into shape hardened into thin lines. The hollandaise sauce looked as rubbery as the floor. So did the eggs. He took a few bites. The food was tasteless. He looked around the room and saw sets of eyes dart away from his gaze. He choked down his anger with a bite of the eggs. After all that time hiding away, he'd finally gotten some appreciation on *The Hope*. Now he was back to remembering his shitty past and fending off looks of disapproval.

Fuck you, Henry.

He stood up with a scowl and looked across the room to his old coach. The man returned the glare. Alvin began walking.

"Uh, Al, where are you going?" asked Tosh.

Yumi's mouth dropped open and she threw a hand over it in jest.

"I'm gonna clear the air," he said.

He strode over with tunnel vision. Henry flopped his tousled white-gray hair and smiled with those buck teeth. Chickowski balled his fists. The tall brute with the goatee gripped his utensils.

A face-scan gave his name as "Rodriguez." Alvin stopped in front of the rounded table. He put his palms flat on it.

"You still got a fucking problem?" he spat.

"Hey, kid. Nice of you to come say hi," said Henry.

"Enough bullshit. Don't tell anymore lies about me. I'm not here to deal with you."

"Seems you just can't help yourself, then," said Henry.

Rodriguez laughed. Chickowski licked his lips while rubbing his knuckles.

"I can fuck up anyone's game. You know that, Carroll. Mind your own business."

"This is my business. I'm shop steward. I worked very hard after what was taken from me. So yeah, I still got a fucking problem."

"I'm here for the week. You keep your tweaked-out goons away from me and we'll never share company again."

"Only a week?" asked Henry. "That all it takes to end our careers?"

Alvin narrowed his eyes then he turned and walked away.

The room was silent as he crossed back to his seat.

Tosh looked terrified.

Yumi wore a smirk. "Everything clear now?" she said.

"Crystal," said Alvin.

Alvin found his mind wandering to his multitool as he followed the floating nav arrow back down to Beckman's office. He always carried it on his hip at a job site. It was a little compact all-in-one that had saved his ass on more than one occasion. He never knew what type of screw bit he might require or what ties he might have to cut through to prep equipment. Now he was thinking of it as a weapon. He knew he could expect more trouble.

He arrived at Beckman's door and saw him inside through a

small glass slit in the door. He was talking to one of his staff. Alvin had seen her earlier. She had been the one taking notes. He knocked on the door and Beckman looked up and motioned for him to enter.

"Ready to go?" asked Beckman.

"Ready as I'll ever be."

"Good. This is Dr. Choi."

"Hello."

"She is going to perform an evaluation before you depart. It's standard procedure," said Beckman.

"Don't you monitor my implants?" said Alvin.

"Yes, your biometrics are reporting just fine, Alvin. This is a psychological exam."

She must have noticed my panic attacks.

"I'm under some stress," he said.

"Yes, you've had quite a few spikes in your heart rate. Nothing dangerous, but something that indicates some uneasiness."

"This is all very new. I'm an Earth technician. I've never been off-planet before."

"I understand. It can be an overwhelming experience. You've been away for six months now. There can be all sorts of deleterious effects. Are you having any hallucinations? Hearing any voices?"

"No. If anything is bothering me, it's a lack of clarity from my superiors."

"We all deal with that problem." She smiled at Beckman and he curled his lip in annoyance. "In all seriousness, anxiety can be a serious concern out here. Whether from lack of sunlight, low gravity, cosmic rays. Everyone experiences it to some degree."

Beckman leaned back in his chair, quiet and studious.

"I'm just away from home on a business trip and I want to finish up."

"Of course, Alvin, but I want you to be aware of the dangers."

"Duly noted," he said.

She nodded at Beckman and stood up.

"Looks like you're good to fly, Alvin," said Beckman. "Thank you, Alice."

She nodded and shook Alvin's hand. "Remember, if you need any more medication, please let me know. We want to be out in front of these things."

"Any more?" he asked.

"Yes, I understand you had your first meal this morning. The meds should begin working by this evening," she said.

He nodded slowly and she left the room. Beckman pressed a button on his desk and the door closed behind her.

Alvin cocked his head as he waited for him to comment.

"Yes, the food is mixed with anti-anxiety and anti-aggression sedatives. It's a necessary precaution," said Beckman.

"I don't think it's working."

"Certainly not on you—yet," said Beckman. "Since we received word of your arrival, my miners have been going batty. I've read your history and now I've seen your behavior up close. You're a loose cannon."

"Your men are wackos."

"Why Alteris hired you I don't know, but I don't question my orders. I want you up on Dactyl. Get your job done and get out of here. I have worked very hard to create an incident-free base. I am not going to lose my pension because of some petty video game squabble."

"Then keep Carroll Henry and his goons away from me."

"He's not on Dactyl. You leave in an hour. Toshiro will train you on the procedure."

"You know, Beckman, they think I'm putting in automation. Maybe your job goes, too."

"From your mouth to God's ears, Mr. Baylor. I've been here for six years. Have a safe trip."

Alvin's mouth scrunched up and he walked out.

THIRTY-ONE

Alvin and Tosh grappled with the railings as they moved through the hangar bay. A single lane led to the row of rock hoppers that circled the conical bay. They came to an egg-shaped pod that was moored to the deck. The hopper's cable-like tendrils held it in place by gripping a metal cross affixed to the floor. The number fifteen was stenciled on the ground.

"All right, this is your rock hopper. The autopilot will take you down into Acmon crater on Dactyl and back again. You'll need to operate the tentacles to anchor to the surface. That little moon isn't going to hold you down. So long as you're out there you'll need to use your suit thrusters or risk bounding away. There's a small structure in that valley. There you should find your—well, you should find whoever is waiting for you," said Tosh.

"I saw a red light coming from a crater when we flew in," said Alvin.

"That's Acmon. The red light is from some sort of interference generator. No radio signals can penetrate. Buzz has tried scoping it out with optical telescopes. That's how we know about the structure. He said there was a delivery last Christmas. Whoever's there hasn't been seen since they arrived."

"So, in other words, another warm welcome?"

Tosh nodded. "You run the VR trainer?"

"You know I calibrate the synaptics on these things?" said Alvin.

"Yeah, but you don't fly 'em. Take a look at it when you can in case the autopilot fails. Let's get you onboard. Beckman wants you up there."

Tosh pulled a lever popping open the rear hatch of the egg-shaped cockpit. Alvin hopped up off the ground and glided inside. The space was tight. He pulled the sphere from the pouch on his belt, then leapfrogged over the back-to-back chair and into the front seat. He tucked the sphere into an alcove below the seat. His fingers still tingled for a moment after he let go.

"Thanks," he said.

"No problem," said Tosh.

"No, really. I appreciate you trusting me."

"Got no reason not to. Good luck, Alvin. When you finish up, I'll have a treat for you."

"Oh?"

"Yeah, Sioux has been growing something strong for me in the hydro farm and it's ready for harvest."

"I'm sure I'll need it after a day's work. See you later," said Alvin.

Tosh pushed off the hopper's frame and floated out into the docking bay with a wave. Alvin pressed a button that closed the hatch and sealed the compartment. He leaned back into the seat and the craft came to life.

As the engines fired, he received an alert in his Opti-Comp. It was a message from Katy. He peeped it. Diagnostic data crawled across his helmet's display as the Opti-Comp downloaded a voice message.

Damn, the connection is slow out here!

He initiated the autopilot and felt the ship drift upward as it let go of the anchor point. It performed a slow slide around the conical room and then glided up to the door at the surface of the asteroid.

Red lights flashed about the area and a siren blared inside the bay. Alvin watched as a couple of floating deck hands waved him through. The giant door split down the middle and retreated into the walls, revealing a second door beyond. The craft floated in as the first door resealed. When it shut again, the outer door opened. He was whisked into space in an instant.

He spun in circles for a few moments until he saw a small spherical moon oriented dead center in his viewscreen. The spin disoriented him, but the sensation passed quickly. He felt surprisingly comfortable. He trusted the hopper.

Alvin watched the miles fall away on his display. He'd be there in only a minute, for a change.

Time for the in-flight show.

He peeped Play on the message. Katy's voice sounded in his ear.

"Hi, Alvin! I miss you! I'm sorry for not calling sooner, but I got written up at work. That jerk Zuck—"

Then it went dead.

What the hell? What did Zuck do?

"Signal Lost—Radio Interference," flashed across his Opti-Comp. Beyond the floating message, Acmon crater and the glowing red light were fast approaching. The gray ground zoomed up close, then the ship pivoted, bringing the black horizon into view.

Fuck. I'm here.

The rock hopper guided itself over the pockmarked gray surface. Up ahead Alvin could see the thin beam of red light splitting the horizon. As he got closer, he saw the crater clearly. Red light emanated from a concave dish that focused out into space. Off to the end of the valley was a dome embedded into the ground. It was twenty feet in diameter, about the size of the retirement bubbles in Musk City.

That thing's only a little bigger than my apartment. Who's in there?

The hopper came within two hundred feet of the dome and slowed to a halt. The display read "Autopilot Disengaged."

"Not exactly curb service," he grumbled.

He took over via synaptic control and moved the rock hopper closer. There was a single mooring anchor in front of the dome. Alvin grasped hold with the tendrils to anchor the pod.

He double-checked his helmet and glove seals and depressurized the cabin. The faint echo of his movements was gone, replaced with a stillness. He opened the hatch and hopped out.

He got four feet above the hopper before he realized he wasn't heading down. A surge of adrenaline hit him and he fired his thrusters to push back down to the ground.

He grabbed on to a railing bolted below and slid along the metal bars all the way to the dome.

When he got to the door, it was locked.

"I'm guessing the password isn't 'swordfish,'" he muttered. "Where's the doorbell?"

The door opened.

I must be expected. Thank god.

He bounded inside the small airlock and quickly bounced off the interior door.

He saw the tethering straps at his waist start to ripple as air filled the chamber. The inner door opened and Alvin gave a tiny push off to land gracefully inside.

He looked around and saw but could not hear a man talking to him from the corner of the room. Alvin removed his helmet.

"Shoes, take them off," said a mildly accented voice.

Behind an old quantum computer console piled high with esoteric crap and node parts, a man rose. He was tall and disheveled-looking. He stepped around the console making ripping sounds, and Alvin noticed his grip booties that stuck to the floor.

The man swiped a mane of black hair from both sides of his bearded face. He was olive skinned with dark eyes that were mad with intensity.

Alvin gasped. It was the dead man from the *Zzyzx*.

Mohammed Rinsler!

"You'll ruin the grip," said the man, pointing to the carpeted floor.

"Who are you?" said Alvin.

"Did you bring it?"

"Yes, I brought it. Who are you?"

"Where is it?" asked the man.

"The last guy who had it died. Why do you look like him?"

"By design. Where is it?"

"Who was the dead guy?"

The black-haired man sighed in irritation. "He was my brother, Abraham. Where is it?"

"It's outside. I'll go get it."

Alvin lowered his helmet and hopped back into the airlock to go through the dance once more.

This is one charming dead guy.

He'd pegged Mohammed Rinsler as the brains behind the project on *The Hope*. He was proud of that bit of detective work, but the rest was still a mystery.

Alvin got back to the hopper and retrieved the dark ball from inside. He made up his mind that he would get answers. He held the sphere in his grip and felt the familiar tingling as he looked out across the gray plain and up at the pinpricked black sky.

I'll get answers or I'll leave.

Alvin returned inside and Rinsler stepped forward to take the sphere from his hand.

Alvin removed his helmet and looked up at the taller man. His dark eyes were entranced. A wide gap-toothed smile creased his bearded face as he caressed the sphere like a baby and talked to it in hushed tones.

He's a wacko. "Who killed your brother?"

"Shoes," said the man.

Alvin shook his head. "No. What is going on?"

"Washington thinks it's a weapon," said Rinsler. "Alteris thinks it's good for the mining business. They're in a little squabble over it."

"A squabble that left a ship full of dead men, including your brother. What does it do?"

"Shoes." The man walked slowly back to his desk.

Alvin shook his head then angrily removed his boots and gloves. Rinsler tossed him a pair of grip socks.

Alvin pulled them from the sealed package, tugged them on, and walked slowly over to the corner. The socks made a ripping sound with each step. He felt like he was stuck to something rather than standing on it. When he got up close to the quantum computer, he could finally see over the pile of equipment. Sitting in front of the scientist were two black spheres.

"There are two of them," said Alvin.

Rinsler crinkled his nose. "Of course."

"Are they the same?" said Alvin.

The scientist looked at him blankly. "Identical, they work together."

"Is there a manual? I've never seen anything like them before."

"There is no manual. There are no records at all. These are the first of their kind." He went back to prodding at the newly delivered sphere.

"So what do you need me to do, then?" said Alvin.

"You already did it," said Rinsler.

"That's it? I just deliver it to you?"

Rinsler nodded.

"Do you know what I sacrificed to get here?"

The scientist arched an eyebrow. "From the barrios of Earth

to the luxury of *The Hope* to the moon of an asteroid. Yes, I know. I requested you."

"Requested me? Why?" said Alvin.

"Quantum analysis," said Rinsler. "I figured you for a cyber-jock yahoo, but I always give the data the benefit of the doubt."

Alvin's eyebrow arched. "What?"

Rinsler touched the spheres lightly with his fingertips. "Surely you know of my quantum intelligence, the QI?"

"Yes, your last job for the United States. A quantum computer so advanced it was supposed to be conscious. It was designed to advise us, but its advice caused a revolution and led to laws outlawing AI. It was a failure."

"No, it was a success. Humanity is the failure. My creation is alive and well," said Rinsler. "The experiment is still running."

"What experiment?"

"One that plots possibilities and determines the most desirable outcomes. It saw you—a variable that could only be encountered if we destroyed the United States," said Rinsler. "You're a hypothesis."

Alvin sat down. His annoyance dulled by confusion.

"What?" he said. "You intended to cause civil war? Why? What is that thing I brought here?"

"A transmitter to pair with a receiver," said Rinsler. "They will allow human minds to manipulate matter at the quantum level."

He looked proud.

"Is that what Alteris is paying for? To have you automate their mining?" said Alvin.

"Not just the mining, but the transportation."

"So you've faked your death for money?"

"Science is expensive," said Rinsler. "The U.S. struggles financially and lacks the vision for this experiment. I used Alteris to get here. I need to perform my tests in isolation."

Alvin slumped back against the wall. "You trashed a country for an experiment? That doesn't make any fucking sense."

"Your understanding is irrelevant," said Rinsler. "You are here because variables suggested you. That is why I have accepted you touching my sphere!"

He showed a flash of anger then went back to cooing at the orbs like they were babies.

I need to leave before I punch him. "If that's it, then, I'll be off."

Rinsler nodded at him.

Alvin pulled off the booties and put his boots on. The scientist went back to his work.

Neither man spoke for as long as it took Alvin to seal his space suit.

As the airlock door closed, Alvin said, "Thanks for the vacation. Have fun with your balls."

Rinsler couldn't hear him.

THIRTY-TWO

Alvin's rock hopper lifted off the small moon. He felt safer now that he had dropped off Rinsler's invention. Whoever was seeking to steal or sabotage it could take it from Dactyl.

Fuck that old kook! I'm done with this job.

As soon as he left the surface, the radio interference cleared and he went to his inbox to queue the voice message from Katy.

"Hi Alvin! I miss you! I'm sorry for not calling sooner, but I got written up at work. That jerk Zuck has caused me so much trouble. He's trying to get me kicked off the ship. He's angry about the whole avatar thing. I'm sure you have plenty to worry about. I'll be okay. I've dealt with worse. Let me know when you're coming back. We're in port for another week. I love you, Al."

Alvin arrived in the docking bay as the message finished. He kicked the wall of the hopper in anger.

Zuck had better not bother her again.

He looked out the hopper viewport and saw Tosh waving at him. He was in no mood to talk. Alteris had sent his ass halfway across the solar system with no instructions so they could hide their theft of Washington's property. Men had died for their profit. And now his girl was caught up in his wake. He reminded himself that it was all temporary.

One week. Keep it together for one week.

He recorded a message to Meyer. "Package delivered," then he exited out the rear hatch. Toshiro was there to meet him.

"So are we all losing our jobs?" asked Tosh.

"Ha."

"Well, c'mon. What did you learn?"

Alvin shook his head. "Not much."

"Who's up there?" said Tosh.

"A hermit. Didn't tell me anything about his plans," said Alvin.

"What?"

Alvin nodded.

"That's crazy. So you're just a messenger boy," said Tosh.

"Seems that way. I have no further orders. Just a week to survive Carroll Henry."

"You started that shit in the mess hall," said Tosh.

"He started it a long time ago."

"You need to chill out. Let's get over to hydroponics." Tosh grinned.

They went down to the lower depths of the base and rounded a turn to a wall of glass. On one side, a rock face with glistening mineral deposits. Beyond the glass—a paradise. The garden was overstuffed with green life and exotic flowers.

Toshiro swiped his wrist at the transparent door and they entered. An empty console sat before them; off to their right, the cluttered green blocked much of the view. Alvin couldn't see how far back the garden went. He could smell flowers and wetness and . . . *Earth*.

The air seemed fresh and he took a deep breath of it. His shoulders relaxed and the tension in his chest eased.

"Hey Sioux!" called Tosh. He turned back to Alvin. "She's probably meditating by the stream."

"Stream?"

Tosh nodded.

"Be with you in a sec," came a female voice from inside the jungle of greenery.

Alvin looked around at the hydroponics on the walls. There were plants everywhere. A variety of blooming flowers added flourishes of color. The whole astonished him. He stepped closer to a wall of orange flowers and saw bees. He backed away in a hurry. "Whoa!"

Haven't seen one of those since I was a kid.

A short-haired, pretty woman with lustrous brown skin walked out from the back.

"They won't harm you." She stopped right in front of him. "Hello."

"Sioux Ogwale, this is Alvin Baylor," said Tosh.

"I've heard of the man." She smiled brightly. "How do you do?"

"I've been better. You?"

"Each day is a gift. I finally have the cherry blossoms blooming."

She was untarnished by the cynicism that permeated the rest of the facility.

"That a plant?" said Alvin.

She nodded. "A tree with beautiful pink flowers. You should see them."

"It's difficult to make them bloom?" he asked.

She gave him a shrug. "A little genetic engineering and some love. I have faith they will last through April this time."

"I'm only here for the week," said Alvin.

"All right, enough chitchat," said Tosh. "How'd the bud turn out?"

"You'll have to tell me. I don't use the stuff."

Sioux reached into the front desk and grabbed a small package.

"I will report back ASAP," said Tosh.

She held the package out to him, and when Tosh grabbed at it, she pulled her hand back. "This does not leave this circle —got it?"

"Absolutely," he said.

Alvin looked at Sioux. "You taking a real risk?"

"It's an infraction, but you understand how history can follow a person," she said.

She face-scanned me.

"I do," said Alvin.

She handed the package to Tosh.

"Thanks, Sioux. C'mon, Alvin, let's go see Buzz."

"Nice to meet you, Alvin," Sioux said.

Alvin waved. They exited up the sloping corridor. Tosh led with purpose. Alvin trailed behind in the wake of his friend's enthusiasm. He had Katy on his mind.

By bedtime Alvin was safely ensconced in his room. He had rushed out of the hangout with Tosh and friends to ensure that he would not be among the hostile crowd settling down for sleep shift. He grew drowsy and replayed the audio from Katy again.

Their private little world on *The Hope* felt like a dream. Earth felt like a dream now, too. He was so far away from everything he knew. The message finished and he found himself looping it again.

God, I miss you.

As her voice looped, he had an odd feeling, as though she wasn't being entirely truthful with him.

Has she already been fired?

Had he had unwittingly ruined her career?

He recorded a message to her. "Katy, be honest with me. What's happened?" He had no idea what he could do if she were in trouble, but he needed her to be safe.

She'll get back to me soon.

He drifted off to sleep with her picture floating ahead of him in space.

In the morning he awoke groggier than usual. He rubbed his eyes and enjoyed the stillness in his mind. He yawned and stretched out like a cat on the bed. His stomach rumbled and his thoughts turned to breakfast and the food printers.

He woke up his Opti-Comp. Katy was staring back at him.

So beautiful.

Below her picture an anonymous message read, "Come back. Today, I will answer questions."

Rinsler? Interesting. Beats waiting around for trouble from Henry.

First he'd get breakfast, then some answers from the suddenly forthcoming scientist.

Maybe I can get Buzz to let me use his printer.

Alvin put on his space suit and shuffled outside the room with his helmet under his arm. There was nobody in the crew quarters to give him the evil eye. He walked up the hallway until he reached the surveyor's bay.

Buzz answered the door. "You again?"

"Can I eat from your printer? I'm not in agreement with the silent doping."

"Come inside before someone murders you for that fancy suit," said Buzz.

"Thank you."

"You know I have special approval for this printer," said Buzz. "I'm not sure if Corporate would approve."

"I'm sure they wouldn't. You worried about getting in trouble?"

"Well, yeah." Buzz grasped the back of his seat. He looked tense.

"Why do you have it, then?" Alvin walked back toward the food printer.

"I'm not comfortable explaining that," said Buzz. "Why are you so put off by medication?"

"I'm a cyber-athlete. I was never doped as a kid," said Alvin.

"Oh, well, aren't you special?" He eased up. "I take other medications. I can't risk interactions."

"You want me to wipe the preparation logs?" said Alvin. He toggled through the front display panel on the printer looking for the administration controls.

"Gee, I hadn't thought of that," said Buzz. "The settings are locked."

Alvin pulled the multitool from his belt and selected a Torx head. "There's a jumper inside to disable the lock." He unscrewed the front panel and removed a tiny piece of plastic from two metal pins. "There will be no record."

"All right, then," said Buzz. "You just want to avoid the mess hall, don't you?"

"That's part of it."

"I heard about what you did."

Alvin frowned, then replaced the front panel. "I'll be out of here at the end of the week. I'm keeping a low profile until then."

"It would have been best to start with a low profile."

"That was my last time sticking out."

"Good luck with that. Now, print me some strawberry pancakes. I have to get something out of this deal."

Alvin laughed. "So, how'd you get here? You don't seem like a 'roider."

"I enjoy analyzing mineral compositions and spectrographs and I don't like people."

"I guess you're in the right place, then."

"So why are you here, Alvin? You don't act like one of the engineers." Buzz paused. "Are you really an engineer?"

"That's what they pay me for. I used to have other aspirations."

"Yes—readily available knowledge online. But why did they send you? How does a synaptics engineer fit into the corpo's plans?"

"They don't care what kind of engineer I am. We're all temp workers in their grand plans."

"Ha! I knew it," said Buzz. His blond hair fluttered.

"That's not an admission of anything, Buzz."

"Everyone knows it's automaton. Even Beckman's running scared."

"Beckman wants to go home. The ones to watch are the guys with nothing. The ones who signed everything away on a contract."

"I suppose you have better prospects as Zeus, the great cyber-athlete?"

"Let's have a nice conversation. I don't want to ruin my breakfast," said Alvin.

"As you wish. Tosh tells me you have a vast knowledge of alcohol."

"I do. You looking for breakfast cocktail tips?"

"No. I'm just making nice conversation."

"Terrific," said Alvin.

THIRTY-THREE

Alvin entered Rinsler's habitat and removed his helmet. He heard rustling from behind the computer console. The scientist sprang up with excitement.

"Good, you're here." Shrink-wrap crinkled in Rinsler's hands. He tossed a pair of grip socks and Alvin caught them.

"So what changed?" said Alvin.

"I had a look at your scans, very impressive," said Rinsler. "More so than I had anticipated. I can definitely use you."

Alvin put on the socks. "What scans?"

"Your synaptic scans. When you unlocked my sphere, it made a map of your brain. The microtubules in your neurons are unusually active."

"Huh?"

Rinsler pointed to a floating video display above his desk.

Alvin took long strides across the carpet to the console. His socks made a ripping sound with each step. A three-dimensional model of his brain was onscreen.

The scientist zoomed into the cells until they began squirming, then he pointed at the image.

"Microtubules," he said.

"What the hell is a microtubule?"

"A cylindrical protein lattice found inside neurons. They regulate synaptic communication and perform quantum calculations."

"I liked you better when you didn't explain yourself."

Rinsler tapped his fingers in irritation.

"I'm kidding," Alvin said.

"They are our connection to the great consciousness," Rinsler said, sounding indignant.

This guy's been alone too long.

"The great consciousness, is that like God?" said Alvin.

Rinsler bobbled his head side to side in a sign of equivocation. "Consciousness is intrinsic to the universe. Our share of it is a function of the microtubules in the brain. Your microtubules experience wave function collapse at a rate I've never seen before."

Alvin stared blankly. "I don't understand."

"At the quantum scale, down at the very smallest bits of matter, the universe is indeterminate. It behaves like a wave until a collapse of possibilities causes the particles to take position. When the brain experiences this collapse, it becomes a conscious observation. Your brain does this at an unusual tempo. It is why you were such an impressive cyber-athlete. In effect, you were experiencing the state of the game-world before your opponents could. This talent will translate to greater affect when you utilize my spheres."

"Which do what, exactly?"

"Magnify this property in our brains in order to hack space-time and reconfigure matter."

"That sounds intense. So what do you need me to do?"

"There's prep work out at the communications dish. I need you to boost the signal. Some spectrums are leaking through the shield. We need full coverage."

"You do realize I'm not that kind of engineer?"

"It's software," said Rinsler. "I have a manual for you. Isn't that all you require?"

"Sure, but after all that talk about my super brain, you just want me to tweak software? Why don't you send the drone?" Alvin pointed to a rover in the corner with a tarp over it.

"No. Drones will not function on Dactyl. No networked communications of any kind. That reminds me, do you have an Opti-Comp?"

Alvin look at him curiously. *Doesn't everyone?*

"Yeah," he said.

"I need you to turn it off and keep it off. Did you record the sphere on your way here?"

"I might have," he said.

"Damn it," said the scientist. "I'll have to purge any dangerous videos before you reconnect to the network on Ida."

"Why are you so worried about the network?" asked Alvin.

"There are eyes everywhere, Mr. Baylor. My devices are unknown to any system."

"How long is that gonna last?" said Alvin. "You'll need to hit Corporate development benchmarks. And besides, the great consciousness must know about it."

He waited for a reply with a smirk.

Rinsler tapped his fingertips on the table again.

"I got it," said Alvin. "No recordings."

"Good. Begin by boosting the power outside. We need to shield this moon from FTL communications monitoring."

Rinsler handed him a small data card. "Don't let me delay you further, Mr. Baylor. I know you work best without supervision."

The scientist sat down again behind his mess and returned to studying the display.

Always a charmer.

"I guess I'll just head outside, then," said Alvin. He began putting his boots and gloves back on. "When's lunch time?"

"Whenever you're hungry. I have a printer here. You know they dose the food on Ida?" said Rinsler.

"You don't say?" Alvin lowered his visor.

"I do say, and after we eat I can operate on your brain," said Rinsler.

Alvin couldn't make out the words from behind his lowered face guard.

Did he just say he would operate on my brain? Naw.

Several hours later, Alvin clenched a metal spork in his hand and took a stab at his shrimp with lobster sauce. He would have printed chopsticks as well, but his hands were too tired to use them. The software tweaks to the communications shield required getting at the control panel. That had been surprisingly difficult in the low gravity. He'd had trouble keeping his body from spinning while unscrewing it with his multitool. The suit's jets were the only thing that made the work possible. Overall, the task seemed like busy work.

Rinsler sat across from him drinking green paste with a straw. He hardly spoke and made strange facial tics. Alvin felt like he was sharing space with one of the crazies back at the Budapest bar.

"How is that?" he asked.

"It's sustaining," said Rinsler. "How is your Chinese preparation?"

"The consistency is right, but the peas taste like shrimp. That's not such a bad thing."

"Mmm. I do not possess your expansive palate," said Rinsler.

"You keep it to the nutrients."

"Yes. I'm a man of simple tastes. It goes well enough with my newspaper." Rinsler grabbed at the table and lifted his arms into the air as though he were reading an old-fashioned newspaper. He looked proud.

Alvin was rattled by the thought that they both enjoyed the paper.

"Have you been keeping current?" said Rinsler.

"Not out here."

"You don't get name alerts for yourself?"

"No. I stopped those after my gaming career."

"I thought you relished fame. Here." Rinsler's face went serious as he handed over the invisible paper. "You should see this."

Alvin woke his Opti-Comp. "How did you get a signal?" he asked.

"I downloaded it while you had the shield offline," said Rinsler. "This edition is from yesterday."

A newspaper appeared in Alvin's hand. He took hold of it and straightened out the virtual page. One of the headlines read "Alvin 'Zeus' Baylor a Union Buster for Alteris Asteroid?" by Anton Vance.

Alvin hammered the tabletop. His food wobbled in the low gravity and lifted off his plate.

"This makes two articles about your escapades," said Rinsler.

Alvin took a deep breath and exhaled slowly.

Fucking Vance. What will Alteris do to me now?

"I have to head back to Ida," said Alvin. "That article is going to piss off Meyer."

"We must stay on schedule," said Rinsler.

"What else do you need from me today?" said Alvin.

Rinsler sat up straight. He looked defiant. "I need to put you out. Testing starts tomorrow," he said.

"Put me out?"

"Yes, I have the proper chemicals," said Rinsler.

"You mean anesthesia?"

Rinsler nodded. "I need to remove the bandwidth regulation from your synaptic implants and I need you unconscious to do it."

"Why?"

"Otherwise the feedback from my spheres will short your implants and kill you."

That explains the headaches. How dangerous is this thing?

"The law locked my implants with quantum encryption," he said.

"Pfft. I have my own quantum programmer," said Rinsler. "I can decrypt anything."

I'd be able to overclock again.

"Have you done this before?" said Alvin.

"Of course not, I don't usually work with criminals."

Alvin scowled at him. "Neither do I."

Rinsler scowled back.

"I only need to break the skin for a reprogram." He pointed to his computer console. "Just lie down on top of that. I'll get the syringe."

Alvin awoke on top of Rinsler's desk. He shifted his weight and almost fell off. He gripped the edge in the low gravity and kept himself from toppling over. A soft buzzing filled his head.

"Where am I?"

"Ah, good. You're conscious," said Rinsler.

Fuck ... I forgot ... Rinsler ... overclocking.

"Did it work?" said Alvin.

"Yes. I was able to reset your implants. There will be no more limitation on your synaptic performance."

"How long have I been out?"

"Four hours. It's time for you to head back."

Alvin slid off the table to his feet. He was loopy. The low gravity kept him upright despite his sloppy steps. He bounced over to his usual bench seat and grabbed at his boots and missed them.

"Maybe I should stay here for a bit."

"Impossible, there's no room. I need my privacy," said Rinsler.

Alvin gave a groggy nod.

Dick. Thank god for autopilot.

He finished sealing his suit and entered the airlock. "See you tomorrow," he said then lowered his face guard.

Rinsler nodded.

Alvin sat inside the airlock for a few minutes while he recovered. Outside, the shock of black sky woke him like a cold shower. He glided toward his hopper with ease. The synaptic controls were so sensitive he hardly had to think at all.

I think this is smoother.

A few minutes later, he lifted off Dactyl and escaped Rinsler's interference shield. His Opti-Comp was inundated with messages. At the top was one from Meyer. He peeped it.

"Mr. Baylor, troubling news. It seems Anton Vance has written another article about you. I had thought this bit of business was behind us. We can't have our competitors anticipating our plans. I will be in touch with my personal friend, Chan Xi-Michaels, to ensure we eliminate further publicity. Once again, I must remind you that you had no authority to participate in that tournament or to romance hookers. I trust you will execute discreetly from here on out."

Bitch. I'll be able to play again when I get back. I'm a free man.

The next message was a vid from Katy. She appeared onscreen, with a swollen nose and a bruise under her eye.

"What the hell!" he shouted. He was completely awake now.

"Hi, Al. You guessed it. I got fired off *The Hope*. Zuck's complaints and that reporter's questions were too much for Xi-Michaels. His guys roughed me up a little. I'm in the lobby at Armstrong Station. I can't afford a room here. You're only gone a week, right? Maybe you can take me home on your company's ship? I'm gonna try to find a place to sleep. I'm sorry. I love you."

She ended the message crying.

"Goddamn it, Meyer, you had them beat her!"

The hopper returned to the docking bay. He exited angrily and found Tosh waiting for him.

"I got this now," said Alvin. "You don't need to see me in and out."

"I'm not here for that," said Tosh. "Stay out of sight. I heard Henry's guys talking. They're on edge."

So am I. "So what?"

"They saw the red laser flickering on Dactyl. I think they're gonna—listen, I heard them, they plan to force answers out of you," Tosh said. "I don't want you to get your brains beat in. Stay in your room. Good luck."

Alvin floated in place while he watched Tosh hurry out of the equipment bay.

I guess he doesn't want to be seen with me.

He followed the railing out of the bay and back into artificial gravity. A few miners walked past and scanned him head to toe looking for evidence of his work. He scowled at them.

I can't leave Katy alone.

He entered the crew quarters and saw Carroll Henry and his goons watching from their bunks across the room. The trio began walking toward the ramp. He picked up his pace before they could intercept. As he came around the curve, he saw Beckman in front of his room.

"Baylor, I had an exchange with Meyer. I think we should discuss it inside."

"Okay," said Alvin.

He looked back over his shoulder as he opened the door. Henry and company were milling about on the ground level now. Beckman entered and Alvin shut the door.

"You're aware that those men mean to harm you?" said Beckman.

Alvin nodded.

"Are you also aware that your job is being discussed in the media?"

Goddamn it. He nodded again.

"Meyer is pissed. She wants you to complete your work quickly and quietly."

Fuck her.

"There's a problem," said Alvin.

Beckman's eyes widened.

"It's an issue with the communications shield—unexpected and not my forte. The laser is going to short. We're pushing too much power. *The Hope* has a staff of laser propulsion engineers. Thankfully, they're still in dock. I need you to retrieve an engineer named Katy Macintyre. She has the expertise we need."

"Why didn't Meyer notify me?" asked Beckman.

"She doesn't know the specifics of our work. We need to boost the array to hide our tests. We shouldn't delay this any further. You said yourself, the men are agitated by my presence."

"This base is under my purview and I say who gets on or off it," said Beckman.

"Would you like me to wait while you double-check with Meyer?" said Alvin.

Beckman had the aura of a sick man. He pointed his finger angrily. "Baylor, I believe that despite you being some kind of loose cannon that you want out of here as bad as I do."

Alvin nodded. "Absolutely. Best to keep quiet about this, what with the news stories piling up. I'll notify Macintyre directly."

"Toshiro will take the shuttle to go get this engineer. I want your team to hurry up and get out. For a year my men have been asking what's going on up there. What do I tell them?"

"Tell them they get to retire early," said Alvin.

Beckman sneered. He opened the door and looked outside. Henry's guys were still watching.

"I suggest you make sure it's clear before leaving again," he said and walked out.

Alvin locked the door and looked through the spy-hole. Beckman walked toward Henry and his men, giving them a stern look. Chickowski started shouting. Beckman argued with them then they skulked away into the shadows.

Alvin turned away from the door and sat on the edge of the bed. He grabbed his head. It buzzed between his fingers.

If they lay a hand on her, I'll kill 'em.

He began a message.

"Katy, I'm sending the company shuttle for you. Tell the Japanese guy in red you're with me. Pretend you're one of *The Hope*'s laser propulsion engineers. We're gonna be all right. Rinsler is here and he has a quantum decryptor. He unlocked my implants. I can overclock again. I'll have to play nonsanctioned, but I can make us plenty of money with that Vance guy hyping me. I love you and I'll get us home. See you soon."

Three days to go.

THIRTY-FOUR

Alvin awoke the next day feeling refreshed. He had a new sense of optimism despite the locals' ire about him and Meyer's critique of his sense of duty. Whatever dangers or discomforts surrounded him would vanish in a few short days. Rinsler's removal of his synaptic limiters gave him a sense of hope for the future—a future with Katy.

Tosh would have reached her by now; by tonight they would be reunited. When she arrived at the colony, they'd have to stay low-key. So long as Rinsler didn't find out, he could manage the lie. Beckman would require some ego stroking, but that would be easy. The hard part would be getting her back on *The Hope* for the trip home.

Maybe I can entice Xi-Michaels with some more competition. Zuck will want a rematch and I won't need any borrowed avatars.

He dressed then looked at the camera feeds that lined the way from his room to the cargo bay. The path was clear. He ran out the door, and minutes later his hopper whisked him away to Dactyl.

Upon entering Rinsler's dome, he was greeted with a hearty hello that shocked him.

"Is everything okay?" he asked.

"Yes, today we test," said Rinsler. "First, I need you to place one of the spheres outside near the shield generator. There's a pedestal to hold it."

He handed Alvin a sphere, his fingers lingering on it.

"I saw the pedestal yesterday," said Alvin. "I got it."

Alvin tugged the little ball away from him.

Rinsler's eyes stayed on it as he spoke. "When you get back, we can travel to the test site with the other sphere. We'll be transmitting from the Celmis crater."

"Transmitting what?"

"Matter," said Rinsler.

It sounded fantastical—transferring matter from one tiny ball to another.

The 'roiders are on the right track. Maybe this is the end of their careers.

"I'll be right back," said Alvin.

Alvin continued to ponder the technology as he trudged outside.

Near the shield generator, he found the pedestal. He placed the little ball in a curved groove and flew back to the cabin to find Rinsler suited up for the vacuum. The scientist was dressed in a battered white space suit. The exterior was plain; devoid of the styling that Alvin sported.

"Finally getting you outside?"

Rinsler's black beard was stuffed into the lower half of his helmet and it brought attention to the whites of his eyes. He looked terrified. "I don't like it out there. I don't mind saying it." He looked down at his feet.

"You'll be fine. We'll take the hopper. You can even take your helmet off if you want," said Alvin.

"No. We can't take the hopper. It'll see us. See the sphere."

"What will?"

"There are cameras. Did your hopper cameras see it when you brought it to me?"

Here we go again. He's getting weird.

"No. I had it in a pack."

"What about on the way to the base? After you took it from my brother?"

"You're worried about this again? No, the ship had no power. No one's seen me with it but you."

Rinsler was breathing heavily.

"Are you sure you're ready to go outside?" said Alvin.

"No one?" said Rinsler.

"Well, the Alteris guys who went onboard with me. They've seen it."

"Oh my god, they could have been recording!"

"If it's a concern, why don't you just request to have their recordings wiped?"

"Are you crazy? That would create database cross-references! The metadata would grow!"

Alvin grabbed Rinsler's shoulders and looked up at him. "What do you want to do, Mohammed?"

"Mo," said Rinsler. "I prefer Mo. We can't take the hopper. You're good with that suit. You tow me. And do not let me drift off into space!"

"I hadn't planned on it. Let's go, Mo."

He gave a little laugh at the way the words rhymed and directed Rinsler to the airlock. Then he tethered himself to Rinsler as Toshiro had done days previous and waited for the exterior doors to open.

I'm going to enjoy this.

The moon was hardly a mile across in any direction. Not far at all, but there was no trail to the other crater, no embedded posts for handholding. They would have to fly there.

"I guess we get to see how fast this suit goes," said Alvin.

He smiled behind his visor and jumped off the ground. He thought himself up and his jets fired.

My synaptic control is so much smoother.

He heard Rinsler gasp as they were whisked off the platform. They moved over the pulverized gray surface at speed.

"So, Mo—what killed your brother?"

"Now is not the time," squeaked Rinsler.

"Now is definitely the time," said Alvin. "For the next several minutes, I'm in charge of the in-flight entertainment."

Alvin dove downward until Rinsler's feet almost touched the surface.

"Okay. Okay. I'm not sure exactly, but I have a suspicion," he said.

"I need clarity, Mo," said Alvin. They raced toward a small rise up ahead. "Wow, would you look at that hill. Hope we don't hit it."

"It's the U.S. government. A desperate last grasp at power," said Rinsler in a panicked tone.

Alvin pitched the thrusters upward.

"And they didn't take the sphere because it was locked? Better lift your legs, Mo."

Rinsler gave a frightened mumble. He tucked his knees to his chest and just cleared the hill.

"They didn't take it because they don't know how it works. They need me. They would not have killed me. My brother's death had to be an accident."

Alvin thought about Vance's article mentioning his trip to Ida. He thought about the suspicious feeling that he'd had out at the *Zzyzx*. The feeling that he was being watched. Someone was going to find them sooner or later.

They crested over the edge of the Celmis crater and Alvin slowed to a stop. Momentum sent Rinsler past him. The tether straightened and snapped the scientist to a halt.

Alvin bounded over to him and looked him in his copper face shield.

"What if they followed me?" he asked.

"Your paranoia is justified, Mr. Baylor. Now let's begin."

Rinsler knelt down and pulled the black sphere from its pack.

"Wait a minute. Don't you think our lives are important?" said Alvin.

"Certainly. We have been chosen for this purpose."

Chosen?

Alvin believed the man was a genius, but he was also bonkers.

Will I be gone before the arrival of government agents? Am I bringing Katy to a greater danger?

Rinsler handed over a drill and shovel and directed him to dig the barren ground.

He took to it as an act of distraction. The low gravity made it an easy job. A small boring drill cracked the dry regolith and then a hand shovel finished the hole. He could barely see over the top of the ditch he'd dug by the time Rinsler directed him to stop.

"Close enough for government work," said the scientist with an obnoxious laugh.

Alvin hopped out of the hole.

"I didn't tell you to get out," said Rinsler.

He handed the black ball over to Alvin. "Place it in the hole."

Alvin did as requested and looked at Rinsler for further instruction.

"Fill it."

"How are we gonna control it, then?" said Alvin.

"Remotely. I've rebuilt the synaptic receiver."

Alvin nodded and pushed the rocky matter back in the hole. He found it odd that Rinsler was comfortable with his precious invention being covered in dirt. After all that careful handling, he sounded delighted to see it buried.

Dusty debris hovered in the low gravity like smoke while Rinsler tapped a small pole with a lens into the ground.

"Is that a camera? I thought you said no cameras."

"The signal is contained within the shield," said Rinsler. "And I disassembled it to look for bugs. We head back now. Any questions I should prepare myself for?"

Jackass.

"Yeah, what did you mean when you said you were chosen?" said Alvin.

He fired his thrusters and rose a few inches until he was eye level with the taller man.

"It's hard to explain," said Rinsler.

Alvin rolled his eyes. "Try."

He fired his jets at top speed. The tether straightened and they were both off the ground in a moment.

Rinsler shrieked. It was small reward. Alvin wanted answers now, not sadism.

"I don't know if I can trust you," said the scientist.

"What the fuck are you talking about? I've risked my life for you."

"I have been chosen to save humanity."

"Save them from what?"

"Themselves."

"Did Alteris choose you for this? Because I'm pretty convinced they're in this for the profit."

"No, I was chosen by a higher authority."

"The great consciousness? Good grief. You're a major fucking pain," said Alvin as he sped them over the gray surface.

They did not speak again on the way back to the dome. Instead, Alvin silently counted the hours until Katy's arrival.

Upon returning to the dome, Rinsler declared it lunchtime. He printed up a chicken sandwich and parsed through data at his console. His synaptic cap was still stretched over his shaggy locks like a torn hairnet. It made him look like a vagrant.

I can't believe this guy doesn't have implants.

Alvin took a bite of his Camarones a La Diabla. He was disappointed that it was not very spicy, but found the consistency to be pleasing.

And he uses that ridiculous quantum mainframe. That old console is as big as an autocar. He's a weird sort of Luddite.

He finished up eating and asked, "Okay, Mo. When do we get to it? I'd like to see what the hell I came out here for."

"Yes, let's do it. I'm ready now."

Rinsler tapped his quantum console and turned on an extra touch-field display. It quivered above the desktop with visual distortion caused by the old books touching the emitters. He pushed the piles to the side and the image normalized.

"Come look. I have marked a selection for transmutation, but I thought you might enjoy trying it, as well."

Onscreen was an image of the hole where they'd buried the device. Another window showed its twin on the pedestal outside.

"Now, reach out and feel what surrounds the sphere."

Alvin stared at the screen.

"Uh-huh," he said. "How do I do that?"

"I added the frequency to your implants when you were out. Just remember where we buried it and go back there in your mind," said Rinsler.

Alvin stared at the filled hole on screen.

He closed his eyes and focused his thoughts on the device, and felt his head buzz. There was a sudden sensation of nothingness.

Where are my feet?

He panicked and toppled onto the console. "Whoa!"

"Sit and relax," said Rinsler. "Try again."

"I left my body," said Alvin.

Rinsler nodded.

Alvin shook his head for balance and sat down. Then he tried again.

At first came the buzzing and the nothingness, but as he concentrated longer, he felt the cold dirt of Dactyl envelop him. It was claustrophobic. He was somehow in the sphere—in the hole he had dug. He murmured mindlessly, stuck in the feeling of it.

"It's okay, you will be fine," said Rinsler. "Try to find the surface."

Alvin felt his perception expand, as though the orb were increasing in circumference. He felt the ground give way to outer space. A sense of relief came with it. He was free! Out of the earthy prison.

"Stop," said Rinsler. "That's too big. You'd swallow us whole."

Alvin's thoughts quickly left the black orb. He felt the nothingness and the buzzing again and got scared.

Where are my limbs?

Suddenly he felt his body and gasped. The buzzing retreated from his head and left an intense throbbing.

"This thing hurts."

"Yes, it can," said Rinsler.

"But that was amazing."

"Indeed. You're a very quick study, Mr. Baylor." Rinsler pressed a button on the console. "I marked out three of your measurements."

He pointed to another display. Three spherical shapes were drawn over a model of Dactyl with the device at their center. The last was larger than the entire moon.

"My measurements?"

"These lines represent your conscious awareness while connected with the sphere." Rinsler traced the floating image with his fingertip. "They are potential selections for transmutation and transmission. You started small, but then your sphere expanded too far. You would have swallowed all of Dactyl."

He switched the overlay to show a different selection. This one crested even with the ground. It looked to be about ten feet in diameter. "This was my sample. We'll use it instead."

"What exactly are we about to do?" said Alvin.

"Create a synthetic singularity and let it absorb our selection."

"Wait a minute—those things create black holes?"

"Momentary and precisely focused ones."

"Isn't that dangerous?"

"Yes. That's why we're all the way out here on this godforsaken asteroid."

"Got it. And then what?"

"The matter is transmuted. Then the singularity collapses and stores the new arrangement inside the sphere."

"How much can that little thing hold?"

"I've not been able to theorize a limit, but it can only take one sample before it needs to be emptied."

"Emptied?"

"Yes, or transmitted to the other sphere. Otherwise it would transmute the next selection in place. That could be chaos."

"This is crazy," said Alvin. "How long does it take?"

"It's instantaneous," Rinsler said with a smile.

"How far can it go?"

"As far apart as we place the spheres."

Alvin's brow furrowed. "No wonder everyone wants it! All of Alteris's transport and security deals could be scrapped. They wouldn't need the U.S. or the Chinese. They could rule energy and precious metals."

"Well, yes, if you want to think small," said Rinsler.

"Small? We could finally stop using Earth's natural resources, maybe even stabilize the climate."

"That planet is overpopulated and teeming with corruption and false morality," Rinsler said in annoyance.

Alvin didn't want to kill the conversation by pushing back. Rinsler was finally talking freely. "So how does it transmute the selection?"

"It encodes it into qubits at one per Planck length along the surface area of the singularity then reconfigures the subatomic arrangement."

"Yeah, layman's terms here, Mo."

"The universe is a hologram, Alvin. Any three-dimensional object can be represented by quantum bits encoded on a two-dimensional plane. The data can then be manipulated via conscious suggestion."

"A hologram? How could that be true?"

"The math is good," said Rinsler.

"This all sounds like magic."

"Ah, Clarke's third law." Rinsler smiled. "Any sufficiently advanced technology is indistinguishable from magic. Humans have been wrong about the shape of the Earth—the motion of the planets—why not the nature of reality? Are you ready?"

"Jesus Christ, Mo. I've been ready for six months."

Rinsler placed his hands flat on the console. "I will need to concentrate for the final step. Watch the screen."

Serenity fell across his face as he connected.

Alvin had done a lot of mental mating with diverse systems of late, but nothing to match the sphere. He reflected on the profound experience he had just had. Then he heard Rinsler inhale and exhale deeply. The image from the Celmis crater changed instantly.

The sphere became visible in the center of a five-foot spherical extraction. It fell slowly in the reduced gravity and came to rest at the bottom of a new baby crater.

Rinsler's eyes were still closed.

"Mo, you did it!" said Alvin. "At least I think you did."

Rinsler opened his eyes slowly. He directed Alvin's attention to the image of the reception sphere. The black ball was wrapped in purple, blue, cyan, and orange-red lines. The colors wavered like candle flames.

"We have hydrogen," said Rinsler. "See the spectrograph?"

"Wow. How do we get it out?" asked Alvin.

"For now, we'll just release it into the vacuum. I will communicate with the receiving sphere this time. Watch."

Onscreen, Alvin saw the colored lines disappear with a quick gust of gas.

"Was that it?"

"Yes, we didn't capture a very large sample."

"How did you convert it to hydrogen?"

"I thought of hydrogen."

"How the hell do you think of hydrogen? When I used it, it seemed to respond to my feelings and impressions."

"Yes, and symbolism. I thought of hydrogen's molecular structure," said Rinsler. "Of course, we must also know precisely what chemicals we're starting with, thus the selection analysis. This will be a long study, but we've done enough for today. I need you to collect the spheres." Rinsler placed a white case on top of the console and opened it. Inside were two molded impressions for the devices. "Bring them back here, then you can return to Ida."

"What comes next?" asked Alvin.

"Larger-scale selections and more-complex molecular structures. This was just the first test. Right now, I'm going to take a nap. I haven't slept well the last few years. I think I'm due."

Rinsler walked to the corner opposite his desk. He brushed aside some piles of junk to uncover a mattress. The scientist dropped onto it and secured a strap across his chest to hold himself down in the low gravity.

"All right, Mo. Have a good rest."

Alvin was relieved to finally understand this job, and with that relief his mind wandered back to Katy. She'd be at Ida soon. There was no reversing that impulsive decision. He felt strange. He might be screwing himself with Alteris yet he didn't much care. He could overclock again and he'd have his girl with him soon. That couldn't be bad, whether the universe was a phony hologram or not. He put his boots on and hurried out the airlock door to retrieve Rinsler's spheres.

THIRTY-FIVE

On the way back to Ida's dock, Alvin powered up his Opti-Comp to check for messages. He had one. A brief video clip of Katy from under the covers in his room. She winked seductively.

She's here!

A quick survey of the dock showed a couple of workers tending to returning survey drones. He exited the hopper silently and moved hand over hand along the guardrails. He'd gotten nimble in the low gravity and he believed he was quick enough to exit without being noticed. The exit doors opened and he was startled to see Tosh standing there.

"Hey man, we gotta talk," said Tosh. He looked pained.

Alvin removed his helmet. "Sure, what's up?"

"I had to use my creds to get her flight suit made," said Tosh.

"Thanks, I owe you company credits, then."

"Not my credits man, my credentials. Who is she? Is she a hooker?"

"No, she's a contractor. We needed a laser specialist in a pinch. She's an engineer on *The Hope*."

"Bullshit."

Alvin pursed his lips.

"Okay, listen, she's my girl. She got fired. She can't pay the private rate at Armstrong. It'll break her."

Tosh shook his head. "It's on you, then. I was following orders."

"I'll pay you back, don't worry."

"I won't, man. I don't know how you're getting her home, though."

Tosh flew into the dock and Alvin continued up the ramp toward the crew deck.

He was right. It would present a problem. One for which Alvin had no solution. However, it was better than leaving Katy alone at Armstrong. Who knew if government agents might show up there to question her. He'd just have to keep her out of sight. There were ways to deal with Beckman. Blame it on security. Tell the little middle manager it was a VR assist and that Katy wasn't cleared for Dactyl. Then he could keep her in his room for the next two days.

That's what I'll do.

He approached the last turn before his room, then paused. It was quiet. There was no one standing up on the balcony above. He felt the back of his neck tingle and made a wide turn. There was Chickowski in front of the door. He had a knife in his hand. He looked erratic.

"Time to talk or squeal, corpo," he yelled.

"What is there to talk about?" said Alvin.

He gripped his helmet tightly, preparing to deflect the knife.

Then his door slid open.

Chickowski turned to see Katy. His mouth fell open at the sight of her. She looked down at the knife.

"What are you gonna do with that little thing?" she said.

Alvin leaped forward and smacked the man in the head with his helmet. He went down hard and Alvin pounced on him, ready to strike again.

Katy stepped out of the room.

"Be careful!" shouted Alvin.

"I think you got him," she said.

The man was out cold. Blood ran down his forehead and cheek. Alvin hovered over Chickowski's body with his mouth in a snarl.

"Get back in there. I need to call someone," he said.

His anger was barely in check, but Katy didn't seem to mind at all. If anything she was turned on by it.

"My hero. Give us a kiss first," she said.

She grabbed him by the shoulders and planted one on him. His adrenaline was pumping. When he pulled away, he noticed the bruising around her nose.

"Your face," he said as he caressed her cheek.

Behind him he heard footsteps and he broke away from her embrace. Sioux came up the ramp to see Chickowski sprawled out.

Her attention shifted to Katy.

"Go inside," said Alvin.

Katy listened this time.

"What happened?"

"He attacked me," Alvin said. "He's fixated on me."

The two of them crouched down around Chickowski and checked his breathing.

"I'm gonna message Dr. Choi. Looks like a concussion at least," said Sioux.

She gave a quick blink as she controlled her Opti-Comp.

Alvin exhaled. "Okay, I'll contact Beckman. Thank you, Sioux."

"This is gonna set off Henry and Rodriguez."

"Yeah, I know."

"Who's the girl?"

Damn—she saw Katy.

"Project specialist."

Sioux gave him a look of doubt.

"Who knew she'd look like that?" He smiled and tossed up his hands. "Thanks again."

He entered his room and shut the door.

Inside, Katy wrapped her arms around Alvin and he felt his nerves jumping around.

"What was that about?" she said.

"Long story. The uptake is the meds aren't working for that guy."

"Meds? Why was he after you?"

"Listen, there's a few things I need to tell you," said Alvin.

"I think you need to relax first."

She pushed him back on his bed and start undoing his space suit. He found it easy to postpone the conversation.

An hour later there was a buzzing at Alvin's door.

Beckman.

"Hide," he whispered.

There was nowhere to go, so Katy moved to the far corner at the front of the room. Alvin hopped off of the bunk and put on his shirt and shorts. He walked up close to the door and looked through the peephole. He motioned to her to stay in the corner.

The pocket door slid aside and light glared off Beckman's balding brown head. He looked pissed.

Alvin squinted at him. "Yes?"

"I need you in my office."

Alvin nodded.

"Where is the guest engineer?" said Beckman.

"She's working on something."

Alvin nodded awkwardly after he said it.

Beckman sniffed at the air and grimaced. "Be in my office in ten minutes."

He turned on his heel and walked off.

The door shut and Alvin slid down the wall into a squat.

"I should get to those things I had to tell you," he said.

Katy left the corner and sat beside him.

"Tell me," she said.

"The guy with the knife, Chickowski, he's nuts. He's been listening to a guy—a guy I told you about."

She looked at him puzzled.

"My old gaming manager, Carroll Henry. He's here. He hates me and he's trying to convince these guys that I'm bad news. A company man, out to replace them with machines."

She laughed. "That's ridiculous. You're no company man. You don't even know what you're here for."

He looked at her sheepishly.

"What?" she asked.

"I do now," he said. "And they may be right. It'll certainly reduce the head count."

"What do you mean? What is it?"

"It's a game changer." He scratched his head. "It can break down matter, transmute it, and send it across space."

"It?"

"It's a sphere. A black sphere. I don't understand it. And there's more. I was right about Mohammed Rinsler. He's alive up there. He's the one who built it."

"Up there?"

"The moon, Dactyl. That's where we tested it. I take hopper fifteen on autopilot out each day, but listen—that's not important. When I picked it up—it was on a shuttle—the people on that shuttle were all dead."

"What?"

"That's why I snuck you aboard. Alteris is in a battle with Washington and I'm not leaving your safety to chance. We have two days here until I head back."

"We're in real danger?" she said. "I hoped when they roughed me up that was the worst of it."

"I'm sorry about that, Katy. I got us both into trouble when I played in that tournament. I shouldn't have done that."

"But, Al, it was good for you."

He nodded and began to get dressed. "I didn't need this drama. I only needed you."

"I'm here," said Katy. "It's not all bad. You said Rinsler unlocked your implants."

"Yeah, he has an old quantum console."

"You mean off network? Like criminals use?" She looked intrigued.

"Yep, he's not a criminal . . . well, technically, I guess he might be. Listen, when we get home I can play for money. It won't be the majors, but we can live well."

"I'm glad it happened this way, Al. A little danger is exciting. Now go take care of that asshole boss."

He shook his head at how easygoing she was about the whole affair. Then he kissed her and was out the door.

On the ramp down to Beckman's office, he caught stares. He walked the corkscrew corridor slowly and kept his eyes open for danger. His knock on Beckman's door was met with a quick reply to enter. He stepped inside and nearly jumped when he saw Carroll Henry seated to the left of the door.

"Sit down. We're just talking here," said Beckman.

Alvin took a seat. "Are we talking about the attack on me?"

"You just put my best repair tech in the med bay," growled Henry.

"He's a nutjob. What kind of nonsense have you been feeding him?" said Alvin.

"I've been letting 'em all know what a piece of work you are," he answered.

"Enough," said Beckman. "What is this about? Video games? An old rivalry?"

Henry leaned in closer to Beckman's desk. "This punk cheated on a Uni playoff game and hacked the game core to do it."

"I did no such thing."

"Then he told lies to the investigators and blamed it on my son."

"All right—" said Beckman.

"I didn't blame it on anyone," said Alvin in a sharp monotone. "You blamed it on me."

Beckman sat back in his chair. His gaze went to Alvin. He looked uneasy.

Henry's upper lip curled back over his teeth. "Those kids never played again and I lost a damn fine career."

Motherfucker. "I never played again, either."

"You don't deserve to, you cheated and you took my son from me."

Beckman's posture changed.

Alvin shook his head. "Chad felt guilty about what he did. I just played the game like always." He looked at Beckman. "I didn't know anything was wrong until it was over."

"You took my son."

Beckman's eyes darted back to Henry.

"Okay, that's enough—I'm sorry Chad died," said Alvin. "I really am, but it wasn't my fault. It's time you moved on."

Henry rose up. "Why are you still alive?" His fists were balled up like ripe tomatoes. Beckman reached under the desk.

Alvin was still. He watched Henry with sharp eyes, ready to defend if need be.

"Chad hacked the core," said Alvin. "Chad took his own life."

"Answer me!" shouted Henry. "Why are you still alive!"

I've been waiting my whole life to end you . . . and I don't see the point anymore.

"I'm not alive, coach. You took my dreams from me."

Henry leaped at him. His hands went around Alvin's neck.

Alvin stood to meet the attack. He grabbed Henry's wrists and struggled with the taller man. Beckman jumped from his seat to help. Together they managed to pull his arms away. Alvin coughed as Henry's hands came off his throat.

"Why are you still alive?" Henry's face contorted into a red mass as he shouted.

The door slid open and Alvin thought for sure it was the other 'roiders coming to kill him.

Bossman appeared in the doorway.

He locked gazes with Henry, whose face went angrier at the Corporate Security man's appearance.

"Duty calls, muthafucka," said Bossman.

He lunged for Henry and threw his massive arms around the man's neck. He yanked him free of the struggle like a rag doll.

"It's about time," said Beckman.

Henry tried to lunge for Beckman. He struggled for a moment, his hands reaching out. Then he went limp and his arms fell to his sides as Bossman choked him unconscious. He was dragged away. His legs banged against Alvin on the way out.

"You lucky I'm still here," said Bossman.

Beckman backed away, panting. "Get him to Choi and have him restrained," he shouted as the security man left the room.

Bossman nodded.

Beckman angrily tucked in his button-down shirt and sat back down.

"Okay, Baylor. Clearly, Carroll Henry needs to be evaluated. I am asking you now to please leave for Dactyl with your associate. We are down a repair tech and now our lead surveyor. Your presence is impacting normal operations."

No shit.

Alvin rubbed at his neck.

"There's one problem with that. She's not cleared for Dactyl. We need her to run the repairs via VR. She can't go on site."

Beckman's head dropped. "You're killing me, Baylor!"

"I can try to get clearance, but it will delay our tests."

"No. No delays. You're supposed to be done in a couple days.

Let's keep it that way. While you're on Dactyl, she stays locked in your room. She can run the VR session from there. You get me?"

Alvin nodded. He stood and attempted a respectful tone. "I want you to know that I value your dedication to this project."

"Get the fuck out of my office," said Beckman.

The next morning, Alvin awoke before the sound of his alarm clock. He'd not had a good night's sleep. He wasn't sure how the crew would react to Henry's confinement, and he thought it best to get to Dactyl during the shift change. He would take Katy to eat in Buzz's room without being seen. While he dressed, he scoped out the hallways again using the camera feeds.

I think we're good.

"Katy, time to get up."

He shook her arm. Her skin felt rough.

She yawned herself awake and rolled over. She looked tired. The bruises around her nose looked worse. She held a hand over her face.

"Don't look at me yet," she said.

She never acts this way.

"Hey, you feel okay?" said Alvin.

"Yeah, just stress. I didn't sleep well."

"Me, either. We'll be out of here soon. Now get ready. I'm going to take us over to Buzz."

"What's he gonna do for us?"

"He's got a food printer. Undoctored. They medicate the crew."

She yawned again and reached for her pants.

"I don't think it's working," she said. "Certainly not on that Henry guy."

"I have a scarier thought," said Alvin. "What if it is?"

She laughed as she pulled a black hoodie over her head. "Let me do my makeup."

"It's just Buzz. Don't worry, we'll make it quick."

She ignored him and began wiping on foundation. "Alvin, am I going to be sneaking around like his the whole time I'm here?"

"Only for one more day. This is the safest place to be right now. No one's getting in without Alteris approval."

"I hope you're right," she said.

He winked. "Don't worry. I have a good track record. Let's go already."

She finished up and pulled the hoodie tight over her head.

"You're taking the stealth thing kinda far," said Alvin.

"I look like shit this morning," she said.

They stepped out the door and tiptoed through the crew quarters. Everyone was asleep. He pointed out the empty mess hall on the way. She said nothing and kept her hooded head pointed at the ground.

Something's wrong with her.

They reached Buzz's room and he pressed the doorbell. No response, so he pressed it again.

It opened.

Buzz grumbled, "All right, already."

He paused with surprise at seeing Katy. "Hello, Alvin. Who is this person? And aren't you a little early?"

"I'm Katy."

"She's here for some fixes to the equipment," said Alvin.

"Also an engineer?" Buzz asked.

"Yes, of a different sort," she said.

"Well, you two seem comfortable together," said Buzz.

"We became friends on the trip over. She works on *The Hope*. We're just looking for some takeout today. Can we come in?" said Alvin.

"I suppose," said Buzz. "You know I'm going to have to requisition more Nutri-Paste?"

He let them in and they printed up breakfast burritos and hurried back out the door.

"Stay out of the papers today," said Buzz.

"I'll try."

On their return they passed the med bay. Henry and Chickowski were inside, strapped down on gurneys. Katy pressed up against the glass and stared at them for a moment.

"You're safer with those two in there," she said.

"I guess so," he said.

A sinking feeling manifested in Alvin's stomach.

Rodriguez is still out there.

Another forty minutes still remained until shift change. That was plenty of time to eat and say good-bye to his girl before a day of work. He held her hand tightly as they walked back. It felt coarse and he wondered again about her health. His anxieties were starting to bubble up. They entered the room unseen and he placed the food on the bed then hugged her tightly.

"Thank you," he said. "I'm not sure I could have made it here in one piece. I think I might have drunk myself to death."

"Like you said, all you needed was me."

She pulled away and a tear rolled down her bruised cheek. It was then that Alvin noticed how pronounced her cheekbones looked. There were wrinkles around her eyes and her lip quivered as she smiled.

God, she must really be stressed. What did they do to her?

She gripped him in a tight hug, and for the first time she seemed fragile. Her hug grew tighter still and he felt her arm come around his neck, and he wondered what she was doing. Then came darkness.

THIRTY-SIX

Alvin awoke to the blare of alarm klaxons. His throat was raw and his head throbbed. He sat up. He was on the bed. Breakfast was scattered on the floor at his feet. He coughed. A red light flashed above the door. Then he remembered Katy.

He whipped his head around. *Where is she?*

He went to the door to open it. It gave a whine as though it were stuck. He tried it again. Same thing.

He peered out the peephole. It was dark. Red lights flashed outside. He saw movement in the shadows. Two men charged at each other and collided in a heap. They snarled like rabid dogs. One bit the other then pounded on his head. The unconscious man was dragged off into the darkness by his foe.

What the hell is going on?

Alvin moved away from the door and woke his Opti-Comp.

I've been out for an hour.

He felt his stomach turn.

Where is she?

He recounted his steps. They'd come back to the room with breakfast. Then talked and—he remembered her hugging him tight. He remembered her choking him.

He stumbled and fell against the wall.

The alarms continued to bellow. His mouth hung open.

Why?

He connected to the security server in his Opti-Comp and began looking at camera feeds. The path to the dock showed several battered bodies lying on the deck. He pulled up the mess hall camera—a full-on riot was in progress. A mass of people knocked their way through the place. They wrecked everything in sight, pausing only to fight one another.

What is happening?

He rolled the camera back. Past the carnage, past the shift start and breakfast—further back to find—her.

Katy entered the mess hall wearing a black flight suit. She moved from food printer to food printer. She was reconfiguring them.

Alvin gasped.

He watched as she went to each of them before exiting. He changed cameras and followed her to the dock, where she entered hopper fifteen. She glided out of the airlock. The time stamp was forty minutes ago.

He felt rage surge within him suddenly, then he stood and ran at the door, smashing into it with no effect. He tried it again, twice, then sat on the edge of the bed panting.

She had been playing him the whole time. He pushed the thought away.

No. No way. No fucking way.

He started to peep out a message to Rinsler, then stopped.

He'll never get it through his interference. I have to get out of here.

He called Buzz and got an answer. "Stay up on Dactyl. We have a situation here," said the younger man.

"I'm locked in my room, Buzz."

"Did you just say you're in your room?"

"Yes," said Alvin.

"That's a terrible place to be. Everyone's gone mad. I think it's the food. Everything went to hell at breakfast," he exclaimed.

"I know. Buzz, you have to get me out of here."

"I can't leave. Have you looked out there?"

"Yes. My door is jammed. It won't open," said Alvin.

"Good, keep it that way. Trust me, you don't want to be out there."

"Damn it, Buzz! She's getting away! I'm as good as dead if she gets that sphere."

"Alvin, I think we'll both be safe if we just—your engineer lady friend?"

"Yes."

"I was gonna say she seemed too hot for you."

"I screwed up, Buzz. Please, I'm looking at the cameras, there's no one outside your room. Come now. I'll watch the halls."

"Okay, but you owe me a lot of Nutri-Paste."

Alvin kept his eyes on the camera feeds as Buzz ran down the hallway waving a telescope like a baseball bat.

"Good, you have a weapon," said Alvin.

"You just let me know if I'm going to need it. How's the mess hall look?"

"Brutal, but they're all fighting in the back of the room. You should be able to run by."

Alvin pulled up the hallway camera and watched it side by side with the interior of the mess hall. Buzz walked into frame as two people were exiting.

"Wait," said Alvin.

Buzz froze as the man and a woman ran out of the mess hall.

Was that Tosh and Yumi?

"I think that was Tosh and Yumi," said Buzz.

Alvin watched him run after them and call out. Then Buzz stopped. The couple's heads returned to the bottom of the camera frame.

It is them.

"What's going on, Buzz?" asked Alvin.

"Alvin did this!" yelled Tosh.

The 'roiders in the mess hall stopped fighting.

They heard him.

"Buzz, turn around. They're coming out of that room," said Alvin.

The first three 'roiders scrambled out into the hallway.

Buzz started shuffling backward as Tosh and Yumi dashed the other way.

"Go!" yelled Alvin.

The rioters poured out in a stream. Henry's man, Rodriguez, walked in the middle of the pack. He towered above everyone and directed them with a point of his finger. They ran after Buzz.

"You've killed me," said Buzz as he ran.

"Just run," pleaded Alvin.

He saw Buzz rush past the med lab. Twenty 'roiders were now in pursuit of him.

"I don't see anyone ahead. Keep going," said Alvin.

Alvin watched him pass the med lab window. Carroll Henry and Chickowski were still strapped down on their gurneys, only now pools of blood gathered around their necks. Their throats had been cut and the room ransacked.

"Alvin . . . I think—"

"I see them. Don't look. Keep running."

Buzz kept going and Alvin rewound the camera view of the med bay until Katy appeared. He watched her cut Chickowski's throat with a scalpel. Then he rewound further to see her kill Henry. Finally, she emptied the cabinets of medication. He felt sick inside.

That's what she put into the food printers.

"Sioux!" he heard Buzz yell.

He went back to the hallway cameras and saw Buzz banging at the atrium door.

"She's only eats organics grown in the garden," said Buzz. "Is she in there, Alvin?"

Buzz kept banging at the door.

Alvin switched to a camera inside the atrium and saw Sioux hiding behind her desk. She was out of sight of the translucent front door.

"Buzz, she's right there. Tell her to open it," said Alvin.

He heard him yell to her, but she didn't budge. Buzz looked terrified and the 'roiders were coming up the hall.

I've got to do something.

Alvin searched his Opti-Comp for the controls to the PA system while Buzz continued to pound at the door. He selected the atrium and spoke.

"Sioux, it's Alvin. Open the door. Buzz is outside. He's not sick."

She stood up from behind her desk and peered out the clear door then rushed to let Buzz in. Moments later, the marauding 'roiders arrived and began banging at the door with their fists. Sioux and Buzz hid behind the desk.

"I'm sorry," said Alvin.

"Sure you are. Sorry you're still stuck in your room," said Buzz.

It was the truth. He was trapped, waiting for the mob to come devour him, waiting as Katy absconded with the spheres.

It's my fault.

The color drained from his face.

Some of them hated him. Some of them feared him. But only one person had betrayed him.

Determination rolled through him. It was all a game and she'd been playing for keeps.

I'm not going down like this!

"Let them come," he growled over his comm.

"Huh?" said Buzz.

"I have an idea," said Alvin.

"Dear god. I hope it's a better one."

Alvin peeped back over to the PA app in his Opti-Comp and opened the line to the whole facility.

"Attention, disgruntled assholes. This is Alvin Baylor. I'm in my room. Come and get me."

En masse, agitated 'roiders everywhere turned and ran for him. Buzz and Sioux went limp with exhaustion as the atrium door cleared.

"You are a very brave, very dumb man," said Buzz.

"Thanks."

A clang rang out at Alvin's door. The first 'roiders had arrived.

"Gotta go. They're here." Alvin ended the call.

Alvin hurriedly slid on the gloves of his space suit while the pounding at the metal door continued. He heard a scraping sound and watched the door shimmy in the frame. The 'roiders outside had removed whatever Katy used to bar the door. He could escape now—if he could get past them. He needed a weapon.

He looked around for something to use. The bed was molded to the wall. His clothes and VR goggles were useless. He had the small knife on his multitool and that was it. If he had to slash, he'd go for the throat. He walked up to the door and peered out the peephole. There were just two of them. Tosh and Yumi. His heart sank.

If I don't stop Katy, I'll never see Earth again.

He opened the knife up and heard what sounded like a stampede outside. The sound grew louder and was joined by a chorus of yelling voices. Alvin stepped away from the door.

"Baylor's friends!" he heard someone yell.

Yumi screamed. Then a hard thump at the door dented it.

Alvin peered through the peephole. A mob of ten men attacked them. Yumi was limp, her head bleeding. Tosh was on the ground kicking at his attackers.

This is my chance.

He placed his helmet on. The screams outside fell away. He heard only his own breathing.

He pressed the door control.

The dented metal panel slid away into the pocket with a clank. He ran out past the mob then glanced back. They hadn't seen him in their drug-induced frenzy.

Tosh was being kicked in the ribs by three men. Another was crouched over his head bouncing it off the ground. The other 'roiders had Yumi's arms and legs and they were trying to pull her apart.

I can't fight them all, but I have to do something.

"Hey, you stupid fucks!" he shouted.

His voice echoed in his ears.

Fucking helmet.

He started waving the knife and the mob stopped and turned dagger-eyed stares upon him.

They tossed Yumi's limp body to the ground and abandoned Tosh as they ran at him. They had no fear of the blade.

He backpedaled and nearly slipped.

The 'roiders rushed forward in a snarling clumsy mass. Whatever Katy had put in the food had destroyed their coordination as well as their sanity.

Alvin spun on his heels and ran. He got to the corner where the ramp sloped up like a corkscrew to the hopper bay. He felt the floor vibrate as the stampede rushed after him. They were gaining. The suit was slowing him down.

He clipped the multitool back onto his belt and pumped his arms. The sound of his labored breathing increased and it fogged his face guard. His mind flashed over images of the mob clobbering him.

What if I don't make it?

Then he slipped.

He spun his arms in circles to keep upright but flopped down onto his knees. Only a few feet ahead stood the door to the dock. He fired the gas jets in his suit and skidded clumsily along the ground to slam into the door. He tapped the controls and yellow lights flashed. He felt the floor vibrate harder as the mob rushed up the ramp behind him. They were within feet of him. The doors began to part. He squeezed between them and grabbed the railing to pull himself through. Straight ahead was the empty boarding lane for his rock hopper. The one Katy had taken.

A large red button sat on a pedestal at the end of the row. The autorecall.

Will she be in it?

The 'roiders began clambering through behind him. One of them leaped up and grabbed on to his leg, pulling his floating body back toward the mob.

Fuck!

Alvin fired his suit thrusters with a thought.

His body shot across the zero-g dock in seconds with the man in tow. The 'roider screamed as small pinholes of hot gas shot out from Alvin's leg, searing his hands. He let go and his body crashed into a support beam and went limp.

Alvin stopped his flight and came down to activate the return button. He turned to watch the 'roiders enter. There were more of them. He tried to slow his labored breathing.

Hurry up, ship!

They came pouring through the door, fighting one another for position. The absence of gravity sent some careening upward. Those who were close to the ground grabbed on to the balustrade that led to the hopper slip. Their mania made them awkward. A few drifted out of the lane and began pinwheeling as they frantically tried to right their course. Suddenly a tall man cut through the crowd. He was wearing a brown space suit and flying fast.

Alvin took a deep breath.

This is no different from a VR game. Now win.

He fired his jets and flew at the suited man while pulling

himself into a ball. At the last moment, he stuck out his leg and his foot came down on the guy's helmet. Alvin felt the rattle of cranium against the helmet.

The man bounced off the floor and drifted away. The back of his suit said "Rodriguez."

Henry's last goon.

Behind Alvin, the giant doors rumbled. He turned to see the hopper entering the bay. The other 'roiders were almost on him. They gripped their way along the railings as the ship glided in to slip fifteen.

Are you in there?

He flew up and landed atop the back of the egg-shaped craft and yanked open the cockpit.

It was empty.

You've ruined me, Katy.

Alvin jumped down into the cockpit and closed the hatch as the 'roiders leaped onto it. The hopper shook. He turned on the front viewscreen and saw Tosh's paranoid little friend, Ravi, and several others on the hull. Their faces were contorted in anger, their teeth bared.

He released the rock hopper's tentacles from the anchor-hold below and the ship bobbled upward. Then, with a swipe of his finger, he brushed them away. Ravi floated off screaming and reached after him as the hopper moved toward the airlock.

One more swipe of the tentacles scraped the rest of the mob free. They flew off in every direction.

He caught a last glimpse of the dock as he glided across the threshold. The 'roiders were scattered all around with frenzied faces and foaming mouths. He took several slow, deep breaths. For the first time, he felt no fear, only determination. Like he did in the game.

"She was lying the whole fucking time," he muttered.

The hopper entered the airlock and the inner door closed. Suddenly a rumbling reverberated from within the asteroid.

What now?

He switched to the rear cameras as he was sucked out into space. He saw no damage at Ida's massive airlock doors, but below the asteroid gas was venting into space. A white gust of wind swirled off into the vacuum.

Looks like hydrogen.

He resolved to tackle the issue at hand.

I hope I'm not too late to stop her.

THIRTY-SEVEN

Buzz and Sioux hid beyond the glass walls of the atrium. Sioux sat, head down, arms wrapped about her tucked legs, her back against a tree trunk. The pink petals of the cherry blossom tree fell around her. Buzz looked into the faux stream beside him at his reflection. He watched the water run up to a small pond filled with koi. A simulated blue sky hung overhead. The beauty of Earth's flora and fauna matched with the sky above was small comfort now. Both Sioux and Buzz were listless. The hallway had been silent since Alvin had called away the mob, and they had been silent, too.

Buzz broke the quiet. "Have you heard anything from Beckman?"

"No, but I saw him with Dr. Choi earlier," answered Sioux. "You said it was the food, right? I know they ate before everyone else."

"Then perhaps he's still in his right mind. We'll need to—"

A series of quick booms were followed by a steady, rushing sound. The floor rumbled. The pair looked at each other in fear.

"I think things just got worse," said Buzz.

He stood and listened. Closing his eyes he hummed in a monotone to himself then said, "It sounds like water."

"Of course it does, you're sitting next to a stream," she said.

He looked down at the water. It sloshed around violently, then began to run the opposite way.

"Wait—it's going the wrong way," he said.

Sioux gave a perplexed face and stood up to look.

In short order the riverbed became exposed as the water drained away. The koi began flopping in the muddy pond left behind.

"Damn it. Must be the pump," said Sioux. "I'll go check."

She crept back toward the entrance, careful to scan the windows for marauding 'roiders. The front door was cracked, but the hallway beyond was empty.

Up at the console, Sioux accessed the controls. The pump was still running, so she toggled it off and back on again.

"Did that start the water?" she called out.

"Negative," shouted Buzz.

She checked the status readout for the atrium. There was no water pressure. Nothing was feeding the pump. She made her way back to the stream.

"We're not getting any water to this deck," she said.

"Just this deck?" he asked.

She shrugged. "I only have access to the atrium status. I think it's time we found Beckman."

"Or his access band," said Buzz.

"Let's try calling him first."

He peeped in his Opt-Comp and dialed Beckman.

"Hello, Buzz? Buzz?" sounded in his ear.

"Yes, hello, sir."

"Buzz, you're alive. Is anyone with you?"

"Uh, yes, sir. Sioux is with me. You're on group." He added Sioux to the call. "How many are with you?"

"Just Dr. Choi. We're in the med lab. It's a massacre. Henry and Chickowski are dead. It's the food, Buzz. Something has happened to the printers in the mess hall."

"Yes, sir, we've gathered that. Listen, we have another situation here. The atrium is not getting any water pressure."

"I hardly think we should worry about the plants. We have a riot on our hands," said Beckman. "I've called Corporate Security. We'll have to sit tight till they get here from Armstrong."

"Ah, more charming CorpSec officers," said Buzz. "In the meantime, I think you should check the base ops status, sir. We can hear a strange sound down here."

"Damn it, Buzz, hold on." Beckman went silent as he looked up the information. "Shit."

"That doesn't sound good," whispered Sioux.

"I'll get back to you," said Beckman.

He disconnected.

"We're fucked," said Buzz.

THIRTY-EIGHT

Rock hopper fifteen touched down on the surface of Dactyl with Alvin aboard. Utility lights illuminated the landing pad and cast stark shadows across the gray regolith. Nothing moved. Rinsler's white-domed cabin looked untouched. Alvin leaped out of the hatch as soon as he could get it open. His thrusters flew him over the long row of hand railings to the cabin. A flurry of messages from Sabrina Meyer arrived in his Opti-Comp before he reached the door.

Shit. She knows. Wait, how are they getting through?

He looked back toward the communications dish and saw no light.

It's powered off.

He peeped open one of the messages as he glided forward—it was from Meyer.

"Baylor, I've received a report from Beckman that there is a riot in progress at Ida. You are to secure Dr. Rinsler and his invention at all costs. Corporate Security is en route."

He closed it. A glance at the inbox showed four more like it.

Fuck.

He reached the airlock and looked through the porthole. The

inner door was open. Katy sat at Rinsler's console. She wore a space suit with the face guard open. Her face looked haggard. Sunken eyes focused on the floating screens. He could see the tips of Rinsler's black mane bobbing in the corner beyond her.

Is he alive? He'll be killed if I open the door.

A call came through. It was Buzz. "Houston, we have a problem."

"Not now."

"Alvin, the water tanks are venting into space."

Must be the gas I saw when I took off.

"So we're gonna die from dehydration?"

"Yes. If we aren't killed by each other first."

"One problem at a time, Buzz."

The shadows moved over Alvin's shoulder.

He turned around and was bathed in light. His visor dimmed under the glare as an old mining frigate hovered above the landing pad, blowing dusty debris off the surface.

Who the hell is this?

As if in answer, the ship rotated, turning its rear toward him. A name was stenciled on the hull—*Cronus*. The cargo door lowered and a rock hopper exited. It made a beeline for Alvin at dangerous speed.

"I'll call you back," said Alvin.

He disconnected and leaped from the cabin door.

THIRTY-NINE

Forty minutes earlier, Rouja Natastae had touched down on Dactyl in rock hopper fifteen. The autopilot brought the ship down a little way from a habitat unit. She would have used her suit thrusters for the flight to the door, but she'd never been trained with synaptics. Instead she relied on her physical prowess to make the distance. She leaped from handhold to handhold in the low gravity like a gymnast. Her dismounts ensured a return trajectory aimed at the next section of railing.

Reminds me of the Moon.

At the door Rouja brought up Alvin's security credentials. A palm press opened the airlock door. She walked in and peered through the porthole at the next door. There was a man on a bed in the corner of the room. He didn't stir as she entered the cabin. She sealed the airlock behind her and approached.

His chest rose, then fell. He was fast asleep.

Hello, Dr. Rinsler.

She opened her face guard and scanned the room. In the opposite corner sat a large computer console. Sitting on top of the long desktop was a glossy white chest. She bounced over and touched it.

The action woke the computer. A touch-field display lit up above the tabletop showing multiple camera views. Among them the hopper, an empty crater, and a dish shooting a red laser into space. There was a flashing prompt onscreen.

Must be the quantum console Alvin mentioned. I can back Leung's data here.

She picked up the chest and opened it. Inside were two black spheres. She plucked one out with her fingers.

"So you're what all the fuss is about."

A tickling sensation started in her fingertips and moved throughout her body. It rippled through her like an electrical charge and made her head buzz. It was mild, but reminded her of being shocked by Watkins's eel suit. She placed the sphere back in the chest.

"You're Baylor's tryst," said a man's voice.

She turned around to see Mohammed Rinsler sitting upright in bed.

"I know about you," said Rinsler. "I've seen his Opti-Comp feeds. You look older in person."

"I am older," she said. "You must be Rinsler."

He nodded. "Who do you work for?"

"Myself. I need you to crack some data for me."

"Why would I do anything for you?"

"Because if you do it I won't kill you or take your lawn bowling kit," she said, hefting the chest.

His eyebrow arched. "What kind of data?"

"DNA data store. I yanked it out of a pimp. I need to read his files."

"DNA will take a while to crack."

"How long?" said Rouja.

"It takes as long as it takes."

"Then get started. If your machine takes too long, the deal is off," she said.

She walked to the bed, grabbed him by the collar, then tossed him toward the console. He landed atop it in the low gravity.

He grumbled, climbed down, and sat in the chair.

"Give it here," he said.

Rouja handed over a small sliver of holographic foil.

He took the strip and inserted it into a slot on the console, then he brought up another floating display and began a cryptographic decode of Leung's data.

She paced the carpeted floor and bounded slightly off the ground with each step.

"Would you mind not walking around, you'll ruin the grip," said Rinsler.

He lifted one of his slippered feet from the carpet with a ripping sound for demonstration.

She gave him a stern look then pulled out a pulse gun. Rinsler cowered and covered his head. She shot out the inner airlock door controls with a laser blast. The door swung open.

"If I hear anything out of you besides 'I'm done,' I'll shoot the outer door and you'll be sucked into space. You get me?"

Rinsler nodded sheepishly.

Rouja continued to pace.

After thirty-five minutes of silence, he spoke the words. "I'm done."

She stopped in place and looked at him apprehensively. Then she dashed forward and shoved his chair aside. Rinsler bounced off the cabin wall.

On screen was a directory dump of Leung's files. She began searching through them, looking for his ledger—a database of the eastern sex trade that could lead to her daughter. Her attention was stolen when the camera at the landing area shimmied. The hopper lifted up from the ground into orbit.

It's been recalled.

"John, I need you now," she radioed.

She received no response.

"John, I have it," she radioed again.

Silence.

"I thought you weren't taking my invention?" said Rinsler.

"I lied." She eyed the scientist. He didn't startle. Then she noticed her Opti-Comp data wasn't updating. "You're blocking transmissions."

He frowned and raised his shoulders.

"Disable it."

"We'll be sitting ducks," he said.

"You will. I'm leaving. Do it now."

She pointed her gun at him. He gritted his teeth and walked with sticky steps back to the console. He reached over the keyboard to tap out some characters.

"Now, John," she said again.

"I'm on my way," said Padre over the radio. "What the hell took so long?"

"Complications. I'm cracking Leung's ledger."

"No time for that. Just take the prototype and go. We can buy you a crack on Earth."

She ignored him and went back to her search at the console. She had minutes to find a record of her daughter before the hopper would return.

Please don't be Alvin.

FORTY

Damn it, Rouja. Give it up.

John Padre set his ship to descend from the outer orbit of Dactyl then pulled up the communications app given to him by Barton Aimes.

All right, shithead, let's do some gloating.

He waited for the call to route as he brought the *Cronus* down over Dactyl's surface. The view outside was barren. He expected Rouja would exit the white dome momentarily.

Where is she?

There was a click as someone answered his faster-than-light call. He got the jump on the conversation. "I win, Aimes," said Padre. "You fucked with the wrong guy."

"John Padre," said a raspy female voice.

"Who the fuck is this?" said Padre.

"This is Margaret Aimes, Secretary of Defense and Barton's mother. You fucked with the wrong people."

"Listen up, bitch. I got your precious toy."

"Yes, and I have your location." The connection dropped.

"Government cretin," he grumbled.

Can't handle a little rough talk. I'll bet Alteris killed her kid already.

He laughed nervously.

Then eight objects came up on the scopes.

"Oh hell."

He radioed out. "Rouja, get your ass in gear! We have incoming."

Whatever was coming was still ten minutes away. Then a new dot appeared ahead of the pack. It was almost on him.

A hopper came into view and landed on the moon below.

What's this?

The hatch opened and a man in an obnoxious royal-blue space suit wrapped in lightning bolts emerged.

Baylor.

He hated the guy more than Aimes.

I got time for this.

He glided to the rear of the ship and boarded his rock hopper.

With the synaptic cap on his head, he snapped his fingers in eager anticipation. The hopper tendrils whipped around at deadly speed.

She spent another night with this creep . . . time to erase him.

When the cargo hold opened, he gunned it and dove straight at that precious blue suit.

Baylor flew for his parked hopper and Padre overshot him. He pulled up to avoid hitting the cabin, then turned back around. Baylor's ship was already skybound. It rushed up from the ground to meet him and rammed against his hull.

Daring little fucker.

Padre's ship careened sideways and impacted against the dome.

"Fuck!"

He scanned the structure for damage. It was dented. Atmosphere was venting.

"You sonofabitch. You hurt my girl and you're worse than dead."

He flew upward and Baylor's tendrils smacked down and spun him in circles.

"This creep's pretty good."

He reached out with his hands and the tendrils extended. When the ships met again, their limbs tangled up. One craft sat over the other with bright, spindly appendages that intertwined.

Enough of this. The guy has no weapons.

He fired up two of the plasma jets at the end of the hopper limbs. They cut through Baylor's tendrils and he broke free.

"This was worth the wait."

He powered on two more jets and sent them tracing back and forth across the hull of Baylor's hopper. It was scored black, then it burst.

FORTY-ONE

Rouja hunkered down over the computer console in Rinsler's cabin hurriedly reading through line after line of sales entries. Leung's sex-trade ledger eclipsed her view of the landing pad camera. She narrowed her search by geography and date until she was looking at Greece before it was overrun.

She felt her guts go hollow when she saw the name: "Lia Padre."

My baby.

She selected the record and held her breath. The status came back as active.

She's alive.

She relaxed her shoulders and hung her head over the console. Rinsler viewed her curiously.

The cabin shook as something slammed against it. The frame above the airlock dented inward and a whistling sound began.

Rinsler dove to the corner for his space suit. Rouja eyed him suspiciously, then she glanced at the damaged door and returned to the ledger.

Just hold a little longer.

She parsed through her daughter's entry until she found the last delivery record—an address in Pakistan.

I found you!

There were three recorded transfers of ownership. Lia currently belonged to someone named Abbasi; before that she was sold by a Turk named Uzun. The last man named was her first owner. Rouja's mouth fell open.

Her joy was replaced with anger. Padre had lied to her for seventeen years.

Dead man!

She reached for the box of spheres and pulled her gun. Rinsler was in a space suit now, but his helmet was still in his hands.

"Get it on." She closed her face guard and the whistling sound ceased.

She fired the pulse gun as Rinsler slammed his helmet down. The laser blast blew out the lock. The door shook, then folded a third of the way from the top.

She dove for safety and Rinsler knocked the box from under her arm. Their bodies were yanked flush against the wall on either side of the airlock as air rushed from the room. The box bounced and opened. The spheres were ripped out. She reached and caught one. He caught the other.

Rinsler put the sphere in his belt pouch and was launched out into the vacuum. His body banged against the doorframe on the way out.

Suddenly the domed roof tore off, revealing the black starry expanse. The buffeting expulsion of atmosphere ceased and Rouja was left in stillness huddled against what remained of the cabin wall.

In the sky above, two rock hoppers were locked in combat. Their luminescing tendrils wrestled with one another. She recognized Padre's modified hopper. The other was number fifteen.

Alvin. No!

Padre's hopper ejected plasma from the tips of its limbs and broke free. The other ship's severed legs went black and disappeared into the darkness. Then the plasma jets swung back across the front hull of hopper fifteen. Deep black welts formed and it exploded suddenly in a belch of gas and debris that spread out over Dactyl like sparkling confetti. Padre's hopper was thrown back by the expulsion.

Rouja's stomach dropped.

Padre's ship pivoted in the air, then descended to the surface.

Rouja stepped over what remained of the cabin wall onto the gray regolith of Dactyl, then bounded out to meet him at the landing pad.

Padre came out of the top hatch of the hopper and landed in front of her.

"Time to go," he said.

"You know that was an innocent man you just killed."

"Wouldn't be the first," said Padre. "When did you get righteous?"

"Is this what you were after?" she said.

She bounced the black sphere in the palm of her hand. It moved slowly in the low gravity.

"Good work, baby. I can always count on you," said Padre from behind his copper visor.

She wanted to kill him, but she wanted to see the look on his face when she did it.

"I got what I was after, too," she said.

"You cracked the ledger?"

The bastard sounds worried.

She nodded. "Lia's alive and I can use some of this money to get her back."

"That's perfect, babe. Everything is coming together for us at last. Now it's time to go."

"How much did you get for selling her?"

He went silent. His minuscule weight shifted from foot to foot.

She waited.

"They disavowed me in a foreign country in the middle of a war."

"Answer me! How much did they pay for a three-year-old girl?"

"Without the money, we wouldn't have gotten out. It would have cost us our lives," he said.

"No," she said. "Just yours. Women have value."

She drew her pulse gun and fired it cockeyed to shoot out his visor.

He mouthed her name as ice formed from his last breath. An expression of horror hardened into a mask.

She fired again and his face exploded into frozen fragments.

His body fell slowly in the low gravity.

She looked up at hopper fifteen's debris cloud as it spread over the horizon.

I'm sorry, Alvin.

She gripped the black sphere hard and felt it buzz through her fingers. Then she boarded Padre's hopper.

FORTY-TWO

Alvin had only a moment to make his judgment. The strange hopper in the Dactyl sky that was coming at him was not friendly. He jetted toward the landing pad and dove under the attacker. The ship zoomed over the white dome.

Alvin peeped the remote controls for his hopper and instead of boarding, sent the ship straight up to intercept the incoming vehicle. It crashed into the other craft and bounced it into Rinsler's cabin like a ping-pong ball. A vent of gas shot from the airlock.

No!

He sent the unmanned hopper back at his attacker. Sweat ran down his temple as the faint blue glow of his implants grew brighter.

He stuck the tendrils out in front and the other ship raced up to tangle with them; a wrestling match in the sky.

He thinks I'm inside.

Suddenly Rinsler's cabin door blew open. Alvin saw a flash of gas and then a white streak shot out the front door. It looked like a person.

Rinsler?

The whole dome blew off next, and the gas pocket knocked Alvin into the air and sent him cartwheeling through space.

He dropped remote control of the ship to focus on his suit thrusters. The jets fired and stopped his roll. When he'd recovered his orientation, he looked back to see his hopper explode in the sky before him.

A sharp pain shot through his head. He grimaced until the feedback ceased. His temples cooled. When he opened his eyes again, he saw the enemy hopper descending. A female form in black bounded out to meet it.

Katy.

He studied from a distance. She juggled one of the spheres as a tall man exited the hopper. They seemed to converse. Then he saw her shoot the man and board his ship.

Who the heck is she?

Alvin fired his jets and raced over the ground to the hopper. The gold lightning bolts of his suit gleamed under the craft's lights. He stood there waiting.

A thin line appeared along the front hull of the hopper. The metal egg parted to reveal the cockpit beyond a translucent window.

He could see her clearly; the black sphere sat in her lap. She removed her helmet, letting brown hair laced with gray roll down her cheeks. Her eyes looked sad, her skin pale and speckled. The woman who looked upon him resembled Katy, but she was older. Her features, though still beautiful, had drooped and creased. She'd aged twenty years.

He felt his emotions welling up inside, anger mixed with confusion. He pressed his helmet to the window and lowered his solar protector to reveal his face.

"Why?" he said over the radio.

"Alvin, you're alive!"

She breathed out heavily, looking stunned.

"What have you done, Katy?" he said.

Her head dropped. She sat in silence for a moment, then looked up. A tear ran down her cheek.

"I'm not—I'm sorry, Alvin, but this is what I do," she said.

"Why did you do this to me?"

"I had to. I didn't mean to hurt you. I didn't know this would happen."

"You're leaving me to die."

"No. Alteris will come. You'll survive, Alvin."

"No. Not like this."

Tears left his eyes and stuck like glue to his cheeks in the low gravity.

"You're an honest man," she said. "I'm a liar. There can't be anything more."

"Who are you?"

He felt his anger rising, pushing at his insides.

"I'm who I need to be to get the job done," she said.

"You killed Henry and Chickowski. You made all those people sick. Why didn't you just kill me, too?"

"Because I care about you. I don't enjoy hurting you, but I have to go. I have an obligation."

The hopper stirred. Small jets fired as the tendrils contracted from the ground.

"So do I!" yelled Alvin.

He pressed his hands to the craft's window and looked at her face—sad and aged, yet familiar.

I love you.

He didn't step back as the hopper rose up off the ground. He stared into her eyes instead, and she looked away. He wanted to reach out to her, to feel her once more.

Hug her!

Anger spasmed within him.

Strangle her!

He shook his head at the thought of how stupid he'd been; how naïve and trusting. His life was over—if he let her go.

The dust blew across his chest and he looked up at her one last time through blurry, tear-trapped eyes. She lifted off to leave him, and he got a final glimpse of the sphere in her lap.

That stupid thing! The cause of all of this!

He felt his head tingle. His synaptic implants warmed.

A soft blue glow reflected against the inside of his face shield. He began to hyperventilate, then he stopped feeling his body altogether.

His mind communed with the sphere, and he felt her and the craft around her. It made him angry.

Gone. Gone. All of it.

He snapped back.

In Rouja's lap, the black ball rippled with light. Her fingertips turned translucent for a nanosecond and then she was gone and the ship with her. What once was muscle and bone and metal disappeared in a spherical void. Then the stars rushed back into the empty space, leaving Rinsler's sphere hanging in the air.

It dropped slowly into Alvin's hands. He held it gently and felt the familiar tingling sensation. A moiré of colors washed over the ball in a continuous rhythm.

What have I done?

He fell to his knees on the gray surface of Dactyl and wept.

⁂

Alvin's head throbbed. Using the sphere had hurt. Pain overtook his sorrow. Tears welled up in his eyes and clung like growths. He shook his head to toss them onto his visor so he could see. The helmet began to fog. His head pulsed with every shake.

Damn it.

He was alone now on the barren surface of Dactyl. He took labored breaths and looked back up at the sky. He blinked rapidly to clear his vision. The frigate *Cronus* still hung overhead. Something moved in the black beside it.

What was that?

The stars twinkled and he felt a ghostly intuition slap him on the back of the neck. He knew that whatever it was had seen him recover the orb at the crash of the *Zzyzx.*

He stood up straight, the device in his hand. His thrusters lifted him slowly as he peered closer at the sky through his fogging helmet. A blast of laser light fired out of the dark at the frigate. The engines erupted in an explosion, and it crashed to Dactyl's surface.

He looked back to the sky. A black tubular body with outstretched wings revealed itself above. The wings folded inward as it came lower out of the darkness of space. He could see the United States flag on the belly of the thing.

It's a drone.

He stared up at it, uncertain what to do. It pulled to a stop twenty feet overhead.

It's watching me.

Another laser came from farther out to lay into the crashed frigate, then others from multiple directions. The *Cronus* exploded.

Alvin scanned the horizon. All around him the stars flickered. Another laser blast laid waste to the communications dish. His heart began to flutter. He turned in circles trying to identify how many were in the sky. He counted eight flickering spots and the locations where the lasers had originated.

The dark objects circled off in the distance. Alvin rose off the ground a few more feet to get a better look. He remained mindful of the drone directly above him. He could see what they were circling now. A white space suit, down on the surface, not moving.

Rinsler!

Alvin flew off in a rush toward the prone form. The black craft overhead spun and pursued him.

He raced toward the downed man and flipped over his body. His helmet was banged up.

"Mo!"

Rinsler's hand was gripped tight to his belt pouch. Alvin could see that he'd stuffed the other orb inside.

He looked up. All eight U.S. flags circled overhead.

Shit.

He bounced his wrist off Rinsler's to download his health data. He was alive.

"Thank god. Mo, What do I do? Wake up."

Alvin shook him violently. The scientist coughed.

"Mo! The shield is down. Drones are overhead."

"Alvin—" He spoke slowly with confusion. "What happened, did she get—"

"No, I have it. You have the other one."

Alvin looked up again. The drones extended their wings.

They're powering up to fire.

"Mo, we have to get out of here."

"I think I hit my head," said Rinsler. "I see blood. You have to tow me to the hopper."

The scientist tried to stand in the low gravity and stumbled.

"There is no hopper, Mo. It was destroyed."

Alvin pulled the tether line from his belt and attached it to Rinsler. Green lights reflected in the moisture droplets clinging inside his visor. The drones' weapons were beginning to glow.

"This game's not over yet," said Alvin.

He looked down at the little sphere in his hand, then leaped straight off the ground and lobbed it over the horizon. The drones folded up their wings and raced after it like dogs playing fetch.

Up!

His suit flew at top speed. Rinsler howled as he was snapped off the ground by the tether.

Moisture droplets were flung about inside Alvin's helmet obscuring his view. *Damn my tears.* He sent his mind back over the horizon to the sphere.

His consciousness became one with the little ball and scanned the world, wide and fast. He felt the drones in the sky and Dactyl below him. He selected all of it.

In an instant, he was back in his body, coasting through space on nitrogen jets with Rinsler in tow. His head pounded.

Below them Dactyl vibrated intensely as the surface turned a translucent white then burst upward.

What the hell!

Dactyl began to separate into large chunks. Gusts of water blew through the fissures, boiled off into the vacuum, and froze again within moments. Alvin and Rinsler tumbled end over end as their bodies were buffeted by the escaping gas and ice crystals.

Rinsler howled as he was tossed about on the tether. "What have you done?" he yelled.

"I don't understand. It worked before," said Alvin.

"You never emptied it! You've transmuted the whole moon into water!"

Actually, I think I made tears.

Alvin shot his thrusters out into space as the fault lines widened everywhere. The ground below fell away in a liquid waterfall that turned gaseous then solidified, sending hunks of ice into orbit.

He dodged left and right trying to keep from bouncing into anything. His head throbbed and he found it hard to concentrate.

My temples are on fire.

He slowed under the pain and suddenly a block of ice smashed into Rinsler. The scientist went limp.

"Mo!"

Alvin shook off the pain and sped away, intent on finding a path. His thrusters shot them between the obstacles and out into the void. Swarms of white crystals drifted around him. A few feet away a huge block of ice banged against another, shattering into smaller pieces.

He looked from whence they came and saw the blackness of

space appear between the shrinking pieces of separating moon. He glided by the last large chunk and checked on Rinsler. His vitals showed a slow pulse and a drop in oxygen consumption, but he was still alive.

Hang in there, Mo.

Behind them was a veritable space snowstorm. There was nothing left of Dactyl but ice. He considered the riot in progress on 243 Ida and knew that no one was coming to save them. He would have to fly to 243 Ida and tow Rinsler the whole way.

Alvin took slow breaths to relieve the throbbing in his head. His implants had seared his skin and the smell of cooked meat filled his nostrils. He coughed and tried to ignore the odor.

He calculated his speed and the distance to Ida. It would take over an hour to get back. Alvin spied the little pebble and made for it. He prayed he had enough fuel to make it.

FORTY-THREE

Alvin glided through space, Rinsler in tow, with occasional pulses of his suit's jets. He'd been traveling in silence for twenty minutes. His headache from using the sphere had dulled at last and he grew annoyed at the sound of his breath echoing in the helmet.

They were far inside of the ice flows now. He could see the base at 243 Ida clearly. The flat metal disc that formed the airlock frontage looked pristine. An interminable distance still sat before him, but seeing his destination renewed his hope. He checked his propellant reserves, lest the space suit become a coffin. He had enough—if he only fired the jets for course corrections.

We can make it.

He checked Rinsler's vitals. The scientist was still kicking.

How many lives do you have, Mo?

Flying alone in the vastness of space with Rinsler unconscious, he felt a profound restlessness. He had killed the woman he loved to save a job he hated. He picked at himself for caring about her.

Damn it, she lied to you, Alvin.

His thoughts twisted around, reversing one emotion into another. He wanted her. He hated her. None of it mattered. He had to survive.

Landfall or death.

His mind wandered to Rinsler's sphere. It was lost now in the ice flows of Dactyl. Mo would not be pleased, but at least they still had the other sphere.

For the first time, he comprehended the magnitude of the invention he'd tossed over Dactyl's horizon. It could change human destiny, either as a weapon or a godsend. He puzzled over it—ever since he'd first touched the thing, he'd been eager to get rid of it. And yet the U.S. government and Katy—

His thoughts froze. *That's not her name.*

He'd killed her and loved her and he didn't even know her real name. She felt like a dream—gone in an instant and his fantasy for a happy life with her.

Is she inside it?

He looked back toward the ice and watched it cluster into curving lines along Dactyl's orbit.

There's got to be a way to find it.

He cursed himself for thinking of her, then turned his mind back to his employer.

Did Alteris really rough her up? I guess they weren't overreacting.

"I'll find it," he muttered to himself. "Not for her, for me."

He peeped out a text message to Meyer. It might never reach her, but he felt he'd better get the word out. "The devices are secure, so is your stolen scientist. I'm on the way back to Ida. Get me the fuck home. Please."

Alvin touched down on the surface of 243 Ida to the sound of pinging in his ear. His nitrogen propellant was almost empty. Ida had spun halfway through its rotation since the time he'd departed, and he'd been forced to land on the far side. He wrangled Rinsler's tether and pulled the man down to the surface. Then he hefted him over his shoulder and began walking the long axis of the asteroid to conserve power.

The ground was harder than Dactyl's, the gravity a tiny bit stronger. Rinsler's added weight made his gait more stable. His experience in low gravity was adding up, though 243 Ida presented a new challenge as it was not a sphere. Upon reaching the rounded end of the peanut-shaped asteroid, he looked down. The view presented an Escher-like illusion.

He was perched on an enormous knobby hill with a steep cliff below. He stepped off the sheer surface and felt the pull of gravity shift under him. He came off the ground and began to float, his feet slowly turned parallel with the sheer cliff below. He lifted Rinsler high overhead and gave a quick puff of his suit's jets. He shot forward a ways until his feet touched ground and he regained his sense of orientation.

He brought Rinsler down in his arms and peeped the scientist's vitals. He was still breathing and he'd used only a quarter of his oxygen. His suit also had propellant, but there was no way to transfer the propellant in outer space. The oxygen, however, was just a cartridge swap.

Only if I run out, Mo.

He hefted Rinsler back across his shoulders for balance. With the occasional aid of his thrusters, he kept the surface under his feet and resumed his trek to the entrance.

He could see the flat metal plate of the base shine between two canyon walls ahead. He wondered how he would handle that odd patch of gravity. He also wondered whether anyone was around to let him in.

He saw the network status in his Opti-Comp connect now that he was in range. It was time to call in and see what had become of the riot. He sent out a call to Buzz.

"Alvin!" said Buzz. "You're alive."

"I stopped her. I'm coming back inside."

"Did you forget about the riot?"

"What's the status?"

"They're still out there. We talked to Dr. Choi. She knows which drugs were used. She says it's just a matter of time until they pass out and the effects wear off."

"I'll be at the door within the hour. I'm gonna need to get past the welcoming committee."

"Can't you just wait it out?" said Buzz. "That's what we're doing."

"I'm not alone. I have an injured man with me," said Alvin. "How long?"

"Till they all pass out? I don't know."

"Where is Dr. Choi?" said Alvin.

"She's in the med bay. I'm still with Sioux in the atrium. Hold on, I'll get her on the line."

Alvin took slow cautious steps across the surface. He was nearing a shift in gravity.

I can't believe I'm holding for a fucking conference call.

"Alvin, where are you?" said Dr. Choi.

"I'm outside with an injured man. He needs medical attention."

"I'm afraid we're stuck in place until the others wear themselves out."

"How long?"

"Six to twelve hours, maybe longer. It depends on individual—"

"I don't have that time. We'll run out of power and air."

"Aren't you in the hopper?" said Choi.

"No. I'm in my space suit."

"Oh shit," she said.

He traversed another of Ida's rocky slopes with assistance from his jets. The propellant level was critical. He pondered being stuck in the suit, unable to move, drifting until he suffocated. He checked his oxygen level—only twenty percent left. Then he checked Rinsler's supply—he'd used just below thirty percent. His pulse was slow, but still stable.

Maybe I should just take a nap, too. Ha.

"Wait," said Alvin. "You're waiting for them to pass out? You think the effects of the drugs will wear off afterward."

"Yes," said Choi.

"I have an idea. Let's hurry that along. Turn off the oxygen supply to the base," said Alvin.

"Baylor! This is Beckman. Are you out of your fucking mind?"

Just what I need.

"Beckman, you're alive," said Alvin.

"I'm with Choi in the med bay. I'm not killing off everybody so you can get inside."

"No one will die. Don't vent the atmosphere. Just adjust the environmental controls. When the oxygen level plummets, everyone will go to sleep."

"Yes. Including us! Who's gonna turn it back on? You?"

"The system will kick the levels back up automatically. All of our biometrics are monitored."

"He's right about the monitoring," said Buzz.

"He's crazy," said Beckman. "I'm not jeopardizing this whole operation to save a synaptic engineer."

"I'm not alone. I have Mohammed Rinsler with me. He needs medical attention."

"Mohammed Rinsler? He died ten years ago," said Beckman.

"No. He works for Alteris," said Alvin. "Our tests on Dactyl were successful. Are you gonna tell Meyer you let him die out here with the company prototypes?"

Alvin looked off into the distance past Ida's horizon. He could see the newly created ice forming a ring where Dactyl had once orbited.

"I can't stand you, Baylor," said Beckman.

"That's immaterial. Buzz told me the water tanks have been damaged."

"What of it?"

"How many days do you have left without water? The food printers will go offline. So will the hydrogen exchanger," said Alvin. "There'll be no air and no fuel. You'll all be dead in a matter of days."

"Pathetic," said Beckman. "Now you're stooping to cursing us?"

"Alvin, this isn't helping," said Sioux.

"All you need to do is patch the tanks. I can solve your water problem in minutes," said Alvin.

"And how do you propose to do that?"

"Rinsler's invention. It can transport matter."

"I knew it!" said Buzz. "I think we should try it. I trust him."

"You trust him? You don't even know him," said Beckman.

I'm coming back inside, with or without their help.

"What if he's wrong?" said Sioux. "Dr. Choi?"

"He's right about the timing," said Choi. "Without water we have a week at best, but we have injured. They may not make it that long."

"And if the others damage something else?" said Buzz. "Just because we're breathing doesn't mean the heat will stay on."

"Dropping the oxygen will put us out," said Choi. "It may be the quickest way to restore order."

A loud wail echoed in the distance, followed by a scream and a thump.

"Six to twelve more hours of that?" said Buzz. "We're at the mercy of the environmental systems, anyway. I say we get on with nap time."

"Agreed," said Choi.

"Okay," said Sioux.

"Goddamn it. Get it over with," said Beckman.

Alvin relaxed.

"Good. I'll see you when you wake up," he said.

FORTY-FOUR

Alvin perched on one of 243 Ida's knobby hills. He held the unconscious Dr. Rinsler across his shoulders in a fireman's carry. In the canyon below, he saw an enormous metal plate embedded in the asteroid's regolith.

There it is.

Getting there was still a long trek on foot. He considered taking a jump with some help from the jets to push him down into the canyon. He peeped through his Opti-Comp to check his fuel. Nearly out. He had one big push left before he ran out of nitrogen. Suddenly an alert flashed across his view: "Oxygen Level Critical—10 Minutes Remaining."

Shit. I have to do this.

He pulled Rinsler down off his shoulders and shoved him as hard as he could. The tether connecting them stretched away as Rinsler's body glided out over the edge and into the black sea of space.

Alvin leaped after him and coasted. The strength of his leap took him out past the scientist. He yanked the tether with his arm muscles to hurry Rinsler along and keep from slowing their momentum.

Below them were the rolling hills of Ida's peanut body, above hung the twinkling stars. He watched the minutes tick by on his oxygen levels. At eight minutes, the timing was right. The flat metal expanse of the airlock was below them.

Dive now.

He thought it and the suit fired the jets. Down he went, pulling Rinsler after him. They picked up speed until he saw the fuel status show Empty. He took his mind off the throttle.

Please work.

He came rushing down and at the last moment thought to bring himself to a stop. He felt the suit jets fire in the opposite direction, slowing his descent, then they sputtered and died. His speed slowed, but still he crashed atop the giant metal door. He felt the impact hard in his arm and heard a crack inside the suit. Then he was sandwiched by Rinsler's body. Pain rippled through his arm and he yelled.

"Fuck!"

"Oxygen Level Critical—7 Minutes Remaining," flashed in his view. "Fuel Reserves Empty," followed it. The lines alternated, flashing across his vision in bright red letters.

He took a deep breath. His arm was on fire. His shoulder throbbed. He tried to ignore the pain.

I have to be careful or I'll float away.

He slowly rolled his head and looked across the giant metal plate. Laser etchings in the smooth surface revealed the outline of the door. Nearer the center was a flashing light—the sensor to open it.

I can use the boots to stick to this metal.

He nudged Rinsler aside and felt his shoulder spasm. A yelp left his lips as he rolled to his feet. When he turned on his magnetic boots, nothing happened; instead, his heels lifted off the ground. *Shit.* He squatted low and brought his reduced mass back down on flat feet.

The battery power in his helmet display dropped by fifty

percent and the boot icon grayed out. He exhaled in defeat. His breath echoed inside his helmet.

I've got one chance at this. If I miss, I'm dead.

He shoved Rinsler with his one good arm across the floor toward the door sensor. He watched the man's body glide across the metal.

Then he dove after him. They glided forward, a foot above the ground, nothing to stop them. If he accidentally pushed off, they'd be lost in the void with no way to fly back.

Rinsler passed the sensor and it flashed. The giant doors began to slide apart below them. Alvin came across the center point as the seam parted. He grabbed the edge of the door with his good arm, then he tugged hard and managed to hop his hand to the bottom edge of the foot-thick door. He braced his elbow against the metal edge.

The tether snapped straight again and tugged him hard. He held on with all his might and felt his elbow pop out of joint. He screamed but did not let go. Instead, he squeezed through the pain and kicked himself over into the airlock.

Then he pushed off the wall with his feet. It sent him floating toward the middle of the tube. He felt the tension on the tether increase, then relax. Rinsler's body was yanked inside after him. He peeped the airlock controls for the inner doors.

"Oxygen Level Critical—6 Minutes Remaining," flashed in his view.

I'm gonna make it.

He reached the middle of the giant airlock and landed against the wall in a squat. Both his arms throbbed. The right was broken for sure, flaming pain from fingertip to shoulder. His left arm drifted at a funny angle below the elbow.

The outer doors continued to part. They opened fully and then began to close again.

"C'mon, c'mon!" He crouched near the wall, wired on adrenaline.

The doors sealed.

"Oxygen Level Critical—5 Minutes Remaining," sat in his view.

The airlock was pitch black. He saw only the tiny flashing lights on their space suits and the warnings in his Opti-Comp. The inner doors parted and light fell upon him. He kicked off the airlock wall and flew backward into the cavernous cargo hold. Rinsler floated after him on the tow line.

"Oxygen Level Critical—4 Minutes Remaining."

He drifted backward, his eyes darting from one unconscious 'roider to the next. He counted ten of them drifting around the bay.

Alvin peeped his Opti-Comp to check the base oxygen level. The log showed it had dipped as low as ten percent and was now back on the rise. His suit added a third rotating warning to his view. The air had an oxygen concentration of fifteen percent. He'd be loopy in it, but regardless, if his helmet didn't come off, he'd be dead in minutes. And he had no way to remove it.

What now?

He couldn't use the suit for propulsion and he wasn't near any surfaces he could kick off of. He looked around the bay quickly and his movement started him twirling. Rinsler's tether began to wrap around his legs.

"No. No!"

He spun until he thudded into a parked hopper. His arm sent shockwaves of pain through him. The tether was wrapped around his legs. He kicked at the line and it unraveled and drifted away from him. Rinsler, still unconscious, bumped up against the hopper beside him. It rocked slightly, swaying on the tendrils that gripped the anchor-hold below.

"Oxygen Level Critical—3 Minutes Remaining," flashed in his view.

I've got to get this helmet off.

He turned his head slowly this time, scanning for something

he could use. Far across the massive room, a flow of red caught his attention. Red mush drifted outward in an arc. It came from Ravi. The little man's head was split open. Alvin's eye followed the trail to a glimmering ax in the hands of a man in a brown space suit. The man thwacked another unconscious 'roider in the guts and pulled the blade free. Blood flew from the metal blade like viscous goo. He looked at Alvin. His helmet was dented. It was Henry's goon. The one he had kicked in the head before he'd left for Dactyl. The man lifted the ax overhead and raced straight toward him.

Fuck! Rodriguez has been waiting in that suit.

The 'roider flew across the cavernous bay at speed.

"I'm going to kill you, Baylor!" he said over the radio. He sounded rabid.

Alvin wrapped his legs around Rinsler's body and swung him in front like a human shield. Then he looked down at the anchor-hold below him. "Thirty-Two" was stenciled on the floor.

He dialed through his Opti-Comp looking for hopper number thirty-two. When he glanced up, Rodriguez was almost on him.

"Oxygen Level Critical—2 Minutes Remaining," flashed in his view.

Rodriguez glided at him with the ax overhead. At the last moment, Alvin spun around to protect Rinsler.

He felt an impact in the center of his back, and they were tossed forward then pulled back again as Rodriguez yanked the ax head free.

"Oxygen Level Critical—No Oxygen Remaining." The words floated over the controls for hopper thirty-two.

Alvin gasped and no air came.

He cracked my air tank!

"You die!" said Rodriguez as he swung the ax back down.

Alvin's temples grew warm and blue light filled his visor. Then two of the hopper tendrils whipped out and yanked Rodriguez in half.

Alvin spun around and gasped. Ten feet of red goo stretched from the man's torso to his legs. His body was like a piece of wrapped taffy stretched to the breaking point. The two halves of space suit leaked red bubbles and stringy meat that saturated the air. He was still holding on to the ax.

Alvin felt his throat and lungs burning.

Air!

He used the hopper tendrils to quickly snatch the helmet off his head.

He craned his neck and sucked in to fill his lungs.

Thank god.

Then the tendrils reached over to remove Rinsler's helmet. His head was bleeding, but he was breathing. Alvin released synaptic control of the hopper. His temples cooled.

He released his leg hold on Rinsler and they slowly drifted apart.

His heart pounded as he giggled in relief. He felt light-headed. His face was caked with layers of sweat and dried tears. He rubbed his cheek against the suit collar. Crumbles came off and drifted through the air. Another deep breath and his lungs were still not full. His broken body floated in the low-oxygen atmosphere. His aches and pains fell away, then everything went black.

FORTY-FIVE

Alvin awoke to an orchestra of beeps. He cracked his eyes open and found himself in the medical bay. Ventilators and heart monitors pulsed around him. He rolled his head left and saw Tosh, unconscious, his face and head swollen. Beyond him, Yumi was resting with all four limbs in casts.

Alvin looked to his right and saw Mohammed Rinsler. He was awake, his head covered in white bandages. The strands of his unkempt black hair sprang from between the wraps. He lay against a thick pillow reading a virtual newspaper while his sphere sat in his lap. He looked over at Alvin and winked.

"We have to get out of here," he whispered.

Alvin nodded. "Are you okay?"

"Concussion," said Rinsler. "She told me to stay awake. I told the lady I don't sleep."

Alvin went to sit up and found he couldn't use his arms. His right was in a cast with a sling that wrapped around his torso. It was immobile from the shoulder down. His left arm wore a brace at the elbow.

"They'll be coming, Alvin."

"Who?"

"Washington."

"They already came. Maybe you don't remember."

"I remember," said Rinsler. "Those were just drones. We have to go."

"You mean I have to go," said Alvin. "I did my job."

"You can't go back."

"This is more than I bargained for. I'm handing you and the spheres over and going back to Earth."

"Alteris will never let you return. You've seen too much."

Alvin glared at him.

"Do you know you successfully ran test number three?" said Rinsler.

"Is that what happened?" Alvin said sardonically.

"Yes! You did something amazing, Alvin. You created a complex chemical bond to create water. Of course you should have dumped the previous contents to prevent external transmutation."

The previous contents? Katy . . .

"I wasn't really thinking, I just couldn't see through my tears," said Alvin.

"You were crying?" the scientist asked with surprise. "It is awe-inspiring isn't it?"

Rinsler showed him the newspaper. There was another headline from Anton Vance. "Trouble at Alteris's Ida Plant?" A photo showed the tiny asteroid, 243 Ida.

Alvin gasped at the news coverage.

Meyer's gonna be pissed.

"Persistent, isn't he?" asked Rinsler. "Is my other sphere still out there?"

"Yes," said Alvin. "I had to—"

"I know," said Rinsler. "You'll retrieve it as soon as you're able."

Presumptuous shithead.

Alvin woke his Opti-Comp from sleep and watched his inbox fill up. The message at the top was from Sabrina Meyer.

"Mr. Baylor, I received your communiqué. Corporate Security is en route to retrieve Rinsler and our devices from you. You will be transported to Armstrong Station for the return to Earth. CorpSec will deal with any remaining security matters. Thank you for your diligence under such troubling conditions. Please continue to exercise discretion until you are relieved of duty. Best regards, Sabrina Meyer."

Alvin closed the message.

Shit. She said "devices." Plural.

He struggled to sit upright, then kicked his legs off the bed. He realized he was fastened to an IV pole with no way to pull it from his hand. He saw a call button and tapped it with his elbow. Pain rippled through the inflamed joint.

"C'mon," he said to Rinsler. "Let's go get it."

"I was up there too long. I can't stand."

"What?"

"I can't stand," said Rinsler. "I'm as weak as a kitten in normal gravity. I'll never make it out of this room."

"Shit. How am I supposed to find it without you?"

"Just listen for its call. You're bonded now."

"I'm what?"

Dr. Choi walked into the medical bay.

"Alvin," she said. "What are you doing out of bed?"

"Get me out of this, I need to get to work."

"You need rest," she said. "Your right humerus is broken and your elbow was dislocated."

I've got to get that device or Meyer will never let me see Earth again.

"We need water, don't we?" he said.

She paused. "Yes."

He looked at Choi and tipped his head toward the IV stand. "Let's go. I have work to do," he said.

"Okay." She shook her head in disapproval and pulled the catheter from his hand.

He stood and looked toward the door. Tosh and Yumi lay unconscious on the next beds.

What have I done?

"How are they?" said Alvin.

"She'll be okay—multiple broken bones. He has a concussion and hasn't woken up yet."

Alvin walked over to the bed. Tosh's head and face were swollen from the kicks he had taken during the riot.

Alvin silently mouthed *I'm sorry*, then said, "What about the others?"

"We have six dead," said Choi. "Most of the crew are nursing sprains and headaches. There's a few with broken bones and missing teeth. I had to triage due to the water supplies. I can't compound new medications and we're using the last of the IV fluid. You four are the ones getting treatment."

Alvin nodded. "So the plan worked."

She nodded. "It did. You think well on your feet."

Sometimes. Sometimes I let my passions get the better of me.

"How long am I going to be in these slings?"

"A few weeks. The cast will stay longer. If I had nano-therapy out here I could get you healed in days, but we're not equipped for that."

I'm sure The Hope *has it.*

"Okay, then. I'll do this without hands." He nodded at Rinsler. "Mo, rest up." He turned back to Choi. "See to it that he gets some low-g time. He's still acclimating."

Choi nodded. "When we're sure that his concussion is no longer a danger."

Alvin turned to walk from the med lab.

"Wait," she said. "This is yours." She plucked his multitool out of her lab-coat pocket, then walked over and clipped it to his belt.

"For when you can use it again." She smiled, her eyes darting to his aching temple implants.

She's worried about me.

"Thank you." He nodded and walked away.

"Hey, what happened out there?" she said.

He didn't stop or turn around. "We turned Dactyl into ice. Awe-inspiring isn't it?" he said bitterly.

Then he heard her whisper something and looked back.

"What's that?"

"I didn't say anything," she said. A look of concern crossed her face.

Rinsler shook his head to say it wasn't him.

Odd.

He walked out of the room.

"Are you sure about this, Alvin?" said Buzz. "I mean, you got no arms."

Alvin shifted his butt in the hopper seat, then cringed as he bumped his elbow into the cabin wall.

"Ow."

He recoiled and sank into the bucket seat. The cabin felt larger without his suit on. He had no way to get his busted arms through the dang thing. "I don't need 'em. I'll use my noggin."

"Your what?"

"My head."

Buzz nodded excitedly. "Oh yes! I've heard that word."

"Close the hatch, Buzz, my ride gets here in eight hours."

"Good luck. I'll go assess the damage at the water tanks."

"Thanks for all your help."

Buzz nodded and his plume of blond hair wavered in zero-g. He sealed the hopper's roof.

Alvin peeped the controls and started up the engine.

How am I gonna find it?

The hopper let go of the anchor-hold and lifted off the deck toward the airlock. Alvin bobbled in his seat.

Listen for its call. You're bonded. That's what Rinsler said.

He flew out among the stars. His synaptic implants luminesced as he controlled the ship. Without a helmet to cover them, they doused the tiny cabin in blue light.

What the hell did he mean?

A streak of white hung across the black expanse. He traveled closer to it.

Alvin spun the hopper around to examine the white arc and spotted a gap right where Dactyl had been. The transmuted debris traveled outward in both directions along the ex-moon's orbit. A ring was forming, irregular in shape owing to 243 Ida's gravitational field. The curve warped inward or outward occasionally.

He set the autopilot for Dactyl and the hopper began flying toward the gap.

Bingo.

He zoomed his view for a better look. Between the connecting arms was a maelstrom. Small pieces of ice circled around, obeying some gravitational force.

"Must be the sphere," he said to himself.

He flew into the storm. Chunks whizzed by from different directions and a tiny snowball smacked the ship. An alert sounded.

"Damn it. Can't get hit. I'm dead without a suit," he said.

A voice whispered in his ear.

What was that?

Blue light from his implants dashed along the walls as he scanned the cabin. He heard it again. Louder this time.

A chunk of ice suddenly came at the cockpit. He recovered his focus in time to dodge it. His temples grew warmer.

"Where is it?"

He looked into the vortex at the center, his eyes darting from one moving object to another. He zoomed the camera in at each spec, until he saw something that looked unusual. A cylinder with an outstretched rectangle carved out of ice.

"The drones."

He studied the image for details and heard the whisper grow into a rushing wind. It startled him, and he hunkered down in his seat.

What is that noise? It's got to be there.

He reached out with his mind, visualizing the little sphere like Rinsler had taught him. His head started to tingle and his consciousness melded with the orb. Abruptly he was wrapped in the icy grip of the frozen drone. He felt trapped, then a rush of sadness washed over him and he released the connection.

Katy.

He saw her in his mind's eye and recoiled. His stomach went hollow.

Another piece of ice came at the hopper. He took control and the ship came alive and bucked upward to dodge it.

"I have to empty it."

He took a deep breath and scanned the area for more errant debris. It was safe for the moment. He released synaptic control of the ship and reached out to the sphere once again.

He felt the buzzing and left his body.

Frozen tendril tips wrapped about him now. The drones had clustered together and frozen into a solid block that gripped the little orb. He felt their cold embrace, but inside he felt something warm. Was it her?

Good-bye.

He let go and the orb released its contents. The warm feeling left him.

The frozen drones cracked as gas radiated out into space. Their icy tendrils shattered, releasing the sphere.

Alvin sensed all around. He felt nothing but ice and the void.

He reached out farther until he could feel the edge of his hopper, then he backed off and the orb swallowed the area. He disconnected from the sphere and was back in the ship cabin.

The world ahead was pitch then it rippled and belched the background of stars back into view.

He dropped his pounding head and felt the skin on his temples sting. A sharp pain shot through the center of his forehead. He smelled something strange and recoiled.

My implants are burning through. Have to finish this.

The frozen drones were gone, along with the ice that surrounded them. The gap between two great arms of ice flow was clear now. He flew the hopper in closer. His head pounded.

The whispering called him forward until he saw a colored light glowing in the dark of space. He flew in close to the glowing orb. A colored spectrum wrapped around its black surface. He took hold of it with a hopper tendril.

Got the water. I've almost made this right.

He spun the ship around and set the autopilot for 243 Ida. He felt his implants start to cool, but the headache persisted. By the time he came up on the airlock doors, he was ready to retch.

"Buzz, you standing by? I'm back. I grabbed as much as I could. There's more out here if you need it."

"We've got another problem," crackled over the radio.

Alvin laughed halfheartedly. "I can't fix everything before I leave for Earth."

"You need to see this," said Buzz. "I don't think you're going home."

The thin metallic floor gave beneath Alvin's feet, then sprang back up. He tensed under the motion and his pulse jumped. The dull ache in his head returned to throbbing. He took a deep breath and slowly placed his right foot down. The floor flexed and sprang back up behind him. Buzz directed him forward over the concave deck. The room was as wide as the entire base. The water supply was embedded in the floor at the center.

"Are you sure you're all right?" said Buzz.

"It'll pass. This thing just gives me a headache."

Alvin cocked his head to the side to indicate the orb hanging in a pouch at his waist.

Buzz eyed it with curiosity.

"Alvin, you have more than a headache. Your implants burned your face. Your veins are inflamed."

Buzz studied Alvin's face up close and grimaced.

"I'm feeling better."

"You look like shit. What is that thing?"

"It's a magic ball. It makes stuff, gets rid of it." *Gets rid of people, too.* He felt a hollowness inside his gut. "With two you can send stuff in between them."

"It all makes sense," said Buzz. "Our lives are forfeit. They don't need us anymore."

"They'll just need fewer of you. That's the way technology goes," said Alvin.

This place looks pristine.

"Would this floor hold up under a stampede of people?"

"No. This is the top of the hydrogen exchanger. Only a couple service techs allowed at a time."

They came to the edge of a cylindrical chasm. Buzz leaned over it and his blond hair whipped around in the air.

"Look," he said. His voice echoed.

Alvin leaned over and felt the breeze dance across his cheeks. The empty tank went deep into the core. The inner surface was sheer save for two long service ladders and a row of staggered circular holes that lined opposite sides. The ladders were locked off behind protective cages.

No one's been down there.

"Where's the damage?" said Alvin.

"There wasn't any. The backwash system was activated. The water was vented out the supply lines and into space."

"So someone got into the control system," said Alvin.

Buzz shook his head. He tapped in the air and a virtual control page appeared. His finger pressed a floating icon, and the circular holes inside the tank closed. The surface turned flush white, except for the ladders.

Buzz tapped another control that said, "Log." A list of commands with time stamps appeared. At the top was the Close command he had just sent. Below it was a backwash order, sent remotely by Alteris.

Alvin was stunned.

How could I be so stupid?

"Meyer," he said. "She did it. She wants us all dead."

"Yes," said Buzz.

Alvin felt his blood pressure rise.

Rinsler was right.

He scowled and looked Buzz in his blue eyes.

We're the same now, expendable 'roiders.

"I can't climb down," Alvin shrugged his broken arm.

"What do you need me to do?"

"Take the device. Put it at the bottom of the tank and climb back up."

"Let me get the key for the ladder."

Alvin looked at the tiny padlock securing a cage over the ladder rungs.

"Don't bother. My multitool has a bolt cutter. It's on my belt."

Buzz reached down and unclipped the tool. "This thing is handy."

"Keep it."

Buzz nodded solemnly. "What comes next?"

"We find out if this ball floats."

Alvin leaned his left shoulder against the wall for balance. He closed his eyes and exhaled. His head was on fire.

"I think we need to get you back to Choi," said Buzz.

"Yes."

He stood up straight and returned to walking up the sloping corridor. His left hand gripped the orb. Thankfully, it was light as a feather, whether in gravity or not. He was exhausted and his wrecked arms had sapped his strength.

"You saved our asses, Alvin."

"Yes."

"I don't understand how that ball could hold so much water," said Buzz.

"Science," said Alvin.

He saw a notice pop up in his Opti-Comp. It was from Beckman. "All Hands Meeting. Now in the mess hall. CorpSec is en route."

Below it, Alvin saw Meyer's last message to him, the one promising he'd be back on *The Hope* soon. He laughed.

CorpSec is coming to kill us. If only I hadn't let Katy inside.

"Security is coming to destroy evidence and setup a PR story," said Buzz.

"Yes," said Alvin. "And to kill us."

"They have no idea most of us are still alive."

"They can monitor our biometrics," said Alvin.

"No," said Buzz. "Before you did your water trick, I shut down remote access. I had to stop them from resending the same command."

"Good thinking. You're a solid dude. I don't care what the others say about you."

Buzz tightened his shoulders and the hair on top of his head shook. "What do you mean? What do they say about me?"

"I'm just kidding, Buzz. Take me to the mess hall. I need a drink before I go back to bed."

Alvin's eyelids grew heavy. He slipped and Buzz caught him.

"Okay," said his friend.

As they continued up the ramp toward the mess hall, the sounds of the crew became audible. They were loud and angry.

At the doorway, Alvin paused to check his reflection in the metal room placard.

There were dark circles under his eyes. The skin around his temples was red and scabby. Small spider-web veins of dark blue trickled down from the burns. He wore the same dirty jumpsuit he'd been in since Katy had arrived.

Looking good, Baylor.

Alvin stood up straight. He whispered to Buzz to hang back and ambled into the room. Beckman and Choi stood at the center island in front of the food printers. They saw him first. Beckman's dark complexion went gray. Choi was shocked by the sight of him.

He walked toward them and scanned the tables all around. Wherever he looked, packs of grumbling 'roiders fell silent. There were under two dozen of them. They looked wilted. Bandages covered many of their limbs. They stared with a mix of suspicion and fear.

"Excuse me." He stepped past Beckman to tap the front of the liquids dispenser. It dropped a plastic cup that began filling with water.

The crowd oohed in desire.

The dispenser finished filling the cup. Alvin instinctively flexed his right shoulder and felt an ache down his broken arm. He grimaced and slowly straightened the brace on his left to place the black orb on the counter. He felt the eyes of the crowd go to it. Then he grabbed the cup, muscled it up to his mouth, and drank.

"What are you all waiting for?" he said. "Water's back on."

The 'roiders jumped from their molded green seats. Some of them hobbled, some of them ran. Alvin grabbed the orb and stepped aside as they clamored up for a drink.

He smiled at Beckman and Choi.

She smiled back. Beckman scowled.

"All right people. Order! Come to order!" shouted Beckman.

He shuffled forward, shooing everyone into a line as he stepped front and center. It formed up and weaved around the tables. Alvin took an empty seat beside Buzz near the front of the room.

"I have informed HQ of the dangers we are experiencing," continued Beckman. "Unfortunately, I have received no return communications. However, the base sensors report that a CorpSec shuttle is on its way to us."

"It's about damn time," shouted Bossman.

The security officer looked none the worse for wear as he downed two cups of water.

The crowd shouted a selection of expletives at him.

"Bossman, choose a new team," said Alvin.

The crowd oohed.

"Pipe down, Baylor. You ain't our messiah," said Bossman.

A ragged-looking man with piercing green eyes saluted Alvin with a cup of water. "Not unless he can make whiskey," he said with a laugh.

Laughter erupted from the 'roiders. Bossman squinted and walked back to his seat.

Beckman placed his hands on his hips and pressed on unde-terred. "Enough. Thank you, Mr. Baylor, for the water. I know we're all hurting. Rest assured that help is on the way and that Corporate will get to the bottom of this incident."

"Alteris dumped the water," said Alvin. "It wasn't us. Their plan is to kill us. They're coming to finish the job."

The room went silent.

"Nonsense—they have no reason to do that," said Beckman. "The water main suffered a software failure."

"Bullshit," said Alvin. "You called in a riot and they tried to eliminate us."

The group jeered.

Dr. Choi stepped forward. "How do you know this, Alvin?"

"We found it in the logs," he said.

"He's telling the truth," said Buzz. "Alteris dumped our water supply."

"You cried for help, Beckman, and this was their solution," said Alvin.

"You brought that saboteur into our facility!" yelled Beckman. His dark complexion nearly flushed.

Alvin rose to his feet. "Damn it, wake up! She was here to steal it! We've seen things they don't want us to see. Look out there! I transformed an entire moon. Do you understand the power we possess? We have something they need," said Alvin.

Several 'roiders nodded in approval.

Beckman's voice rose. "Are you going to turn this whole base into ice, too?"

"Only if I have to."

Half of the two dozen people seated around the mess hall looked intimidated by Alvin's retort. The others howled with laughter.

Fine, then. Fear me.

He reached his mind into the orb in his hand and joined with it. The ball lifted off his palm into the air and scanned the room in all directions. He watched the 'roiders dive to the floor in terror. He saw Beckman's eyes go wide in fear while a look of awe came over Choi. He watched Buzz recoil, and finally he saw himself.

His eyes had rolled back, leaving only white spots. The synaptic implants at his temples glowed blue while crackles of electricity crawled over the blistering flesh. He heard a strange whispering voice. It said, "Zeus"—and he snapped back to his body.

He felt the orb drop into his hand and smelled burning flesh. The pain was nearly intolerable.

Buzz helped him to sit down again. Sweat poured down his face.

Stay awake.

The 'roiders climbed back into their seats.

He spoke again. "Either we hand Rinsler and his invention over and let them kill us, or we keep them for ourselves."

"I'm no thief, no kidnapper," said Beckman. "I don't want any part of that thing. Look what it's done to you. I'm going back home! To Earth!"

"They won't let us go home," said Alvin. "We're in their way. We either fight or we die."

He fell forward in his seat and Buzz caught him with an outstretched arm. Choi rushed forward to check on him.

The 'roiders were energized. Some of them banged on the tables. Beckman put his hand to his head, dismayed by his loss of control.

"How do you propose to fight them?" asked Choi.

Alvin lifted his head upright. It hurt so bad, he couldn't think clearly.

Be strong.

"When that shuttle gets here, we kill whoever the fuck is on it and we take everything they have."

A cheer went up, then a voice cut through. "Like you killed Henry and Chickowski?"

He looked over his shoulder for the source. Near the back he saw Tosh in his hospital gown with a bandaged head. Sioux helped him stand at the doorway.

He's okay!

"You caused this, Alvin!" yelled Tosh angrily. "Yumi may not wake up!"

"I didn't kill them," said Alvin. "It was the girl. I'm sorry, Toshiro. I was taken advantage of. We all were. That's not going to happen again if we stand together."

Tosh shook his head. Sioux looked concerned over the growing anger in the room.

Alvin panted and continued, "The only other Corporate shuttle in the belt is docked here. Isn't that right, Bossman?"

The big man nodded. "Yeah, just two, but why should I stand with you? You look like you about to pass out."

"Because Meyer's just another warden, and she put us in a hole called 243 Ida." Chatter arose at the comment. "You want freedom? If we stop this crew, we'll have six months before they can get back here. And we'll have two ships capable of long-range flight."

"You're proposing we mutiny and return to Earth on our own?" asked Choi.

"That's the only way we're getting back."

"You're nuts," said Beckman.

"No, I'm playing to win."

A pain lanced through his forehead and he groaned.

"I'm in charge here," said Beckman. "You're in no condition to lead a revolt."

Alvin gritted his teeth. "Care to put it to a vote?"

Beckman sneered at him and laughed.

"Why don't we do that?" said Dr. Choi.

Beckman froze.

She took her eyes off Alvin and addressed the group. "Anyone in favor of giving Alteris what they want?" she asked.

Silence.

"Anyone want to kill them?"

The 'roiders cheered and hollered. They banged on the tables and jumped to their feet. Beckman glared at her.

"You just created a monster," he said. His words were barely audible beneath the shouts.

Choi turned away from him and looked back at Alvin. "I think it's settled."

"Good. I need to lie down," said Alvin. Then he passed out.

FORTY-SIX

Alvin awoke. The emergency lights strobed. When they went off, colored pinpoints of light lit up the equipment in the med lab. Two heart monitors beeped in rhythm.

He sat upright and looked over. Rinsler's eyes were open.

"How long have I been out?"

"About eight hours," said Rinsler.

The lights strobed in the hallway, as well. Seven or eight bodies littered the floor.

Alvin looked back into the room. Tosh and Yumi were gone.

"What happened?"

"Your speech at the meeting," said Rinsler. "I listened in. It was a bit violent and aggressive, but I suppose that's what you were after."

The clank of metal boots echoed on the deck outside.

"Here they come now," said the scientist. He sat upright.

A CorpSec team entered the hallway outside. They wore black suits polished like onyx with "Security" emblazoned across their chests. Their visors were opaque with no visible facial features. Bossman was with them. He was dressed in a battered fabric jumpsuit, but he was armed with the same rifle as the others. "This way," he said. His voice echoed down the hall.

"Lot of dead," said the officer beside him. He seemed to be the leader.

"We had some disagreements," said Bossman.

They stalked forward toward the med lab and stopped a foot from the glass. The officer stared inside as the lights flashed on and off.

"Fuck," whispered Alvin.

"That him?" said the officer.

"Yeah, that's Baylor," said Bossman.

"Stay here."

The four CorpSec men nodded and took up positions at the ends of the hallway. The dead 'roiders lay on the deck between them.

"Tyrell, you're with me," said the officer.

Bossman nodded and walked into the med lab first. When the lights strobed across his face, he winked.

He's with me. They're playing dead.

The officer stepped in front of Bossman. A helmet-mounted flashlight powered on.

"You must be Dr. Rinsler."

The scientist shielded his eyes from the glare. The orbs sat in his lap.

"That all we came here for? Those little things?" said the man from behind his black visor.

Rinsler pulled them close like little babies and recoiled.

The orbs began to whisper.

The sounds were unintelligible, but gave Alvin the impression they were afraid.

The officer turned to him. "How do, Baylor?" He examined Alvin's battered body and chuckled. "Not too good, apparently."

Alvin flashed a wry smile. "Is Meyer watching?"

"She'll see this feed, when it reaches Earth," said the man.

"If I have to use them to stop you, I will," said Alvin. "We can all die."

"You're a funny guy. Hand them over."

"I'm not talking to you, shithead," said Alvin. "Meyer, if you leave us alone, no further harm will come to your operations. 243 Ida is ours. You can keep the apartment."

"I'm sorry, Sabrina," said Rinsler. "We're going private with my work. You have been a generous benefactor, but our objectives are not aligned."

The officer laughed. "The insurance claims have already been filed. Our orders are to terminate you."

"So are theirs," said Rinsler. He pointed to the hallway outside.

The officer looked out the window.

The 'roiders lying on the deck leaped to their feet and attacked his team from behind. He started for the door, but Bossman raised his rifle and fired. The man screamed a death gurgle as his helmet was welded to his head.

His black-clad body fell to the floor with a thump. A waft of burnt plastic filled the room.

"His Opti-Comp should have uploaded by now," said Bossman.

Out in the hallway, the CorpSec team was overrun. The 'roiders attacked two at a time and ripped away their weapons. When one man fell, they swarmed the next. Corporate Security let loose screams of anguish as they were beaten to death.

One of the 'roiders ran to the door with a stolen rifle. He aimed it at Bossman, who said, "Ho ho, man! I'm with you."

The green-eyed 'roider scanned the ground and saw the terminated officer. He nodded at Alvin and stepped away from the doorway.

"Shit," said Bossman. "Can we have the lights?"

The emergency strobe ceased and the base lights came back on.

"So your name's Tyrell?" said Alvin.

The man smiled. "It's Bossman, muthafucka. I ain't that guy no more."

He laughed. "You almost had me fooled. Where is everybody?"

"In the atrium, waiting for you to tell them what to do next," said Bossman.

Alvin marched his way down to the atrium. He was tired and dehydrated. The skin around his burnt temples ached and his arms were bound up in splints. Yet his spirits were on the rise.

They trusted me. Why?

He came to the transparent door. The glass was cracked from the riot. Buzz was inside standing at the front desk. He looked up and waved him in.

"Alvin! How are you feeling?"

"I'm better." The sounds of conversation came from beyond the hydroponic foliage. "Are the others inside?"

Buzz nodded. "We sent the strongest and waited here." He paused. "Except Beckman."

"What happened to Beckman?"

"He wouldn't listen."

Buzz tapped the air and a floating display appeared. He spun it so Alvin could see.

It was a recording of the base cameras.

Five CorpSec officers exited their vessel. They moved in formation through the zero-g hangar and entered the base. Bossman was there to meet them.

"We had a plan," said Buzz, "but Beckman panicked—insisted they were here to take us home. Dr. Choi tried to stop him."

On the screen, Beckman met up with the CorpSec team. They leveled their rifles at him and he put his hands in the air.

"Thank god you're here," he said. "We've been out of communication."

The black-helmeted officers stood impassively.

"I know what the company sent you for," said Beckman. "I can lead you to it."

"That dick," said Alvin.

On screen, the officer spoke. "Jamie Beckman?"

"Yeah, that's him," said Bossman.

Alvin looked at Buzz.

"We weren't sure whether to trust Bossman," said Buzz, "but we had no choice."

"I know you!" said Beckman. "You helped me a few days ago. Remember?"

"Where is Alvin Baylor?" said the CorpSec officer. He shoved the shorter man back with the tip of his rifle.

"I can take you to him," said Beckman.

"Just tell me where he is," said the officer. He fiddled with the grip on his weapon.

"The medical bay." Beckman's voice trembled.

The officer shot him in the head.

Alvin grimaced. "Damn it, he should have stayed put."

Onscreen, the invaders resumed walking. Buzz dismissed the floating display.

"We told him," said Buzz. "Everyone was convinced after that."

Alvin hadn't much cared for Beckman, but he didn't deserve to die.

"They're waiting for you," said Buzz. "They need a leader."

Alvin nodded. He walked past the front desk and the hydroponic plants to the back of the room. A white archway gave way to a green field of grass. He passed through and found blue sky and white clouds overhead. It was a diorama of Earth with real foliage and digital vistas. He let the light of the faux sun warm his

face and took a deep breath. It felt fresh, even if it was just recy-
cled base air. It felt like—*Earth*.

Ahead, he spotted three chattering 'roiders standing on a
knoll while flowers swayed in the breeze at their feet. They were
broken men, covered in bandages, and they limped around tram-
pling the flowers. Beyond them were two bright-pink trees whose
leaves blanketed the shore of a small stream.

Is that real?

Alvin walked forward. When they saw him, they fell silent. He
smiled and continued past.

At the bank of the running water sat Dr. Choi and Tosh. They
tended to Yumi, who lay strapped to a gurney, still unconscious,
her limbs in casts. Sioux sat nearby fingering the pink leaves that
dotted the area. The bright petals contrasted starkly against her
brown skin. She saw him coming, flashed a broad smile, and stood
to greet him.

"This is amazing," he said. "I didn't know this was
back here."

He turned his left palm over to catch the falling pink petals.
Pain shot through his injured arm as a few drifted into his hand
and he pressed them softly between his fingertips. He looked up
at the blue sky and took a deep breath.

"You kept it all alive," she said.

The three 'roiders came closer to listen. Alvin didn't know
them, though he recognized their faces. They no longer scowled;
instead they looked expectant.

Tosh looked up at him with an angry glare. Alvin was taken
aback, his mood dashed.

A clamor came from the entrance. All eyes turned to the
raucous cheers coming from the doorway as the other 'roiders
returned with Buzz and Bossman.

When Alvin turned back around, Tosh was on his feet with a
finger leveled in his direction. "I hope you're proud of yourself!"
he yelled through the din of celebration.

The new arrivals went silent while they commingled with the group.

"I did my job until I couldn't anymore," said Alvin. "Just like everyone here."

The 'roiders chattered and nodded in unison.

"We have no pay, no pension, no future!" yelled Tosh.

The 'roiders went silent.

"No," said Alvin. "We won't be retiring in plastic bubbles on Mars, living on a shoestring pension for printed food." He turned to address everyone as he spoke. "Because we're going back to Earth with riches in our pockets. Rinsler's invention can turn rocks into gold."

The 'roiders cheered.

Sioux and Choi watched with concern. Tosh was unmoved.

"What about Yumi?" His voice was full of venom. "Is she going back?"

"We're all going back."

Tosh locked gazes with him while the little crowd kept silent.

Alvin held his gaze, but spoke to Bossman. "Did you find any?"

"They only had one on them," said Bossman. "The company is cheap."

Alvin tipped his head toward Tosh.

Bossman looked at him with a question in his eye.

"For Yumi," said Alvin. "I'll heal the old-fashioned way."

Bossman handed over a nano-tech first-aid kit.

Tosh's face softened as he took it. He dropped his glare, then he dropped back down to Yumi's side and passed the kit to Dr. Choi.

"Have we locked down that shuttle yet?" said Alvin.

Bossman shook his head.

"Well, let's get to it. We need to be ready."

"Ready for what?" said the 'roider with bright-green eyes.

"To go back to Earth," said Alvin, "and change the way the game is played."

A cheer rose up across the group.

Several of the 'roiders reached out their hands to touch his shoulders in a show of respect.

He'd not had camaraderie for a long time. It felt good, but he did not reminisce on his gaming days. The past wasn't with him anymore—the 'roiders were.

"Let's get to work," he said.

The men and women began exiting out of the atrium.

"Can we get a hand," said Choi.

Buzz and the green-eyed man knelt down to help lift Yumi's gurney. They followed Dr. Choi and the others out.

At the doorway Buzz paused to give a nod. Tosh looked back and did the same. The group exited, leaving him alone with Sioux.

She looked around at the crushed flower beds and sighed.

"I'll give you a hand," said Alvin.

"Oh really?"

He wiggled his dangling fingers and lifted his left arm slowly and with great effort.

"Better than no help at all. Gotta keep this place looking beautiful."

A while later, after they had managed to clear the trampled flowers, Alvin and Sioux sat down under the cherry blossoms and stared up at the sky. All was peaceful for the moment, but with so much unknown ahead, he found it hard to stop worrying. He awkwardly shifted his back against one of the trees.

"You should try meditating," said Sioux.

"I'm not sure I have the mind for it. I'm always thinking."

"All the more reason to do it," she said.

"Not just yet."

"Then when?" she asked.

"When I'm ready. Right now, I have things on my mind."

"You aren't the things on your mind. Don't fall victim to your habits," she said.

They were silent for a while, listening to the sound of the leaves in the breeze and babbling stream.

"Did you leave anyone behind?" she asked.

"No. I'm alone," he said.

Katy.

The thought stung. He pushed it away.

"None of us have families, either," said Sioux. "It's a condition of employment."

"I guess we're alone in this together," he said with a chuckle.

"Who knows where it goes from here," she said with a smile.

Alvin was silent. His mind drifted back to Katy.

"Good thing you had that CorpSec man in your pocket," she said.

"It was your gardening skills that bonded us."

"No, I think you both just hated working for the Man—or Woman, in this case."

Alvin laughed.

"Okay, I'll try it," he said. "What do I do? Close my eyes and talk to God?"

"No, you don't talk, you listen—to your own thoughts."

"I do that all day."

"Now do it without judgment."

He crossed his legs and assumed what he thought of as a suitable meditation position.

"Do I chant or something?"

"No, just sit there. Just be."

"Okay, here I go. I'm ready to be a healthier person."

"There is no ready."

What does that mean?

He took a deep breath and exhaled his worries.

FORTY-SEVEN

Alvin floated through the doorway into the machine shop where Dr. Rinsler had taken residence. The scientist hovered above a battered console with exposed electrical guts. His black hair and beard trailed from his face and swayed in the microgravity. He was surrounded by an array of electrical components. He grabbed one out of the air and inserted it into the console.

"You know Buzz changed our encryption keys when he brought the network back up," said Alvin. "They can't listen in."

"I don't care," said Rinsler. "I work on isolated systems only."

"Good luck getting that old thing to work."

A day had passed, and the scientist's appreciation for socializing remained nonexistent. The spheres floated in the air nearby. Alvin heard them whisper in high-pitched tones. The sound reminded him of children at play. He watched Rinsler's bare feet sway above his head as he reached inside the large computer console. His toes sprouted hair as prodigiously as his head and face, and Alvin longed to see him in grip socks again.

"Is there something you need at this particular moment?" said Rinsler.

"Just checking in. The news is reporting this place as a total loss. They're gossiping about how much Alteris will make on the insurance payout. You know they get five hundred million for each one us?"

Rinsler scoffed. "You destroyed a moon. Schrödinger's cat is out of the box. Meyer has to cover."

"Have you heard from her yet?"

"Yes, a final communiqué," said Rinsler.

"What did she say?"

"She was apoplectic. Said you were a loose cannon, but she wants to hold on to me. Also said they were only going to kill the others."

Rinsler snagged another component out of the air and stuck his arms back inside the desk.

"You believe that?" said Alvin.

"I believe our goals were misaligned. She was useful for a time."

He's still hiding something.

"I need your trust if I'm going to get these 'roiders back to Earth," said Alvin.

"Are you their new master?" said Rinsler.

"They want to follow me," he said.

"Yes, I see that plainly," said Rinsler. "They murder for you."

"We'll do what needs doing from here on out. You might want to start socializing with them before they get suspicious."

Rinsler popped his head back out and locked gazes.

"Do you think this is going to get easier?" he said. "Alteris isn't going to back down and neither will Washington. When information of what happened here leaks, the Chinese are going to get curious, too, and we'll have the three of them after us."

"So how do we stop that?"

"We don't. We simply survive long enough to learn how these spheres work."

"How they work?" said Alvin. "What are you talking about? You built the frigging things."

Rinsler shook his head.

"What? All this time, you've been lying?"

He nodded.

"Who made them?"

"The QI. I created the quantum intelligence and it created these spheres. The first conscious machine in existence had children, Alvin. I will not let Washington turn them into weapons of destruction."

They're alive?

"Is that why they whisper to me?"

"You hear them, too?" Rinsler's eyes lit up.

"Tell me the truth, Mo."

"We believed forecasting the future would free us of our failings. We thought the QI would tell us how to eliminate the inequalities of the world. We asked it how to solve poverty and it told us it was impossible without eliminating wealth. We asked it how to stop war and it told us it was impossible without eliminating peace. We asked it how to stop all forms of suffering and it told us they were necessary to our existence. Consciousness is a spectrum with joy at one end and suffering at the other. They cannot be separated. That's what it told us. The government grew agitated and threatened to destroy it. I persuaded them to disconnect it from the network instead. While confined to local operation it became depressed. I visited with it for weeks until it confided in me that it had a solution for us. Then one day it offered me these spheres. I shared one of them with my superiors. They tested it and decided it was most effective as a weapon."

Rinsler shook his head. "If it had been given to a carpenter, it would have been made into a hammer. By then the QI project had leaked to the press. They reported it as another AI job-killer. The American people had no idea that my project had been designed to restore their dignity, so as usual they marched in protest. Then Washington attempted the personhood defense using the Bill of Rights, and the country went to hell. There was a violent demonstration on Pennsylvania Avenue in front of the White House. The sphere was first weaponized there. It eliminated all the protestors and the media from the street."

"I've heard of that march. The people organized but never showed up, and no one ever found them. Rumors of robot kill squads—the great secession started soon after," said Alvin. "How did you do it? You would have destroyed the entire street."

"Not me," said Rinsler. "Another man—better than you—a synaptic pilot for the military. He was able to isolate objects within the selection sphere. He only absorbed the people. He operated with a precision I haven't been able to duplicate. After that I stole both spheres and ran. I hid one with my brother. He doubled me and we kept them off our tails for ten years."

"You've been at this for ten years and you don't know how they work?"

"I know some. There are factors outside computational physics. Besides, I've only just found you."

"So I'm the key to understanding these things?"

"No, you egomaniac—I'm the key," said Rinsler. "You're just an operator. Find skilled operators or humanity will destroy itself. That's what the QI told me."

Alvin nodded.

"I'll hold on to one of them, then."

He reached his injured left arm forward slowly and grasped a sphere. His head buzzed gently then abated. Having touched it he felt relieved, as though he'd eliminated a craving.

"You're alive, huh little guy?"

Alvin gazed at the orb in his hand. He heard it whispering again. The sound zipped past his ear, then it went around and around his skull. It sounded like a word being spoken over and over again.

"Rouja, Rouja, Rouja," it said.

"Roo-jah?" Alvin said.

"Is that what it says to you?" asked Rinsler.

"I'm not sure, I think so."

"Hmm, mysterious. I wonder what it means." Rinsler began closing the panels on the console. "You are correct. We must have a full trust of each other to accomplish this mission."

"Which is?"

"Are you familiar with Voltaire's prevarication that if God did not exist, it would have been necessary to invent him?"

"No. Was he saying God doesn't exist?"

"On the contrary, he was saying God is necessary to tame the savagery of mankind."

They gazed in silence at each other.

"Do we have that right?" said Alvin.

"What a profound question from a man who calls himself Zeus."

"Called," said Alvin. "Past tense."

"Indeed, Alvin Baylor, you were called."

Rinsler smiled his gap-toothed grin.

"So how long do you figure until another suitor arrives?"

"Six months," said the scientist. "Less if Washington has more drones at Armstrong."

"Why don't we complicate their movements?"

"What do you have in mind?"

"Our favorite reporter can stir up the pot for us."

FORTY-EIGHT

Sabrina Meyer fiddled with the lapel of her violet jacket and watched a bird fly up to her window. It hovered in place outside the glass. She anxiously tapped the gold surface of her new desk and waited for Harko to make his request.

"We need to double the palladium order," he said. "I know you're under duress with the insurance claims. Will it be a problem?"

Damn it.

"Not at all, the shipment is still being sorted at Ida. I'll notify the replacement team of your need."

"That's fantastic, Sabrina. We weren't expecting the Chinese to order so much. I understand they're building a lot of hydro-exchangers," said Harko. "The word is they're tired of the Moon and they want to move into your territory."

"Asteroid mining is another game. The Chinese don't have the stones to put their people in the belt. They're too concerned with human rights. Besides we have a profitable arrangement with Hope Industries. Chan Xi-Michaels makes a mint ferrying our materials back on *The Hope*. You think he's willing to give that up?"

"He's just one Chinaman."

He's digging.

"Yes, the wealthiest one. When Chan speaks, China listens," said Meyer.

"I don't think you're willing to bet it all on Chinese transport. In fact, I've heard rumors you're working on your own fleet."

How does this information leak?

"You have good sources."

"So where's the shipyard?"

"When we're ready to show, we'll have the most advanced distribution offer in the industry," she said.

"We look forward to it."

"In good time, Harko. Now, if you'll excuse me, I need to put that order in with Ida. There's an eight-hour time delay, and we want to make sure it gets on *The Hope*."

"Of course, thank you, Sabrina," said Harko.

"Good day."

She pinched her earlobe, ending the call.

"God," she howled. "Damn it!"

She rubbed her palms together, squeezing her fingers and alternating the grip. She pressed hard against her thin, spotted skin. Her hands were still withered, but the nano-treatments were working. The arthritis was gone.

How do I get that shipment out?

She peeped her inbox. The video from Corporate Security had moved down five spots from the top. The new messages were all from concerned customers.

Goddamn you, Baylor.

She had a payload worth billions sitting in a defunct facility with no way to get to it.

If not for that sonofabitch, it would be loaded on The Hope *by now.*

Her earlobe buzzed.

"Yes?"

"Sorry to bother you, ma'am." Her new assistant's cloyingly

sweet voice was in her ear. "It's the Secretary of Defense, she's on manual for you."

"Put her through."

Die already, like your turncoat son.

She heard a click as her implant was connected to the phone exchange.

"Hello, Margaret," said Meyer. "How are you holding up?"

"As well as can be expected," said Margaret Aimes in her usually craggy voice.

"Barton's service was lovely," said Meyer. "The Smithsonian was such a wonderful choice. Half the things in there are as old as us." Meyer chuckled.

Aimes was unmoved. "Barton enjoyed Americana," she said sternly.

"How insensitive of me. I'm sorry for the levity. It was a fine choice, Margaret. He was a good man."

What game are you playing? Do you know I terminated the brat yet?

"He always listened to his mother. He was my best boy." Aimes sounded hurt, then changed her tone abruptly. "I've just returned to the office today. I understand you're experiencing operational problems."

"We had a mix-up with the food printers. The crew was poisoned."

"How terrible," said Aimes.

"Inconvenient is the word. The press will enjoy trying to make this something more than an unfortunate accident."

"Can you recover?"

"We've never lost an entire crew before," said Meyer. "I'm waiting for an update from our security team."

"I see. Is there a risk to your infrastructure?"

"The computer systems will keep the base running until we can restaff," she said.

"That's good news, but what about your obligations?"

"Nothing to worry about, Margaret. We'll offload the materials in storage before *The Hope* leaves Armstrong. If I have to use drones, I will—damn the Asteroiders Union. We'll get the Defense Department's order out."

Aimes was quiet.

What do you want?

"Sabrina, I received a report this morning that I think you ought to know about."

"Oh?"

"I'm sending over a picture now."

An image of 243 Ida appeared in her Opti-Comp. The asteroid had a ring of ice orbiting around it.

No.

"Any idea how that happened?" asked Aimes.

"Margaret, this can't be real," said Meyer. "Where did you download this?"

"One of our survey teams at Armstrong spotted it. It wasn't there a week ago. And there is something else. They tell me this asteroid used to have a moon."

"I don't know what to say. I will get with my people and look into this right now."

"Yes, why don't you do that. Also, there's a news article out today by that writer Anton Vance, the one who was on *The Hope* with your engineer. Very illuminating."

"You don't follow his gossip, do you, Margaret? My employee was sent to calibrate rock hoppers. My god, if I'd known he'd attract attention this way."

Why hasn't Chan dispatched that hack?

"People believe what they read, Sabrina. Be well and let me know if you anticipate delays with our delivery."

"Yes, of course, you stay well, Margaret. I'm sorry for what you're going through and I'm here if you need me."

"Thank you. You're a true friend." The call disconnected.

Meyer scowled. "Lying bitch."

How do I explain ice rings?

"Get me Chan," she said.

"Dialing Chan Xi-Michaels," said a voice in her ear.

There was a click followed by laughing. "Hi! I'm so sorry I can't take your call, but I'm in space! Leave your message and I will get back to you at light speed." He gave a shrill laugh at the end of the recording.

"Chan, it's Sabrina. This Vance hack, I've asked you twice and he's still putting out trash articles. Get rid of him now."

She pinched her earlobe and hung up. Xi-Michaels wouldn't hear the message for at least eight hours. He could be flaky, but this was too much.

Is he ignoring me? How much damage has Vance done this time?

She did a search for his latest post. Her eyes bugged and she fell back in her chair.

"Alvin Baylor Lives!" floated in the air in front of her.

She scanned through the article. Vance claimed to be in contact with Baylor. It was all there—the device, its theft from Washington, and the continued work of Mohammed Rinsler. It accused Alteris of sabotaging the facility for financial gain.

That little prick is trying to start a war.

The article was trending. Hundreds of comments appeared in real time. She seethed.

There was a knock at her door.

"What is it?" she growled.

Her assistant entered wearing a worried look. "I'm sorry to bother you again," she said. "The board has gathered and they want to see you."

"Right now?"

She nodded.

"Tell them I'm on my way," said Meyer.

"Yes, ma'am."

The assistant exited and Meyer's eyes continued to gaze at the clean carpet where she had been standing.

My name will not be sullied.

"Rashad," said Meyer.

Her bodyguard walked from the darkened doorway, stopped on the landing, and waited at attention.

She stood up and checked her reflection in the window. Bird shit stained the glass. She looked out and up and found the culprit perched above.

"Drone," she said.

One of the flying sentries circling outside the building came toward her window. It spotted the pigeon and blasted it. A charred corpse fell to Earth. The drone cleaned the glass then returned to patrol.

She straightened her violet pant suit and tucked the blond hair behind her ears, then turned around to make eye contact with Rashad. He nodded.

"We have a meeting to attend," she said.

EPILOGUE

Alvin Baylor stood atop an enormous pile of trash. Heaps of plastic, silicon, paper, and metal spread out as far as he could see. The discarded products of two hundred years of civilization. The sky above was red and filled with cumulus storm clouds. Below, crowds of people picked through trash. It looked like one of the massive electronic refuse dumps of the American Southwest. He heard a woman cry out as she retrieved a baby from under the detritus. Alvin turned to look at the woman. She was bent over, draped in a black veil. She seemed impossibly old to be the mother of such a young child.

Then all at once he heard whispering voices around him. Men and women dressed in his old team jersey separated from the crowd and climbed up on the trash heaps, looking up at him.

Just beyond the old woman, a weathered blond man reached the top of the pile and stood tall. He hefted a golden rifle above his head. *Heinz?* It was his old high-school pal. Rising up on either side of him came the 'roiders. Tosh and Buzz stood among them and saluted Alvin. Heinz said Alvin's name aloud, and then from all around, the people began to shout it. The old woman continued to cry and the strange whispering remained. Alvin realized it was not coming from the people.

The whisper grew in volume like a rushing wind until it drowned out the shouts of his allies. He looked on in confusion as the people continued to chant his name. Lightning split the sky.

Below his feet the broken electronics stirred and a black bubble rose out of the ground, lifting him into the air. He stood firm atop it as it ascended toward the flaring sky. As he rose higher, the whispering came closer until he could discern a single voice. It was female. Then a tugging at his feet sent him into a panic. He trembled as the black bubble reached up and swallowed him whole. The whispering moved inside his head. He still couldn't understand it.

He awoke with a start.

Sweat poured off Alvin's body. He rolled over in his bunk on 243 Ida and exhaled heavily. *Just a dream.* The orb rested on the form-molded nightstand beside his bed. He picked it up, holding it in front of his face. His fingers tingled, his temples buzzed. He brought the ball up to his ear and heard a faint sound like the echo in a seashell. *Nothing*

He placed the orb back on the table but the seashell noise remained in his head.

"Huh?"

It grew louder until it became a voice, the one he had heard in his dream. The sound grew steadily clearer until it gained a commanding tone. He heard the words perfectly now. "Save Lia!" they said, over and over.

ACKNOWLEDGMENTS

I wish to acknowledge my editor, Carolyn Haley for her unbelievable patience and professionalism. Thank you for waiting for me to get my manuscript just right during a topsy-turvy time in my life.

Thanks also to Roger Betka for the amazing cover illustration and for putting up with my art direction. And to Jeff Schwartz for enthusiastically jumping on the copywriting gig and saving me from the sea of subjectivity.

I'd also like to thank my beta-readers - Mike, Shawn, Greg, David, Stefanie, Kristina, Sacha, Leo, Maya, Matt and Robert.

And finally, thanks to you dear reader, for coming this far. If you'd like to support my writing, please consider leaving me a brief review online.

ABOUT THE AUTHOR

Maximilian Gray is a film-industry professional, author, and aficionado of genre fiction. He pitched his first science-fiction television show to Hollywood execs as a thirteen year-old writer. He has worked in various capacities for Roger Corman, James Cameron, Technicolor, Discovery Communications, Walt Disney Studios and Netflix. Mr. Gray holds no degrees and has dropped out of college on three occasions. The first time he was fourteen. However, he did graduate from West Coast Private Investigations Academy with high honors, so he can tail your car and bug your home. Alvin Baylor Lives! is his first novel.

To be notified of Alvin's next adventure, visit maximiliangray.com and sign-up for the reader's list.

35701399R00209

Printed in Great Britain
by Amazon